Montana Surprise

Center Point
Large Print

Also by Caroline Fyffe and available from Center Point Large Print:

Heart of Dreams
Montana Dawn
Texas Twilight
Mail-Order Brides of the West: Evie
Mail-Order Brides of the West: Heather
Moon Over Montana
Mail-Order Brides of the West: Kathryn
Montana Snowfall
Texas Lonesome
Montana Courage
Montana Promise
Montana Reunion

MONTANA SURPRISE

A McCutcheon Family Novel
Book Twelve

CAROLINE FYFFE

CENTER POINT LARGE PRINT
THORNDIKE, MAINE

This Center Point Large Print edition
is published in the year 2025 by arrangement with
Caroline Fyffe.

The text of this Large Print edition is unabridged.
In other aspects, this book may vary
from the original edition.
Printed in the United States of America
on permanent paper sourced using
environmentally responsible foresting methods.
Set in 16-point Times New Roman type.

ISBN: 979-8-89164-692-6

The Library of Congress has cataloged this record
under Library of Congress Control Number: 2025940785

Dedicated to our newest granddaughter, Elizabeth. Our hearts are overflowing with love, and we can't wait to see what joy and wonder you'll bring to the world.

Chapter One

Y Knot, Montana Territory, July 1888

Justin Wesley, deputy sheriff of Y Knot, nodded amiably to the passing riders as he walked along the boardwalk. He enjoyed the rustic, frontier community. Nothing much out of the ordinary happened here aside from an argument between merchants or rowdiness in the saloon. Today, the town was quiet but felt even more so since all the hullabaloo from almost two months before. First, Flood McCutcheon's historic birthday party occurred. Second, a twister threatened to blow Y Knot off the map.

Justin had been at home, playing checkers with his father, the day a hellish, howling wind sent twigs and pebbles pattering violently on the windows and roof. Carlie, his little sister, ran down the stairs from her bedroom and crawled into their father's arms, her eyes the size of harvest moons. Aunt Pauline had dashed from the kitchen, dishcloth in hand. His three family members had followed him to Y Knot from Denver a year earlier, when he'd accepted the deputy position from Sheriff Crawford, and they'd not seen such a storm since. Curious, they'd stepped outside to find the day was black as night and had a greenish tint churning the clouds. Seconds later, the roaring wind swallowed every sound. The sky had opened with force, battering everything with huge drops of rain and hail.

Justin smiled, shaking his head, thankful the tornado had veered right at the last second, leaving him a town to watch over. Pushing through the batwing doors of the Hitching Post Saloon, he went to the bar where Abe, clipboard in hand, was taking inventory. The bartender's slender frame always reminded Justin of a banty rooster. The establishment was deserted. The piano sat quiet on the far wall. The scent of fresh brewed coffee mixed with aromas of stale sweat and horse manure. "Mornin', Abe," he said, leaning his elbow on the long, walnut bar top.

Abe made two hash marks next to a column.

Justin stifled a grin. The Hitching Post wasn't like the large saloons he'd known in Denver, with men crammed into every crevice. He wondered if Abe went through two cases of whiskey a month.

"Deputy."

Justin bobbed his head and chuckled. "Inventory time? Don't let me distract you." No more than five hash marks were on his sheet.

Abe glanced up sharply. "Young pup! You *got* to know your numbers. A man who don't soon'll be parted from his profits—even if that ain't much."

The barkeep was right. He should've kept his mouth shut. "Sorry, Abe, didn't mean any disrespect."

Abe laid aside his work, the irritation on his face a moment before now gone. "I didn't mean to bite your head off, either, Justin. Been slow, is all, with so many fellers out of town. What can I do ya for? Beer? Whiskey?"

Abe was just being polite. He knew Justin didn't drink while on duty. "Just a glass of water. My throat is a mite parched."

Abe's smile was back. "Temperature's rising, all right. Gonna be a hot summer. Water comin' right up."

Three fellas appeared in the doorway—Sam Green, Dennis Oats, and Chet Fender. The boozers nodded as they staggered by and went to a table in the middle of the room.

Dennis ran a hand through his thinning brown hair and then broke out a deck of cards. "Beers, Abe!" he called as he shuffled.

"That we have," Abe responded. He plunked Justin's glass of water on the bar and went for the mugs. "How's Brandon doin'?" he asked over his shoulder, filling the first mug. "Heard tell he's still woozy." Abe shook his head. "That break was a doozy."

If Brandon's accident wasn't so serious, he'd smile at Abe's humor. As it was, Brandon had taken a mean fall from a ladder and broken his left femur. The break was clean, or so said the doctor, and given a good prognosis. Brandon and Charity were staying out at the Heart of the Mountains while he recuperated, where Charity's mother could help in the process. Caring for a bedbound man of Brandon's size was no easy task, and Charity was in the family way. "I was out there yesterday. He's sleeping a lot."

Abe balanced the three beers on his beat-up, round tray. "That right?" he said as he passed Justin by. "Seems a trifle odd."

At the time, Justin had thought so, too, but hadn't said anything to Charity in her delicate condition. Didn't want to feed her fretting. He wasn't a doctor, and Dr. Handerhoosen was. The physician said all was well.

Abe was back with the tray tucked under his arm. He stopped on Justin's side of the bar. "You let me know if there's anything I can do. With Flood and most of the ranch hands gone from the Heart of the Mountains, the women might be anxious."

"They're not *that* shorthanded, Abe. Luke, Matt, and Mark, plus Francis, Lucky, Nick, and Hickory stayed back from the cattle drive to Miles City."

Abe shook his head knowingly. "There you go again, young pup, shooting off your mouth over something you're ignorant about. Seven hands on a sizeable spread *is* a skeleton crew. You just tell Claire and Charity I'm available, if need be."

"Will do tonight, when I go out to report to Brandon." *If he's awake.*

"Where's Fancy?" Sam Green hollered.

Justin watched the three through the mirror behind the bar. Something about Sam always reminded Justin of a goat with his scruffy black hair and sloppy clothes that hung every which way. In contrast, Chet was clean-cut and his garments formfitting.

Sam downed half his beer and wiped his mouth on his sleeve.

By the looks of the money in front of the other two, he'd just lost.

"I need her to sing," Sam said. "I have better luck when she's here."

"Tuesday and Thursday she has a few hours off in the morning—you know that. She's off doing something, somewhere."

The man bit out several curses, pushed back, and came to the bar for a refill.

Abe complied.

Sam turned.

"Pay up now, before you lose the little money you have," Abe stated firmly. "No more tabs for you."

"Real friendly, ain't' ya, Abe?" He tossed down twenty cents. "Can't imagine where a saloon gal goes, but I can imagine what she does," he mumbled as he returned to his table and took a seat. "I *surely* can."

Justin gazed into his glass. He hated lewd talk—especially about Fancy Aubrey. She was a good woman and a great conversationalist. She kept him abreast of all the undertones around town. Helpful information, especially now, with Brandon indisposed. Being somewhere in her mid-to-late thirties, she treated him like a little brother.

The rumbling racket of heavy wagon wheels belonging to the stage, if he was correct, drifted into the room. Curious to see any new arrivals to Y Knot, most townspeople came out when they heard the jingle of the harness and call of the driver. Justin was no exception.

He left his water at the bar and stood at the batwing doors, watching as the stage rocked to a halt in front of the Cattlemen's Hotel.

Bradley Renfro, the thirtyish shotgun messenger with an easy smile and mad sharpshooting skills, climbed down and placed a small stool beneath the door.

Must be women inside.

A tall, slender woman, somewhere in her forties or fifties, clambered out with the help of the stagehand. Dressed in a yellow calico dress and matching bonnet, she wobbled once before she hit solid ground.

Justin feared she might fall. Now successfully anchored, she took a moment to straighten her skirt and then hurried to the boardwalk, where Ina Klinkner was waving a cheery welcome. The two fell together like long-lost hens, clucking and laughing while they waited for the luggage to be brought down from the top of the stage.

One second later, another woman was handed out. Young, pretty, and all alone. In such a fine, tailored dress, she was sure to stand out. He'd not seen a pair of crocheted gloves since he'd left Denver. A light blue hat, the same color of her dress, sat forward on her head.

"Wonder who *that* is?" Abe breathed from behind Justin's shoulder. "Doesn't look like she's searching for anyone. Wooheee, a woman like her doesn't come to Y Knot every day!"

Justin lifted a shoulder, noticing the same thing. "Looks like a startled deer. Not sure what to do next . . ."

Abe nudged his back. "Mayhap someone should go out and welcome her. That's what Brandon would do."

At his and Abe's interest, Sam, Dennis, and Chet scooted back in a racket of scraping chairs and hurried from their table, the card game abandoned.

"Good idea." Sam hitched up his dusty pants and was just about to push through the door.

Justin caught his shoulder. "Welcoming newcomers is *my* job, Sam. I wouldn't want to scare her away. You go back to your cards and pray for your luck to turn."

Chapter Two

This whole day felt like a dream, *or nightmare,* depending on how Madison's stomach presented from one moment to the next. Grit from the long, tortuous trip from Waterloo coated her cheeks. When she bit down, a crunch grated between her teeth. The inside of the stagecoach had been stifling, making her corset pinch mercilessly. And the bench! She could feel each spring ready to push through the worn-out fabric and assault her. The poor old transport needed an upgrade.

As the stagecoach rocked to a halt, she glanced out the window to the shops and businesses lining the road. A warm, dusty scent wafted into the window. Y Knot resembled many of the small settlements she'd passed through to arrive here. What did her future hold in store?

"Age before beauty," Belinda Bowie exclaimed. The middle-aged woman had boarded in Waterloo, as well. She claimed to be the second cousin to a woman in Y Knot named Ina Klinkner and was visiting for the first time. She stood, as best she could, and moved toward the stagecoach door. "I can't believe I'm finally here." Without further ado, she climbed out into the sunshine.

Now Madison's turn at the door, she took Mr. Renfro's hand and allowed the shotgun messenger to help her to the street. Her legs wobbled like warm taffy and her innards jiggled, bringing to mind the undercooked Christmas pudding she'd baked last year. The lengthy stagecoach ride, emphasized by bumps, jolts, and curves, had been an ordeal she didn't want to repeat anytime soon. Was making this arduous journey a huge mistake? Did Y Knot hold the key to her hidden past? Or would all her planning come to naught?

Annoyed with her negativity, she straightened. She was in Y Knot. The trip was ineluctable after the truth came to light thirteen years ago. Ignoring the hustle and bustle around her, she glanced up at the large, flat-bottomed clouds. Anticipation, and something akin to awe, swirled within. Something good was on the horizon!

"Miss Plumb?"

Madison turned.

The shotgun messenger, who'd been solicitous to her every need, stood on the boardwalk, his face a pleasant pink from unloading several large pieces of luggage from the top of the stage. He smiled and gestured downward. "Your trunk."

"Thank you so much, Mr. Renfro," Madison replied. "I appreciate everything you've done along the way. You've been incredibly kind."

The color of the man's face deepened. He removed his hat and rolled the brim. "It's been my pleasure, miss. Is there any other way I can be of assistance before we pull out?"

"Would you happen to know where the post office is?" That was where the letters from her father's attorney would have arrived. A very important place, indeed.

His face brightened. "I most certainly do. Just two doors down inside the mercantile." He pointed. "Lichtenstein's Provisions. You can't miss it."

"Renfro!" the grizzled-faced stagecoach driver barked. "Get them livestock watered! You ain't paid ta stand 'round socializin', son. We got us a schedule ta keep!" Mumbling something unintelligible under his breath, the driver marched across the dirt road to the saloon where several men stood inside the doors, watching.

Mr. Renfro nodded once, pushed on his hat, and took his leave.

A kicked dog couldn't look as sad. With him gone, Madison felt a surge of panic. Besides Belinda Bowie and the stage-line employees, she didn't know a single soul. She was completely alone. Laughter made her turn and glance up the street to where two women were talking outside the mercantile.

Like magic, a man appeared at her side. Being distracted, she'd missed his approach. He was tall, had impossibly wide shoulders, and his eyes matched the blue of the sky. A metal star glinted on his chest. Since beginning her journey from Kentucky, she'd seen many men dressed the same, as well as their weapons—rifles, handguns, and knives. This was the first time she'd seen a coiled whip attached to the other side of a gun belt. Somehow, the look enhanced his appearance, and she decided he'd be a good man to know in a fight. For a moment, he looked reluctant to speak. As she'd been taught, she pulled back her shoulders and smiled. "Good day, Sheriff."

"Welcome to Y Knot," he replied in a clear, strong voice, touching the brim of his cowboy hat. "May I be of help?" He gestured to Miss Bowie and her cousin as Mr. Renfro loaded the woman's belongings onto the back of a fringed-top surrey. "Are you waiting for someone, miss? I'm Justin Wesley, *deputy* of Y Knot. At your service."

"Thank you for the warm welcome, Deputy Wesley," she replied, truly appreciative of his presence. The men watching from the saloon made her uneasy. She'd heard too many scandalous stories from her roommate about the West and the uncivilized men and women who lived there, especially in drinking establishments. "I'm not expecting anyone, but thank you for asking."

His raised eyebrows lowered as his smile vanished. "Where're you staying?"

She glanced between the hotel and boardinghouse, knowing she should make her funds stretch, but first impressions were everything, particularly if one had an important endeavor, as she did. Feeling his expectant gaze, she made a quick decision. "Cattlemen's Hotel, of course," she replied. "For the time being."

Her alibi for arriving in a small western town—where she didn't know anyone—was a little unbelievable. But she couldn't just blurt out her true reasons for coming. They were personal. Might even cause undue pain. She needed to be discreet. She'd been raised to be truthful, so weaving a deception, to anyone, and especially someone who was being so kind, felt wrong. She didn't like being a shyster, the kind of person her father spoke of during his work for William Lindsay, senator and judge, but it was too late to change course now.

"Cattlemen's is a nice establishment. You'll like it. May I help you with your trunk? That's the least I can do."

Before she could reply, he'd wrestled her wide trunk into his arms, strode inside, and placed it next to a counter where a young woman flipped through the pages of the hotel register.

"Miss Hallsey, this is—" He glanced at her expectantly as he removed his hat.

"Miss Plumb," she supplied, feeling very grown up. When the deputy smiled, it felt as if the sun had popped through the door and lit up the hotel lobby. She discreetly moved her gaze away from his pleased expression, realizing she liked his face immensely. He seemed so much taller than the young men back home, requiring him to look down when they spoke. The hat he was now holding had marked his hair, and the crease went around his head in the most interesting way.

"Very well, Miss Plumb," Miss Hallsey said. "Please sign here." She turned the ledger and handed Madison the pen after dunking the implement in a small pot of black ink. "How long will you be staying?"

Madison's heart galloped off. "I'm not exactly sure," she responded softly. "But I'd like a room for at least four days."

The girl and the deputy exchanged a look.

"That'll be fifty cents a day. Warm water for a bath is a dime extra. The recently renovated top floor is more expensive at a dollar a night. At the moment, the hotel is only a quarter full, so you can have your pick."

So many decisions. She didn't need anything fancy, but she *did* need a room with a view of Main Street. She'd clandestinely studied every woman since she'd arrived. The person she sought could be anyone from her early thirties—if Madison stretched the possibilities to the limit—to a mature woman of fifty or sixty years old. Before answering, she turned and gave the deputy, who was listening intently, a brief smile.

He stepped back. "Well, I'll just be on my way,"

he said quickly, still holding his hat. "Welcome to Y Knot, again, Miss Plumb. If you need *anything* at all, the sheriff's office is conveniently next door." His smile deepened. "I'm there early and most days stay late. Don't be shy."

She waited until she and the clerk were alone. "I think I'd like to be on the second floor with a room facing the street."

Miss Hallsey gave a wink. "I've a pretty corner room that overlooks Main Street. And if you're up early, and glance above Berta May's Fabric Shop, there's just enough of a break in the pine trees on Creek Street to give you a beautiful view of the sunrise. I think you'll enjoy it."

"That sounds perfect," Madison said breathlessly. After all her planning, she couldn't believe she was actually here. She'd taken the first step to see her plan through. "And a restaurant?"

"Absolutely. If you're hungry now, our restaurant is still serving breakfast and lunch. Dinner starts at five. There're two other eateries in town, the Biscuit Barrel and Lou and Drit's Boardinghouse. The latter charges thirty-five cents for a family-style meal at one long table. The other is a café." Miss Hallsey tapped a silver bell several times.

A young man appeared from a door behind the counter.

She handed him a key. "Harold, please take Miss Plumb and her trunk to room twelve." She looked at Madison. "I'll be up in a few minutes with fresh towels and water."

"Thank you," Madison replied. She followed behind the young porter, giving him ample room as he struggled up the stairs.

A giddy excitement erupted inside.

I'm here in town. Can you feel my presence?

Her heart quivered. The chance she wouldn't be kindly received was real. She'd better prepare herself for any outcome. This journey could end either way.

Out of breath, the young man plopped the trunk on the carpet runner in the narrow hallway and fished the key out of his pocket. After opening the door, he handed the guest key to Madison then waited as she preceded him into the room.

The furnishings were sparse but clean. A bed with a nightstand and oil lamp. A small table and straight-back chair by the window. A washstand with pitcher and washbowl. Empty towel rack. A soft braided rug. The accommodations were charming, but nothing at all like her bedroom back in Frankfort. The feel was closer to her dorm room at Mary Sharp College. "Thank you," she said, digging in her reticule.

Harold brought her trunk inside, being careful of the doorframe. He placed it at the foot of the comfortable-looking bed covered with a simple patchwork quilt.

When she offered him a few coins his eyes lit

up. "Thank you, miss, but that's not necessary."

"Of course, it is. I appreciate your help."

Taking the money, he smiled and backed out of the room, softly closing the door behind him.

Madison crossed to the window and pushed aside the powder-blue curtains. Miss Hallsey had been right. She had a perfect view of the fabric store across the street, as well as the bank, the saloon, and the telegraph office. If she stretched her neck, she could see all the way down to the boardinghouse. Past that was one more small building she thought might be a firehouse. On her side of the street, beside the hotel, and more difficult to see, was what looked to be the sheriff's office the deputy had mentioned, a livery she'd noticed, and then a row of small houses.

Yes, she'd be comfortable here as she decided her direction for the next few days.

A woman appeared on the opposite side of the street. She looked young and walked along, holding a toddler by the hand. Her dress swished with each step, and she looked down when the child must have said something. The tiny family passed the bank and slipped into the fabric store.

Could that woman be her mother? Only time, and a bit of detective work, would tell. Oh, to have a family unit again. Be a part of a group to whom you were special. Where your absence was noticed and triggered a response. A small bubble of desperation threatened to ruin her excited mood. On family day at college this year, she'd been alone. Her friend had invited Madison to join her large group of eight, but Madison had discreetly declined, still mourning the recent loss of her father and barely remembering her adoptive mother's voice. Maybe, just maybe, with some digging, and a sprinkle of luck, Madison Ann Plumb might meet her birth mother face to face. Whatever reason her mother had had for arranging the adoption, Madison held no resentment. They could get past anything. Be friends, as well as family.

Glancing above the rooftops, Madison studied the sky. What would tomorrow bring? Without finding her past, she had no real future.

Chapter Three

The following morning, Justin made an early call to the Heart of the Mountains, intending to speak with Brandon and let him know the news from town. Seemed each day, a new challenge arose. He reined up in front of the bunkhouse, chasing away a cat sharpening its claws on the hitching rail post. He dismounted, tied his horse, and started for the house.

Francis came out of the barn. "What brings you out this morning, Justin?" he asked in his ever-present calm demeanor. "You were here last evening."

Word was Francis had been a foundling years ago and had grown up on the ranch. If he wasn't here in the barn, or out riding fence, he was usually in town, wooing the schoolteacher, Ashley Adair. Never knowing his last name, he accepted the McCutcheon's generous offer to use theirs.

"Just here to check on Brandon. He was drowsy last night, and I'm not sure how much of what I said he heard. It's understandable, with what he's been through. Anyone stirring in the ranch house yet?" he asked, hitching his head toward the building. "Don't want to intrude. Didn't realize the hour until I was halfway here." He'd lain awake most of the night, pondering different matters, one being a new feller hanging around town. Normally, a stranger wouldn't be a concern, but with Brandon incapacitated, Justin needed to be ready for anything. Another was the attractive young woman who'd arrived yesterday. She'd been vague and less than forthcoming about coming to Y Knot unchaperoned. His suspicions had been stirred. Still, this was a free country, and he had no real right to know everything about her—even if he'd like to.

Francis shook his head. "Nope, none I've seen." He turned for the bunkhouse at the same moment Nick Petty came out the door, wet hair slicked back and a coffee mug gripped in his hand. When he saw Justin, his eyes lit up. "Wesley. Just the man I wanted to see."

Justin stifled an inward groan. The middle Petty brother was known for his short fuse, and smart mouth. He was nothing like his younger, calmer brother, Tanner Petty, or his older, more responsible brother, Shad Petty. Justin liked Nick well enough, and except for the fact of him being only one year older than himself, he enjoyed challenging Justin. Justin mostly ignored him, but sometimes Nick could be a real burr under his saddle. "Mornin', Petty. What's on your mind? I *can't* imagine this early in the day . . ."

"No? Word's got around about the new woman come to town yesterday. Said you spoke with her and even took her belongings into the hotel. Who is she? She married? Heard she arrived alone." Leaning his shoulder against the porch post, he sipped from his mug. "What's her business here in Y Knot? I was told she's a real looker."

Nick never disappoints. Justin wondered who Nick had spoken with. The information could've come from anyone. Miss Plumb's pretty face appeared in his mind. *Parting was such sweet sorrow,* he thought, playfully changing the Shakespeare quote just a tad. "Pretty early in the morning for a game of twenty questions, isn't it, Nick?" He looked Shad's younger brother up and down and then put out a palm. "To ease your mind, I didn't inquire about her private business the moment she stepped off the stage. But, if I had, I wouldn't pass *anything* on." *Especially to you.*

Nick took a drink from his mug and narrowed his eyes over the rim. "You're no team player, Wesley."

Justin lifted a shoulder. "Never claimed to be. Now, if that's all, I have matters I need to discuss with Brandon. You have a nice day."

Justin tapped the threshold of the open bedroom door, wondering if Brandon was asleep or just lying there with his eyes closed. He'd met Charity in the kitchen, and she'd told him to go on up. Brandon was awake. Right now, his boss looked about as tough as a crushed daisy. Almost comical, stretched out in Charity's bed. His casted leg stuck out of the covers and was propped up on a tall stack of pillows. A dark, grayish-black bruise shadowed the left side of Brandon's face. Only four days had passed since the accident. He must still be in a good deal of pain. But, knowing Brandon, he'd never say as much.

The day of the accident rushed back to Justin with force. He'd ridden out to see the progress on the barn on Charity and Brandon's new ranch. Brandon stood on one ladder with Colton holding the base. Luke was on another, with his nephew, Billy, steadying the legs, one of the boy's feet wedged against a rock. The plan was to walk the twenty-foot beam on their shoulders to the top of the new construction. Not wanting to be a distraction, Justin halted a good distance away. Even the breeze moving the leaves seemed to hush for a moment as the men slowly worked their way higher, placing each foot on the next rung, arm muscles straining with the weight.

But Colton looked over his shoulder for the briefest second and must have relaxed his grip, or maybe Brandon's weight shifted. Whatever the reason, the outcome was the same. In the blink of an eye, the men fell in a jumble of shouts. Brandon ended up on the ground with the end of the beam jammed into his thigh. Justin heard the snap of bone from thirty feet away. Luke was knocked off his ladder, as well, but he hadn't sustained anything more than a bruised side and arm.

Just when Justin decided to go back down to the kitchen and accept the offer of coffee while he waited for Brandon to wake up, he saw his boss open his eyes, and the peace of sleep eased off his face. He looked worse than he had last night. Tense lines ringed his mouth, attesting to the level of pain. The dark bruise on his face melded into the whiskers covering his jaw. "Didn't mean to disturb you," Justin said. "Charity told me you were awake. She'll be up soon with your breakfast."

"Not disturbing me." Brandon glanced at the chair beside his bed. "Make yourself comfortable. I'm glad you're here."

At least, he seems more lucid today. Justin took the chair and got comfortable. "Much pain?" he asked, taking in the expanse of the heavy cast weighing Brandon's leg.

"Only when I breathe." Brandon tried to chuckle, but the sound faded away.

That explained his boss's corpse-like stillness. On the end table was a small tray with a mug and plate, crumbs strewn across it. "How you feelin'?"

Brandon's brows drew together. "Good as a man can with a busted leg. How's Y Knot, and what's transpired since I ended up here?" His gaze moved around the room, but he stayed completely still.

Doesn't he remember my visit last night? "Pretty quiet, for the most part. A new man, a gambler, maybe, rode in yesterday morning on a flashy horse. Goes by Cole Mercer. Took a room at the hotel. Has a dog. I noticed he made two trips to the bank. I've been keeping a close eye on him."

Brandon stretched back on the pillow and grimaced. "And the woman?"

"News travels fast," Justin replied. Made sense Nick Petty might have heard, the way information of a pretty, young woman got around the bunkhouse like the crack of a whip. But the news reaching Brandon so quickly surprised him a little. "Not much to tell, really," he conceded, embarrassed he hadn't learned anything more than he had. "Her name is Miss Plumb."

Brandon gazed at him, eyebrows high. "And?"

"That's all I know."

"She arrived alone," Brandon stated.

"She did."

"Why's she here in Y Knot? Visiting relatives?"

Justin felt a bit protective. "She was close-mouthed. Didn't volunteer much of anything during our short conversation."

Brandon slowly, carefully, lifted his arm and scrubbed a hand over his whiskered jaw. "Any possibility she's working with the new fellow, the gambler you mentioned first? They both came into town alone without much of a reason. Maybe they're taking the lay of the land before they make a move."

"Can't imagine that from the proper young lady I met." *But she is staying in the same hotel with the stranger.* Somehow, the thought hurt. "She looks about as deceptive as a kitten."

"You're pretty quick with your assessment." Brandon pierced him with a gaze. "The innocent kittens are the ones who bite the hardest. Keep watch. Try to learn more. She stayin' at the hotel, too?"

As much as he hated to, Justin nodded.

"Need I say more?"

Charity arrived with Brandon's breakfast tray laden with a plateful of savory foods. He wouldn't die of starvation. Two eggs smothered in Mexican-style beans and several tortillas, as well as roast beef, already cut into small pieces. She handed the tray to Justin to hold briefly while she helped Brandon lean forward and placed more pillows behind his back for support. Finished, she situated the tray on Brandon's lap and sat gently on the bedside, preparing to help him eat. She glanced back at Justin. "Are you sure you wouldn't like some breakfast? There's plenty downstairs. Esperanza told me to be sure to offer you a plate. Brandon's been beside himself with boredom. Eating with him will keep you around a little longer."

Charity looked as pretty as usual this morning, with her hair pulled back and braided down her back. The apron covering her flowing blue skirt appeared rather snug as her pregnancy progressed. "No, thanks, Charity. How's he doing? I couldn't get a straight answer out of him pertaining to his injuries. He's a stubborn man."

She smiled into Brandon's eyes as she fingered his napkin into the *v* of his sleepshirt. "Don't I know? He slept better last night. Not too much groaning and shifting. He even seemed to rest. That's something I can't wait to pass on to the doctor."

"I can tell him when I return to town, if you'd like," Justin offered. "Or leave a message, if he's not there."

"Thank you. That'd be helpful." She pushed the hair off Brandon's forehead.

Justin was surprised his boss was so submissive. He stood. "I best be on my way." He'd done what he'd been instructed to do—keep the sheriff informed about events in town. Brandon was wrong about Miss Plumb. No possibility existed she was connected with Cole Mercer.

Chapter Four

Madison's feet ached with fatigue. She'd walked every inch of Y Knot, checking with every business and shop looking for work. She'd brought a tidy sum of her inheritance with her, so she wasn't in danger of going hungry, but to stay in town without looking suspicious meant she must find employment, just like any other self-reliant young woman would do. Gone were the days when she *had* to marry to survive. Times were changing. In the city, women worked at the county courthouse in Frankfort, typing and answering the phone. Single women were everywhere, minding their own futures, and she intended to be one of them.

Her explanation was somewhat plausible. She planned to say she'd picked Y Knot out of the bag to write about for her next and final year's term paper, but in the meantime, she needed to find work. Her reasoning might sound far-fetched for a city-raised girl who knew little of western ways—but she'd not been able to come up with anything else. Hopefully, when her newness wore off, people would accept her. Once she was gainfully employed, she'd investigate other accommodations. If one presented itself, she'd prefer to live with a nice family somewhere close. Doing so would be safer and easier to learn about the women who resided in Y Knot. She could also ask questions under the pretext of curiosity about the town.

Now, though, she felt discouraged. Plopping on a bench in front of the bank, she glanced both ways to be sure she was alone and then unlaced her left boot. The relief was instant. Quickly slipping it off, she rubbed her aching foot. Like a fool, she'd left her old, well-broken-in boots at home, thinking they appeared too worn. Tucking her sock-clad foot beneath the hem of her skirt, she withdrew a small notepad from her reticule and put a line through the next name on her list.

Butcher Shop.

She'd learned the butcher and his wife ran the small shop easily. Madison hadn't been upset. Working around raw meat all day would make her feel sick. She'd felt queasy just standing in front of the counter filled with chops, severed legs, and steaks for fifteen minutes. While speaking with the shop owner, she'd surreptitiously studied his wife. There might be a tiny possibility, because of her age, the woman could be her mother, but the resemblances ended there. Where Madison was slim, and of an average-to-tall height for a woman, the butcher's wife had been short and a bit husky. She possessed a narrow face and jet-black hair. Her voice bespoke German ancestry. Madison was slightly built and fair-headed. The woman did have vivid blue eyes—much like her own—which sparkled with kindness.

Madison lined through the butcher shop, since they needed no help, but put a question mark, as well, for the possibility of the woman being her mother. Albeit small, the kind woman's age made her a candidate.

Feeling disheartened, she realized she hadn't spotted any woman she'd entertain as a strong prospect. Prior to her arrival, she'd thought finding her mother would be an easy matter. Now she wasn't so sure. Sadness made her glance into the sky, thinking about the last year. Preparing. Making lists. Letting her dreams run away with her to the possible outcome. She'd loved her adoptive mother and father with her whole heart. But she could love her birth mother, as well. Doing so would never distract from them. And what if she had half sisters and brothers? The heady thought made her smile and chased her fatigue away.

In the street, a heavy wagon rumbled by, drawing Madison out of her musings. If she was successful, and she found her mother, Madison was aware the woman might not want Madison to be a part of her life. Madison promised herself she'd accept any outcome. She wouldn't be hurt. She only wanted to know where she was from and her real identity and lineage. If the woman wanted her to leave town, Madison would leave her in peace. All she wanted was a chance to say hello. She wouldn't expect anything more.

Pulling on her boot, she tied the lace and stood. Her next stop was the fabric shop, the sign proclaiming Berta May as the proprietor. Would she find work here? Or, perhaps, her mother? Her one-dimensional world back in Kentucky had opened into a kaleidoscope of possibilities.

Chapter Five

Open Range, Montana Territory

Shad Petty contemplated the wave of brown, black, and cream cattle undulating slowly over the meadow. The doleful lowing sounded pitiful to his ears. The bovine didn't know they were headed to the stockyards in Miles City. He didn't like to ponder their future. Doing so made him sad. He'd volunteered to ride drag today. Eating dust and shooing flies for hour after hour was right in step with his present mood.

He hadn't wanted to make this trip. Hadn't wanted to leave Poppy when she was feeling so low. But the McCutcheons had been darn good to him, better than any ranch hand deserved. They treated him like family. When he'd been chosen for the task, he'd been loath to ask to stay back. He owed them mightily. First, they'd hired on both his brothers at a time when outfits usually pared down their manpower for the winter. And then they'd taken in stride each time he and Poppy changed their wedding date. Each instance he and Poppy had good reason, yes, but the thought still made him uncomfortable. He didn't like to put them out. Luke and his family had taken the ever-changing plans and rearrangement of his and their schedules with a smile, assuring him his job was secure, even when he moved out of the bunkhouse to the Preece Farm. Where he resided made no difference to them, or so they said.

Spotting two steers grazing behind a short wall of sagebrush, he nudged his gelding and made quick work of bringing them back into the herd. Finished, he pulled up, unscrewed his canteen lid, and took a long drink. The temperature was hot and would grow hotter by the end of the fourteen-day trip. After work finished in Miles City, the men had been promised a few days off. Everyone except him, Roady Guthrie, and Chance Holcomb had been elated by the prospect of free time. He shrugged. With nothing else to do, he'd use the time to find a unique wedding gift for Poppy. Something to mend her broken heart.

A shout went up.

He turned to see Flood McCutcheon loping his way. Smokey had told Shad last night this drive was the first time in ten years the head boss was taking the herd and leaving his sons at home. Said he'd missed the trail. The smell of the July grasses crushed by so many hooves. The nights under the stars with someone on the guitar or harmonica.

Flood reined up. "Shadrack—that you? Don't recognize you under all the dust." He chuckled and then stacked his palms on his saddle horn and stretched his back. He groaned with pleasure and then a wide smile split his face. "I'm just making the rounds. How you doin' back here, eating dirt?"

It was the standard joke to the drag rider. Spread way out in front, the other ranch hands were only dots intermingled with the herd.

"Just fine, Boss. How's *your* day goin'?"

There must have been something in his tone, because Flood turned from looking at the cattle and searched his face. "What is it?" he asked. "You've been quiet since setting out." Flood rubbed his arm across his sweaty brow and then pulled up his neck bandanna to swipe his cheeks. His weather-roughened hands reached for his own canteen, unscrewed the lid, and he took several long draws. Finished, he sat his horse, waiting. When Shad didn't promptly answer, he asked, "Are you and Poppy postponing the wedding again? I have four sons of my own, and a daughter, plus all their significant others. You can tell me. I've heard it all."

Shad would have chuckled at Flood's heartfelt attempt, but he didn't even have a smile left inside. "We're set for three weeks, Flood. Nothin' will stop us or make us postpone. We've waited long enough."

"You know what they say, absence makes the heart grow fonder. By the time you return, she'll be giddy to run down the aisle. Trust me. I've had years of experience. Spicing things up is actually one of my reasons for making this trip, myself. To give Claire a little space without me doggin' her heels. I can just imagine how young we both will feel when I finally ride back into the yard. I see how all my sons' wives rush into their arms."

This time, Shad *did* chuckle. "You wily old fox."

Flood puffed out his chest. "And don't you forget it." He stretched up in his stirrups and scanned the empty horizon and then back over the many long miles they'd just covered. "Look at it, Shad," he said, low and reverent, his voice filled with awe. "Where else can a man experience such freedom? The autonomy of the prairie. Nothing but land and sky and the good Lord above. I was born for this life. Touches something in me. Something deep down inside." He settled back in the saddle. "But freedom and the open prairie are not what we're talking about now. What's troubling you, son?"

Shad sucked in a deep pull of air. "You heard a relative—an aunt—responded to one of the advertisements we placed in several newspapers? The young'uns will be going there."

"I did. On one hand, I was sorry to hear it, but on the other, you must be happy for the children. Family really *is* where they belong. As much as you love 'em, trust me on this. You need to let 'em go."

"I know you're right. Poppy, though, is taking the split real hard. She's had 'em over a year now. With the approaching wedding, at a time when she should be her happiest, she's not. Far from it. Her eyes are always red from crying. She tries to hide her pain but doing so is impossible. And, truth be told, I can't imagine a day without July or April and May." He shook his head. The cattle had moved on and they should, too, but he made no effort to comply. Shad's horse pulled on the bit to follow the herd.

"That's tough," Flood responded, his brows drawn together. The sun was moving low to the horizon and what was left of the daylight illuminated Flood's face under his hat brim. "I understand your feelings. But, as soon as you two wed, things will change. Give her a babe of her own to coddle. Once she's in the family way, the pain from losing the others will ease up some. I *promise* you, it will."

But I can't give Poppy a baby. Not now, not ever. He felt like a fraud. And worse, he couldn't stand the thought of Poppy living her life without a child of her own. She'd assured him he was what made her happy. Even without children, she'd be satisfied. He'd circled this a thousand times.

Flood reached over and gave his arm a friendly

punch. "Hell, Shad, fill the house to the rafters with children. You're the man to do it! Nothin' brings a man more pleasure or such a grand feeling of accomplishment. My children are my greatest prize."

Shad forced himself to smile at Flood and nod. If he opened his mouth, all his deep-seated grief would tumble out onto the well-beaten ground. "You're right," he finally replied. "I'm making too much of this. We can visit July and the girls anytime." He had to look away from Flood's relieved smile. "It's not like we'll never see 'em again."

"Good. I hope you feel better."

Flood was a fine man. An exceptional father. Shad had few memories of his own father because, when Shad was just a boy, his parents had bundled up him and his brothers—Nick and Tanner were just little tikes then—and left them with their grandparents, where they'd lived until the time of their grandparents' deaths. After the last of the two died, Shad took over as mother, father, and sibling. A boy could surely grow under a man like Flood. He surely could. Even today, Shad liked how Flood spoke to him with respect and love. Just like he did with his own sons.

Flood raised his arm and pointed ahead. "We best get movin'."

Shad nodded.

Flood nudged his horse and loped away.

Shad did the only thing he could. Pushed all thoughts of children out of his head. Nothing would stop him from marrying Poppy—even though doing so might be wrong. If only he'd stuck to his guns back when he'd first explained his condition. She'd be over him by now and probably married to someone else—and maybe even in the family way. But now it was too late. After losing the Sanger children, he couldn't pull more of the rug out from under her feet.

Chapter Six

Seven hours later, full of dismay and with shooting pains torturing her feet, Madison tugged on the sticky door of the Biscuit Barrel, remembering the heavy entry was difficult to get open. Other than the door, the white clapboard café, with blue-trimmed windows and a colorful banner waving off the porch, was as cute as a pin. She'd visited earlier in the day and been told no, they weren't looking for another waitress.

She stepped inside to several mouthwatering aromas enticing her taste buds. The multilayered pie shelf behind the counter had been almost empty on her first visit but was now completely full. Her stomach rumbled. She hadn't eaten since morning, some eight hours ago. Being three thirty and between lunch and dinner, diners occupied only two tables, so she had her pick of seats.

Without making eye contact with anyone, she walked, trancelike, to a table and sat with her back to the wall. Withdrawing her hankie, she blotted her forehead and cheeks. How she wished she could also unfasten the first three buttons of her shirtwaist neckline. Indeed, the day had grown quite warm, but the temperature was nothing compared to Frankfort this time of year. If she'd been outside all day at home, she'd be drenched in perspiration.

Taking a deep breath, she glanced around. This was the first establishment where she'd inquired in this morning. The cheerful exterior had drawn her, as well as the customers streaming in and out. The café seemed like a much-loved destination. If she were employed here, getting to know the townsfolk would be easy. She could hunt for clues about her mother as she earned a wage. If only Mrs. Larson had hired her. Instead, she'd said the two waitresses and herself were more than enough for the business she had—but thanked her anyway for stopping in.

One of the young women she'd seen this morning headed her way. She wore the establishment's cerulean-blue gingham dress. The color reminded Madison of the vivid Montana sky, which had stolen her breath at her first glimpse in Waterloo.

The waitress smiled and withdrew her paper pad from a pocket. "You're back," the waitress said, her green eyes searching Madison's face. "Have any luck?"

Madison shook her head. "Not yet, but I'm not giving up."

The waitress gave her a smile, her eyes softening. "Something will turn up, you'll see." She poised her pencil to write. "Do you know what you'd like to eat? Most customers know our menu by heart, since it's limited."

"Oh, I haven't even looked yet." She plucked up a small, printed menu inserted between the salt and pepper shaker in the middle of the table. "But I *would* love a cup of tea while I decide. My throat is parched from my unsuccessful salesmanship."

The young woman tapped her pad twice. "Coming right up."

As the waitress crossed the room, the smallish man at the other table, the fella she remembered from the telegraph office, lifted his cup.

"I'll be right back with more coffee, Mr. Tracy. Would you like your usual pie?"

"Indeed, I would, Ethel," he called back. "Leaving the Biscuit Barrel without a slice of apple cinnamon would be a sin. I'm not willin' to risk my eternity, at least, not today."

Madison smiled to herself, looking forward to the tea as she enjoyed the homey feel of the place. She couldn't become defeated her first day out. She was made of stronger stuff. *Just set your mind to whatever you want, Madison,* her mama used to say. *And keep your chin up. God hears your prayers.* The woman who'd raised her was of Swiss descent. Kind, but forthright. Finding her birth mother wouldn't lessen the love she held in her heart for Albina Plumb.

After ordering chicken and dumplings, Madison sipped from the cup of steaming peppermint tea enjoying the tangy taste. She studied the table of diners across the room. One man, a woman, and a little girl. The man had been sweeping in the woodshop establishment she'd inquired within earlier.

After taking another sip, she opened her reticule and took out her own tablet of paper. Quickly exasperated with her list, which had gotten her nowhere, she shifted her attention to the long counter at the back of the café. Ten leather-upholstered stools, bolted to the slightly sloping wooden floor, stood in front. Square and rectangular tables were scattered throughout the dining area and were draped with blue-and-white checked tablecloths. The walls were decorated with cooking utensils, cake and pie tins, and other interesting paraphernalia. A pretty blue-and-white apron, stitched with a large *BB*, was tacked to the wall by the cash register, a price tag dangling from one sash. Madison was too far away to read the amount.

Mrs. Larson, the owner of the café, and the two other waitresses wore the same garments over their matching dresses.

After wolfing down his pie, the small man, Mr. Tracy, stood. "See ya later. Money's on the table," he called out to the room and the table of three occupants.

They waved him goodbye as he went out the door.

The deputy who'd welcomed her to town yesterday entered. Before she could look away, their gazes met. His eyes widened, then he nodded and smiled as he took off his hat.

Madison returned the gesture, then dropped her gaze to her cup, hoping beyond hope he would pass her by. She didn't want to speak with anyone right now. She felt grumpy and tired and had things to figure out. All she wanted was to eat her chicken and dumplings in peace and go back to the hotel and fall into bed the second she closed the door. Tomorrow was another day. Things would look brighter. But, right on cue, she heard footsteps heading her way.

"Miss Plumb? What a pleasant surprise, running into you today."

With nothing else to do, she glanced up, feeling heat prickle her cheeks. His thick, dark blond hair reminded her of a pitcher of sweet tea. "Deputy," she replied, as if surprised at his appearance.

He shifted his weight from one foot to the other. Taking a breath, he said, "It would be an honor if you'd join myself and my family." He gestured to the only other table in the room. "You're new in town. Might be nice to know some names and faces." When she didn't respond right away, he added, "I promise we don't bite."

Is the darling little girl his daughter? A moment

of disappointment lodged inside, thinking who else she could be.

She was gazing at them with a wide grin and rounded eyes.

"Thank you, but I couldn't intrude. Anyway, I've ordered, and my meal will arrive any moment." She shook her head, hoping he wouldn't press the point. A boyish smile appeared and pulled up one side of his lips then spread all the way up into his eyes, making him look exactly like his daughter.

"I'm sorry, but I must insist," he said. "Brandon Crawford, sheriff—*and* my boss, is adamant about welcoming newcomers." He used his hat to point to his table. "My pa ordered for me, and we're waiting on our meals, as well. Everyone'll be disappointed if you decline. And I know Carlie will be heartbroken. She's about to fall out of her chair with excitement."

The others at his table watched their conversation wide-eyed.

He was right about the little girl. Capitulating with a smile, she returned her things back into her reticule and stood. Before she could pick up her teacup, he did it for her and ushered her over.

At the large table, they made room between his seat and the girl's.

The woman was too old to be his wife, so Madison figured she must be his mother. He set her cup of tea on the tabletop as she got comfortable, or as comfortable as she could be, considering. The woman's stare burned a hole through her forehead. She was impeccably dressed, much more so than anyone else Madison had seen in town, so far.

"Let me introduce everyone," Deputy Wesley offered. "My father, the Honorable Harrison Wesley, my aunt, Pauline Backus, and my little sister, Carlie."

Little sister?

He turned and smiled into her face. "This is Miss Plumb. She arrived on yesterday's stage. She's new to Y Knot."

A judge! How fortuitous. Madison had grown up around judges and senators. She felt the most at ease when she was walking the halls of the capitol or in a courtroom on an errand with her father. "Judge Harrison, sir," she replied, slightly dipping her chin at the deputy's father. "I'm honored to meet you." She looked at the woman and then the little girl. "Mrs. Backus. Carlie."

"It's *Miss* Backus," Deputy Wesley corrected. "My aunt never married."

Hiding her reaction, Madison didn't think Deputy Wesley knew the effect his words had on his aunt. Women didn't take kindly to being reminded of their unmarried status or introduced in such a way. She took a quick glance at the stoic woman, who ignored the comment, and then the judge, who reached for his coffee cup, his face a graying white. He knew . . .

"I noticed when you came into the furniture shop where I'm working," the judge said quickly. "You spoke with Morgan Standford, the proprietor and craftsman. Being his assistant, I do whatever he needs me to do. I'm retired from law in every way, shape, and form. I like the smell of pine shavings and the prospect of a game of checkers at lunchtime."

"Your son has taken up the gauntlet for you?" She glanced at Justin with a smile.

"I tried to direct his desires elsewhere, but he was having none of it. He can be stubborn, when he wants to be."

She turned and looked out the front window. "I remember seeing you at the woodshop, Judge Wesley. The building is right across the street. I didn't hold out much hope of employment there but didn't want to leave any stone unturned. I thought, perhaps, the owner might be looking for someone to sweep the sawdust or manage the counter. I'm good with sums." She peeked at the deputy, who seemed quite content to allow everyone else to carry the conversation.

The judge grinned. "Then you'd be taking *my* job. But actually, the law is calling me back to Denver for a few weeks. I'll be leaving tomorrow, and I'm not looking forward to a minute of it." He waggled his shaggy eyebrows.

Madison softly laughed, liking the judge greatly.

"What's your first name?" his adorable little sister blurted. "I bet it's something pretty. Because *you* are. I love your beautiful dress, too."

Madison didn't miss Justin's gaze briefly touch her rose-colored dress, the high buttoned neckline, the fitted sleeves. She smiled as her face warmed.

"She's right, Miss Plumb. The color suits you."

All gazes at the table fell on her.

"My given name is Madison." She smiled, then took a sip of her tea, wishing their meals would hurry up. Her face must be as red as a tomato.

Miss Backus straightened. "Well, it's a pleasure to meet you, Miss Madison Plumb. My sister was Carlie's mother. Where are you from? Please, do enlighten us."

"From Louisville, Kentucky, ma'am." Madison had decided to say she was from Louisville instead of Frankfort, to keep her true identity hidden, just in case. She wasn't sure how much her birth mother knew about her—if anything. She was sure her name, or her parents' names, had never been revealed.

"And why have you come to Y Knot?"

Judge Wesley cleared his throat. "Pauline, let's not interrogate Miss Plumb with a hundred questions before she gets her meal."

Pauline harrumphed and looked down her nose. "Every young woman I know *enjoys* talking about herself, Harrison. And I enjoy listening. We don't get many new faces in town." She smiled sweetly and looked around the table.

The woman's pressure, as well as wanting to protect her real reason for being in Y Knot, fought inside Madison. "I don't mind," she finally said. "I'm on summer break from Mary Sharp College, a women's college in Winchester, Tennessee. I've come to do research for my final paper next year." *A bit of a stretch, but close enough.* "About the western way of life."

Pauline sat straighter. "Your parents don't worry about you taking such a dangerous journey alone?"

"My mother and father are both deceased."

"I'm so sorry," Deputy Wesley murmured.

"Thank you. My mother passed thirteen years ago, but my father more recently, at the beginning of this year. Actually, I needed this trip to soothe my soul. My professor, Mr. Galbraith, encouraged me." She fought back hot prickles behind her eyes that always threatened whenever she remembered finding her father in his bed, his face peaceful in eternal sleep.

"College," the judge commented, both his brows high. "That's commendable."

"Yes," Miss Backus added. She clasped her hands together and leaned forward on the table. "What are you studying? I'm extremely impressed."

Madison glanced at the quiet deputy. Seemed she'd shocked him speechless. Before she had a chance to reply, a rumble of angry voices sounded from the kitchen. Everyone at the table glanced at the kitchen door, but, just as fast, the commotion faded away.

Judge Wesley shrugged, then gave a small laugh.

"What did your father do for a living?" Pauline went on.

Mr. Wesley lifted a brow, but this time he didn't criticize his sister-in-law.

"He was a clerk for the Honorable William Lindsay, a judge and senator in Frankfort." She cut a glance at the judge and smiled before she realized her mistake. If her father worked in Frankfort, her living in Louisville would appear farfetched. The trip from Louisville to Frankfort was grueling and took a full day to travel. Looking at the trusting faces, all smiling her way, pricked her conscience.

"A judge," Pauline exclaimed breathlessly and beamed at Harrison. "Miss Plumb fits right in. She'll have much to speak about with you. Imagine such a cultured creature residing *here*. I've seen nothing but wagons and cowboys for days on end."

"Y Knot's a *fine* town, Aunt Pauline," Justin protested. "I work here, and we've all relocated. Carlie's young. Most of her memories will be made here."

Aunt Pauline groaned. "I know those facts all too well, Justin. But, if you're honest with yourself, you must admit Y Knot can't compare to Denver. There's no opera or museums, and only a minimal number of shops. You must travel all the way to Waterloo to catch the train. Even as young as Carlie is, your little sister enjoyed the culture of Denver. Here, she'll grow up lacking—"

Madison held up a palm as the two debated. The tension made her uneasy. "My father was *only* a clerk, and *not* a judge, but I did hear my share of motions, judgments, and summaries." She gave a small laugh, remembering. "Of postponements and adjudications. When I was little, he would regale Mother and me with stories about his work in the court. Then, when I was older, he'd sometimes let me tag along on errands or watch cases of attorneys he knew. Those times were exciting, and I enjoyed them."

That was all the truth. By the look on Miss Backus's face, everything she'd said sat better than well with her.

And the judge was giving a slight nod to Justin.

Carlie reached out and touched her hand. "Will you be my friend, Miss Madison?" The child's dancing eyes moved around Madison's face. "Papa allows friends to visit, sometimes. Can you come over someday?"

Madison let out an embarrassed little laugh.

“Of course, Carlie. Thank you for the invitation. As soon as I find a job and get settled.” She glanced around at all the faces. “The reality of employment is looking pretty bleak, at the moment.” She shrugged. “But I’m not losing faith just yet.”

Chapter Seven

The sound of breaking glass reverberated loudly from the kitchen in the Biscuit Barrel. Angry voices erupted again, reminding Justin of the caterwaul of fighting cats. Renee Cannon marched out, slamming the door against the wall with a loud crack. In a show of defiance, the redheaded waitress ripped the apron over her head, hurled it to the floor, and commenced to stomp it with both feet.

Everyone at his table jumped to their feet and stared.

Mrs. Larson, who'd followed, watched open-mouthed. "Renee," she barked. "What on earth? You're acting like a spoiled child. Stop this instant. You're scandalizing our customers."

Renee spun a quick circle. "What customers? The place is practically empty! What's Justin going to do? Arrest me?"

Justin felt his face heat. He'd spent many a slow afternoon in the Biscuit Barrel, drinking coffee and chatting with the two waitresses. He liked both, though Renee did have a bit of a temper. He remembered the time she grasped a drunken cowpoke by the ear and propelled him out the door after he'd patted Ethel on her derriere, causing her to drop a tray of dishes.

At the moment, Ethel stood back, her eyes the size of saucers. She held several full plates stacked up one arm with another in her free hand.

"I quit," Renee scoffed. "And I'm taking my little brother with me. I've had enough of your complaints and overbearing control, Mrs. Larson. 'Renee, look at your sloppy job, do it over!' " She mimicked her boss in a sweet voice. " 'Faster, Renee, we have hungry people to feed. Are you half turtle?' "

For one second, Renee made eye contact with Justin and her cheeks darkened, then she shifted her fury back to Mrs. Larson. "No self-respecting person should work for you. Come on, Sammy," she shouted to the kitchen area. "Get your things and let's go. Mrs. Larson can wash her *own* dishes and wait on her *own* customers. We've had enough of the Biscuit Barrel."

The whole place—which was just his family and Miss Plumb—watched in silence as Renee stormed out the door, followed by Sammy, his head bent over, watching her heels.

"But what about tonight?" Mrs. Larson hollered at the closed door Renee and Sammy had just exited, her face turning beet red. "It's *Wednesday!* The day the whole McCutcheon clan comes in. We need you, Renee." Her voice had withered to a whisper. "*I* need you. Please, reconsider . . ." She wrung her hands, her mouth agape. "What am I going to do?" Only two heartbeats passed before she turned and frowned at Ethel—still stunned into silence against the wall. "Ethel, serve the judge and deputy their meal before their food is ice cold. You know how unappetizing sticky, cold potatoes are."

Ethel bolted forward, the white porcelain dishes clinking together. "Yes, ma'am," she said, placing their meals before them.

A red-faced Mrs. Larson approached. "I apologize for such a horrible display of temper. I'm terribly embarrassed. Renee has a habit of flying off the handle. This isn't the first time she's quit and probably won't be her last. She'll be back . . ."

Justin glanced at Ethel, but the young woman's expression gave nothing away. Struck by inspiration, he gently nudged Madison's foot with the toe of his boot. Seeing her glimpse his way, he looked at Mrs. Larson, tipped his head, and lifted an eyebrow.

Her eyes went wide. Madison gently cleared her throat.

Ethel hurried away to the kitchen for the remaining meals.

"Excuse me, Mrs. Larson," Madison said softly to the owner, still standing a few feet away. The woman's gaze was riveted out the window, as if she could summon Renee and Sammy back with her thoughts. "I couldn't help but hear you're now shorthanded for tonight—and maybe from here on out. I failed to find employment elsewhere today and wondered if you might reconsider me for the job? I'm a fast learner."

Aunt Pauline's head snapped up. "What an excellent idea, Opal. This young lady is educated and refined. I don't think you'll find better."

Opal Larson's face brightened. "Yes, I totally forgot you came in earlier. Would you be able to begin right away, Miss . . . ?"

"Plumb," Justin filled in for her. "Madison Plumb." Madison briefly glanced his way again—this time with a smile on her face. He sat a little straighter.

Mrs. Larson nodded. "Thank you, Deputy. I mean after you finish eating your meal, of course, Miss Plumb."

Miss Plumb twisted the napkin in her lap. "I can."

She didn't sound too confident.

"I'd just need to return to my room and change into a more serviceable dress, but doing so won't take long."

"Wonderful. Enjoy your meal, and I'll find a uniform to fit you, plus an apron. You can get changed and return. I like to be set up and ready before everyone begins to arrive, usually around five or six o'clock."

After witnessing Renee's outburst, Justin hoped he hadn't landed Miss Plumb in a difficult position. Besides today, he'd never really witnessed any other problems between Mrs. Larson and her employees. Smiling into Madison's face, he felt proud and a bit protective, because he'd been with her when all this transpired. His father's rental house, where he lived, as well, was only around the corner from the Biscuit Barrel, barely a three-minute walk. He sliced off a chunk of his golden-brown chicken breast and forked the food into his mouth, thinking how much more exciting Y Knot had become in the last few days.

Justin lifted his gaze to find his father watching him as the judge slowly chewed. His father's brows lifted as his gaze tracked between him and Miss Plumb. He smiled knowingly.

Seemed everyone liked Miss Plumb. *Madison,* he corrected himself. And not just him. Winning Aunt Pauline's favor was not an easy task. She'd put up a fuss whenever Justin had even looked at a pretty woman. Madison, though, was a different matter, altogether. She'd won over his grumpy aunt with just a blink of her eye.

Chapter Eight

As Madison took in the bustling dining room, she gulped down a knot of fear. Why had she been headed to the kitchen? She couldn't remember for the life of her. Laughing voices mingled with the sound of forks and knives clinking against white porcelain plates. Noise reverberated from every corner of the room. She'd been a fool to think she'd have even a second to contemplate the women of Y Knot while working here, let alone *think*—at least, on Wednesday evenings.

After finishing her meal with Deputy Wesley and his family, she'd hurried back to the hotel to change into her uniform. The garment, with its large pockets, was a smidgeon too loose, making it extremely comfortable. Unfortunately, she didn't have any other shoes to change into, and her feet screamed for mercy.

After a quick description of what was expected of her from Mrs. Larson and Ethel, she stood behind the counter and watched through the large front windows as buggies and riders had begun to arrive. Now every table was occupied. Others milled around outside on the porch, waiting for a table to open up.

Ethel pushed out of the kitchen, a dinner plate in her right hand and three more stacked up her left arm. She stopped at Madison's side. "What do you need?" she whispered.

"I'm not sure. I've forgotten why I was headed to the kitchen."

"I'd say it's your order for table ten. It's up and on the counter. Mrs. Larson gets angry if you let the food get cold."

Panicked, Madison glanced around the room, trying to remember which table was number ten. Ethel had pointed out the McCutcheon families as they'd streamed in, but recalling any names was impossible. She felt surrounded by McCutcheon adults and a bevy of offspring. Some ranch hands and others were also present. The place was a madhouse. Granted, a happy madhouse, but she didn't want to do anything to change the atmosphere by messing up on her first night employed at the Biscuit Barrel.

"The middle table by the left window," Ethel whispered. "The one with the four boys. Now, get moving."

"Thank you." Madison rushed away, searching her mind for the names Ethel had mentioned twenty minutes ago. She remembered Billy McCutcheon, because she'd had an acquaintance back in Kentucky named Billy. And Hickory, because the name was so unusual and reminded her of the hickory-flavored beef from Pat's Steak House on Brownsboro Road. *Home.* A surge of homesickness threatened to crush her. Whenever her family traveled to Louisville, they'd disembark the stage in front of Pat's and eat.

"These have been ready for five minutes, Madison," Mrs. Larson barked as she ladled up mashed potatoes on several more plates stacked behind her order.

Madison could tell her boss was holding her temper at bay, probably because Madison was new, and she didn't want to run her off the first night.

Mrs. Larson frowned. "Nothing worse than cold potatoes!"

Right!

Mrs. Larson worked in the kitchen with the cook, who was her adult son. The fella was always red-faced and sweating—and looked like he could use a bath and a shave. At times, Mrs. Larson delivered food, as well, if the orders were backed up. As much as Madison didn't like to think it, her boss could be a candidate for her mother. But that would mean the cook was Madison's half brother. She shuddered. The possibility didn't bring waves of happiness.

"Come right back for your next order," Mrs. Larson said. "We're plating table six as soon as these are cleared." The woman glanced up and tried to smile. "Don't worry, dear," she said, gentling her voice. "The night'll be over before you know it. Just keep going. You're doing a fine job."

Dirty dishes stacked both sides of the sink. Harold, the young man who'd brought her trunk up to her room, had taken over for Sammy. He was bent over the dish pan, scrubbing as if his life depended on it.

Mrs. Larson came around the workstation in front of the hot oven and helped her load the plates.

Madison's eyes blinked wide when her boss began to stack the plates up her arm as Ethel had done. "Ma'am? I don't feel ready to take so many. May I please make two trips?"

Mrs. Larson's brow puckered. She looked down at the dirty apron she wore and shook her head. "I guess it can't be helped. I'll follow you out."

"Thank you, ma'am."

At the table, the boys' talking hushed as she placed her dishes first, making a mistake and having to switch Billy's with the other boy close to his age. Colton, she heard Billy say. Hands now free, she took one plate at a time from Mrs. Larson.

Once served, they all thanked her respectfully.

Mrs. Larson rushed away, leaving her to ask if they needed anything else.

At the same moment, Deputy Wesley tugged open the resistant door and stepped inside. He removed his tan-colored hat, hanging it on the hat rack. Close in proximity, he caught her eye and smiled. "Take a deep breath before you pass out," he said softly. "No one here will bite you if you make a mistake."

His gaze roamed her heated face. She thought she must look a mess. She prayed the moisture on her forehead didn't glow overly much. Following his directions, she paused and took several deep breaths, enjoying the humor in his eyes.

"Better?" he asked.

"Much. Thank you. Now I must run off before table six's food gets cold." She hurriedly glanced around. "The only available spot left is the stool at the end of the counter."

"Perfect. The end stool is my usual seat. Go on, we can talk later."

Invigorated with a new spirit, she hurried away.

The men called hellos to the deputy sheriff as he made his way through the crowded café.

Justin slowed, just now recognizing the man sitting on the stool next to the one he was about to straddle. *Cole Mercer.* Justin had questioned Abe about him only fifteen minutes before.

The bartender said the newcomer had come in once or twice but hadn't stayed long. He'd been invited into a few card games but hadn't partaken.

Isn't turning out to be the gambler I'd thought. Abe stated he liked a whiskey but didn't drink to excess. *Cole Mercer is a riddle.* Justin spanned the stool and sat. "Mercer," he said in a friendly tone. A good chance existed the man was just drifting.

Cole Mercer turned. "Deputy. What has the town all fired up about this café? When I saw all the wagons and buggies, I had to come find out. They cooking something special?"

Justin lifted a shoulder. "Not so much. Wednesday nights just became a routine with the Heart of the Mountains ranch. The owners and ranch hands all come into town for supper and pie. Other townsfolk joined the tradition and sort of made Wednesday nights a special occasion."

Cole glanced behind him and gave a low whistle. His thick, chestnut hair was salted with gray. A scar pulled at the corner of his bottom lip. "The proprietors will turn a tidy sum tonight."

"True enough. The rest of the week, the place just perks along. If you don't like waiting for a table or service, *or crowds,* you might want to avoid coming in on Wednesday evenings."

He gave Justin a long look. "Don't mind crowds."

Justin smiled amiably. "You belong to the dog waiting out front? Seems I remember one following the heels of your fancy gelding when you rode in." The dog sat by the window, gazing in. The animal hadn't even looked Justin's way when he'd taken the stairs and reached for the door. Of medium size, he had a glossy, long black coat with white-tipped paws, tail, and a narrow stripe down his face.

A sentimental smile appeared on Cole's face. "Name's Major. Been riding with me for two and a half years. Found him tied up in an alley in Pendleton, Oregon, half-starved to death. Poor fella was all eyes and ribs. I cut him free and gave him something to eat. He's been my shadow ever since."

Justin raised his brows at the dog's name. "Major, huh? I'm guessin' you're an army man."

Mercer nodded. "And you'd be right. Twenty years."

This time, Justin gave a low whistle. "Long time. Should I be calling you Colonel or Lieutenant Mercer?"

Mercer chuckled and shook his head. "I was promoted a few times but was demoted almost as fast. Didn't always agree with how the army dealt with some things, *especially* Indians. I issued out a captain—and I have no complaints."

"All right, then," Justin said, not really knowing how to respond. The man didn't seem inhibited, speaking about his past. "I'm surprised Hildy lets you bring your dog into the hotel," Justin commented, going back to the subject at hand.

"Took some fast talking, but she relented when I assured her he's housebroken and well mannered. Of course, he sat quietly when she met him and licked her hand. Now he all but ducks out of sight when he sees her coming. Pretty smart for a mutt. Out of sight, out of mind."

Madison appeared before them behind the counter. "Sorry to keep you waiting. What can I get for you?"

Justin didn't miss the charming smile Mercer sent Madison's way.

"How about a menu?" Cole asked.

Madison blinked several times. "Oh, I'm sorry. Didn't realize . . ."

"I don't need a menu, Miss Plumb," Justin called to her retreating back.

One second later, she handed Mercer a ratty menu spotted with gravy.

Justin could tell she was completely rattled.

She looked at him.

"While my friend here's deciding," he said, "and only when you have time, I'll take the meatloaf and a cup of coffee, if the pot is fresh."

She bit her lower lip.

"Skip that. I'll take the coffee any which way."

"Madison!" The sharp call came from the kitchen. "Order up."

She glanced at the swinging door.

"Never mind," Justin said, shooing her away. "My coffee can wait." Seeing her wobbly smile that warmed Justin to his bones, he watched her go.

Chapter Nine

Charity read quietly at the side of Brandon's bed, the bed she'd slept in as a child. She'd had a cot brought in so she could stay close and not disturb his broken leg.

Bachelor's buttons, Lady's smock, And the Lady Hollyhock . . .

Her attention faltered as the lines of poetry wavered before her eyes. Ashley Adair, Francis's intended and Y Knot's new schoolteacher, had given her *A Child's Garden of Verses* by Robert Louis Stevenson as a gift as soon as the news of her pregnancy had become known. The sweetness of the rhymes touched Charity. She couldn't wait to share them with their baby.

The ranch was quiet. Most everyone who had stayed back from the cattle drive had gone into town to eat at the Biscuit Barrel. Her mother had stayed behind with her, and also Lucky, the bunkhouse cook, claiming a toothache that made him crankier than an ol' bear.

She stole a glance at Brandon. *Still asleep.* He appeared calm, his face relaxed and his fingers laced together over the white sheet with an embroidered edge. This morning, after Justin had taken his leave, Brandon became unusually drowsy, even more so than he'd been the last couple of days when his pain had been at its greatest. Charity encouraged him to rest, so his body could mend more quickly, but now she missed him. Even in his battered condition, he did his best to lessen her worry by making silly comments and keeping a running dialogue going. When he was awake, he assured her he was fine—and she tried to believe it. No broken bone was going to slow him down. She adored his deep voice. His boyish, quick smile.

Contemplating how much she loved him sent her heart trembling. She set the book on the end table and gently caressed her tummy, marveling at the thought of their baby growing inside her. Life was a miracle few people took the time to ponder deeply enough. Elements of her and Brandon mingled together, creating a whole new person. Beautiful.

They shall be joined together, and the two will become one flesh.

"Charity?"

Turning, she found her mother at the door, a small frown marring her forehead. She held two cups of tea. "You need some rest, too, sweetheart. Don't forget about the baby. You've been in here for three hours. Let me sit with him, and you take this tea and enjoy it downstairs. After you're through, take a little walk. Stretch your legs. It'll refresh you."

Smiling, Charity stood and stretched her aching

muscles. Maybe only about five months along, she noticed how keen were the differences in her body. Her stamina was gone, and she tired much more quickly. She could fall asleep in the blink of an eye.

After one quick glance at Brandon, she approached her mother and took the cup of tea held out in offering. "I know you're right. I just can't seem to leave him. He looks so young when he's asleep like this. You remember he lost both his parents when he was only five, them murdered by an outlaw? He didn't have an easy life. Not like me. I want to make up for those times. Make sure he knows just how much we *all* love him." Glancing at Brandon again, she longed to go to him and hold his hand. He meant more to her than life itself. And now, she had his baby to love, as well.

"He knows, sweetie. We can't love him any more than we already do." Claire slowly rubbed Charity's arm. "He'll be up and around in no time. You're the one who needs to be careful. You have someone very special to look out for."

Her mother smiled into her eyes.

Claire put her arm around Charity's side, easing her closer. "You can't take the best care of him if you get sick from exhaustion. I'll sit with him. Then it'll be time for dinner. He'll be fine. I won't take my eyes off him. I promise."

An aggravated moan came from Brandon,

jerking her out of her pondering. They both snapped their attention back to the bed. Brandon had been in pain since the break but hadn't complained overly much, even when Charity knew he must be drowning in it. Rushing to his side, she set her teacup next to the poetry book and Brandon's glass of water.

His head turned from side to side, and he moaned again. This time, he clenched his body as if his stomach hurt.

Frightened, she laid a hand on his forehead, and heat radiated up into her palm. This was something new. She turned to her mother in alarm. "He's hot! He's not had a fever before."

Claire leaned in, touching Brandon, herself. She pulled back, studying his face. "Fever usually means an infection . . ."

Fear streaked through Charity. The process since the accident had gone smoothly, she now realized. After his leg had been set and a cast applied, he'd spent two days at Doc Handerhoosen's. Then, going slowly, the men had transported Brandon by wagon back to the Heart of the Mountains, and they'd been staying there since.

Turning to Claire, she gripped her mother's arm. "What if something else happened to Brandon when he fell? This morning, I questioned Justin more fully since he witnessed the accident. Saw Brandon and Luke fall. He said Brandon landed on his side, twisted, when the beam broke his leg. Could Brandon be suffering from something more?"

Moisture shimmered on Brandon's forehead.

"We mustn't think the worst, Charity." Claire glanced at her son-in-law for several long seconds, her brows drawn down in a deep V. "You stay with him, and I'll run out to the bunkhouse and send Lucky into town to fetch the doctor."

Her mother's face had gone white. She was frightened, too, but was trying not to frighten Charity any more than she already was.

Headed for the door, her mother turned. "I'll send Esperanza up with a basin of cool water and a washcloth. Bathing his face and chest will help keep his temperature in check until the doctor arrives. Don't fret too much. Everything'll be all right. This is just a tiny setback."

Brandon moaned again, and this time he made as if to sit up but cried out.

Charity eased him back, knowing something terrible had happened to her husband. She'd seen horses colic. She'd seen them die. It was tragic, but not uncommon for a ranch with many animals. Their intestines got twisted or blocked. The horse had to be walked nonstop until the twist or obstruction passed. The accident flashed through her thoughts. Had something happened to her love? A pain sliced through her. She bit her bottom lip so hard she tasted blood.

She *must* stay positive—for his sake. Anything less would be weakness and went against her nature. She wouldn't lose Brandon! She couldn't. The possibility was unthinkable.

Chapter Ten

Madison glanced around the faces of the large table the McCutcheon men made by pulling two others together. Their wives sat by their sides, chatting excitedly. They'd already had their supper and were ordering dessert. As she scribbled their choices on her small pad of paper, her gaze kept returning to Rachel McCutcheon, the smiley young woman married to the eldest brother, Matthew. If Madison were to guess, the woman must be in her early thirties, maybe thirty-two or thirty-three, which meant Rachel would have had to be extremely young, twelve or thirteen. She'd heard such stories before. Rachel's hair was brown but had golden highlights. And something about her eyes looked familiar. Could she have given birth to Madison and given her up for adoption before she'd met and married Matthew McCutcheon? "Ma'am," Madison said, gesturing to Rachel. "Do you know what kind of pie you'd like?"

Rachel smiled. "I have two favorites, and today I'd like blueberry crumble."

Seemed the Biscuit Barrel was big on crumbles, as most of the choices were exactly that.

"My mouth has been watering all day at the thought," she added, winking at Madison. "Please tell me you have some left."

"Oh, yes. Plenty." Madison scribbled down her order and looked at the fella who'd been introduced as Luke McCutcheon. "Sir?"

He smiled warmly. "Apple for me, and a generous slice."

This was a welcoming bunch. Everyone had been good-natured when she'd mixed up a few details on their supper order, and she'd had to go back to the kitchen three times to correct her mistakes. She nodded and felt her lips tip up in answer. "You, ma'am?"

"I'll have what my sister-in-law is having—blueberry crumble," the pretty woman at Mr. McCutcheon's side replied.

And so the evening went. Madison was convinced Rachel McCutcheon was her mother until she met Berta May, the fifty-somethingish lady who owned the fabric store. The way she tipped her head back and forth as she laughed reminded her of herself. She would have been in her twenties, nineteen years ago. Much more plausible than the tender age of twelve or thirteen. Such a traumatic experience so young would be difficult to get over. And Rachel McCutcheon didn't seem traumatized in any way.

Only ten minutes earlier, she'd met Lynette and Saralee, the wives of Ralph and Jed Hicks, the lumbermen who supplied logs to the Klinkner Mill. The two women were friends with Ethel, who had quickly introduced Madison as she'd passed their table. Somewhere in their later thirties, both were the right age to be considered. Where Lynette was darker skinned, plump, and had a waterfall of straight, black hair, Saralee was slender, with frizzy strawberry-blond hair. Three children sat between them, two boys and one girl, all under the age of about sixteen, Madison guessed. One boy, a tall, rangy fella with dark black hair, appeared to be slow, because the other boy, his cousin, helped him speak to order his pie.

How on earth would she ever learn the histories of something so private? She felt more confused than ever. Before she'd arrived in Y Knot, she'd thought finding her mother was just a matter of time. But, after meeting some of the many possibilities, she realized the task would be much more difficult than she'd ever believed.

Chapter Eleven

Dr. Handerhoosen ushered Claire and Charity into the hallway where Brandon couldn't overhear what he was about to say.

Charity had never seen the man so serious. Lucky had fortuitously met the doctor already in his buggy on their side of the town. Sending him on ahead to the ranch, Lucky then continued to the Biscuit Barrel for Luke and the rest of the McCutcheons, who should arrive any time.

"My best guess is Brandon has some sort of infection. If he'd broken something internally, the pain would have presented itself on the day of the accident."

Shocked, Charity couldn't believe her ears. "Your *best guess,* Doctor? Don't you know?"

He wagged his head, his face grave. "I can't be sure of anything. I'm only able to eliminate what's not causing his pain and temperature. I believe he's sustained a rupture somewhere, probably in his abdominal wall, stomach, small intestine, or perhaps his bowels. Worst case scenario is he's developed peritonitis."

Peritonitis! "What's to be done, Doctor?" Claire asked in a hushed voice, her expression grave. "Surely, there's something you can do."

Thankful for her mother's presence, Charity took a deep, soothing breath. She didn't have the will to speak with all the horrible possibilities running through her head.

"There is. If I'm right, he needs surgery immediately to remove the injured section before the infection worsens. I'm sorry, but I'm not qualified to do such a detailed procedure."

Charity's eyes went wide. The life of her husband was ebbing away. Clenching her fists, she dug her fingernails into her palms.

Dr. Handerhoosen put out a placating hand. "There is a hospital, a *fine* hospital, in Helena. I've heard St. John's has some of the best surgeons in the land. Since Brandon's fever and abdominal pain only started today, I believe you've caught it in time. But he needs to get to Helena immediately."

Charity felt her mother's gaze on her face. "We'll leave tonight," she said with conviction.

Dr. Handerhoosen nodded. "The sooner, the better. You'll need to prepare a wagon so Brandon will be comfortable and able to make the trip lying down."

"Charity," her mother said softly. "You *must* think of the baby. You should stay at the ranch. Your brothers and I will accompany Brandon."

Charity couldn't believe what she'd just heard. "I'm *going,* Mother. Nothing you can say will change my mind. My baby's place is with his or her father. Brandon needs us. To give him something to live for. If the tables were turned,

I'd want him with me." Charity knew she must ask the question causing her throat to constrict with fear. "What are his chances, Doctor? Is this surgery risky?"

Frowning, he slowly shook his head. "*Every* surgery is risky. And if I was to give you some numbers, they'd just be another guess. I've only read about peritonitis. This is the first case I've seen, if, indeed, I'm correct."

Well, at least the doctor wasn't mincing words. Brandon needed all her support and prayers.

"Please remember," he went on. "Brandon is strong. The body is a great healer, if given a chance. I'll stay until you're ready to depart. Help prepare him for the journey. Work to keep his fever at bay with the ice Lucky is fetching. I'll send laudanum to ease the pain during transport. The wagon ride to Waterloo will be the worst." He removed the stethoscope from around his neck, folded the instrument, and placed it back in his small, black bag.

"Thank you, Doctor," Claire and Charity said together.

He scrubbed a large, wrinkled hand over his face. "I wish there was something more I could do. As soon as Lucky returns, we should send him back to town with a telegram to St. John's in Helena and alert the surgeons Brandon is on his way. They'll be ready for surgery the moment he arrives."

Chapter Twelve

By eleven o'clock the next morning, the wagon carrying Brandon pulled into Waterloo, every dip and bump in the road making the buckboard jostle and Charity's heart constrict. Brandon lay on a stack of folded blankets with a thin sheet to cover him. For the most part, clouds had shielded the sun, but it was now shining with gusto. What was left of the ice puddled around him. When Brandon was awake, his eyes were bleary with fever, although chills racked his body. Charity, Luke, and Matthew sat in the wagon next to him as Mark drove the team.

Francis rode by their side, intending to drive the wagon back as soon as he helped them board the train.

Once the McCutcheon clan heard from Lucky about Brandon's situation, they'd rushed home and spent several hours preparing to transport him to Waterloo as pain-free as possible. Their wives packed necessities and prepared food for travel. Charity's mother had fought tooth and nail to keep her at home, to no avail. She'd not stay behind.

With Flood and most all the ranch hands away on the cattle drive, someone of authority needed to stay back at the ranch. Claire McCutcheon was the only choice. She'd have Francis, Nick, Lucky, and Hickory to look after things on the Heart of the Mountains. Matthew, Mark, and Luke wouldn't hear of staying back. They loved Brandon like another brother, and Brandon would need their strength—and so would she.

When the train finally pulled out, Charity nodded to Francis as the ranch hand stood grave-faced on the station platform, seeing them off. The outcome of this journey was in God's hands. She was already weary and bone-tired, and they'd only just begun. Through her watery gaze, she studied Brandon's strained face. He'd been trying to hide the fact his pain had slowly increased since yesterday. His temperature stayed elevated, despite the ice-packed night and wagon trip.

Her heart trembled, seeing him so weak. Never in all the years she'd known Brandon had he ever been sick, had a sniffle, or broken a bone. She glanced at the large cast sticking out at an odd angle, making passing in the aisle difficult. Overnight, Matthew and Mark had constructed a small platform to place between the train seats so Brandon could ride lying down, as Dr. Handerhoosen had instructed. They'd rounded up all the extra blankets from the bunkhouse for padding.

The passenger car was already half-full when they arrived. When the seated travelers saw the men carrying Brandon, preceded by Francis lugging the wooden platform, they gathered their things and moved, giving them room.

The conductor assured everyone Brandon was not contagious in any way and there was nothing to fear.

Charity felt a hand on her shoulder and looked up.

"Stop worrying so much, Char." Luke spoke softly, his forced smile wobbling. "Brandon's too cantankerous to stay down for long. He'll be back to badgering us and all the doctors, as soon as he's had the operation, and . . ." Unable to go on, Luke snapped his mouth closed.

She watched as her brother slowly took in Brandon's sleeping face, the train chugging along the track maddeningly slow. Wasn't there a way to make it go faster?

Matt came down the rocking aisle, carrying two cups of coffee.

Mark followed with the same.

"Found these up front," he said, handing a mug to Luke and another to Charity. "The engineer's rigged up a handy-dandy contraption so the fire powering this train can also perk a pot of coffee. Quite ingenious."

Charity smiled her thanks. She blew on the hot liquid, touched to see hers was laced almost white. Where her brothers found milk was a mystery, one she'd ask them about later. Right now, she was too exhausted and heartsick to talk. She'd almost been done in by the all-night wagon ride. Brandon had come around several times in the wee hours on the way to Waterloo. She'd held his hand as they studied the predawn stars. As much as her brothers tried to get her to ride up front on the seat where she'd be more comfortable, she'd refused. Now, her back ached in protest.

"Still the same?" Mark asked quietly.

She nodded. The train trip was hours long. And they'd have to change lines twice more. *God in heaven, have mercy. Don't take Brandon. We've only just begun. We have a lifetime of love to share. You've blessed us with a baby. And a baby needs a father as much as I need my husband. Dearest God, I'm begging you. Please, hear my prayer.*

Chapter Thirteen

Lenore Saffelberg busied herself putting the finishing touches on the living room of her tiny rental. She made sure the coverlet over her couch was wrinkle free, the pillows in her two chairs nicely plumped, and every speck of dirt or dust swept off her rug. The water in the kettle was hot and ready for tea. Measured out on her kitchen counter, and waiting to be mixed and baked, were the ingredients for a classic Southern buttermilk pie.

She did a full turn and stopped, gazing at her sole living room window. A smile crept across her face. Tipping her head, she took in her handiwork. The striking difference the new curtains made in the room was astonishing. They should have been changed years ago. She didn't have one of those fancy-dancy sewing machines like Berta May. Each evening, after her shift at the restaurant, she put her feet up on her small stool and stitched away by hand until her eyes hurt and her fingers ached. Once she was in bed, the challenging task relaxed her enough she fell asleep instead of tossing and turning until dawn, contemplating her what-ifs and what-nows.

Where was her life going? At one time, she'd

thought Trent Herrick might be sweet on her, since he'd come into the restaurant daily, but now everyone knew Hildy was the woman who'd caught his fancy. There'd also been Morgan Standford, when he'd first arrived in town, but possibilities of him being a beau lasted all of five minutes.

The lovely fabric beautifying the window once again made her smile. Sea-green brocade with a small, raised pattern. Speckles of gold and crimson scattered throughout. She'd fashioned a puffy valance stuffed with old newspapers and stitched flowing panels that cascaded down and puddled on the floor. The double-sided tiebacks finished off the look. And she'd always been good at tying a proper bow.

She harrumphed. If her window were larger, she'd not have been able to afford the expensive material in the first place. Disappointingly, Berta May held firm with the price on the textile, even though much hadn't remained on the bolt to make anything else.

Except my curtains.

At the sound of a soft knock, Lenore was jolted out of her reverie. She hurried to the door, an excited little skip making her smile.

"You *sure* you don't want me to cancel my trip to Denver?" Harrison stood before his bedroom mirror, tying his tie. "I'd like nothing better than to have a valid excuse not to go." Finished, he turned with a wide smile.

Justin stood behind him, a coffee mug in his hand. He knew that look—the one his father got when he thought he'd won the argument. "I'm proficient enough to watch over Y Knot by myself." He pushed aside his disappointment. *When will he realize I'm not a boy any longer and am capable of doing a man's job?*

"Of course, you are, son. I didn't say different. I only offered because Brandon is incapacitated. Such a crying shame about that fine young man. We can only pray his surgery goes well. And now, all the McCutcheon men are out of town, too. You don't have *any* backup. I'd just feel better staying here."

Justin took a slug of his lukewarm coffee, telling himself to tamp down his temper. His father was only trying to help. Maybe a year ago, Justin would have said yes to the offer, but not now. He didn't need, or want, his father watching over his shoulder. "You're retired, remember? Besides, there're lots of men still in Y Knot. Morgan Standford, Hayden Klinkner, Trent Herrick, to name a few. I've been here over a year, and all I've had to do is arrest a few drunks, dig people out of the snow, and go looking for lost livestock. What could go wrong?"

"A lot," Harrison threw out, all pleasantness gone from his tone. "Those men have never faced down a gun pointed in their face. Or pulled the trigger when there was no other option. And they shouldn't have to. They don't wear the star. *You* do."

Justin paced to his father's bedroom window, looked out for all of one second, and then turned to face the man who'd sired him. The judge was formidable. Men shook with fear when they saw the Honorable Judge Wesley headed their way. His father's shoes were large and would be difficult to fill, but if Justin never got a chance to test himself, he'd never know where he stood. "I wish you'd put some faith in me. I hoped your coming to Y Knot was to retire and not to secretly look out for your little boy."

Harrison shook his head. He wiped a hand over his newly shaven face, the scent of shaving lather still lingering in the air. "I wonder if I was this stubborn when I was your age? Somehow, I don't think so."

Aunt Pauline appeared in the doorway. She looked between them, her eyes narrowing. She was a woman of medium build and height and always wore her hair up. The small, brownish mole at the edge of her left ear always drew his gaze for a second or two. She'd come into Justin's life when he was eighteen, when his father remarried her younger sister. At first, Aunt Pauline had been indifferent to him, perhaps not wanting to step on any toes, since he was practically grown. But since then, she'd taken an interest in everything he did. Offered advice in certain situations, suggesting how to dress appropriately when they'd gone to the opera and such back in Denver. He liked her well enough, except when she nitpicked and harangued his father.

"Don't have an argument right before leaving town, Harrison. Justin," Pauline said, coming into his father's bedroom and closing the door. "I'm surprised at you. I heard your voices all the way down in the kitchen."

Justin shared a long look with his father. He didn't want his father to leave on bad terms, either. "I don't want to argue. I just want you to go on your trip and have a good time."

"Good time? I'm performing a wedding for the daughter of the clerk who used to drive me to distraction," Harrison replied. "That fella was the most irritating employee I ever had. For some reason, he took a shine to me. Then, twelve years ago, he made me swear on my grave that, when the time came, I'd perform his daughter's wedding. How was I to know he'd remember and call in the promise?"

"Or that you'd move all the way to Montana Territory?" Aunt Pauline quipped. "I still can't believe you uprooted all of us the way you did, myself, Harrison. And," she went on after a deep exhale, "if you recall, he sent you a message every Christmas to make *sure* you didn't forget. He's a man who knows how to get what he wants." She handed Harrison his satchel. "I've packed you some goodies in case you get hungry on your way to the train. Hurry up now, you don't want to miss the stage." She shook her head. "Please take the pained look off your face, Harrison. You have other appointments you've set up, meetings with old friends, and a dinner here and there. You'll have a wonderful time. I can tell you this . . ." She glanced at Justin, her brow winging high. "I wish *I* was the one going on the outbound stage back to civilization. I surely do. Denver, with its multitude of culture. Museums, the arts, sumptuous dinners over candlelight. And my women's club doing everything we could for the downtrodden." Her eyes fairly glazed over, and then she pinned Justin with an ominous stare. "Young women who knew how to dress, act, and conducted themselves with dignity."

Justin knew what was coming next before the words passed her lips.

"Like our dear, *wonderful* Miss Plumb. Isn't she a delight? Justin, you really should snap her up before someone else has a chance. She's head and shoulders—"

"Pauline!" Harrison barked. "Stop with your delusions of grandeur. There are many fine young women here in Y Knot. They don't have to be up to *your* standards."

“Oh, you don’t like Miss Plumb?” she asked, her face coloring.

“That goes without saying. We *all* like Miss Plumb, including Carlie.” His gaze snagged Justin’s. “All I’m asking is for you to stay out of my son’s personal business. He’s a grown man and can make his own decisions without your tutelage. Now, I *will* miss my stage if I don’t walk out of the room this instant.” He went to the bed, snatched up his Stetson, and made for the door.

Chapter Fourteen

An hour after he'd seen his father off on the stage, Justin sat in the sheriff's office, Harrison's parting words still fresh in his mind.

"Goodbye, son. I've every confidence in you, despite my earlier offer to cancel my trip. You're right, of course. You've been at this a year and have a fine head on your shoulders. Just follow your instincts. Sometimes, overthinking a situation can be a mistake." He'd shaken Justin's hand and then tugged him into a hug. "I love you."

Climbing into the coach, the driver made ready to go.

"I'll see you safe and sound in a few weeks. And," he added as the conveyance pulled out, "please keep an eye on your aunt. Help her with Carlie. You know how overbearing Pauline can be."

And then he was gone.

Overbearing, yes, but his aunt meant well. He glanced at the envelope lying on the desk. She'd given him the sealed missive this morning, meant for Miss Plumb. He leaned back in his chair and looked around. The room was shipshape. Not a thing out of place. He almost wished something needed to be cleaned so he'd have a chore to do. If the day proceeded as uneventfully as the morning had, he'd be bored to tears.

At least, when Brandon was here, the sheriff had Charity with him most of the time. Lately, the two had been working on their house plans, as well as the layout of the rest of the ranch. Sometimes, the conversation got a mite spirited between them, but it was fun to listen to. Other times, Justin excused himself and went to the leather shop to pay a visit to Trent Herrick or down to Standford's Fitting to chat with Morgan and the judge. His father had taken incredibly well to retirement. Justin had had more than a few doubts he'd be happy with an easier life, leaving the law to him and Brandon—but he had. The tension had eased out of his face, and he was getting more sleep.

Mr. Tracy came through the door. "Telegram from Luke." He handed the paper over. "Came in this minute."

"Do I have time to send a reply?"

Mr. Tracy shook his head. "Don't think so. This was sent when they was changing trains. Most likely gone by now, I'm sure."

The McCutcheons had promised to keep Justin informed on Brandon's condition as much as possible along the way, and in turn, he'd pass on the information immediately to Claire out at the ranch.

Flood and the ranch hands were somewhere

in between Y Knot and Miles City and were impossible to reach.

HALFWAY THERE. STOP. BRANDON HOLDING HIS OWN. STOP.

Poor Brandon. How fast his life had changed. Justin couldn't imagine anything except a complete recovery for his friend and boss. He stood and walked with Mr. Tracy to the door. The next few days would be crucial for Y Knot. Everyone, as well as himself, would be devastated if anything happened to Brandon. The thought was unthinkable. "Have you seen Harold? I need him to ride out to the Heart of the Mountains and deliver this telegram to Mrs. McCutcheon. Send him my way."

"Saw him a few minutes ago, dumping a bucket of dirty water outside Lichtenstein's. If I can't find him, or someone else soon, I'll let ya know, Deputy. You have my word." The small man nodded and stepped out the door.

Buzzing caught Justin's ear. A horsefly was trapped inside on the window, bumping every which way to try to escape. Fetching an old newspaper, he rolled it and gave the insect a thwack.

Outside, Cole Mercer rode by the window on his good-looking sorrel. The gelding was tall, with four white stockings and a wide blaze. The sun glimmered on a small silver concha attached to the browband. Mercer's dog was nowhere to be seen.

Who *was* Cole Mercer? Justin's appraisal of him as a gambler or drifter was changing. The mystery Justin felt on the man's first day in town only amplified, and he recalled Brandon's last words to keep watch.

Intent on Mercer, Justin hadn't noticed Madison coming up the boardwalk from the opposite direction at a nice clip until she was right in front of the window. Without seeing him, she stopped and was about to cross the street. When she looked both ways, he had a moment to study her profile. Tall, sloping forehead, straight, petite nose, nicely formed lips. *Enchanting.* Before giving much thought to his action, he tapped on the window.

She turned.

He put up a hand in greeting, just remembering his other hand still held the crumpled paper with the dead fly. Breaking his own rule of orderliness, he tossed the swatter behind him and strode for the door. "Good morning," he said. "How'd you fare last night? The Biscuit Barrel was still quite busy when I left."

"I'm still alive to speak about it," she said with an impish smile. "And I'm headed back for the lunch shift a little later today."

"Are you mad at me for setting you up at the Biscuit Barrel?"

She pretended a scowl, and then laughed. "Not at all. I needed a job and now I have one, thanks to you." She stuck her foot out from under her hem and waved at her new shoes. "Tonight, I'm prepared. My other shoes are extremely uncomfortable. I bought these today at Lichtenstein's. Hurrying about won't be quite so painful." She wiggled an eyebrow. "I'm breaking them in."

He glanced down and then up into her face. "Good idea. Oh, I almost forgot, I have something for you."

Her brows rose in anticipation.

"A note from my aunt. I'll just grab it off my desk. Do you have time to wait?"

"Of course."

He returned to the desk for the note. Back outside, he handed it to her. "I have no idea what this is, except that it's from my aunt Pauline. She's taken a strong liking to you." Embarrassed, he felt his face heat. "As we *all* have," he amended quickly.

Her smile rose into her eyes. "That's nice to hear. I'm delighted to have some friends." She put her finger under the flap. "I like your aunt, as well—and all of you."

He chuckled at her quick wit as his curiosity over the message intensified. And now worried him a little. Knowing Aunt Pauline, the note could say anything.

Miss Plumb's gaze held steady on the page and then lifted toward his face.

"Good news? Bad news? Like I said, I have no idea . . ."

"My first formal invitation."

He stifled his gulp. What had his aunt gone and done, now?

"To dinner. On my first night off, which is tonight. I'm supposed to let you know."

"Dinner? Tonight?" He put out a placating hand. "You don't have to accept, Miss Plumb, if you'd rather not, or have other things to do. My aunt will understand. She is, ah . . ."

Madison's brow fell as color came up in her face. "I don't *have* to comply, Deputy. If you'd rather I didn't, I do have things I could do, like work on my paper. I've been remiss, what with settling in and then working at the café, and haven't written one word. If you want me to decline, I understand." She blinked a couple of times and then looked away. "We've hardly met, and I'm sure you're busy, with the sheriff being hurt and out of town—the poor man. I pray he makes a speedy recovery."

How could he explain himself without sounding like a dolt? He didn't know, but he was willing to try. "I'm sorry, what I said came out all wrong. We all would love for you to come, but I just didn't want to put you on the spot in case you had other plans." If she hadn't taken a step back, putting some space between them, he might have picked up her hand. "I assure you, having you for supper would be delightful—if, er, well, we used to have a woman who did the cooking when we lived in Denver. Aunt Pauline does her best, but sometimes, her meals don't quite turn out as she plans. Let me just say, her dinners don't taste like the food at the Biscuit Barrel."

Madison's wary expression faded away. "If that's all, you have nothing to worry about. I'm sure anything she prepares will be excellent. And I'll get to see your little sister again. She's absolutely darling, which you already know." She glanced across the street at the fabric store. "Now, if you'll excuse me, I'm on my way to Berta May's. I'll see you tonight, around five o'clock." She studied the invitation a moment longer. "Clove Hitch Street?" she said softly. "The next street over?"

"Right. On the end by the gazebo. We can see the Biscuit Barrel from our front porch."

A smile peeked out. "That's handy."

He grinned. "Indeed." A strained silence hummed between them. "I'll let you get to your business." Justin doffed his hat, annoyed Aunt Pauline hadn't given him the opportunity to ask Madison first. Or, at least, let him know her intentions. The last few moments could have been handled much better. "Miss Plumb," he said. "Until tonight."

With a nod and smile, Miss Plumb swished across the street in a flutter of yellow and blue, making Justin's heart skip a beat as she went. He had some planning to do.

CHAPTER FIFTEEN

"Have you always been a writer?" Pauline asked.

Madison, perched on a chair in the front room of the Wesleys' small home, smiled. She could tell Pauline was intent on impressing her. Justin's aunt sat straight, with perfect posture and a slight tip of her chin. She was kind and had taken a deep interest in her. The home and furnishings looked more suited for ranch hands than a distinguished judge, or even a deputy. Along the wall, closest to the kitchen, was a well-worn chesterfield where Justin sat. The faded green fabric matched a painting of a meadow hung on the wall above. A long, brown bench under the window that gave a view of Clove Hitch Street was spruced up with two green plaid pillows. Madison and Aunt Pauline sat opposite the sofa in matching cream armchairs. Madison understood things were different here in Montana. Pauline went to great lengths to explain the house was a rental and had come furnished. Most of the few family pieces they'd brought from Colorado were up in the bedrooms.

"For as long as I can remember," she responded to Pauline's question, satisfied from the meal of roasted chicken and mashed potatoes. "Mostly just in my diaries or short stories. And, of course, my schoolwork the last few years." The dinner also included creamed corn, small, round biscuits, and vanilla cake with sugar cream frosting for dessert. Belying Justin's warning, she'd thought everything delicious. "I'm determined to, at least, finish the first draft here in Y Knot." She took a small breath and looked between Justin and Pauline. "Renee returned to work, as Mrs. Larson mentioned she might, so I won't be working as much at the café—which gives me more time to write." *And search for my mother*. She thought of her sore feet. They were happy about the turn of events, as well.

Justin smiled and nodded in her direction.

Seemed the deputy was a man of few words. Or, at least, when he was around his family. Like the day in the café when she'd first met the judge and Pauline. The older woman had insisted they be on a first-name basis.

Carlie skipped into the room, her face rosy from running upstairs to her room and back again in just a few seconds. "I found it." She hurried to Madison's side, holding a square of fabric made in the log cabin quilting pattern. The stiches were loose and uneven, but Carlie beamed as if she had won a grand prize at the county fair. "See?" she said. "I did it all by myself."

"You did?" Madison responded with surprise and awe in her tone. "It's lovely. I like the colors you chose."

Carlie nodded with enthusiasm. "Miss Sinclair is teaching me to quilt."

Madison tipped her head, thinking. She hadn't yet heard the name. "Miss Sinclair?"

"That's Berta May," Justin supplied. "Owner of the fabric shop opposite the sheriff's office. You went there this morning."

"Oh, yes, Berta May. I've not heard her last name before." *And I've been wondering, too. For my search.*

Carlie nodded vigorously again. "I go once a week on Tuesdays, and she's teaching me. With two other ladies. It's fun."

Madison glanced at Pauline. Children usually learned domestic arts from their mother or grandmother. But a small class was a nice idea.

"I never learned to quilt, and Carlie expressed an interest. Carlie's mother took more to socializing than sewing and quilting. Besides, Carlie was still quite young when Agnes passed."

Justin looked to the door for the fourth time in the last few minutes. He seemed impatient to be away. She really didn't want to hold him up if he had something pressing. The past two hours had been a treat. She'd been welcomed into their home and to the supper table like long-lost family. "Justin, if you're needed elsewhere, please don't let me hold you up . . ."

Caught out, a stain of embarrassment climbed up his face.

"Am I so transparent? I can assure you, I didn't mean to be. It's just, with Brandon out of town and his condition worsening, I usually only take a moment to eat and then stay in the office." He gestured to the walnut pendulum clock on the wall. "Really should get back."

She stood. "Please, I don't want to interfere with your work. And I should leave, as well. Thank you for such a lovely evening." She glanced at Pauline. "The supper was delicious. And it was nice to be off my feet for a few hours. I can't tell you how much I've enjoyed the evening."

Carlie's smile vanished at the prospect of their guest leaving.

"Then the timing is perfect." Pauline followed Madison and Justin as she rose to her feet. "Justin can see you safely to the hotel."

"I'll be happy to."

How fortunate she was to meet Justin as soon as she'd arrived in town. His friendship meant so much. Passing by his office a few times a day gave her an opportunity to lean in and say hello. And now she knew his family, too. She'd be quite lonely without them. Reaching down, she gave Carlie a brief hug.

"Promise you'll come back again, Miss Madison," Carlie said softly. "Next week."

"I will, sweetie."

Justin helped her on with her shawl and then he

strapped on his gun belt, as well as the bullwhip. Securing his hat, he opened the door to a gust of wind.

Leaves from the front porch scattered inside.

Pauline took a quick step back. “No matter my efforts, I can’t seem to keep this place clean and presentable.”

Madison grasped the ends of her shawl to keep them from flying in her face. “It’s blustery out here.” Her hair whipped around and soon felt like a mess.

Justin stood on the top step, looking down the quiet street. “I noticed the clouds this afternoon. Just a little summer storm on the way to water the land. Won’t be much.”

Pauline and Carlie waved as she and Justin headed down the road, twilight slowly giving way to darkness.

“That was lovely. I enjoy speaking with your aunt. She’s an intelligent woman and has a lot to share.”

He smiled and then tipped his head into the wind so as not to lose his hat. “Well, it’s easy to see she’s taken a liking to you. A tiny word of warning. She’s a gracious woman and means well, but she can become quite controlling.”

Madison glanced back at the house, where golden light illuminated several of the windows. “I’ll keep that in mind.”

“That may sound ungrateful, but you’ll understand more fully as you get to know her." He slapped his hand over his heart. "We all love her dearly . . . but . . ."

Nothing could spoil the homey, cared-for, and included sentiments Madison felt inside. A result of the special evening. Justin hadn't said much, because Pauline was fond of talking. The woman commandeered most of his dialogues until he just sat back and let her speak, giving Madison a conspiratorial wink behind the woman's back. Justin did have a point. "So, Justin," she began slowly. They had a whole block to walk. "You must know everyone in town, by now. Am I right?"

He glanced in her direction. "Pretty much. Except for a few who come and go without settling." His brows drew together. "Do you have a reason for asking?"

They had just passed the gazebo. Should she trust Justin with her secret? He was her closest friend in Y Knot. And perhaps doing so would lighten her anxiety. "Just making small talk, I guess," she finally replied. "I've noticed there are many more men than women." She lifted a shoulder, trying to look indifferent. "You know, for my research paper. Are there many women living outside of town?"

He nodded.

But she felt her questions had stirred his curiosity.

"Most do."

That endearing, boyish smile appeared on his lips and chased away the questions in his eyes.

"*Research*. Any time you'd like to know more, seek me out. I'll be happy to tell you what I know—to a certain extent, of course. I can't divulge anything personal."

A happy thrill almost made her do a little skip. Could she trust Justin? Should she? Having an advocate, especially one who knew everyone in town, would be such a boon. She'd sleep on the idea tonight and decide in the morning. Time testing an idea was the best course of action, her father often said. Who was she to disagree?

Chapter Sixteen

The train pulled into Helena at six o'clock at night as a soft rain began to fall. Using the blankets as a makeshift stretcher, her brothers carefully lifted Brandon and carried him along the aisle of the now-empty passenger car. Completely worn out, Charity followed, offering a silent prayer of thanks Brandon had hung on this far. And, too, that all her brothers had insisted on coming along. She couldn't have made this journey without them. They assured her Brandon was holding his own, but to her, her husband seemed weaker, the hours spent on the train draining away what little strength he had left. She was petrified of what might come next. She couldn't live without him. The thought of him dying was impossible to contemplate.

"Bring him over here." The porter, a man in his sixties, waved them over the platform toward the station doors.

Her brothers, with Brandon carried between them, moved so quickly she had a difficult time keeping up. She wanted to shield Brandon from the rain but couldn't keep pace.

The porter held the door wide.

Matthew, Mark, and Luke hurried through, laying Brandon inside on the wooden floor.

"This is the last train tonight," the porter said. "You can leave him here if you need to arrange transport to the hospital, which is about twenty to thirty minutes away. I'll show you to the telegraph office and the livery. They're just down the street."

The appropriately named Mr. Porter had been extremely kind the whole way. Charity had learned the man had a son Brandon's age who resembled her love. She wanted to tell him what his kindness meant to her, to them, but he was already hurrying away with Matt and Mark. Luke would stay behind with her and Brandon.

"Here, Charity," Luke called softly in the empty lobby, the high ceiling giving a slight echo. Helena Depot was much larger than any they'd passed through along the way and made Waterloo's look as small as a henhouse. "Rest here while I fetch the platform we built before the train moves away. I'll be right back."

She glanced to Brandon, who was ten feet away. "I don't want to leave his side. I'll stay by Brandon on the floor."

"You can't. You need to rest." He narrowed his eyes. "I don't have time to argue with you. We'll need the contraption to take Brandon home."

Those sweet words flowed over her like melted honey. *Brandon home.*

"I can pull him closer, but we shouldn't move him if we don't have to." Without waiting for her response, Luke gently took her arm and walked her several paces to the long bench where travelers usually waited for their train. He sat her down and then lifted her feet.

After hours spent on the clackety train, the position, even on the hard bench, was a relief.

"Thank you." She barely got the words out before tears erupted. She hadn't thought she had any left to cry.

"Just stay put. You'll be safe, and I'll be back as quick as I can."

Unable to do anything else, she nodded. Steeling her nerves and heart, she watched her brother walk away, more thankful than ever he was here to help her through this crisis. "Thank you for coming, Luke," she called.

Turning, he briefly smiled and then hustled away.

In the stillness of the empty station, Brandon's shallow breathing sliced over Charity's nerves. She recalled accidents the ranch hands had experienced over the years. They'd fallen or were hurt, but not badly. Smokey had caught his boot heel and tumbled off the bunkhouse roof one year when he'd gone up to see what was clogging the chimney flue and causing the bunkhouse to fill with smoke. And Chance had gone over a fifteen-foot drop when his horse tripped and went head over tail. Neither man had been seriously hurt, receiving only scratches and bruises. Then there were the countless sprains, and kicks by horses and cattle, alike, but still, nothing life-threatening. Well, except when Amy lost her baby—that heartbreak Charity never wanted to experience again. Mark almost drowned, she reminded herself, and Rachel had her difficult birth and Faith had to help. And now, Brandon had twisted something inside when he'd fallen from the ladder. Because of it, he might die.

She hadn't taken her eyes off him for a second. *Not Brandon, God,* she silently begged. *Please don't take him from me.* Her hand rested on her tummy, protecting the tiny babe growing inside.

Chapter Seventeen

The time was nearing midnight when Justin closed his copy of Benjamin Franklin's autobiography, stood from behind the desk in the sheriff's office, and stretched. Wariness hummed through him. He felt uneasy, tense, and realized perhaps he *had* kept the notion of his famous father in the back of his mind as a source of backup and support. Brandon, as well. His father's parting words had hit their mark.

Tonight, with everyone out of town, he felt edgy sitting here alone in the quiet jail. He wasn't afraid, just uncertain of his abilities. He'd tried reading, but his restless mind wouldn't settle down. What would he do if faced with a life-or-death situation? A panicked lawman was dangerous. A hundred thoughts nipped at his mind. He glanced out the window, thinking the night had never looked so dark.

Father came to Y Knot on my invitation.

Justin had no siblings besides his young half sister. He hadn't wanted to miss watching Carlie mature. As well, he'd known his father had been considering giving up his work and settling somewhere to live a quiet life. Justin had thought, *what better place than here in Y Knot,* where they could once again be one big family—or so he'd told himself. His mother had passed when he was only ten, but he had many wonderful memories of her soft blue eyes smiling into his. She'd adored the ground his father walked on. She'd been strict, but loving, with Justin and taught him to persevere in all aspects of his young life. And, since his father was often away, she'd counted on Justin to be the man of the house, and he'd taken his job seriously.

Were these the only *reasons I wanted Father here in Y Knot? Or am I counting on him when I should count only on myself?* He scrubbed a hand over his face. *Why are these thoughts bothering me so much tonight?*

Five hours had passed since he'd dropped Madison at the hotel. Her infectious chatter had kept him laughing all the way around the corner and down the street. They'd talked more in those few minutes than in the whole two hours at the house with Aunt Pauline domineering the conversation. Madison had begun opening up regarding her father's death and about her family, but they'd soon reached the hotel.

Madison seemed to have something important bottled up inside and maybe even wanted to share. If that were true, he didn't think she'd hold out much longer. Until she trusted him completely was just a matter of time. He'd like to help her, if he could. The thought sent an exhilarating zip around inside him, waking him from his lethargic boredom. She was a beautiful young woman. She planned to return to Kentucky for her last term in college. And she'd mentioned a Mr. Galbraith, her professor. Justin couldn't stop himself wondering how old this professor was and how well they knew each other. He'd like some way of asking, if possible.

What does Madison think of me? Maybe Justin was putting the cart before the horse, wondering what she thought of him in any way besides being the helpful deputy of Y Knot . . .

He shook his head and went to the window. The wind had kept up, littering Main Street with leaves and debris. They'd had a light smattering of rain, creating a dusty aroma from the hard, parched road.

Three hours prior, Mr. Tracy had delivered a new telegram from Mark. The group had arrived in Helena and were now working to get Brandon to the hospital. The surgeons would operate as soon as they arrived, no matter the hour. After the telegram, he'd walked his rounds, trying to dispel his worry, and then he'd gone to the livery and saddled Scout and ridden out to the Heart of the Mountains to pass on the news. After which, he'd ridden to the Klinkner Mill, and then the Holcombs' and Preeces', just wanting to make a full sweep.

Justin dug his thumb and forefinger into his gritty eyes. He didn't like to think of Brandon dying. He'd only known the sheriff a little over a year, but they had a strong, binding friendship. Right now, Brandon's prognosis sounded just about as bad as it could get. Crossing his arms, he yawned and leaned a hip against the window jamb, half-asleep.

In the middle of his musings about how soft his mattress was going to feel, Justin heard the *clop, clop, clop* of a horse's hooves followed by a lone rider appearing out of the darkness a moment later. The man rode in the middle of the murky street. Justin couldn't make out the rider's face. His coat collar stood up against the wind and his hat pulled down low.

The stranger halted in front of the sheriff's office and dismounted.

Justin met him on the boardwalk, all senses alerted to the situation.

Chapter Eighteen

"Evenin'. You're new to Y Knot," Justin said, trying to get a read on the fellow. The man didn't feel threatening. "What's your name?"

"*My* name? I say, what's *your* name?" The fella glanced around and then back at Justin, an insulted tilt to his brows. "Where's Brandon? The sheriff have the night off?"

Feeling no threat from the stranger, even though he wore a 45 Colt strapped to his leg, Justin relaxed. "The sheriff's out of town. I'm Deputy Wesley."

"Wesley? Any kin to Harrison Wesley? I've known the circuit judge serving this territory for years!" He looked Justin up and down and shook his head. "Brandon's hirin' 'em awful young these days."

Irritation rippled inside. But facts were facts. Justin was younger than most for a deputy position. And his father *had* earned the respect of every lawman in the territory and beyond. Perhaps this tall, rangy fella wasn't the shady sort. Then, still, he could be someone his father had sentenced to the penitentiary and was out for revenge. "He's my father," Justin replied, gauging the newcomer's reaction. A lot could be learned from a man's eyes. "I asked you before. What's your name? You've yet to say."

The stranger leaned an elbow on the hitching rail as if he owned the place. "You're probably the only man in town who doesn't know."

"Enlighten me."

"Jack Jones."

"Jack Jones!" Justin barked, stepping forward to the edge of the boardwalk.

"I can see my reputation has preceded me."

"I promise you, it has. I'm surprised you have the nerve to show your face here in Y Knot, after all the ways you've managed to earn the scorn of just about everybody here. How, in Priest's Crossing, you jailed Luke for days, even though he was innocent. He almost burned to death in your jailhouse because you lost the keys!"

Jack took a deep breath and slowly let it out. "I had my reasons. Followed the law. No one can say different. The victim identified Luke. I had no other choice but to lock him up."

Justin gripped the porch post. "A *lying* victim! The same one who turned out to be the perpetrator. And you never investigated anything to corroborate or expose her false story or to find the real killer. If the ranch hands and my father hadn't shown up when they did, Luke might have swung from the end of a rope for something he didn't do—or died in the fire."

Jack scuffed some dirt with his boot, the first tell he might be more self-conscious than he was letting on. “It wouldn’t have got that far. I have no taste for a lynching or vigilante justice.”

Justin smirked. “Oh, you would have risked your own neck to stand up to an angry mob? Somehow, I don’t think so.”

They stared at each other.

Justin realized he’d not get anywhere arguing like magpies, and the night was late. He needed to get at least a little sleep tonight to be able to function tomorrow. Keeping Y Knot safe was up to him. “Fine,” he said. “You passing through?”

Jack shook his head. “Not passing through. I’m here to stay. I like Y Knot. Ever since I left, my life’s gone downhill faster than a sled on ice. One of the last things Luke told me when he was locked up in Priest’s Crossing was I should try some other line of work.”

“He didn’t mean *here!*”

“I’m not so sure. I aim to prove everyone wrong about me and set up shop—here in this town where I know the people. Luke will be *honored* I took his words to heart.”

Honored? Jack Jones must be touched in the head. Justin knew exactly what Brandon and Luke thought of his bungling, slothful ways. Justin had heard an earful. Lazy, dense, and many times—sneaky. Brandon wouldn’t be happy to have Jack Jones back among them—especially when he, himself, was out of town and incapacitated. Maybe Justin could do something to help the former deputy see the truth of the matter, before Brandon returned. But doing so wouldn't happen tonight. "What new work are you talking about?"

"I'm holding those cards close to my vest, Deputy," he said, a small smirk on his lips. "When I'm ready to say, you'll be the first to know. Ain't no law stating I can't, is there?"

Justin shook his head. "Where're you staying?"

Jack perked up at the question, probably thinking he'd won Justin over.

"Lou and Drit's Boardinghouse, for the time being. I have my eye on a small place I'll need to enquire about later."

"I'm just about ready to wrap things up here," Justin said, suddenly feeling the enormity of Brandon's absence. "I'll walk with you to the livery, so you don't give June a fright. Then I'll see you to Lou and Drit's."

They looked across the way to the dark barn housing the forge and livery. He'd keep a close eye on Jack. Maybe the former deputy was out for revenge on his old hometown. He might be speaking out of both sides of his mouth.

"Whatever makes you happy, Deputy," Jack said on a half chuckle. "Might be difficult, though, holding my hand all day long." He shrugged knowingly. "Tomorrow, you'll see I'm not the hated pariah you think I am. I have friends. They'll be pleased as punch to hear I'm back."

He gathered the reins of his sleepy horse. “It’s a free country, last time I checked.”

Jack Jones was right. And Montana was a free territory, as well. They’d see what happened tomorrow, when Y Knot woke up to find the prodigal son had returned.

Chapter Nineteen

St. John's Hospital, Helena, Montana Territory

Charity knelt in the small chapel of St. John's Hospital, exhausted. The small of her back ached terribly, and her temples squeezed like a vice. An elderly couple had been here when she'd entered, but now she was alone. With her arm draped over the walnut back of the pew in front of her, she rested her forehead. She was out of tears and out of prayers. God knew what was in her heart. She just needed some time alone, away from the probing eyes of Matthew, Mark, and Luke. Her three brothers took up a lot of space in the narrow hall outside the surgery, and the walls had been closing in.

Nine hours had passed since Brandon was wheeled into surgery. As promised, the doctors were ready for him as soon as they'd arrived. Her once-virile husband had been as limp as a weathered old bandanna by the time they'd found a wagon to rent, got him settled, and then made their way through Helena in the dark. They'd lost their way once and lost precious time.

Although starving, Charity knew if she took even one bite of anything, she'd throw up. Moving slowly, she carefully lowered herself to the hard surface of the pew bench. Laying on her side, she pillowed her cheek on praying hands. The spicy aroma of the tiny room filled her senses. A small altar and a crucifix stood up front. The two rectangular stained-glass windows on each side of the altar were narrow and now glowed with the coming dawn.

What was happening in surgery? Why was the operation taking so long?

As they'd rushed through the doors, her brothers—carrying Brandon with the blankets—were met by a group of nuns who ushered them to the second floor. Once there, a team of three surgeons told them they'd do an examination first, to be sure Dr. Handerhoosen's diagnosis had been correct, and then one of them would come and report the findings. If, indeed, Brandon suffered from peritonitis, they'd perform the operation immediately. Time was of the essence.

Charity didn't recall much of the conversation except the words peritonitis, dangerous, immediate, and only option. She'd heard they'd done the operation many times before. And she and her brothers shouldn't fret if the procedure took a long time. They would do all in their power to save her husband.

So many thoughts tumbled around Charity's mind as she laid on the granite-hard bench. She recalled the day she'd decided Brandon was the man for her. She rode into town with her father to take care of banking and other errands. The blustery weather made her horse skittish, and Charity had a time keeping the mare under control. When Brandon had stepped out of the sheriff's office, the wind caught his beloved, new, black Stetson. Before he had a chance to clap it to his head, the hat sailed off like a kite. It tumbled a few times and landed beneath her horse, causing the animal to rear and come down on the Stetson, smashing it in the dirt. When he caught her amused expression, Brandon had frowned, and she'd known right then and there she would marry him or die. He was young, strong, handsome—and mightily irritated by the way she smiled through her apology. That day had begun their on-again, off-again love affair.

We were destined for each other.

Our love is so true, nothing can ever break us apart—not even death.

She stifled the sob pushing up her throat. "Brandon," she whispered. "I love you, my darling. Keep living. Come back to me. I can't survive without you." Forcing herself to relax, she thought of the upper meadow last spring where they'd made love under a sky filled with sunshine and clouds. Calming, her thoughts drifted. She relaxed.

Was God real? Or a myth made up thousands of years ago? Minutes ticked by, and Charity drifted off to sleep.

"Look, sweetheart," her father said, pointing. "About the prettiest thing I've ever seen."

He sat straight in his saddle as they watched golden beams of light spread out over the mountaintop, illuminated by low, dangling clouds. In the next few moments, the sky all but exploded with color, bringing a gasp from her throat. The sight was so beautiful, enough to steal her words. She could do nothing but stare in wonder.

"No eye has seen; no ear has heard what God has prepared for those who love Him," her father said low and then glanced at her. "I remember that whenever I get to questioning. If God can do this*"—he motioned toward the horizon—"I can't wait to see what comes next. This sight never ceases to inspire me and strengthen my faith."*

With a jerk, she came awake. For a moment, she lay still, struggling to hold fast to the dream. Someone had spoken into her ear. She was sure of it. The voice hadn't been her father's. Had someone joined her in the chapel?

Slowly sitting up, she looked around, the stiffness in her body painful. In the dimness, she spotted Luke in the last pew, his hair creased from his hat and looking much older than his years. "Luke?"

"Nothin' yet, Char. But I'm sure we'll hear something soon."

Feeling almost numb, she rubbed a hand

across her face and pushed strands of her hair from her eyes. "How long have you been here?"

"Arrived a few minutes ago. Sorry if I woke you."

"Did you say something to me? I heard a voice as clearly as we're talking now."

He shook his head. "You were dreaming."

"I was dreaming, yes, but this wasn't part of it. There was a voice. One I've not heard before." When she went to stand, her numb legs buckled, and she caught herself on the fall.

In an instant, Luke was at her side and swept her into his arms.

The gesture made her feel all of six years old again.

"You're lying down, this instant. In a bed. Not a bench in the train station or a pew in this chapel. Enough of this foolishness. You can pray for Brandon just as well from there. You have your babe to consider."

Content to let him take charge, Charity laid her head on Luke's chest and listened to his heartbeat as he carried her out the door and along the quiet hallway. Nuns in their nurses' outfits passed them, keeping their gazes to themselves as they went about their business. A few moans reached her ears as patients woke up. Someone shouted something at the end of the cool corridor, but Charity couldn't understand it with one ear pressed to her brother's heart.

Who knew how much longer Brandon would be in the operation room—or what the outcome would be when he was out.

Adjusting her in his arms, Luke asked, "What did the voice say, Char? You never said."

She took a deep breath, savoring how safe her brother made her feel. "No eye has seen, nor ear has heard what God has prepared for those who love Him . . ."

Chapter Twenty

"Charity, honey, wake up."

Charity tried to roll away from the disturbance, but the voice called her again, making her eyes flutter open. She was in the hospital in Helena, waiting for Brandon to come out of surgery. What time was it? How long had she slept?

"Charity, I hate to wake you, but Brandon's out. You should come and see him right away."

She sat bolt upright in the stiff bed. White walls surrounded her, and scurrying sounds came from the hallway. Mark stood at her side. She blinked again to clear away the cotton fogging her mind. "Brandon?"

"The doctors are finished. The operation is over, and he's awake—but they aren't sure how long he'll stay that way. You must come immediately."

Charity's heart beat faster. *They're afraid he'll die before I get there.*

Swinging her legs over the bed, she swayed.

Mark caught her and lifted her into his arms.

"Mark! I'm fine. Put me down."

"This'll be faster."

His tone brooked no argument.

Brandon's awake, but they fear he won't live but a few minutes. Her heart cried with the injustice. "How long has he been out of surgery?" She held tight to Mark's shoulders as he strode quickly through the hallway, nurses with their bleached white aprons and pointy white caps stepping out of his way without a word of question or complaint. Charity was reminded of the time when she was little, not more than five or six, when a bottle-fed calf she'd taken to mothering got cornered in the paddock by an ornery mule. The long-eared beast began kicking her darling for no apparent reason. She'd screamed.

Mark appeared out of nowhere. A tall and muscular teenager, he'd easily hopped the fence and scooped up the white-faced calf, carrying him out of the corral and into the barn, with just as much purpose as he carried her now.

He'd been her champion that day, drying her tears and then making sure the little critter was doctored to the best of their abilities.

This Helena hospital was not the Heart of the Mountains, and her brother couldn't fix what ailed her or Brandon. Spicy scents of medicine, as well as other smells, assaulted her senses, and she knew she wasn't on the ranch any longer.

Stopping at door eight, Mark set her on her feet and held her until she gained her balance.

"You strong enough to walk?"

She heard hushed conversation coming from inside. She nodded. Wouldn't her brother have prepared her for the worst if Brandon was about to die?

Mark reached for the knob and opened the door.

Luke and Matt stood on the far side of the bed, looking at Brandon. Their gazes rose to meet hers.

A doctor and a nurse speaking at the back of the room turned.

"Mrs. Crawford," the doctor said, holding out a hand as he came forward.

She didn't respond but rushed to Brandon's side and bent close to his face.

His eyes were barely open.

"Brandon? Brandon?" She glanced up at the doctor.

"He's still groggy from the chloroform. The surgery lasted longer than we anticipated."

"What does *that* mean? He's going to be fine, isn't he?"

"That's what we hope."

Hope! Don't they know? Again, she bent low to Brandon's face and tenderly caressed his balmy cheek, still warm to the touch. She looked to Luke and Matt, searching for some sign of good news, but they hid any kind of reaction in their eyes. Straightening, she asked the doctor, "You've already given my brothers his prognosis?"

The doctor nodded. "I have, Mrs. Crawford. The surgeons here at St. John's Hospital have done all in our power to remove the injury. Now it's up to your husband to fight any new infection. His prognosis could still go either way."

"And if he hadn't come here. Hadn't had this surgery?"

"Most certainly, he would have passed."

She had to toughen up. Her brothers wouldn't be carrying her anymore. She'd walk and stand on her own two feet. "I see. When will you be back to check on him? What should we expect in the next few hours?"

"One of the other doctors or myself will stop in every three to four hours. If your husband's condition changes significantly between then, one of the nurses will alert us. He'll begin to come around more fully as time passes."

She struggled to keep tears at bay—at least, until the doctor had left the room. "Thank you," she managed to push out through her strangled throat. "Thank you for saving my hus—Brandon's life."

With a small bow, the doctor took his leave.

Shortly after, the nurse left, as well.

Mark had circled the bed and stood with Luke and Matt. Silence wrapped around everyone. With their wide stance and their hands clasped identically before them, not knowing what to do or say, they looked like soldiers, unable to make this right no matter how hard they might try. They'd watched over her all of her life. And on this harrowing journey. They'd done their best. How she wished she had the words to ease their hearts. Remove the worry from their eyes.

But she didn't . . . and couldn't. All she felt was a blatant fear. She glanced at Brandon, his eyes still small slits in his beloved face. Whiskers covered his jaw, all the more chiseled by the fact he'd lost a significant amount of weight since the accident. The hair on his forehead stood up, and she realized he must have worn some kind of headband during the operation.

She needed to be strong now more than ever. She took a deep breath and slowly let it out. "You boys go get some rest," she said, trying to sound firm, like her father. "I'm rested, thanks to you three, and will stay with Brandon."

Luke shook his head. "We can't, Char. I'm staying."

"Not on your life, little sis," Matt remarked.

Mark, wiping a tired hand over his face, struggled to stifle a yawn. "Nothin' doin'."

She pointed toward the door. "You're all dead on your feet. Besides, I'd like some private time with Brandon. No one knows what's coming next. You'll need to be rested, too. Brandon and I both might need you more than ever in the days to come." She offered a loving smile. "You're no good to us now." She took in their tired faces and hitched her head at the door. "I won't take no for an answer." Her lips wobbled. "But, thank you for everything. For taking care of Brandon and for taking care of me. Now, go. Get some sleep."

They glanced amongst themselves.

“As much as I hate to admit we’re human, she’s right,” Luke mumbled.

“We’re just across the street,” Matt said. “The kind nun took care of getting us a room. They can send word to us, as well, if you need us.” His expression spelled out everything.

“I’ll let you know if there’s any change.” She glanced at Brandon with a sinking feeling in her breast and then back at her magnificent brothers. Without them, she’d never have gotten Brandon here so fast, if at all. She owed them *everything*.

Listening as her brothers left the room, Charity again felt like a child. She might think she was a grown woman, and even be expecting, but in the face of danger and death, and the inability to change it, she was nothing but their little sister.

If the worst came to pass, how would she ever survive?

Chapter Twenty-One

Jack Jones stormed into the sheriff's office, making Justin jostle his first cup of morning coffee as he lifted the mug to his lips.

"Why didn't you tell me about Brandon last night? Or that all the McCutcheons are out of town? You kept the information intentionally to yourself." His face was red with annoyance.

Justin jerked his handkerchief from his pocket and angrily wiped his face. "Because it was none of your business, Jones! And it's *still* not. Have you so soon forgotten you're not the deputy around here any longer? Get on with your day and leave me in peace!"

"The hell it's *not* my business. I know everyone in Y Knot. You have no backup. Even your father is out of town." He glanced about, taking a deep breath. Retrieving the straight-backed chair by the iron stove, he plopped it down backward and straddled it. "You need my help."

Justin set his mug down and stood, now taking his turn to lean over the slacker. "You're dreaming, Jones. You know better than *anyone* Brandon would never, and I mean *never,* hire you back. And I won't, either. The town doesn't need the kind of help you give."

"I'll work for half pay."

"You won't work at all! If something comes up, there're plenty of men here in town I can count on. I don't need you. Who told you, anyway?"

"Told me? I told *you* I intended to reside at Lou's until I was settled. Lou and Drit's Boardinghouse should be your first stop when you're looking for information. See—you don't even know that. Brandon and his accident were the topic of conversation over the breakfast table. Word is Brandon arrived in Helena alive, and has had, or is having, the surgery he needs."

Justin wondered if Jack's concern was all for show, to get into Justin's good graces so he'd hire him back. "You're not telling me anything I don't already know, so wipe that look off your face."

Jack's gaze hardened. "Be reasonable, Wesley. You can't be here twenty-four hours a day. You need to sleep sometime. And when you do, you leave Y Knot vulnerable. I'll only work until Brandon gets back."

"We don't stay in the office around the clock. You can't talk me into anything—so just save your breath."

Jack's chin jutted, and his eyes narrowed. "That's because Brandon lives behind the jail, only fifteen steps away. He's available most always, and if he's not, I'm sure you're close. Where do you live, anyway?"

"I can't believe I'm being interrogated by Jack Jones!"

Jack threw back his shoulders. "Tell me."

"One street over on Clove Hitch. I'm just about as close as Brandon ever is."

Jack stood and paced over to the coffeepot and helped himself.

"Make yourself at home." Justin smirked.

"Thank you, I *will.* I've worked here for years. Much longer than you ever have. I know things you don't."

Justin had just about had enough of his bravado when Trent Herrick stepped inside.

The leather worker's eyes widened when he saw Jones. "Jack?" he sputtered.

"Hey, Trent. Good to see ya."

Trent looked to Justin with an eyebrow raised.

"Just chewing my ear, trying to get back on the payroll. Nothin' doing. Now, Trent, what can I do for *you?*"

Trent's brow furrowed. "We had us a visitor last night in the leather shop. I must confess, I'm embarrassed to admit I didn't hear a thing. My pa wouldn't, of course, because he's deaf. The thief jimmied the back lock and got inside. Stole a couple bridles and what little cash I left in the cash box downstairs. Wasn't much, but every little bit adds up."

A crime! The first real offense since Justin had become deputy. Justin went over to Trent. "Any clues left behind? Or anyone loitering around the last few days, watching the store?"

"Isn't that something *you* should have noticed, Deputy?" Jack Jones now stood by their side. "Seems news has gotten around Brandon and Harrison Wesley are out of town. Y Knot's wide open for easy pickin's." He nodded and grinned. "Just like I was saying."

Justin clenched his jaw. "Shut up, Jack. I'll be over in a few minutes to have a look around," he said to Trent. "Hope your pa wasn't too rattled by the robbery."

Trent shook his head. "Naw. Just talkin' about blowing a hole through the culprit's noggin if he dares to return." He chuckled, but the sound quickly died away. "I would like to get my merchandise back, as well as the money."

" 'Course you would. I'll stop by shortly." But was Jack right? Did the townsfolk and strangers alike think the town was unprotected now with Brandon gone? Or was Jack the culprit and had broken into Herrick's to put a scare into everyone? Make them feel vulnerable so he would be rehired. Justin didn't put anything past the man—as well he shouldn't. Justin rubbed his palms together in anticipation. Having something to sink his teeth into was kind of exciting. At least, nothing too big had happened, like a bank robbery or murder.

Trent stepped toward the door. "I better get back before my pa does something crazy. He already said he intends to sit by the door in his rocking chair with his shotgun—a kind of warning for whoever done it not to come back." He chuckled again, but the sound held no mirth.

"I'll be by, too," Jack called over Justin's shoulder. "Brandon often said I had a sharp eye. I don't mind looking around, as well—before tending to my own business." When Trent just kept walking, he added, "And no need for thanks. What are friends for, if not lookin' out for each other?"

Justin's anticipation over an active crime to investigate was chased away by an annoying irritation—Jack! Did the man really believe he'd be his shadow until Brandon or Luke returned? That would be intolerable. Justin went for his hat.

Madison stepped inside the sheriff's office.

She looked as pretty as ever. She smiled at him, but when her gaze found Jones, her eyes went wide. "Deputy," she began slowly.

He rehung his hat and returned her smile. He got the distinct impression she'd just stopped in to say hello and, because of Jones, was now trying to think of a reason for being here. "Good morning, Miss Plumb. Did you receive the message I left at the front desk?"

Tension eased out of her face. "I did, thank you. I came in to let you know not to worry." Her face tinted pink.

"You're welcome. As I passed the Biscuit Barrel this morning, I was met by Ethel who ran out and asked me to make sure you got it. I hope it wasn't anything too distressing."

She smiled, seemingly now at ease since he'd rescued her from her dilemma. "Not distressing at all. Just a change in my shift. I'm not due now until four o'clock today. That gives me plenty of time to work on my term paper."

"Term paper?" Jack Jones asked, his curious gaze looking her up and down. "What's this about, miss? Your comment makes me think you're attending a school of higher learning. My name's Jack Jones. I used to be the deputy of Y Knot." He glanced at Justin and smiled. "I've returned and am here to stay. Everyone must be delighted to have such an accomplished young woman residing here."

Oh, brother.

Madison turned to address Jack. "Not an institution of *much* higher learning, a regular college for women in Tennessee." She turned to the door. "Thank you again, Deputy Wesley. You have a nice day. You as well, Mr. Jones."

Jack blinked several times. "That's astounding enough."

With a smile, Madison took the sunshine from the office.

Jack went to the window and watched her walk away. "Miss Plumb, you say? When did *she* arrive?"

"She's no concern of yours, Jack."

"Who is she? Where'd she come from?" He turned back and faced Justin with bright eyes. "Is she courting anyone?"

Justin scowled. Jack's interest was easy to see. "You're amazing, you know that? The stories I've heard didn't completely prepare me for who you really are. Do you think Luke McCutcheon, when he returns, or any of the other McCutcheons, for that matter, will stand for the man who almost killed Luke living in Y Knot? They'd be reminded of the charade every day. You have nerve a mountain high." Grumbling, he lifted his mug and headed to the coffeepot but found it empty after Jack refilled his cup. Muttering words he'd never say in front of Madison, Justin headed for the back door to toss the coffee grounds into the trash barrel.

"It's a free country, in case you've forgotten," Jack called. "And I was only doing my job. How was I to know Pink Kelly—crazy as a loon—would set the jailhouse on fire? Foreseeing his actions was impossible. No one blames *me* for the fire. Lou and Drit, and everyone at the boardinghouse, were welcoming. Excited, even, to see me. Mark my words, Wesley. I'm back in Y Knot to stay."

At the trash barrel, Justin shook his head, trying not to hear all Jack Jones was spouting. What a pest! Life would be pure drudgery if he planned to hang around the sheriff's office all day long.

Justin would have to devise some plan to get rid of the parasite—short of murder, of course.

Returning, he filled the pot with water and coffee grounds and put it back on the stove.

Mr. Tracy stuck his head in the sheriff's office door. "Got another telegram this morning," he said, holding out the beige note.

Justin unfolded the crease, scanning the few lines.

"You need me to fetch Harold to ride out to the Heart of the Mountains?"

Justin shook his head. "Thanks, but no. I'll take this one myself."

Jack's eyes went wide.

No telling what he might think, but Justin wasn't about to dispel his misconceptions, not before Claire McCutcheon knew what the telegram said. "I'm warning you, Jack," Justin growled. "If you breathe one iota of anything about Brandon and what you *might think* his condition is to anyone, and I mean *anyone,* I'll lock you up so fast your head will spin. And then I'll conveniently lose the key, like someone I know. This town is already stirred up enough." He'd never felt more animosity toward anyone in his life than he did to Jack now. Still, with Jack Jones in town, Justin was loath to be gone long, even to the ranch. He might come back to the sheriff's office to find the lock changed and Jones proclaiming himself rehired. He wanted to avoid any type of altercation, even a verbal one, if he could. “Are we understood?”

Jack scowled.

“Jack!”

“Understood. My lips are sealed.”

Mr. Tracy, who’d remained in the doorway throughout the contentious conversation, nodded. He turned and hurried back down the boardwalk.

Justin took one more sweeping look around the office. He strode over to the desk, opened the top right drawer, and pulled out the ring of keys and stuffed them in his pocket. Better to be safe than sorry.

Chapter Twenty-Two

Claire McCutcheon went around the main room of the ranch house with a duster in her hand as if in a trance. She didn't usually do house chores, but to keep her fears at bay, she had to occupy her mind. Her stomach tightened every time she thought of her dear son-in-law. If only Flood were home, passing her days would be so much easier. As it was, all her daughters-in-law and grandchildren were doing their best to keep her busy. The little ones were too young to understand what was happening, but Billy, Adam, Colton, and even Dawn understood Grandmother was tense, even when she tried not to be. The ranch, for the most part, was quiet with Nick Petty, Francis, and Lucky watching over things.

And Hickory. For being so young, he was incredibly astute. Maybe living alone on the street for so many years had shaped him. Whenever they were together, he watched her eyes and was sure not to ask anything about Brandon or Charity—or mention anything about Charity's brothers. Two times this week, he'd brought her a small bouquet of wildflowers he'd collected in the pasture the cattle had missed.

At the sound of a horse arriving, Claire's heart took off at a gallop. Harold, the mop boy, had been bringing telegrams whenever Luke or the others had a chance to send a message. Each time she heard his arrival or saw his face, she expected the worst. Setting her duster on the coffee table, she hurried to the door. Expecting Harold, her heart plummeted when she recognized Justin at the bunkhouse hitching rail, speaking with Francis and Lucky. Gathering her skirt, she ran to the waiting men, praying earnestly with each step she took.

When he saw her approach, Justin whipped his hat from his head.

"Justin," she said on a frightened breath. "You have news?" The look in his eyes confirmed her suspicions weren't unwarranted. Being short-handed in town, only bad news—something he'd want to break to her gently—would bring him out in person. "Don't keep me in suspense. Please, what do you know?"

In what felt like a dream, he reached slowly for the telegram in his shirt pocket. He didn't hand it over immediately, but instead, said, "The worst hasn't happened. Brandon survived surgery. The doctors give him a fifty-fifty chance. He was awake for a few minutes and then fell back into a deep sleep and hasn't woken up since."

"Oh . . ." Claire reached for the hitching rail to support her buckling legs, but Francis caught her first. He helped her to the porch and sat her in one of the wicker rocking chairs.

"That's not all bad, Miss Claire," Francis said. "He'll come around. Just takes a little time. Brandon is strong—always has been."

She nodded, feeling foolish for acting so weepy. "And Charity?"

Justin handed her the telegram. "It only says she's enduring. Eating and resting."

"I know Charity." Claire gazed at the short message. "She's taking Brandon's accident extremely hard, and those boys of mine don't want to worry me more than I already am. I have a mind to go to Helena myself, like I should have done right from the start."

Hickory and Nick had joined the group, having come from the barn.

"I'll go with ya, Mrs. McCutcheon," Hickory offered. "I'm young, but I can get the job done. I know these other fellas are needed at the ranch."

"And you are, too," Lucky said gruffly, frowning at Hickory. "You're not going anywhere, and neither is Miss Claire."

Claire hadn't heard such authority come from Lucky in years, but he was making his feelings clear now. She wasn't going anywhere.

"When Flood gets home will be soon enough," he went on in a softer tone. "Miss Charity has her brothers. They're taking fine care of her."

Justin cleared his throat. "There's more news."

Everyone stared at the deputy, heads tilted.

"Jack Jones is back."

"What?" Francis barked. "How dare that beef-headed idiot show his scruffy hide in Y Knot after what he did to Luke? You sure it's Jack?"

"Can't be any more sure than sitting across from him in the sheriff's office, arguing over every sentence out of his mouth. He wants to lend me a hand while Brandon's away."

Lucky spat a glob of tobacco juice over the railing. "That skunk! I'll give him an earful when I see him. Never thought he'd be brazen enough to return. Just goes to show how numb-brained he really is."

Nick's face turned white, and he balled his fists. "He won't be asking for a job the next time I see him. He'll beg to ride out of Y Knot."

"Not only Luke," Claire went on. "Remember how Jack treated Hickory when Luke first brought him here from Waterloo?" She smiled at Hickory, who was still listening. "That was a short time before Brandon fired him. Jack did his best to poison the whole town against our boy." She put out a hand and Hickory actually came to her side. She caressed his back.

"Don't forget about Sally Standford," Francis grouched out. "That young lady might have froze to death because Jack was lazy and called off the search. Good thing Roady found her in the hunting cabin." A small smile formed on his lips. "And now she's Sally Guthrie."

Lucky inched closer. "That man has earned our

scorn. Killin' by tiny cuts. I just couldn't abide how he kept Brandon's office, no matter how much Brandon preached." A frown pulled his lips.

"He plannin' to stay?" Nick asked.

"Says he is. Says it's a free country, and he never broke any laws. Also claims Luke, at some point when he was locked up in Priest's Crossing, told Jack he should go into some other line of work. Jack took his statement as an invitation to come back here and do just that."

"Do *what?*" Lucky barked out. "I can't imagine."

"Don't know. He won't say."

Claire shook her head. "Jack Jones is the least of our problems. Just keep an eye on him and make sure he stays out of trouble." She searched Justin's face. "You're not thinking of letting him help, are you?"

"No, ma'am. He already knows how I feel."

"He'll be leaving soon enough," Francis proclaimed. "Once we have our little talk."

Claire rubbed her forehead. "I really don't want or need anyone fighting, Francis or Nick. Cut Jack Jones a wide berth." She took in both young men's faces. "Please don't go looking for trouble."

"I won't instigate trouble, Miss Claire," Francis said, "but I'm not holding my tongue, either. Seeing Luke behind bars, day after day, was the most gut-wrenching experience I've ever had to live through. Jack Jones shouldn't be let off scot-free. Goes against every moral code of the West."

Lucky drilled both the younger men with a snake-eyed stare. "You listen to Mrs. McCutcheon. What she says goes. Let's just get Brandon and Charity home. We can deal with Jack Jones later."

Chapter Twenty-Three

Bright and early Saturday morning, the dining room of Cattlemen's Hotel hummed with hungry lodgers and other townsfolk intent on a strong cup of coffee and a hearty breakfast. Clinking and clanging sounded from the kitchen's door. The buzz of happy voices filled the air.

Standing at the entry, Madison noticed a few familiar faces, but many people she still didn't know. Exhausted from her shift the evening before at the Biscuit Barrel, she scanned the room. Her feet ached. Fuzziness squeezed her head. By the time the Biscuit Barrel finally closed, and she'd completed all her closing tasks—refilling the shakers, wiping the countertops, bringing up from the basement anything they'd need in the morning that wouldn't spoil overnight, *and then* folding fifty napkins—she couldn't dredge up even one ounce of energy to pick up a fork and eat supper. Her empty stomach had made falling asleep near impossible. Then, once she drifted off around midnight, she'd tossed and turned the rest of the night. Sometime in the wee morning hours, laughter and the sound of hoof-beats jolted her awake. She'd stared at the ceiling until dawn.

Lesson learned. *No going to bed on an empty stomach . . .*

Harold, the mop boy, who'd stayed on at the Biscuit Barrel even after Renee, along with her little brother, Sammy, asked for their jobs back, had escorted her back to the hotel. Along their quiet stroll, Madison had hoped they'd run into Justin making his nighttime rounds, but that hadn't transpired. The evening had been serenely pleasant, with only a few people still out. Music from the saloon across from her hotel serenaded their progress. For one moment, the saloon girl named Fancy Aubrey had looked out through the doors, and their gazes met briefly. Madison, now ashamed for her action, had quickly glanced away. Spotting an empty booth along the far wall, she hurried forward and scooted in.

"Good morning," Lenore Saffelberg said as she approached. She carried Madison's usual request of a pot of hot water and an infuser of orange tea. "You look exhausted, Miss Plumb. Did you work late last night?" She turned over Madison's clean cup, which had rested upside down in its saucer, set the infuser inside, and poured the hot water.

Madison smiled and nodded. She liked Lenore. The waitress always looked nicely put together, with freshly coiffed hair and a white apron, clean and starched. She spoke well and used correct English. Over the days, they'd become friendly.

Since they were both waitresses, they had stories to share. Madison had noticed Lenore could be prickly or stern with some, and most always with men. But not with her. The older waitress's face seemed to brighten a little when the two talked. At least she was special to *one* person in Y Knot.

Maybe those thoughts weren't quite right. Justin came to mind. *He likes me well enough,* she told herself. *We're friends.* Maybe I'm a little special to him, too. Everything about him made her smile. Should she confide in him? Tell him her true reason for being in Y Knot? Doing so felt right. Not because finding her mother would be easier, but because she'd have someone to share her disappointments with. Her successes, too. "The latest I ever have," she responded to Lenore's question. "The Biscuit Barrel was packed. Mrs. Larson sent word for Renee to come in to help. With the third waitress, Mrs. Larson was able to assist in the kitchen, which makes everything run smoother."

Lenore's brow jerked up. "I'm glad Miss Cheapskate finally opened her purse and employed a third waitress. Those girls work hard over there. I know how hectic waitressing can be." She shrugged and a smile replaced her frown. She glanced at the other tables.

"I'm relieved she hired me, too," Madison said. "Since I've secured steady employment, I won't have to move to the boardinghouse quite as soon as I'd planned. I love my corner room, and I've enjoyed eating my meals here. Feels like home." She smiled at Lenore. "Have you worked here long?"

Lenore nodded. "Long enough."

The waitress had responded a little too quickly. Madison got the impression the woman wasn't looking for sympathy, but maybe a friend. "Do you have any days off?" she questioned softly. Every time Madison had visited the dining room, she'd seen Lenore working.

Lenore's brow dropped. "Sunday," she said slowly. "As well as a couple of lunch shifts—that makes for a nice morning, but I'm here for dinner six nights a week."

"Maybe we can have a picnic sometime," Madison said on an inspiration. "I'm sure you must have some tips to make my job easier. I've seen you carry a stack of plates up your arm. You must have several other little suggestions. I'd be grateful."

A moment of indecision crossed Lenore's eyes before she shook her head. "I'm sorry, I'm usually busy. Besides, Ethel or Renee can show you the same things. Most chores aren't difficult, just takes some practice."

Had she done something to offend the woman? "Oh, all right."

Lenore looked again over her shoulder at the

dining room. “Duty calls. I’ll return to get your order in a few minutes.” A forced smile appeared. “Enjoy your tea.”

A bubble of sadness for the woman made Madison sigh. Perhaps Madison wasn’t the only one in Y Knot who had secrets to hide.

CHAPTER TWENTY-FOUR

St. John's Hospital, Helena, Montana Territory

"Charity."

The raspy plea pulled Charity out of a dream. She sat close to Brandon's bed with her forehead resting on the side of the mattress, her thoughts jumbled and memories murky. Brandon had regained consciousness the first few minutes after the operation, but they hadn't talked. Since then, he'd been in a deep sleep and failed to awaken all night.

Doctors and nurses came and went.

She feared he'd rouse when she wasn't there, so she'd spent most of the night right here in this chair—only returning to the hotel to take one short nap and gobble down some soup. The nuns had been incredibly kind, allowing her to stay past visiting hours. She wondered if their leniency had to do with her three large brothers looking like outlaws with thick stubble and bloodshot eyes.

"Charity?"

The weak plea came again, and she forced her aching back straight. Was her mind playing tricks on her? Brandon appeared to be peacefully resting, his arms straight by his side, his eyes closed. Would she ever see the light in his beloved eyes again?

"Char . . ."

This time, Charity sat bolt upright. By her guess, and the shadowy light beyond the window, she presumed the time was about eight o'clock in the morning. Standing, she gently lifted Brandon's hand and pressed several kisses onto his fingers. She leaned close. "Brandon? Brandon? Did you say something?"

His eyes fluttered once. Then again.

She held her breath. "Brandon," she whispered with urgency. "Oh, my *love*. Are you awake? Please, Brandon, say something." Hot tears scalded her eyes, and she couldn't hold them back a second longer.

Brandon opened his eyes, and their gazes met.

"My love, my love." She carefully laid her cheek next to his, breathing in his essence, his life, his beloved face. *Everything*.

"How . . . where . . . ?" The question died on his lips.

"We arrived in Helena Thursday evening, and you went right into surgery. Today is Saturday morning. Almost two whole days." *Long, gut-wrenching hours*.

At first, his lips moved slowly without words. Then, he finally got out, "Explain."

Charity glanced around. She ran to the back of the room for the pitcher of fresh water the nuns switched out often in hopes he'd awaken and be thirsty. She poured half a glass and helped him take a few small swallows. After which, she told him everything that had happened. All she'd learned from the doctors, keeping nothing back. The dangerous journey and his slim chances, even after the operation. Brandon was a fighter. He needed to know what he was up against. "Thank you for coming back to me," she whispered close to his ear. "I love you, my life. I . . ." A clog of unshed tears stopped her voice, and her legs felt weak, but she wouldn't release his dear, warm hand.

"*Promise* me," he said with a voice she had to strain to hear.

She kissed his lips softly, tasting the salt from the fever. "*Anything,* my love."

"If I die, promise me you'll go on with your life. Promise me you'll marry again." He seemed to rally, his earnest gaze searching hers. "You're young. Beautiful. You have your whole life ahead of you. Don't waste a minute mourning me. Regretting what might have been."

A chill washed over her. "You're not going to die, Brandon Crawford. Stop talking foolish. I won't hear another word. Even in your weakened state, you're an extremely strong man. The doctors said as much. I'll not entertain even *one second* of this thinking. I can't and won't . . ."

But her words faded away as she searched his eyes. *What if Brandon* does *die? Me, remarry? I won't be able to breathe even one minute, let alone go on with my life.*

His head turned restlessly, and his mouth moved but no words came out.

Frightened, Charity looked around the room, wondering if she should run for a nurse. They'd emphasized several times, if he awakened, he must remain still, so the sutures inside keeping his intestine together were not ripped.

"Promise me! Promise me . . ."

To quiet him, she took his hand. "I can promise we'll grow old together. Sit in rocking chairs on the front porch, holding our grandbabies. I promise you *that,* Brandon Crawford. And nothing else."

Hearing her promise, he calmed considerably. "We don't *have* a front porch."

"We don't *yet,* but we will. At the new house. We can resume building as soon as you're better and we return to Y Knot."

"I never believed I'd die inside four walls," he said softly. "Bury me on the ranch, Char. Not our new place, but up on the upper crust of the Heart of the Mountains, by the river. I've always loved that spot. Remember? Where we made love?"

At the sweet memory, she broke down, crying uncontrollably. Unable to be brave a moment longer, she carefully laid her head on his shoulder, taking in his dear scent.

Brandon lifted his hand and stroked her hair. "Shh, little darlin'. Don't cry."

His voice was so soft, she had to quell her sobs to hear him.

"I've loved you more than life itself," he said sadly. "Maybe I'm being punished." He continued fondling her hair. "Loving you too much."

"Don't say such things. We have a child on the way. You must be the daddy. Teach him or her all you know." She wiped the wetness from her cheeks with the back of her hand. His eyes were now closed, but he was still lucid. "Oh, Brandon, I wish you could feel what I do when the baby moves. I sometimes think a tiny butterfly is inside me. Sometimes, it tickles. It's beautiful."

He rolled his head and looked at her, as if her words comforted him. Bathed him in love. "Let me feel."

The baby wasn't stirring now, but still, Charity carefully climbed on the bed and laid alongside him. She pressed his hand to her midsection, silently begging the babe to wake up and move. Do a somersault. Surely, their child was much too small for him to distinguish the movement like she did, but this was a morning of miracles. Who knew? He'd awakened, and they'd shared such loving words. What was life, really, but sharing love with your soul mate? Like the geese that mated for life, she knew without question, if Brandon was called home tonight, she'd never love another man. Their child would be enough for her for the rest of her life.

Chapter Twenty-Five

Francis took the four steps of Y Knot's white, clapboard schoolhouse two at a time. Being as the ranch was shorthanded, he'd not seen Ashley for five whole days. As soon as Justin had ridden out, he'd hitched up the buckboard and headed into Y Knot for supplies.

Wanting to surprise Ashley, Francis opened the door quietly. She'd gotten the school teaching job, just like he thought she would back when she'd been living in Priest's Crossing. Mothers were singing her praises, and he wasn't surprised in the least. School was out for the summer, but more often than not, this was where she could be found, doing this or that, or writing in her journal as she planned out the coming school year.

She looked up from behind the desk at the front of the room and smiled.

A cross breeze flowed in through one open window and out the other on the opposite side of the room. The blackboard was chalk free, and the inside of the rectangle-shaped room had a new coat of light yellow paint—a chore they'd completed together a few weeks before Brandon's accident. Still smiling, she stood as he anxiously crossed the room.

"Francis," she breathed out on an excited sigh.

"I wasn't expecting a visit. I'm delighted to see you."

"And I, you, darlin'." Without another moment's delay, he gathered her into his arms and kissed her soft lips. They remained close for several moments, him enjoying the feel of her smashed up against his chest. Her little mewing noises were driving him to distraction. Courtship was fine and dandy, but he was eager to say his vows to make Ashley his wife.

She finally pulled back, her breathing uneven. "I'm surprised to see you today. I thought you'd be in on Monday to pick up supplies."

He stepped back, keeping hold of her hands. "I know. Mondays are my usual supply day, but I got to hankerin'. All the sad faces at the ranch are hard to take. Poor Miss Claire. This tragedy is especially hard on her with Charity in the family way and her not being able to look after her. Make sure she's eating properly and getting enough rest." Dispiritedly, he shook his head. "Justin brought out another telegram. Brandon's had his surgery and only has a half-a-hundred chance of pulling through."

She tipped her head. "Half a hundred?"

Francis felt his face prickle with heat. Ashley was so intelligent, with so much book learning. He didn't want to look stupid in her eyes. He'd been trying to sound smart. "Fifty-fifty."

"Oh, no." Her brow creased. "Sheriff Crawford

is one of the nicest people in Y Knot. He went out of his way to make sure my mother and I felt welcomed when we first arrived. I've been praying for him every night and morning. I hope he pulls through."

Emotion clogged Francis's throat, and he nodded. "Never thought it would go this far," he finally replied. "We all just thought he had a broken leg. How wrong we were."

She slipped back into his arms and laid her head against his chest.

He slowly rubbed up and down her back as he considered what life in Y Knot would be like without Brandon. "I have more news, too. Or, perhaps, you've heard already."

She stepped back, waiting.

"Jack Jones is in Y Knot."

She slapped a hand over her mouth.

"He came in Thursday night, late. Have you seen him around?"

She shook her head. "I haven't. And I've not heard a thing. But I haven't been here much. Mother and I've been out at the orchard. Making sure the saplings have enough water during this heat. Berta May's been generous about giving her time off from the fabric shop to help me."

Francis felt bad about leaving chores at the orchard up to her, for now. Her face was sun kissed, and a few new freckles had appeared on the bridge of her nose. Until the ranch hands were back from the cattle drive, there was no help for it. "I'm sorry you're carrying all the weight. I'll get out there as soon as the—"

She shushed him with a finger on his lips. "I understand, Francis." She rose up on tiptoe and gave him a brief kiss. "You don't need to explain."

She smiled to make him feel better, he was sure.

"Have *you* seen Jack yet?" she asked. "I know there's bad blood between the two of you."

"Not yet, but I plan to look him up. Justin said he's staying at Lou and Drit's, for the time being." Francis couldn't keep a scowl off his face. "Miss Claire doesn't want us fighting, but I don't see how that can be avoided. He fled in fear the night of the fire when Luke almost died. Because he turned tail and ran like the yellow-bellied coward he is, I never got to tell him exactly what I thought of his lawman ways."

Ashley rubbed both hands up and down Francis's chest. "Please listen to Mrs. McCutcheon. Nothing good ever comes of fighting. There's already enough heartbreak in town to last a lifetime. Promise me you'll steer clear of Jack until you cool down. Jack Jones is just a pathetic windbag who goes around making trouble. Why, I almost slapped—"

Francis straightened. "What did you say?"

Ashley's face changed to the color of the paper

apples glued to her cutout apple tree in the back of the room. She tried to turn away.

But he caught her shoulder and gently brought her back to face him. "You mind repeating yourself? What's this about slapping Jack Jones?"

"I *didn't* slap him, I said I *almost* slapped him. When we were in Priest's Crossing before he was sheriff and long before you and I had met. He was new and trying to make friends. At the Christmas social, he made a pest of himself, is all. Getting me punch, following me around like a forlorn puppy, and then, like a mean guard dog, chased away any other gentleman who tried to dance with me. I didn't appreciate his attention." She stopped and nibbled her bottom lip.

A sure sign there was more to the story she didn't want to say. "Go on."

"At the conclusion of the party, I was cleaning up, since I was the head of the social committee. I reached into the broom closet for the empty boxes to pack away the decorations when he ran his hand down my back, coming dangerously close to my . . ." She briefly snapped her mouth closed. "Jack Jones is the only man who'd dare try such a disrespectful action. He was ready for my response when I whirled around, and pulled me into his arms. He tried to kiss me. I raised a hand to slap him, but he caught my wrist before I could complete what I intended."

Fury rippled through Francis. "Why, that low-down . . ."

"No, Francis. He's been a *perfect* gentleman since. I have no idea why he didn't start out that way. He's not bad looking . . ."

Francis just stared, unbelieving.

"What I meant was," she hurried on, "young ladies flee from scoundrels. At least, the young women I know." She shrugged and glanced at the floor. "Please don't make more out of this than what I meant."

The schoolhouse door opened, and Justin stepped inside. He looked back and forth between them. "Should I come back?"

Ashley stepped away and waved Justin in. "Of course not."

Justin held his hat in his hands. "Just stopped in to make sure Miss Adair knows about the break-in at Herrick's Leather Shop. Until the culprit is found, I'm warning everyone to keep their eyes open and doors locked."

"What's this?" Francis asked.

"I meant to say something at the ranch yesterday, but Mrs. McCutcheon looked as if she had more than enough to worry about without adding fuel to the fire. Herrick's had an unwanted visitor Thursday night. The thief took two bridles and about eight dollars in coins from the cash box. I've searched the place for clues but didn't find much to go on except a broken lock and a half-eaten peppermint ball—the kind Lichtenstein sells. Trent says it wasn't his or his pa's."

"I heard about the break-in from Berta May," Ashley said. "Shocking."

Justin nodded. "I'd like to catch whoever's responsible so the Herricks can recover their property."

Francis raised his brows. "That happens to be the same night Jack Jones rode in."

"I thought the same thing. I'm not ruling out anyone. He might want to stir up trouble."

Ashley looked like she wanted to say something but held her thoughts to herself.

"There's another thing," Justin said, directing his attention to Ashley. "A new young lady has come to town. Miss Madison Plumb. She's about the same age as you. Have you met? She's staying at Cattlemen's."

"Not yet, but I've seen her a time or two crossing the street or going into a shop."

Justin stood there like a statue, as if he'd painted himself into a corner and didn't know how to get out. Clearly, he must be sweet on this new woman. Why else would he bring her up to Ashley? "Why?" Francis still felt surly. All his good feelings had flown out the open window when Ashley almost said Jack Jones wasn't bad looking. Was she having second thoughts about getting married? She was young and said he was her first sweetheart. "Do you have a reason for bringing up Miss Plumb?"

"Maybe the four of us should go on a picnic," Ashley offered quickly, a wide smile splitting her face. "Tomorrow, after church. Ina encourages me to use her kitchen. I can fry some chicken. Justin? Francis?"

Justin let go a deep breath. "Sounds mighty good."

"You already know her age?" Francis asked, surprised. "You're a fast worker."

"No," Justin shot back. "Not exactly. Guessing by her looks isn't difficult. If the idea sits well with you both, I'll speak with her sometime today. If she says yes, I'll get you a message. How's that?"

Francis didn't want to be angry over Jack Jones anymore. At least, not until they were face to face. If he wanted Ashley to share things, he couldn't get mad or jealous if she mentioned another man. "That'll work." He glanced at Ashley to find her gazing up at him approvingly. When she smiled, he couldn't stop one of his own.

Justin turned for the door as he secured on his hat. "I'll see if Aunt Pauline will bake a cake."

Sunday was usually a day off at the ranch, but since they were shorthanded, Francis might have to trade with Nick if he wanted to spend the day with Ashley on a picnic. He'd like nothing better. One way or another, Francis knew he should find more time to spend in town, especially since Jack Jones, a *handsome* man, according to Ashley, had shocked them all by returning. Francis didn't put anything past the nosey imbecile—like trying to sweet-talk his intended away.

Chapter Twenty-Six

Open Range, Montana Territory

"I'll be glad to reach Miles City," Shad said, his hands folded around a hot cup of Arbuckle's. A few feet away in front of the chuck wagon, a fire crackled and popped. Several ranch hands lazed about. The soft lowing of the cattle was ever present. He took a sip and waited for the strong coffee to put some kick back into his bones. Being it was Sunday, they were taking the morning hours off. Flood read a few pages from the Bible before the shift changed. "This coffee ain't half-bad, Ike," he called. "Better than any you've made so far. Lucky will be proud when we tell him you survived as cookie."

"He won't be *too* happy to hear it," Roady replied, striding into camp and going for the chuck wagon. "Wasn't pleased at all to be left behind." Roady took a mug, looked inside, and then wiped something with the end of his shirt. "You might try doing a better job of washing, though."

"Little tailings never hurt no one," Ike threw back. "Additional nourishment."

Shad eyeballed Ike over his mug. The ranch hand had drawn the short straw and ended up driving the chuck wagon and doing all the cooking. A few months back, Lucky's gimpy leg began to give him more trouble than usual, and since this was a relatively short drive to Miles City, Flood had told him to stay home and rest it. Much to Lucky's consternation. Wasn't any secret the fella was growing older, as they all were.

Chance ambled into camp. His red bandanna was tied neatly, and the ends were tucked into the collar of a clean, but wrinkled, white shirt. He'd shaved and combed his hair back with water. Shad held his comments to himself.

"Wearing your Sunday best, Chance?" Tanner chuckled. "Who'd you dress up for? The cattle?"

Chance was pouring his coffee. He straightened, turned, and smiled. "I'm not embarrassed to say I've dressed proper for the Lord. Before we pull out, you'll recognize me again, back in my dust-covered gear."

Shad shot his little brother a *walk lightly* glare.

Tanner shrugged. "What? I was only making an observation, is all."

"Another astute reflection from a greenhorn," Jonathan Burg called out on a laugh. "Used to be Francis, and now it's you."

"Take note, Tanner," Smokey said. "See what married life does to a fella. Makes 'em nice and respectable. Like Chance said, nothin' wrong with respectable."

Tanner shrugged. "How come *you* never married, Smokey?"

"I was in love once, but her pa liked me about as much as a festering tooth. I never had a chance."

Shad investigated the bottom of his coffee cup, hoping someone would change the subject. Once the topic of marriage and weddings got started, babies and children were sure to follow. That was all the talk last night before he went out to ride nighthawk. Flood had been no help at all. He'd sat back with a wide grin and let him, Roady, and Chance deal with all the questions and comments about marriage and children—even though he and Poppy had yet to marry.

What foods did a woman crave when she was expecting? When was best to start toilet training? Hell, he had no clue about any of it . . . only doubts and fears he'd never know at all.

He wished Poppy were here to quell his misgivings. One little quirk of her lips and all doubts fled his mind. She'd assured him she loved him, no matter what, one hundred times—or more. He needed to believe her. Once they got home, wedding preparations would be in full swing.

"Come and get it while it's hot." Ike stood between the chuck wagon and the campfire, stirring a large pot of beans. He'd added the leftover, tough-as-boot-leather beef they'd chewed on last night. Off to the left, tortillas were stacked a foot high.

Smokey was the first through the line. He looked around the chuck wagon and then placed his hands on his slim hips. "No biscuits?"

Ike dished two large scoops onto Smokey's plate and then tapped the long-handled spoon on the side of the pot. "Not this morning." He flipped him two tortillas.

"No biscuits." Smokey grumbled as he made his way to the bench. "No biscuits on Sunday morning? No biscuits *or* flapjacks with butter and syrup? Can't get home quick enough to the Heart of the Mountains."

"If you want biscuits, get up earlier tomorrow and help me. I'll gladly trade my spot for yours."

Shad and all the cowhands looked at anything except Ike as they waited in line. No one wanted his job.

"I'll help tomorrow, *gringo*," Pedro volunteered, his spurs jingling as he stepped forward. "My biscuits are light and fluffy. Just like Lucky's."

Pedro? Shad wouldn't have thought it of the hard-faced Mexican.

"Why you so quiet, Petty?" Chance whispered into Shad's ear from behind. "Been meaning to ask. You got something stuck in your craw?"

"Nothing's bothering me," Shad said quietly over his shoulder. "Nothing at all."

"Eeeeyuck!" Smokey spat a mouthful of beans

over his plate and into the fire. "What in tarnation did you put in these, Ike? An ocean of salt?" He lifted his coffee mug and chugged down the contents. His tongue went in and out, as if he were trying to flick rancid goose grease off.

"Sorry," Ike boomed, his face turning a deep shade of pink. "This is only my third mishap—a man's got to learn. Just thought I'd spruce the beans up with sugar, being it's Sunday. Mistook the salt, is all. The print on the label is impossible to read."

Tanner chortled. "The print's as big as a barn door."

"You know I need spectacles." He waved Smokey over. "Come get some more beans. There's plenty left. Don't be so hard on me, fellas. My heart's in the right place."

When Shad was up to bat, he shook his head at the beans and took four tortillas and several slices of beef. He thought of Poppy and all the Sunday dinners they'd shared at her sister's house. Kathryn and Tobit were the perfect host and hostess, and Kathryn was an exceptional cook. Their marriage was a true picture of domesticity. Poppy was learning from Kathryn, too. She wouldn't have any problem holding up her end of the marriage. He just wished he felt as confident in himself.

The group grew quiet.

Plunked on the camp bench, Roady said softly, "I wonder what Sally and Gillian are doing today. Sure wish I were at home with 'em. Sunday mornings are always special."

Jonathan harrumphed. "No talk of home. You know the rule. Only makes us cowpokes homesick. Sally's probably baking cookies with the women at the ranch, and Luke and Mark are playing cards with Brandon in the upstairs bedroom. They don't miss you at all."

"Yeah, Brandon's got it made," Tanner spoke up. "A pretty wife and all the other women to fuss over him. I wouldn't mind busting *my* leg if I could spend my down days there."

"Hush," Shad barked. "Or I'll put a muzzle on you. Brandon's not the kind to like languishing his days away in bed."

Tanner's lips curled in a rueful smile. "I didn't mean nothin' bad."

"And I'll help you, Shad," Smokey threw out, now chewing on a strip of meat. After he'd filled his plate with more beef, he'd picked a spot on the ground with his back against a wagon wheel. He stretched his legs out before him and crossed his ankles. "Not much happens in Y Knot in the middle of July. Can't take the heat. Everyone hunkers down in a cool spot to while away the day. I'll bet Francis and Nick both gain five pounds, just laying around. We'll be home soon enough, so stop your whining."

"I wasn't whining," Roady responded. "Just thinking aloud."

Flood, who'd returned to camp a few minutes before, laughed. "Oh, how my ranch hands have changed since hitching up to a woman."

Back to the marrying up and baby talk. Finished with his meal, Shad stood and scraped the little bit left on his plate into the slop bucket. He missed Poppy heartedly, but he'd not say so. "I'm saddling up," he remarked, glancing around. "Ride out to the herd early and give one of the others a little more time off before we start pushing the cattle. I wonder how Brandon and Charity's barn is coming. Think it's up?"

"Knowing my sons and Brandon the way I do, I'm sure the barn's built, and several of the outbuildings, as well."

"I 'spect you're right, Boss." With that, Shad ambled toward the ramada, still carrying the weight of the world on his shoulders.

Chapter Twenty-Seven

Justin stood back and watched as Madison and Ashley unpacked their picnic baskets onto the old oak picnic table beneath the shade of a maple tree. Not far away, sounds of children playing and laughing could be heard. The small, blue church, full only minutes ago, stood quiet in the meadow, the double doors now closed. Some townsfolk lingered around the stairs as they often did after Sunday service, while others loaded into their buggies and left straight away.

The girls laughed.

Justin turned his attention back to the women. He couldn't take his eyes off Madison. She'd never looked so pretty. Her light green dress complimented her dark blue eyes. Like she'd settled a spell over him during the church service. All he could think about was her. He needed to keep his wits about him. He was responsible for Y Knot, and he dared not allow himself to become distracted. The town had to be his first, *and only,* responsibility until Brandon was back. He'd keep his priorities straight.

"I wonder where Francis is?" Ashley glanced east, as if she could see over the miles to the Heart of the Mountains ranch. "I really don't feel like eating a picnic without him."

"He'll be along," Justin answered, stepping forward. Justin didn't really want to eat the picnic without Francis, either. He'd be the only man between two beautiful women, and keeping an easy conversation flowing would be a challenge. Watching Madison and Ashley, he recognized the girls seemed to have hit it off nicely. "Here comes Aunt Pauline."

Justin's aunt approached, carrying a picnic basket over her arm. When she spotted him from across the expanse of the churchyard, and after the women had smiled a welcome to her and then looked away, his aunt wiggled her eyebrows, as if he were still twelve years old. He appreciated her willingness to bake something for the picnic, but he wished she wouldn't treat him like a child.

Running past her aunt, Carlie bounded up to their table, huffing and puffing. Her cheeks were bright pink, and a few strands of hair stuck to her moist forehead.

"Hey, squirt. What're you up to?" he asked, feeling conspicuously empty-handed.

Ashley was unpacking a platter of fried chicken, cooked to a golden brown.

A delicious aroma drifted up, and a moment later, his stomach loudly rumbled. Embarrassed, he slapped his midsection.

"You're hungry," Carlie blurted. "Me, too."

"I guess I am," he responded sheepishly.

"I'm glad." Ashley looked over her shoulder again, searching for Francis. "I made plenty for everyone. Once I got permission from Ina, she helped me with everything."

Madison unwrapped a medium-sized bowl. "I purchased potato salad from Cattlemen's restaurant. I asked if they'd allow me to purchase the supplies and make it myself, but the cook said no." She lifted a shoulder. "I can understand but was disappointed. My mother used to make the best potato salad in Kentucky. It's all in the amount of vinegar you add. We like a lot." She glanced at Justin. "I remember when I was little, eating our evening meal outside, and then when darkness fell, chasing the fireflies." She also pulled out a sack of golden-brown biscuits and smiled. "From the Biscuit Barrel."

Justin's mouth watered. "Everything looks delicious."

Aunt Pauline arrived with the chocolate cake Justin had asked her to make. She set the confection on the table, taking a moment to turn and arrange it until she was satisfied.

Do cakes have one side better than the other?

She perused the small group, her eyes twinkling. She'd told Justin again this morning how much she admired Madison Plumb and encouraged him to be bolder where she was concerned. His aunt had been amazingly agreeable about almost everything since his father had gone away.

Perhaps she liked being head of the household, so to speak.

"Carlie, you've torn your dress!" Aunt Pauline frowned as she picked up the hem and examined the damage. "Didn't I warn you to act like a proper lady—especially if you wore this dress? Shame on you."

At his aunt's sharp tone, Madison and he exchanged a look.

"I couldn't help it, Aunt Pauline. Dodger Hicks likes to chase me. My hem got caught on the berry bushes, and I had to get away. He's scary."

Justin put his hand on Carlie's shoulder. The rip was tiny. He didn't know how his aunt even saw it.

All three women now scanned the playground area where several young girls ran, screaming in fun, as a handful of boys followed in pursuit.

"Why, Dodger Hicks is sixteen years old. Hardly a boy to be chasing little girls. Especially if the girls are frightened of him." Aunt Pauline scowled at the group of children still romping around the yard. "And *especially* on Sunday."

Justin remembered all the times he'd done the same. "They're just running," he remarked, not wanting to cause a scene over normal play. "I'll keep my eye on him. And the other boys. If they get too aggressive, I'll send them home."

Pauline stared. "And Carlie *tore* her best dress."

He held his temper, commiserating with his

father for all the years he'd had to do the same. "By accident. And it's a small rip. I can barely see it. The boys chase the girls every Sunday. It's normal."

The scowl on Aunt Pauline's face eased away as everyone waited on her reply. "I guess you're right, Justin," she said. "I'll just leave this cake with you three and walk home. The day is quickly heating up. You young people have fun."

"Can I stay?" Carlie sang out. "I don't want to go home yet."

Justin glanced at Madison and Ashley.

"Of course," they sang in unison.

With a wide smile, Carlie ran back to the children and took up where she'd left off.

With that answer, Pauline wiggled her fingers and turned and headed for the road, meeting Jack Jones as he rode up.

Jack gave Pauline a nod and quickly dismounted. "Sorry I'm late." He smiled at the women and then glanced at all the delicious-looking food. "This sure is a nice spread."

"J-Jack," Ashley sputtered.

"Nice to see you again, Miss Adair. I was wondering when we might run into each other. How've you been? Nice to see you, too, Miss Plumb. Hope you've been enjoying the town."

Ashley's face turned beet red, from anger or embarrassment, Justin didn't know. Justin stepped forward, working to hold his temper again. "What're you doin', Jack? You know you aren't invited. Just mount up and ride away."

Jack lifted a shoulder. "Never hurts to try. And I've been wondering when Ashley would come out of that school. I've wanted to say hello. Here"—he waved his hand across the table of food—"you have enough eats to feed an army. All I want to do is help you out."

"Forget it. We're waiting on Francis. He's due any minute." Actually, he was an hour late. "I suggest you make yourself scarce, if you know what's good for you. He was none-too-happy to hear you've shown up in Y Knot."

"I'm not afraid of Francis."

Jack was spoiling their nice Sunday. "Every time we speak, I'm more amazed," Justin gritted out, feeling his face heat even more. "You don't have the sense of a chicken."

Chapter Twenty-Eight

A happy buzz surrounded Madison, Ashley, and Justin as the time drew on. Unfortunately, Francis never arrived. Carlie had skidded to a halt for all of five minutes to eat and then was off again to play with the few remaining children. To Madison's relief, Dodger Hicks had gone home with his family, and once he had, the whole area quieted down and became quite peaceful.

And what about poor Ashley? Madison could tell Francis's absence had her worried. Justin tried soothing her, saying any number of things could have turned up on the ranch to prevent his leaving. She'd smiled and nodded, but the young woman was antsy, pushing her food around her plate more than eating. Thank heavens, Jack Jones had taken Justin's words to heart and made a polite exit. Seemed no love was lost between the two—*or three*—if what he'd said about Francis was true.

Ashley, sitting across the table, dabbed her lips and then set her napkin back into her lap.

Justin, at her side, reached for another piece of fried chicken. He'd already had three, plus two helpings of the potato salad she'd brought, and three biscuits. That man could eat.

"This is *such* a fine meal. Thank you for pulling out all the stops."

Ashley smiled. "You brought the chocolate cake." She looked over to the sweet. "Should I cut a few slices?"

"But you've scarcely eaten a thing." Madison gestured toward Ashley's plate. The drumstick was barely nibbled, and she hadn't touched the biscuit. She had, out of politeness toward Madison, she was sure, consumed most of her potato salad.

Ashley gave a little huff. "I know. I'm sorry. I don't mean to be a stick in the mud. I'm just not very hungry."

Madison quickly wiped her fingers. "No need to apologize. I completely understand." She glanced at Justin, who nodded.

"Would you mind terribly if I left early? I'd like to see if the livery buggy is available and drive out to the ranch."

Justin straightened. "I can ride out there for you, if you'd like. Check on Francis."

She waved him off. "I'll enjoy a buggy ride this morning. I've driven myself several times."

Justin set the chicken leg he was holding back onto his plate. "Only if you're sure."

She nodded. "And let me take Carlie when I go. I'll drop her by your house. She looks ready for a nap."

Madison glanced over to see the little girl collapsed in the grass on her back, along with two other children, giggling about something.

"We're friends," Ashley went on. "And she'll be in my class next year." When Justin went to object, she put up her hand. "Please. I'd enjoy getting to know her better. Besides, the walk is only a few minutes. It's on my way. I just feel bad I'm leaving our picnic early."

"Will you, at least, have a slice of cake before you go?" Madison asked. "It looks so good."

She shook her head. "I'll take one with me to enjoy later. And one for Francis."

"Take more," Justin offered. "A slice for Ina and Norman, too. We can't eat this all by ourselves." He stood and cut a healthy portion, setting the chocolate confection on the clean plate intended for Francis. He also cut a slice each for Madison and himself.

Ashley packed the cake carefully with her chicken in the basket. "Thank you. It'll be a nice surprise." Finished loading her things, she rounded up Carlie, who didn't hesitate at all, and headed toward town.

Madison watched them go. "Well, that's too bad," she said, struggling for something to talk about. The picnic table was set away, and the church grounds were almost deserted. She and Justin were alone. "I wanted to get her ideas for my school paper. Once we got eating, I forgot."

Justin looked at her. "Ideas?"

"Since she's a teacher, I thought she might have some suggestions. What angle or direction would be interesting to take. Western life is too large of a topic. I'd like to pare the subject matter down. Since I'm a woman, I thought I'd slant the plotline toward how women take to living in a rustic setting. Difficult responsibilities, or aspects they love. That kind of thing."

Justin drummed his fingers on his chin. "Why don't you interview the three mail-order brides who live in Y Knot? Might make interesting reading."

She felt her eyes go wide. "Thank you. What a wonderful idea. Maybe they'll sit down with me together. Do you think they would?"

"Absolutely. I *know* they would."

That idea had just popped right out of Justin. Was not telling him her real reason for being in town a mistake? He seemed privy to all kinds of information. Maybe he already knew a woman who'd given up a child twenty years ago.

Should she trust him? *Everyone needs to trust somebody. No one's an island.* Her father's two favorite sayings. The thought made her miss her father, so recently gone, and her chest squeezed. She'd been the one to find him. He'd slept late, which wasn't like him at all. *Always up with the birds, before sunrise, to get a jump on the day,* was another.

He took a large bite of cake and chewed, a smile appearing.

Who *better* to trust than Justin? She'd known

him the longest. If she was honest with herself, she thought of him as her *best* friend—kind of silly, him being the deputy. She was sure he'd never betray her trust.

"Justin?"

He looked up. Eyes searching her face, he swallowed and set his fork back on his plate. "Yes?"

"There's something I'd like to tell you. Something extremely important."

He sat back and gave her a nod. "Go on, Madison. You can tell me anything."

She tamed her wobbly smile. Nerves skittered inside. "I do trust you, Justin. That's why I brought this up. There's another reason I came to Y Knot, something other than the paper I need to write. Actually, what I'm about to say is the *real* reason."

Chapter Twenty-Nine

Right then, the doors to the church squeaked open, and Reverend Crittlestick stepped out, the strap of his leather satchel draped over a shoulder. Closing the doors, he took the stairs. When he spotted them sitting alone under the maple tree, he headed their way.

Frustration zipped through Justin as he watched the minister approach. He liked Reverend Crittlestick and respected him, but Madison was about to share something important. *Her real reason for traveling to Y Knot?* Justin had guessed there might be other reasons she was hiding.

"Deputy." Reverend Crittlestick smiled at Madison. "Miss Plumb, it's a pleasure to see you again. Beautiful day for a picnic." His gaze roamed between them with a not-so-obscure sparkle in his eye. "I'm happy to see you two enjoying the weather while you still can. Days are growing hotter."

Madison nodded. "I enjoyed your sermon today."

"That's good to hear. I never tire of sharing the fruits of the Holy Spirit. If you stay in Y Knot long enough, you'll see what I mean." He looked at Justin. "Any progress on the break-in at Herrick's? I spoke with old Mr. Herrick yesterday. He's still grumbling."

Justin swung his leg over the bench to sit more comfortably facing the minister. "The only progress I'm making is weeding out persons of interest by getting a statement of their whereabouts that night. I won't say who, but so far, everyone has an alibi." He shrugged.

"Well, keep at it. I'm sure you'll find the thief if he's still in town."

Madison looked around. With the interruption, was she impatient to go? They still had their cake to finish and whatever she'd been about to say.

As uncharitable as the thought was, Justin wished Reverend Crittlestick would be on his way. He didn't want to lose this chance. Maybe he'd seen the cake, was hungry, and hoped for an invitation. "Reverend, would you like a piece of my aunt's chocolate cake?" Justin asked. "We have more than enough. Francis never showed today, and Ashley left early. I see by your satchel, you're on your way home. You can take some with you. We're happy to share."

The preacher's eyes lit with pleasure.

"That answers my question." Justin quickly cut a generous slice from what was left of Aunt Pauline's cake, set in on an extra napkin, and handed it to the preacher.

"Thank you. This looks delicious." He dipped his head. "I'll leave you two to your conversation.

Oh, and I'll drop this napkin by tomorrow. Is it your aunt's, Justin?"

"I brought it," Madison said. "Hildy let me borrow it from the restaurant."

"Then I'll take it back there." A grin split his face. "God Bless your generosity."

Madison picked at her cake as Reverend Crittlestick walked away.

Justin forked in a bite and chewed.

"This is delicious," Madison said. "Please tell your aunt, again, how much we appreciated her offering."

"I'll be happy to."

"I will, as well, when I see her," she added quickly. She stared at her cake.

"Madison, you were about to tell me something important before Reverend Crittlestick arrived. Would you like to tell me now? I'm ready to listen." He gestured toward the empty church grounds. "And we won't be interrupted, like we usually are in the sheriff's office." He gave a smile he hoped would encourage her to open up. "My lips are sealed."

She set her fork on the side of her plate and then used her napkin. "I do trust you, Justin," she said again and looked off.

The sounds of laughter came from somewhere down the road. The sun had momentarily gone behind the clouds, dropping the already-moderate temperature for July a couple degrees. Madison shivered, and he wondered if the weather change was the cause or what she was about to say.

"I *do* intend to write my school assignment," she said softly, "but that's not the principal reason for my arrival last Tuesday. You see, I was adopted just days after I was born. What I told you about my mother dying years ago is true, and my father dying more recently, as well. They were my adopted parents. The nanny who took over seeing to my needs is Mrs. Goodheart. She has grown daughters, and even grandchildren, and was always so kind to me—and still is. She's the one who encouraged me to make this trip."

Justin sat quietly, letting her get her story out. He wondered how this figured into anything. Adoption was a fact of life. He didn't think any less of her for it, not in the least.

She watched a bee circle the uncovered cake and settle onto a crumb on the side of the platter.

"And?" he encouraged. "Many youngsters have the same fate. It's nothing to be ashamed of."

She smiled. "Yes, I know. And I was blessed not to go to an orphanage. My mother, what I can remember of her, was a loving parent. I guess she'd longed for a child for years, and once I came along, she treated me like a princess until the day she died."

"See?" he said with a smile. "How old were you?"

"Seven. One day, my mama and I set out to

take a pot of chicken soup to our elderly neighbor who wasn't feeling well. Crossing the woman's porch, my mother stepped on a rusty, exposed nail, piercing her light day shoe."

Madison's crestfallen brow ripped at him.

She looked up, her eyes swimming in unshed tears. "A week later, she developed a fever, followed by aches in her knees. By the time the doctor arrived, her jaw had tightened. Talking or eating was painful. She began to have spasms and pain everywhere. Unsure what to do, the doctor sent for help, and at the same time, my father sent me away to stay at a friend's house."

"You must have been frightened."

"I was terrified. And I didn't want to leave her. It's the first time I can remember my father raising his voice to me when I refused to go."

"But you did?"

She nodded. "I didn't have a choice. She passed away two days later."

"Lockjaw?"

Again, she nodded. "Something the medical community was just coming to know, at the time. If the first doctor had known what he was dealing with sooner, she might still be alive today."

Justin didn't understand what this had to do with her coming to Y Knot. He longed to hold her hand and chase away the clouds in her eyes. Instead, he discreetly scanned the area to make sure they were still alone and wouldn't be disturbed.

"Father was never the same after mother died. He hired Mrs. Goodheart to care for me while he was at work. She was kind and knew just what to say to a grieving seven-year-old. Or what to bake to take away the sting for a few, fleeting minutes. About a year later, I overheard a contentious conversation between Mrs. Goodheart and my father. As I passed my father's closed office doors, I heard my name. Being curious, I pressed my ear to the wood. Until that moment, I never dreamed I was adopted. Mrs. Goodheart was refusing to write a letter he'd said was required each year. The attorney who'd arranged my adoption, would send the correspondence on to my birth mother. Mrs. Goodheart said for her to write such an important letter was morally wrong. He contended my mother had always taken care of the yearly correspondence, and doing so now was too painful for him. The letters contained my milestones and were to continue until my twenty-first birthday."

Justin reached forward and plucked a tear lingering on her cheek.

She gave a sad smile. "My parents were older than most. So, when I was nineteen, my father was sixty-two and lay in his bed, slowly dying from a weak heart. Until then, I kept the truth and questions to myself, dreaming about my real mother and father, but not wanting to hurt the man who raised me. Christmases and birthdays came and went, and I imagined every fantasy any little girl might dream up. As I grew older, I no longer needed Mrs. Goodheart, but she stopped by on occasion for tea and conversation. We're close. I finally told her what I'd heard. Surprised, and then happy, she encouraged me to speak with Father before he passed on."

"Did he tell you everything?"

She nodded. "Indeed. He and Mother tried for a child of their own for years. Being unsuccessful, they'd finally adopted me. They never learned the name of my natural mother or the circumstances."

"And you believed him?"

"Yes. My birth mother was never told my name, either. The only stipulation was my adoptive mother and father send the letter once a year by January twelfth, telling them about me." Her voice fell away, and she took a deep breath.

Justin still couldn't understand Madison's trip to Y Knot and why she felt so compelled to keep everything a secret. He reached over and took her hand. Had she learned something terrible? Was her mother a murderer?

Madison gave a determined little huff. "I'm sorry to drag this out. You see, my mother lives in Y Knot. The last address the attorney had for her was from here."

"Y Knot." Now everything made sense. "How did you learn that information?"

"My father just knew. I guess knowing the town

where she resided wasn't against the contract, and the attorney informed him several times when the address changed. If she's still living, I want to find her. Meet her. That's all I've dreamed about for years." She glanced away for a few seconds, gathering her emotions. "Maybe we look alike," she whispered. "I'd like to hear her voice. I want to understand why she gave me away and didn't try to raise me herself. Mrs. Goodheart saw my inner turmoil. She thought I should, at least, try to find her. If not, I'd always wonder and regret. After my father passed, I went to see his attorney. He wouldn't divulge anything further, saying doing so was against the law."

Madison gazed at him with her deep blue eyes, as if searching for understanding. As if she thought he would reprimand her for her desires.

"So, Y Knot is the only thing you have to go on?"

"Do you think I'm wrong? Will my showing up disrupt her life? Perhaps she's married and has a family. Maybe my coming into her life now would be a hardship. Or worse, might open wounds her husband—if she's married—never knew about. That's the only reason I can think of for all the secrecy."

Those were all good questions. Ones he had no idea how to answer. He sat there, trying to digest everything she'd just said.

"You see? My taking the job at the Biscuit Barrel has given me a way to meet more people—

women, to be exact. I've been asking a few questions to try to determine if any can actually be her. I'd suspected maybe Ina Klinkner, until I learned she had a son quite a few years older than myself—although that does not fully rule her out. There could be reasons she didn't want a second child. I'd thought finding my mother would be easy . . . until I arrived. I haven't made much headway."

He stared at Madison, amazed at the mission she'd taken on. How heartbreaking and exciting at the same time.

She blotted at her eyes with her napkin. "Please say something."

His mind raced for the best answer. "First, let me say, I know somewhat what you're feeling, although in a very small way. I lost my mother when I was ten, and I've never really gotten past the hurt. Mothers are special."

She nodded, her eyes swimming again with unshed tears.

How fast they could reappear only showed how raw her feelings were. "All your concerns are true. I don't have an answer. I can't imagine how difficult it's been for you. I'll help you any way I can."

She took a deep breath and slowly let it out on a shiver. "But what about me interrupting her life?"

"You won't know until you find her. But,

if your arrival is a disruption, you should be prepared not to go forward, if that's what she wants. She made sure you ended up with a good family all those years ago. A couple who wanted you and could afford to give you things, like an education and a nice home."

Madison's face clouded over.

"On the other hand, she might have had a change of heart, but with the binding contract, she had no way to find you. Your showing up might be the blessing she's been praying for." Still holding her hand, he caressed the backs of her fingers. When he didn't hear anything, he laid his other arm around her shoulders and drew her into his embrace. Compliant, she placed her head on his shoulder and gave a sigh.

"I'm so thankful for your friendship, Justin," she said in a small voice. "I feel like I can tell you anything." She took a deep breath. "I don't know what I'll do if I'm not successful, because I don't allow myself to think in that direction."

She felt perfect in his arms. "You can always get married and have a family of your own. That's what most young women want."

"That's true. But the trust and inheritance my parents left makes other choices possible. Right now, I'm just trying to make friends." Her head still rested on his shoulder. "I invited Lenore Saffelberg for a get-together, but she rebuffed me."

She sounded so lost. "Don't take Lenore to heart. She rebuffs everyone."

At the sound of a horse loping up the road, she pulled back, and they both glanced around.

Francis reined up, looking a bit worse for wear. He dismounted and then smiled at Madison. "Miss Plumb, I presume?"

Madison took a shaky breath and then nodded. "And you must be Francis."

"Yes, ma'am. It's a pleasure to meet you." His brows lowered. "Where's Ashley?"

"I believe she was worried about you and left about a half hour ago," Justin said. "She was headed to the livery for a buggy and intended to go out to the ranch."

Francis shook his head and beat his hat against his chaps. "I was afraid something like this might happen. We discovered a fence down in the back pasture."

"I'd think you'd have passed Ashley," Justin said. "On the road to the ranch."

"Didn't take the road to save time. I was miles away. I wouldn't have seen or heard a buggy."

Justin looked down the road to town, sleepy on a Sunday. "Could be she changed her mind and went home. I'd check the livery before you ride all the way to the ranch again."

"That's good advice." Francis repositioned his hat and mounted up.

Justin slid his gaze over to Madison. What if she found her mother and the fears she'd spoken of came true? She'd run back to Kentucky, and he'd never see her again.

Chapter Thirty

St. John's Hospital, Helena, Montana Territory

Luke stepped into the Victorian-style guest house across the street from the hospital feeling agitated. A sense of alarm swirled inside, pushing him into action. What action, he wasn't quite sure yet. He just knew something had to change, or Brandon would die. He and his brothers hadn't come all this way to let that happen. Even the thought would destroy Charity. She was being brave but also growing shakier as the days drew on. Almost a week had passed since his surgery. Something had to be done.

"Mr. McCutcheon?" a soft voice asked as he came in through the door. "I didn't expect you back quite so soon."

The pretty, middle-aged woman, who reminded him of a graceful swan, glanced at the walnut pendulum clock on her wall. Several worry lines appeared on her brow.

She knew his and his brother's schedule as well as they did. Somebody was always at St. John's with Brandon and Charity. They never left them alone. This was the first time.

"It's only six o'clock," she went on. "You're an hour early. I hope your brother-in-law hasn't taken a turn for the worse?"

Luke didn't have the heart to share what he was thinking and shook his head. "No, nothing like that."

A smile blossomed on her face. "Good. I have fresh-brewed coffee. I'll fetch you a cup." As she headed for the kitchen, she glanced over her shoulder and gestured to her comfortable parlor chair.

Mrs. Hardie had been incredibly kind since he and his brothers had rented the largest room on the top floor of her boardinghouse. She'd sent out their laundry for them and even picked it up. She went to and from the telegraph office as often as they needed, which was two blocks away, sending and retrieving messages. Whenever any of them missed one of her meals, she'd set a plate aside in the warmer until they returned and were able to eat. She'd even asked what their favorite meals were and tried to comply. She insisted she routinely accommodated all her tenants, but Luke had seen no such evidence with the several other businessmen who had come and gone during their weeklong stay.

Mrs. Hardie had also held a room for Charity, even though his sister was more or less living at the hospital with Brandon. Luke had assured her they could afford the second room, but Mrs. Hardie insisted she kept it free at no charge. When their sister needed to rest, or even sleep overnight, it would be clean and ready. Luke wondered how much longer Charity could keep up her demanding schedule at Brandon's bedside before she collapsed from exhaustion.

"And Charity?" Mrs. Hardie called from the kitchen. "I worry about her and the baby."

Don't we all?

"As well as can be expected, ma'am," he replied, rubbing a hand over his face. He needed to bathe and shave. He'd gone over to sit with Charity at eleven last night and remained all night, which was his normal shift.

Thank God for Mrs. Hardie. He appreciated all the woman's thoughtfulness more than he'd ever be able to express. The three-story staircase winding up the back of the parlor of the gingerbread-trimmed house was lined with old daguerreotypes, grainy photographs, sketches, and paintings of a working cattle ranch. Large herds were scattered everywhere. When asked, she'd shared she'd been raised on a large ranch west of Helena called the CCC, run by her parents and six brothers. She, being the only daughter, had moved into Helena when she married at nineteen. Said a day didn't go by she didn't miss the gentle lowing and sweet aroma of the livestock. Luke figured he and his brothers reminded her of home.

"That's good, don't lose faith."

He glanced at the staircase, now feeling the need to speak with Matt and Mark. They must take action of their own. Seemed the doctors were puzzled with Brandon's weak recovery and were just waiting to see what transpired.

He ambled through the parlor. The stairs were in the back of the room, with the opening to the kitchen and dining room just beyond. He'd wait for the coffee. Sounded good, and he needed several cups to keep him awake and moving today. He had no time to lie down and sleep.

"Charity's more exhausted than she lets on but won't leave his side." He gave a defeated chuckle. "She's a McCutcheon, through and through." The woman stuck her head out of the kitchen and nodded as he inched toward the stairs. He needed a meeting with his brothers.

"Go on up, Mr. McCutcheon. I can see you're anxious to get to your room. I'll bring a tray for the three of you."

"Oh, no, I can wait. You make the tray, and I'll take it up." Good-smelling aromas wafted in from the kitchen. Besides bacon, something sweet was in the oven. His stomach let out a loud rumble.

"I insist."

One thing he'd learned about Mrs. Hardie through interactions with her other boarders, she ran the place with an iron fist. What she said went. Mark relayed, a few nights prior, after he'd come in from his shift at eleven and hadn't yet fallen asleep, one fella tried to get in after the twelve o'clock curfew. The innkeeper had stuck her head out the window and told him to find another bed for the night, because he wasn't coming in to disturb her other guests.

At the thought Luke hid his smile. "Thank you, ma'am. Much obliged." Like a sleepwalker, Luke took every motion by habit. He headed for the stairs and climbed them, one foot in front of the other, until he'd reached the top.

Both Matt and Mark looked up wide-eyed when Luke strode through the door an hour early and tossed his Stetson onto the dresser, not even taking the time to properly hang it on the peg beside his brothers'.

"Brandon?" Matt asked quickly. Shirtless, he stood in his long johns in front of the mirror and washbowl, his face lathered and razor in hand.

Mark, who was already dressed, turned from the window.

"The same," Luke responded. "Last night, around two, he stirred some. We thought he was going to wake up, but he didn't. This can't go on much longer. The doctors are just waiting him out. We've got to try something else."

Mark crossed the floor and sat on the side of the rumpled bed.

The room held two double bedsteads, but since one of them was always over at the hospital with Brandon and Charity, no one had to share.

"I agree," Mark said. "But what? The doctors keep telling us to be patient. I'm like you, I'm done waiting, but what can we do?" The three looked at each other.

Luke paced the room. "First things first. Matt, you need to get over to the hospital. I don't like leaving Charity alone."

His brother nodded, wiping the shaving cream from his face with a white hand towel and pulling on his pants.

"I have an idea," Luke continued. "Circled it all night. I hope you two will agree with what I'm about to say, but I have my doubts. I'm not saying the doctors want Brandon to die, but I get the feeling, whenever we're around, they're nervous. And will tell us anything to keep us appeased." Luke stopped and searched the concerned faces of his brothers. He felt as helpless as they looked. "Damn, I wish John was here. Then, at least, we'd have an educated opinion to toss around."

"Our little brother has been as helpful as he can be from Texas." Matt pulled on his shirt and worked the buttons. "Should we take him up on his offer? He still wants to hop a train and come to Helena. Might be a good thing since he has a medical degree."

Mark shook his head. "That would take six to seven days. I don't know what more he can tell us he hasn't already by telegram and phone. He spoke to the surgeons. There's nothing more they know to do except wait and keep spoon-feeding him the best they can."

"*I* have an idea," Luke stated.

A soft knock sounded.

"That's Mrs. Hardie with coffee," he said. "As soon as I down a few cups, I'll be off." Standing, he went to the door and opened it.

The lady of the house came inside and set the heavily laden tray on the small table. With quick hands, she arranged a full loaf of fresh cinnamon bread and butter, plus three cups. The aroma of fresh-brewed coffee drifted from a white porcelain coffeepot. She finished with a few small plates and a knife. "Here you are. Breakfast is ready downstairs whenever you are. No rush. This will hold you over."

"Thank you, ma'am," they all said in unison.

"You've taken as good care of us as our own mother," Matt said with a chuckle. "We can't thank you enough."

She took the empty tray and headed for the door. "No thanks are necessary, other than that fine man across the road getting better and putting a smile on your sister's face." She gazed at them warmly and left the room, closing the door behind her.

Mark poured the coffee, handing the cups around. "What's your idea, Luke? I can't fathom."

"You can't fathom because it's rather unlikely—

but hear me out. Something different *must* be tried. I'm finished with waiting around another day. As soon as you get over to the hospital, Matt, to sit with Brandon, and you, Mark, bring Charity back here to rest, kicking and screaming, if you must, I'm renting a horse and heading out of town." He took a long draught from his cup and let the red-hot coffee scald his throat all the way to his gut. "Last night, when I went to the privy, I overheard a couple of men talking about a Cheyenne tribe somewhere in the hills north of here. They're mostly ignored because they keep to themselves and never bother any livestock or property from ranchers. They belong to one of the reservations, but the powers-that-be, for some reason, are looking the other way."

Mark was slicing several pieces from the aromatic loaf, but his hands stilled. "Luke?"

"I'll bring back the medicine man. See what he thinks."

"What?" Matt and Mark blurted out together.

Nodding, Luke said softly, "We've all heard the stories. Don't tell me we haven't. Amazing recoveries that can't really be explained."

"But that's all they are. Stories." Mark's hand was still frozen over the cinnamon bread. The look on his face said he couldn't believe Luke had just brought up herbal Indian medicine for Brandon.

"I'm not so sure," Luke said, taking a slug

of his coffee while irritation with his brothers sizzled inside. What other options did they have? None. Neither Matt nor Mark had come up with any solutions, except getting a second, and then a third opinion on Brandon's condition, which they'd done two days ago. All the doctors said the same thing. The surgery was done, and now they had to wait. "Gray Eagle has had countless examples of fever, as well as other ailments, being driven out. The doctors claim the injured, infected part of Brandon's intestine has been cut away. Nothing more is wrong with him. His body just needs to heal and grow stronger." Finished with his coffee, Luke stood and stretched to full height. He'd go, regardless of what Matt and Mark thought.

They stood, as well.

"Don't go gettin' angry, Luke," Mark stated. "We're just as frustrated and worried as you are. If you take off to who-knows-where, we won't know how to find you if Brandon has a turn for the worse."

"My being gone won't change anything. He could have a turn for the worse no matter where I am, and that's why I'm compelled to at least try. I believe a medicine man can help. I regret I didn't consider the idea sooner." Luke's heart pounded noticeably in his chest. Why? He hadn't felt such a feeling since the long-ago night when his mother, sitting with him on the top rail of the corral fence, had told Luke about his natural father, *Netchiwaan*. What a night—burned into his heart and soul. Just thinking about it now, with such impending doom concerning Brandon, brought gooseflesh. Then, the night in the jail-house when he was almost burned alive. The Cheyenne death chant had come to his lips, out of nowhere. The whole thing was a mystery. Was he being foolish now, believing he could ride into a camp and request help from the medicine man?

A look of admiration began in Matt's eyes and was repeated in Mark's. They both nodded.

"You'll tell Charity." Luke went to the wardrobe and gathered money. He'd need supplies, and possibly some buckskins, if he could find any to buy. "I didn't mention this to her."

"Because you didn't want her to skin you alive." Mark placed his hands on his hips. "You know she'll be upset, worrying over you."

Luke shook his head. "She'll be angry, all right. Not because I went, but because I didn't think of it sooner and take her along."

CHAPTER THIRTY-ONE

"Justin, I'd appreciate if you'd walk Carlie down to the fabric shop for her quilting lesson." Aunt Pauline's hair was tied back with a kerchief and a long apron covered her dress. "I'm up to my elbows in this bread dough. The time just got away from me." She glanced up at him as he descended the stairs. "It's not out of your way to the office."

Justin smiled. His aunt was becoming a regular domestic provider. In Denver, Mrs. Drier did all the cooking and cleaning. All Aunt Pauline used to do was keep track of his father's social schedule and meet with her lady friends. He couldn't ever remember her stepping out with a man. Here in Y Knot, she was doing her best to fend for her family. "I'll be happy to, Aunt Pauline." He glanced around the kitchen and front room. "Where is she? Is she ready to go?"

For the last three days, he'd not spoken to Madison past hello and goodbye. He didn't know if she'd orchestrated the distance because she regretted sharing about her birth mother or something else. If he left early enough, he might be able to catch her on her way to the Biscuit Barrel. Now, with Carlie at his side, having a private talk might prove difficult.

Aunt Pauline let out a gasp of annoyance. "She was just here a moment ago." Pauline went to the stairs and called up, "Carlie, Justin's walking you to class. If you don't hurry, you'll be late. Berta May gets annoyed if you're tardy."

Justin buckled on his gun belt and then his bull-whip. "Does Berta May really get upset? She's not the type to let anything bother her."

Aunt Pauline dropped her gaze to the dough in her hands and shook her head. "No, not really. I just wanted Carlie to stop what she was doing and come down directly. You know how distracted your little sister can be sometimes."

But the untruth will make Carlie anxious. She's just a little girl. He went to the stairs himself. "You ready to go, little mouse? I'm walking out the door."

"Coming, Justin. Just gathering my sewing into my bag."

Aunt Pauline clucked her tongue loudly. "I told you to do that last night, young lady!"

Clattering sounded from above and then Carlie fairly flew down the stairs, her chestnut locks swishing around her face like an unruly horse tail.

"Your hair."

"Justin'll braid it on the way. As we walk." With a pleading stare, Carlie searched his gaze. Her hairbrush and a bright-yellow ribbon dangled in one hand, and the cloth bag Berta May had given her to hold her quilting work, swatches of fabric, and needle and threads was clutched in the other. Her face was still damp from a quick wash. She was dressed, but her boot laces weren't properly tied and drifted out from beneath her hem. Somehow, she hadn't tripped coming down the stairs.

This would not pass the Aunt Pauline inspection. He knew because he'd contended with those since he'd been eighteen years old—much too old to be told what to do by an aunt who wasn't really a blood relative. But his father had bidden him to go along with her to keep the peace.

Hands on hips, Aunt Pauline glared. "I'll *not* have you go about town looking like something the cat drug home, Carlie. First, tie your laces properly, and then I'll have to wash my hands to fix your hair. You could yourself, if you were so inclined." She rolled her eyes to heaven. "I guess being late today will teach you a lesson. Perhaps Berta May will cancel your session." She glanced at the clock and shook her head.

In a blink, Carlie's shame-filled gaze dropped to the floor.

"There's no need to be so cruel, Aunt Pauline. Carlie's only six years old."

"Plenty old enough."

Justin counted to three as he corralled his temper. "Come here, little mouse," he said with affection. He gave his aunt a brief, censuring look. “Sit on the stool.” His little sister did his bidding. He quickly had her laces tied and hair brushed back into a ponytail. Knowing his aunt was fussy about bows, he took his time getting the ribbons just right. “There. Perfect.” He chucked her affectionately under the chin. What a beautiful woman she’d grow up to be.

“I’ll say it again,” Aunt Pauline muttered from the sideboard. “You and your father spoil that child to no end. She needs to learn responsibility. Put her things where she can find them easily. Then we wouldn’t run into this problem so often.”

His aunt had gone back to her baking and was greasing the bottom of her bread pans with fingers slickened with butter. Thank heavens, Aunt Pauline hadn’t come into his life earlier, or he could just imagine the vocal haranguing he’d have had to put up with. He’d been small for his age. Until his growing spurt in his midteens, he’d been the target of bullies. He was picked on at school, in the church grounds, and out and about, unless his father was around. His mother, God rest her soul, lovingly assured him he’d grow at some point, being she was tall for a woman and his father stood six foot four. When his mother died, and his father left to ride circuit, he was most often left at his grandfather’s ranch.

Justin’s heart warmed at the memory. He’d learned so much from his grandfather. From ranch work to the love of books, and more pointedly, *Shakespeare.* He became adept at branding calves and shoeing a cranky horse. Sensing Justin's difficulties with the older, larger boys, his grandfather, a righteous man, began to teach him the art of the bullwhip. The more Justin practiced, the more his confidence grew. When Justin was good enough, his grandfather entered him into competitions. Several in and around the Denver area had a large winner's purse for first and second place. Justin won two. By the time Justin was sixteen, he stood six foot one and towered over most of the boys who'd given him trouble earlier. Even better than his height, the continual practice built his muscles. He had a quick, scholarly wit from all his reading and was deadly with his friend—the whip.

"All set?" he asked a now-smiling Carlie. She was good at hiding her feelings. He'd do his best to help her navigate childhood during rough seas. "Let's see if we can spot Miss Plumb on her way to the Biscuit Barrel."

Carlie's smile widened. "Does she work on Thursdays?"

"Sometimes." They made their way out of the kitchen and into the living room. "Only way to find out is get out there before she slips by."

"Oh, do say hello to her for me," Aunt Pauline called. "She's *such* an outstanding young woman. So knowledgeable about the law, and so well-bred, and properly put together. She'd fit in this family *perfectly*. I wish with all my heart the two of you would fall in love and get married."

"Married!" Carlie sang out, excitement dancing in her eyes. "That would be better than anything, Justin. Yes, please marry Miss Plumb."

Justin jerked to a stop and turned back to his aunt, openmouthed. Anger sizzled within. "We've only known each other for *one* week, Aunt Pauline." *But in all seriousness, I know I could love her. Actually, I already do. Aunt Pauline is right about one thing, at least.* "Please don't say such things in front of Carlie. She might slip and mention something to Miss Plumb. If Madison heard either of you, she'd be shocked. And embarrassed."

Carlie's eyes widened, and she slapped her hand over her mouth. "I promise I won't."

At the topic of Madison Plumb, his aunt had followed them into the living room. "Fine. I won't mention her again, but I'm free to think anything I want. You can't begrudge me that."

Not wanting to get off on the wrong foot and spoil the rest of his day with irritated feelings, he relented. "You're right. If I see Madison, I'll pass on your greeting. Now, I need to get to the office." He opened the door.

Carlie hurried out before him.

"And Carlie needs to get to her lesson."

Chapter Thirty-Two

Luke lost little time procuring a mount. The livery didn't have any to rent so he'd been forced to buy the only gelding the portly fellow had available. The chestnut paint stood fifteen hands and rode well. His only fault was a constant tossing of his head, a habit many horses developed after dealing with too many heavy-handed riders.

A buckskin shirt had been more difficult to find. Finally, after two dead leads, the son of the mercantile owner had overheard his request and sold him, for an inflated price, the shirt Luke now wore. With several grease spots, it wasn't as fine as the shirt Luke had at home, but it would do to help him blend in. He needed to gain the trust of the people he had to track down, and then convince the medicine man to help. The task seemed almost overwhelming. Especially since he hadn't any idea how long Brandon could hold on. Was this venture folly? Were his brothers right in saying some of the accounts of Cheyenne medicine were hogwash? Being raised in a white man's world, sometimes he'd struggled to feel the Cheyenne blood humming through his veins. But hum it did, and with it, the notion that his Native American heritage was special. *Something more, something spiritual.*

Luke reined up and relaxed in the saddle. He

felt more at home out here after the days spent on the train and in the hospital. He studied the landscape. A multitude of different varieties of trees and vegetation dotted the gently rolling hills of the outskirts of Helena. The men he'd talked with, the ones he'd accidently eavesdropped on talking about the Cheyenne tribe, had turned hesitant to give information once they realized they'd been overheard. Luke had to loosen their tongues by an offer of five dollars each for any helpful suggestions on locating the tribe. Bringing plenty of money was good forethought by him and his brothers. Luke was spending it like water.

"Let's go," he said to the horse, scanning for a morass surrounded by a grove of maples. From there, he'd need to track west. A well-worn trail existed somewhere close after. Seeing a grouping of maples, he nodded, his chest filling with a rush of accomplishment. He clucked to the paint, and they headed off, one head toss after another. He circled the swampy footing and found the small trail concealed in tall grass. Now he was on to something. He loped off to the ticking clock ever present in his mind.

Madison needed to hurry if she didn't want to be late for her afternoon shift at the Biscuit Barrel. Lifting her skirt so as not to trip, she hastened into the mercantile and stopped at the counter.

Not seeing Mr. Simpson anywhere, she rang the little bell on the wooden top.

"Be right with ya," the man called from somewhere in the back of the room. "I'm helpin' another customer at the moment."

Feeling anxious, Madison slowly drummed her fingers on the counter, wondering if she'd receive a letter today from Mrs. Goodheart or perhaps her professor, Mr. Galbraith. She'd sent posts to each the day after her arrival, letting them know she'd traveled safely, and all was well. Even though the possibility of a return letter from either was slim, she still felt the need to check. Or, perhaps, knowing Madison's destination, one might have sent a letter on ahead, thinking she might be lonely. Mrs. Goodheart was known for thoughtful acts. The woman had known the importance of Madison's mission. But more notably today, Madison was discouraged she'd made little progress. She needed encouragement from home.

Girlish laughter sounded from the back of the room.

I wonder who Mr. Simpson is helping?

Clomping signaled someone's approach. Mr. Simpson appeared, followed by a young woman. She was in the family way, with dark hair and a pleasant smile.

"Thank you so much, Mr. Simpson," the young woman said. "I can't wait for Ina's birthday.

She'll be so surprised." She carried a black-and-silver gadget in her hands. "She's been speaking about these Crocker Farnsworth reversible fuel irons for months. Hayden and I appreciate you tracking this one down."

Mr. Simpson harrumphed. "Can't imagine something so complicated bein' much good. I'll stick with the old, tried-and-true model I've used for years. Heat it on the stove and press it on my shirt. That's good enough for me. Iffin she has trouble, I can't give ya your money back, bein' it's a special order. I can just see Ina when the oil leaks out onto her good linen." He shook his head and gave a long whistle. "She won't be happy no more."

Not wanting to appear to be listening to their conversation, Madison glanced at a pocketknife in the center of the display case as they drew closer.

"Howdy, Miss Plumb," Mr. Simpson said in greeting when he reached the counter. "What can I do ya for?"

"I'm just checking to see if I've had a letter addressed to me at general delivery?"

"I've yet to get around to putting out the mail." Reaching down, he lifted a white cloth bag marked US Mail from below and opened the drawstrings. "You go ahead and chat with Heather Klinkner while you wait, and I'll have a look-see. Have you two met?"

Madison recognized the name. "Not officially, but I've heard about the mail-order brides several times." A happy sparkle of warmth made Madison smile. "Belinda Bowie, the woman who rode in on the stagecoach, is staying with Ina Klinkner and told me how you and your husband met." She put out her hand. "I'm so happy to meet you, Mrs. Klinkner. I'm Madison Plumb."

"And I've heard all about *you,*" Heather replied. "And I've seen you, as well. I'm happy I came into the store today. You're in college." She winked. "Word gets around quickly in a small town. And, please, you must call me Heather."

Madison admired Heather's pretty, robin's-egg blue dress, so fresh and springy. "Deputy Wesley mentioned you and the other two mail-order brides might be willing to speak to me for a paper I'm writing."

Heather's eyes lit with pleasure. "I'd love to. And I'm sure Evie and Kathryn would, as well. I'll talk to the others and see. Are you staying at the hotel?"

Mr. Simpson stood behind the counter, going through the mail piece by piece. Sometimes, he turned to the side and stuck the correspondence into a numbered box. Other times, he set the letter aside.

With only a few more envelopes to go, her hopes began to dwindle. "I am. But I might move to the boardinghouse in a week or so. Or you can leave a message for me at the Biscuit Barrel, where I'm employed."

"I'll do that, Madison." Heather glanced at the clock on the wall.

Madison was about to say goodbye when an envelope in Mr. Simpson's hand caught her eye. Made from fine linen paper, it stood out from the rest and resembled the correspondence she'd seen many times in her father's office from his lawyer. And the return address greatly resembled the same firm's insignia, but she wasn't quite sure.

Without looking, he reached over his head and slid the letter into slot number three.

Could it be? And why now? This is July, and Father passed on in January. Is the letter from Father's attorney, alerting my mother of his passing?

Excitement and questions swirled around inside Madison, making stars dance in front of her eyes. Who was the holder of box number three?

Chapter Thirty-Three

Justin stood and stretched his back, intending to make a quick walk around the quiet, sleepy town. He liked to think of Y Knot as a slumbering child, relaxed and confident in the person keeping watch over him until morning.

Tonight, that's me.

For years, the watchmen were Brandon and Jack Jones. A bit edgy since he'd not made much progress on arresting the culprit who'd burglarized the leather shop, and then last night, the butcher shop, he vowed to increase his efforts as much as possible. At midnight, he planned to make a show of walking home but intended to circle back. Keep watch. Someone was taking advantage of Y Knot's sheriff being gone, and that angered Justin to no end.

At the window, he glanced outside as he lifted his jacket from one of the pegs. Over the last few hours, a wind had blown in. Leaves tumbled around the darkened street, visible by lanterns burning in windows or hanging on porches or eaves.

Stepping outside, he made a sharp right and walked down the alley to check on Brandon and Charity's vacant home behind the jail. He rattled the doorknob and inspected all the windows. Satisfied, he turned on his heel and headed back the way he'd come. The break-in at the butcher shop last night beleaguered his mind. The butcher, Mr. Barkley, said he'd taken their earnings upstairs when he and his wife had turned in for the night. All the intruder got was a rack of lamb, which was old and something Mr. Barkley intended for his hogs, as well as some old bacon headed for the trash. Just like at the Herricks', the back door lock was jimmied, and the perpetrator got in and out unnoticed.

Feeling peevish over the unsolved situation, Justin rounded the corner and almost bumped straight into Madison hurrying toward the sheriff's office door. With both hands to her shoulders, he caught her and stopped her in her tracks. He let his hands fall away. "Madison! Why're you out so late?" He looked around to see if one of the boys from the Biscuit Barrel had, indeed, walked her this far to the hotel. "And *alone*." He was mystified why she had searched him out. Delighted, but surprised.

"I was anxious to leave. Couldn't wait for Harold to finish up. As soon as I could, I completed all my closing work and ran all the way here."

It was true. She was breathing hard, and her hair was a mess. "Why? Has something happened?"

She nodded and blinked into his face. "Oh, yes,

something has happened, all right. Something big."

"Do you want to go in and sit down? I was just about to make my rounds, but a few minutes won't matter. Madison?"

"I'm too keyed-up to sit. Can I walk with you? How far do you go?"

"Up Main Street, the way you've just come, then around the corner to Clove Hitch Street. I continue up and down Half Hitch. Takes about thirty to forty minutes." *Or longer, if I find something to investigate.* "Aren't you too tired after work?"

She shook her head. "Not in the least. I feel like I could run a race. And win."

He smiled, not knowing what to make of her strange mood. He'd never seen her so animated and yet apprehensive, as well. "Fine then, let's go. You can tell me what has put a bee in your bonnet as I check the shops and buildings. We had another break-in last night."

Her eyes widened.

"At the butcher shop. Didn't get any money this time—just meat." He chuckled. "I'll have to keep my eye out for a well-fed criminal, and possibly a sick one, since the meat was turning. I've spoken with everyone. No one has noticed anything out of the ordinary. I don't think Jack Jones would go this far for employment. Also, I sort of have a hunch the culprit might be young. With what's been taken, or *not* taken. And no one's been hurt. Anyway," he said, nudging her with his elbow. "Go on and tell me why you're walking on air before you float away or burst with excitement. You've hardly heard a word I've said."

"I think I've found her!" Madison blurted, then hid her mouth behind her hand as if frightened to say the words too loudly on the dark, quiet street. "My mother. A letter in the mercantile. The envelope matches the ones my father's lawyer has sent to him over the years."

An envelope? I hope she doesn't get her hopes dashed over something as common as a lookalike envelope. "Who was the letter addressed to?" he asked, feeling unease slip through his veins.

"I don't know." Madison told him about the letter she saw while checking for any messages from Mrs. Goodheart or Professor Galbraith. She recognized the envelope and possibly the return address as belonging to her late father's attorney. She assumed the suspected letter was about her father's death. And most importantly, in which letter box Mr. Simpson had filed it.

Professor Galbraith? "Did you ask Mr. Simpson about the recipient?"

She nodded. "Yes, but I shouldn't have. He got annoyed and then watched me like a hawk for the rest of the time I remained in the store. Made sure I didn't try to peek. I tried not to act too excited, but doing so was difficult. He said his most sacrosanct duty was keeping all aspects pertaining to the mail secret."

"He said *that?*"

"Not exactly, but in different words."

She gazed into Justin's face, her hand still warm on his arm. He knew what she was thinking. This was a predicament he hadn't expected. He wanted to help Madison. He'd do anything to assist her, but he didn't want to go against his duty of upholding the law. *For everyone.* Including Madison's birth mother. Maybe the woman didn't want to be found. But how could he refuse Madison's hopeful gaze? Saying no might break her heart, and most assuredly turn her against him. He patted her hand and resumed walking. She was silent, the yipping of a coyote somewhere far off being the only sound.

"Mr. Simpson is right, Madison," he finally said. "That's personal business. I can't walk in and ask about the mail, as you're hoping I will. My position as deputy ties my hands. I'd not divulge the private conversation we shared during our picnic after church. The *real* reason you came to Y Knot. It's the same thing. Your business is your business and nobody else's. Same for the holder of the upper-right box."

Her hand fell away, but she stayed in step at his side.

They'd progressed halfway down Main Street and had just passed Herrick's. He stopped at

Lichtenstein's Provisions and tried the locked door. He put his face to the window and cupped out the light from the burning lamp inside. His gaze slid around the dark room and landed on the mail slots. The white corner of an envelope was still visible. The occupant of the box had yet to retrieve the post.

Madison had her face pressed to the glass, as well.

He knew what she was looking at. Leaning back, he turned her toward him with a touch to her arm. "Madison?" He saw her swallow. The smile and excitement he'd seen only minutes before was nowhere to be found. "Just because I can't inquire doesn't mean you can't watch. The letter is still there. I'm sure you saw it, too." Unable to stop himself, he caressed her arms. She looked fatigued. He'd seen her earlier through the window at the Biscuit Barrel, rushing around serving customers. Waiting tables was no easy job. She felt small and vulnerable. He wanted to help her, be her champion. But doing so went against his code of honor. "Madison?"

Finally, she nodded. "I know. I was pretty sure of your answer. Still, I was hopeful. If you did, by tomorrow, I'd know the identity of my mother." She shivered with delight. "She's here, Justin. And I'll find her, if I must stay in Lichtenstein's all day and night." She gave a little laugh.

"I guess I can help watch, too. Doing so doesn't

go against any law or moral code." She looked so beautiful. He wanted to kiss her but knew the timing wasn't right. Moving too fast might scare her off. "Since you've shared your big surprise, I'm taking you back to the hotel so you can get some rest. I'm sure you'll want to plan your course of action for tomorrow." He'd like to keep her by his side, but tomorrow would arrive in the blink of an eye. He was sure as the stars above; Miss Madison Plumb would get little sleep tonight.

Chapter Thirty-Four

Open Range, Montana Territory

The Heart of the Mountains cattle drive reached the outskirts of Billings as the sun was about to set. Around one hundred and fifty miles to go, Shad thought, tired to the bone. He was mentally tired, too. The whole time he'd been on the trail, all he could think about was Poppy and what had transpired with the Sanger children. As many times as he told himself the children were happy with their newfound aunt, his heart was having a difficult time accepting it. More so because of Poppy and how much she loved those children.

He reined up and allowed several steers Roady was pushing to run by him and join the herd. Slouching in the saddle, he forced himself to smile when Roady reined to a halt. Too many men had noticed his demeanor. Talk had begun around camp. Judging by their cautious questions, they believed he was getting cold feet and didn't want to get hitched. Nothing could be further from the truth. He just wanted to give Poppy a baby of her own. Always the optimist, she talked circles around him, and he usually enjoyed the ride—except with this subject. She did a good job of convincing herself, and him, a pregnancy would happen. She'd said, more than a few times, she'd not pin her happiness on an *ol' sawbones* who'd given Shad the painful diagnosis all those years ago.

Shad shook his head. He should have made getting to some large city and being examined again a priority before he and Poppy had gotten so serious. But they'd fallen in love when they'd been snowed in eyeball deep at the hotel. After those days, no other woman than Poppy would do. He should have been more responsible.

Roady pulled a packet of tobacco from his pocket and began to roll a cigarette. "I still see that dark cloud hangin' over your head."

"Thought you stopped smoking."

"Did. Around Sally or Gillian." He licked the side of the paper and smushed the two edges together. "Or any of the other women, for that matter."

"Exactly. Because they'd tell on you."

Pulling out a match, Roady lit the end of the smoke, drawing in a deep breath. "I'm not stupid. Of course, they'd tell. Is a robin red?" In an exhale, he allowed the smoke to circle his face. "Tastes good, but Sally can't abide the smoke. Says her head pinches tight like a squeezed lemon." He shrugged. "And if smoking makes her head hurt, it might do the same to Gillian. I don't mind. Makes cattle drives all the more attractive."

Shad chuckled. He'd do the same. Since meeting Poppy, he realized he'd do anything to protect her and make her happy. Anything at all.

Anything? Like seeing a doctor when we reach Miles City?

He jerked straight.

It's the largest city around. More than a few doctors work there, I'd think. Good doctors, too. We ranch hands have been granted some time off, not heading back to the ranch for several days.

With his arms crossed over his chest and the cigarette hanging from his lips, Roady glanced at him. "What's wrong?" He squinted from all the smoke wafting around his face and glanced around. "Did a bee sting you? I saw you jump."

Shad didn't answer.

"I'm good at keeping my mouth shut, Petty. If you have something you want to get off your chest, do it. Everyone's noticed. I even asked your little brother. He didn't know."

That rankled. "Everyone?" The men needed to worry about the cattle, not him. He didn't like to be the subject of chatter.

Roady puffed a few more times, put the cigarette out on his blackened, worn chaps, and tossed the smoke to the ground. "Don't growl at me. I'm only trying to help, but I can see you don't want to talk." He lifted a shoulder. "Plenty fine with me." From twenty feet away, Smokey waved them over. "Time to make camp." With a nudge to his horse, Roady loped away.

Shad watched him go. Seeing a doctor was a two-edged sword. Yes, the man might give Shad good news and he could go ahead with the wedding in good conscience. That diagnosis would make Poppy the happiest woman on earth. On the other hand, he might confirm what the ol' sawbones had thought. He'd have to tell Poppy. With a confirmation, no telling what she'd do. But not sharing the news would be dishonest. A violation of trust in the worst way.

A niggle of happiness blossomed inside his chest. He'd get a second opinion and share what he found out. They both had to go into this marriage with an open mind and clear conscience. Any untruth between them would build an unseen wall. His grandma Girdy, white-haired and skinny as a rail, always said that without trust, love couldn't abide. Trust and truth went hand in hand. One without the other was a hollow gong. He didn't much understand her words back when he was a boy, or even as a young man, but now he did. Not a reason, wish, or bribe existed in this world that could make him lie to Poppy about anything, and especially about something as important as his ability to give her a baby.

He hadn't thought much about the prognosis when the accident happened. Just wrote the bad luck off to happenstance. An unfortunate roll of the dice. Once the pain had faded, the incident pretty much never entered his mind. Until one magical night, when he'd been snowbound with the most beautiful city girl who'd stolen his heart and soul.

Chapter Thirty-Five

Abe took a stumbling step back and dropped the bottle he'd been pouring. He caught his elbow on the backbar, keeping himself upright, but barely.

Shocked, Fancy rushed behind the bar noting the look of distress on his sallow face. Clutching his arm, she struggled to keep the wobbling man on his feet. "Abe, what's wrong?" She placed her hand to his forehead, feeling to see if he was hot. "You feel sick?"

"It's nothin'," the small man croaked. "My head's been a little dizzy since I rolled out of bed all them hours ago. Just give me a minute to catch my balance."

She gazed into the face of the man who'd been kind to her since she'd come to town. He wasn't like her other bosses, and for some reason, she almost felt like they were on equal footing. He couldn't weigh more than one hundred pounds. *Has he lost weight in the last month? Surely, yes. Shame on me for not noticing sooner.* "Jack," she called to the man nursing a whiskey at the end of the bar. "Help me take Abe up to his room. He's a little tired and needs to lie down."

Jack Jones glanced up having missed the incident.

"Sometime today, Jack! Abe might be small, but my arms are getting tired."

Jack hopped off his stool and hurried behind the bar to Abe's other side.

"I ain't going to my room, Fancy. Who'll run the bar? Thursday nights get busy sometimes."

Only Jack Jones and two other men she didn't know were sitting at the bar. The strangers leaned forward, listening to the scene playing out before them.

"Silly goose," Fancy said as Abe allowed her and Jack to guide him from behind the bar lining the whole east side of the room to the second-story staircase. "I've worked at the Hitching Post for over two years. I think I can handle pouring a few whiskeys and refilling beer mugs." *If any more customers come in.* "I can take money and make change. You're going to bed and not getting up until I give you permission."

"But men come to the Hitching Post to hear you sing."

"I can sing while I pour."

Abe stopped arguing and slumped between them as they helped him up the stairs. His worn-out boots, with the slouching heels and cracked toes, revealed his none-too-clean toenails and made a soft *clomp-clomp-clomp* as they went.

Jack looked over Abe's head and caught her gaze, a troubled tilt to his brows.

Abe was sicker than he was letting on.

Several someones, by all the racket, barged through the batwing doors downstairs, laughing and carrying on. "Hey, where is everybody?" A few seconds passed. "Abe?"

From the second-story landing, Fancy glanced over her shoulder. Sam Green, Dennis Oats, and Chet Fender. "Just hold your horses, boys. I'll be down in a minute. Take a seat and shuffle your cards. I'll have your beer before you ante up."

All three glanced around as if wondering where her voice was coming from.

Seemed they already had a snoot full.

Jack opened Abe's door and helped Fancy lay Abe down.

She looked up at Jack. "Will you go down and make sure those fellas don't help themselves to anything they shouldn't? Keep an eye on the cash box. I'll be down directly."

"Want me to pour 'em a drink?"

She shook her head. "They can wait for me," she responded as she pulled off Abe's boots. "I won't be long. Just want to make Abe comfortable so he's able to sleep."

Jack nodded and closed the door behind him.

Fancy had never been in Abe's room before. Where the barkeep made sure her room was livable, with a pretty water pitcher, new bed-coverings every so often, and a shade to pull down, his was barebones. A tattered, gray blanket was suspended from a nail at the side of his window. Two shirts, the ones he sent out to the washhouse now and then, hung on wall pegs. A badly chipped water pitcher didn't match the bowl. A substantial crack crossed his mirror in the shape of a lightning bolt. She wondered how the looking glass even stayed on the wall. The only bright color in the room were three pairs of red suspenders, the accoutrements draped neatly over the top of his highboy.

Her heart lurched. *Abe deserves better than this!*

She glanced down into his face. Would he mind greatly if she put him in his nightshirt? His eyes were closed, and he seemed to be resting. The garment wasn't anywhere to be seen, and she didn't feel like snooping through his drawers. There was a limit to what he'd stand for. Everyone was entitled to their privacy.

"Abe?"

He opened his eyes. A small smile appeared. "This bed sure feels good, Fancy. My head's been spinnin' all day."

"Shame on you for not saying something sooner," she responded softly. "Is there anything else I can do for you? Put you in your nightshirt? Might as well, since you're not getting up until morning."

He palmed her cheek with a shaky hand. "You're a good girl, Fancy. Thanks for looking after me."

Hardly a girl anymore. When her eyes pricked with heat, she looked around. "Where is it, anyway? In your highboy drawers? You'll be a lot cooler out of your clothes, since the weather's turned hot." Standing, she went to the window and tugged the pane open a crack, letting in the warm night air. His view took in the outhouse, a broken-down wagon, and then the open lot fronting Clove Hitch Street, the next road over.

"Don't have me one. I usually just sleep shirtless in the summer." He attempted to sit up and work his buttons but crashed back and closed his eyes.

Fancy sat on the edge of his narrow bed and made quick work of unfastening his shirt. She slipped the garment under his frail back and laid it atop the highboy with his suspenders. After pulling up his sheet, she gazed down at him. What hair he still had resembled puffs of cotton rimming the bottom of his head. "I'm going down to get the boys their drinks, and then I'll bring you a nice pitcher of fresh water. I'll be back in a minute. You're not to worry about a thing."

When he didn't answer, she figured he'd already fallen asleep. Rest was the best thing for him now. What was ailing him? He'd always been healthy. Never been sick. Not even during the big snow they'd weathered last winter. Halfway down the stairs, Fancy pulled up.

He was back again.

The good-looking fella who'd appeared last week. She'd purposely avoided speaking to him, and he'd seemed to have done the same with her. In her line of business, she didn't want to recall the places where they might have met. She was thirty-five years old. Had seen much of the world and had met more than her share of men. A big hurt inside didn't allow her to look back. She was at her best when she was living in each moment. The past was a deep, dark ravine filled with emotion. She didn't intend to tumble inside. She'd clawed her way out too many times.

Lifting her chin, she straightened her shoulders and proceeded to keep her gaze far from the end of the bar where he casually leaned on one elbow. But there would be no help for it tonight. He was here for a drink, and she was pouring.

A few feet from him, Jack Jones had returned to his spot. "I helped myself to another whiskey, Fancy," he said as she descended. He pushed some coins forward on the bar.

Gathering her courage, she plastered on the smile she'd perfected over the years and breezed into the room as if she didn't have a care in the world. Before she could chicken out, she marched straight for the newcomer and stopped before him—the bar located safely between them. "What can I get you, stranger?"

Chapter Thirty-Six

Finally close enough to be sure, Cole Mercer couldn't believe his eyes. He'd been looking for Fleurette for several years. Just a dream, really. He never expected to actually find her and never working in a saloon. Fancy—the name she went by now—had a pretty figure and was just as beautiful as she'd been as a girl. She'd caught his eye his first night in Y Knot, but being as he'd found her working in the Hitching Post, he'd believed she couldn't be the person he was looking for. Now, this close, there was no doubt. Only one woman had eyes that blue. But, honestly, after living through the Civil War, he came to believe nothing in a person's history mattered—even a tainted past. She'd moved on, lived her life, and now here she was. *Just like me,* he thought with a wry smile. She also found a way to stay alive. He'd not judge her. His twenty years in the Union Army gave him ample memories he wished to forget. "You don't remember me, do you?"

She blinked and took a step back as if he'd just stuck a scorpion in her face. She swallowed and slowly shook her head.

He didn't believe her. The way her eyes darkened gave her away. "Been twenty-three years. You were just a young girl." He chuckled and removed his hat, setting it crown-side down on the bar.

She watched his actions, still ignoring his question.

"I've changed a lot," he admitted. "Been through some hard times, seen and done things I wish I hadn't." He fingered the scar pulling at the corner of his bottom lip received from a Confederate bayonet. He'd filled out, and gray peppered his normally chestnut-brown hair.

"I can hang that on the hat rack, if you'd like," she finally said, gesturing to his hat.

Is she staring at my hat so she doesn't have to look at me? Or, perhaps, she doesn't want to believe I'm really here. Or she remembers but isn't interested anymore.

"Don't bother. My Stetson's been through worse." He fingered a smudge on the bar top on the opposite side of his hat. "Whiskey, please."

"Fancy! We're done being patient," a man sitting at a table in the middle of the room hollered, none-too-nicely. "We're thirsty, and we're anteing up our *third* hand. You lied when you said you'd be right down. Took ya a little longer than you thought to put him to bed?"

Cole didn't like the suggestive tone.

"Fancy," the gambler called again.

One thing for her to have to work there, but every woman deserved respect. Turning, he sized up the men at the table. He didn't really feel like fighting tonight . . .

Justin Wesley walked into the saloon. The young lawman continued into the room and stopped at Cole's side, unaware of what just transpired. "Mercer," he said, looking around. "Quiet in here tonight."

Fancy, using the deputy's arrival as an excuse to escape, rushed down the bar to fill three mugs from the beer tap. Serving the gamblers, she ignored their raunchy comments and suggestive jokes, collected their money, and then did as he'd asked and filled a generous glass of whiskey.

Cole pushed out a quarter, which she picked up without saying a word.

She took herself a short distance down the bar to gaze into a sink filled with dirty glasses.

"Where were you last night?" Wesley asked, talking quietly.

As he took his first taste from his glass, Cole bristled and glanced over. "You askin' for a reason?"

"Maybe."

"And here I thought we were friends."

A crooked smile appeared on the deputy's face. "We had another robbery."

Cole nodded, remembering the year he'd spent enforcing the law after he retired from the army. This young pup was just doing his job. "In that case, I took my dinner in the hotel and went to bed early. My head hurt, and I didn't feel like joining the crowd at the Biscuit Barrel. Ask Miss Hallsey. She saw me go into the restaurant, stay there for about an hour, and then head up the stairs. I remained in my room all night."

Wesley nodded. "Good enough."

"You believe me?"

"Have no reason not to—*yet,*" the deputy responded. "Not like those three, who find trouble faster than a chicken after scratch." He tipped his head toward the gamblers. "Y Knot would be better off without 'em, but I think Abe wouldn't. They're in here almost every night." Finished, Justin wandered over to the man Cole had met as Jack Jones.

Jones must have been eavesdropping, because he seemed ready with his answer.

"I wouldn't break the law to get my old job back," he proclaimed, a hurt tone in his voice. "I'm not *that* stupid."

"Just doing my due diligence, Jack, and asking everyone. You're the next one on my list. You'll slip up in time, if you're up to your old tricks."

"I don't have old tricks."

"I've heard different. Where were you last night?"

"I went to the Biscuit Barrel. Everyone saw me."

"And later? After the town was tucked up tight?"

"At the boardinghouse. Lou and Drit will vouch for me. I didn't go out." Jack's bruised tone turned insolent. "I've been here a week, and you've hardly seen me."

"I know. Why is that?"

Jack huffed. "I haven't caused any trouble. You have no right to suspect me of *anything,* except moving back to the town where I've lived for years. By the way, what's the latest on Brandon? I haven't heard much. The surgery was days ago. When do you expect him home?"

"You're snooping again, Jack. You'll have to hear it from a McCutcheon, not me."

Cole thought the sheriff's absence was dragging on longer than it should. He'd seen more men die in the military hospitals than he'd like to remember. Civilians, too. He didn't put much stock in the medical profession.

His gaze drifted over to Fancy to find her watching him intently, as if she were in deep thought. Her cheeks colored, and she glanced away. She remembered, all right, but was pretending she didn't. That was fine with him. He had all the time in the world. He hadn't lived forty-three years by making rash decisions. He'd bide his time. Let her settle into the thought Cole Mercer was back in her life.

Chapter Thirty-Seven

St. John's Hospital, Helena, Montana Territory

"Here, here, young lady, you must have a seat. You look exhausted." The elderly nun took Charity's arm and attempted to pull her toward a row of chairs lining the reception area.

Charity knew she looked a fright: uncombed hair, dark circles under her eyes, a frown she couldn't turn upside-down, no matter how hard she tried. She'd left Brandon's room for only a few minutes, as nature was calling and she'd waited as long as she should.

It was Friday morning. A week and a day since Brandon's operation. Matt had tried to escort her, but she'd insisted he stay with Brandon in case he awakened and didn't know where he was. She was weary, but not so much so she couldn't make a trip to the privy and back alone. Oh, how she wished she'd allowed her mother to accompany their group to Helena. Charity needed her mother's unwavering strength and confidence. She knew the right words to say to calm Charity's raging fears. Right now, her own faith in Brandon's recovery had slipped to its lowest level since the accident. Each day, he remained sick and warm.

The old nun, still wearing a nurse's cap even though she must have left the service in the hospital years ago, held her arm firmly. "I insist," she said, giving a gentle tug. "Just rest for a couple of minutes. I've been watching you every day. Exhaustion isn't good for the baby."

Exhaustion like this wasn't good for anyone. How she wished Luke was here. His leaving distressed her deeply. On top of Brandon, she worried about him alone in unfamiliar country, trying to find a Cheyenne medicine man. Since his leaving, she'd been plagued by a morbid thought Brandon would die before Luke returned. "Thank you, Sister, but I need to use the toilet," she said, her voice sounding like somebody else. "I'll rest when I get back to Brandon's room." She felt a slight twinge below she'd not experienced before. "I'm fine."

The woman, whose face was as wrinkled as a year-old pumpkin long forgotten in the garden, gave a sympathetic smile. "Then I'll come along. Just in case you need something." As Charity began to object her brow furrowed. "It's my duty. Please."

Charity relented and allowed the old woman with a slight aroma of mothballs to accompany her along the quiet hospital hallway. They passed the chapel and a room where someone inside was moaning.

She couldn't wait to have Brandon better and

back at home on the ranch. The day before the accident, they'd taken a stroll around their land, imagining and dreaming. The house, the barn, the outbuildings. How their sons and daughters would grow and thrive. How smart they'd be. Handsome like Brandon and beautiful like their mother, filled with the McCutcheon brawn and the Crawford cleverness and bravery. Their children would have a bundle of aunties and uncles to teach and instruct them. Life had been so sweet, so promising. If she could just turn back the hand of time. She'd keep Brandon home in Y Knot the whole day. Never let him climb that ladder. If she could just hear Brandon chuckle one more time . . .

The hospital had an indoor water closet with a high pull chain tank and bowl below. The room was spacious, and Charity had enjoyed getting acquainted over the days. A small table and chair stood inside, where she'd sat a time or two for privacy from concerned gazes. Moving slowly, Charity lifted her skirt and was gathering her petticoat when a large, crimson splotch of blood caught her eye. Frightened, her legs almost buckled as she cried out sharply.

What's happening? Do I dare use the toilet? Am I losing our baby?

A sharp rap sounded on the door. "Ma'am? Mrs. Crawford?" The rapping came again. "Is everything all right? I heard your sound of distress." The rapping persisted, and then the doorknob rattled. "Unlock the door so I can help!"

A half hour later, Charity found herself across the street at the Victorian Inn in the comfortable bed Mrs. Hardie had saved for her. She pushed down in the mattress, enjoying the softness.

I must have fainted. How long have I been here?

How had they unlocked the door?

Mark sat at the side of the bed, his head held in his hands. As if sensing she'd stirred, Mark looked up. "You're awake."

His voice was shaky. Had she lost her and Brandon's sweet child? If she had she didn't want to live. She wished she could remember so she wouldn't have to ask. Her eyes filled. "My baby?"

"Is fine. You didn't lose it."

She felt hot tears on her cheeks. "Tell me what happened."

"You fainted. The nun ran for help when she heard you cry out. They brought the master key and unlocked the door. Brandon's doctor gave you an examination. The baby is all right, but you've been put on bed rest and are forbidden to get up for anything. He gave you laudanum to help you sleep."

Anxiety sliced through her as she realized she

did still feel groggy. If she shut her eyes right now, she was sure she'd fall back into sleep instantly. "But I *must* be at the hospital. I can't stay here. Brandon might need me."

His mouth straightened into a firm line. "You've got to obey, Char. There's no two ways about it."

"Why can't I stay in bed in Brandon's room? There's enough space for two more beds, if need be. They've been good about me staying, so far."

"Because the doctor said the fear and fatigue you're experiencing, sitting with Brandon day and night, have worn you down and stretched your nerves. You're in a delicate way. You need bed rest *away* from the hospital. Too many doctors and nurses coming and going."

"But, I—"

"There's no other way, Charity, so just save your breath. Think of your babe. A tiny little combination of you and Brandon, swimmin' around inside you, all warm and happy. You need to do everything in your power to protect him or her. Brandon would want you to. No, he'd *expect* you to. Amy and I used to talk about our little one all the time when she was expecting. It's a time I'll never forget."

An endearing expression crossed Mark's face, and she remembered Amy had lost their first child, the one she'd been carrying before the wedding. The horrible experience had crushed her for months—Mark, too. Straining their marriage and almost breaking them apart. Since then, they'd gone on to have two more children, an adorable little daughter and toddler son.

She wiped her tears. The image his words created of a tiny baby, not more than a few inches long, swimming inside her womb made a small smile creep onto her lips. "How's Brandon? Has anything changed?"

Mark shook his head. "The same. And you're not to worry. The moment anything changes, we promise to let you know. We won't keep anything from you, if you swear to rest and sleep."

A wave of grogginess made Charity take a deep breath and lower her eyelids. The bed was comfortable. With one more quick prayer for Brandon, she quit fighting the blessed sleep and allowed the darkened bliss to take her away.

"Good girl."

She thought she heard her brother croon in a soft, love-filled voice. "Sleep tight . . ."

Chapter Thirty-Eight

Walking slowly, Luke led his mount along a narrow game path, watching for tracks. Matt and Mark had been right. Finding the Cheyenne would be difficult, if not impossible.

Feeling culpable for laying the responsibility of Brandon and Charity on his older brothers, Luke stopped and studied the cloudless sky. The sun, directly above, beat down relentlessly. Dry grasses—wild oats, switchgrass, Indiangrass, and blue bunch wheatgrass—gave off an enticing aroma, reminding Luke of home. He liked it. He'd been warring with himself for the past three hours on whether he should cut his losses and head back. Maybe Brandon had taken a turn for the best, had awakened, and was growing stronger. But something in his gut said that was wishful thinking.

Frustrated and angry with himself, he continued onward, brushing his forearm across his sweaty brow. He hadn't seen another living soul since starting out, and yet he did now and then come across a horse track, and once a mark made by a moccasin. Scaling the shale front of a hillside, he'd found an abandoned campsite, the campfire about a week old. How could he find the Cheyenne if they didn't want to be found?

Coming to a split in the trail, he opted to take the ascending path. Going down felt wrong and was too disheartening. He'd continue just to the top of this ridge, and if something substantial didn't present itself, he'd turn back and return to the hospital as swiftly as he could.

Topping the rise, he took several minutes to study the territory around him. Dense vegetation to the west and open, greener grasslands to the east. Stymied, he thought about Fox Dancing and the days his Cheyenne half sister had lived in his house. She'd remained stoic but joined in when she could, trying to get a better grasp of English. In return, she'd taken time to teach anyone interested a few Cheyenne words. Little Dawn took to the language as if she heard it every day. He'd learned quite a few words, too, as well as a handful of short, useful phrases. Maybe he should try them out now. Nothing better came to mind.

He easily remembered the Cheyenne pronunciation of his sister's name. Dismounting, he cupped his mouth and called out in a loud voice. Turning in each direction, he repeated the name at the top of his lungs, keeping a tight hold of his reins when his horse spooked and tried to run off. Fox Dancing had said her grandfather was named Talking Tree and had taught Luke the name in Cheyenne, too. Luke did the same with that and then Painted Bear Stone, the young brave Fox Dancing had married.

Then he thought of his father's name, one he'd known before he'd ever even knew he had a half sister roaming Montana Territory and staying off the reservation with a small band of Indians.

Netchiwaan. What would happen if he called out the name of the man who'd sired him? Did he live around these parts? Fox Dancing hadn't given more than a general idea of where they had their settlement, because the less he knew, the safer everyone would be. Only one way to find out. Since arriving at the top of the hill, he felt the back of his neck prickle several times, as if someone was watching.

He cupped his mouth and hollered out his father's name. What were the chances he'd get to meet the man in the flesh? He repeated the process.

Minutes ticked by. His horse, still agitated from his shouting, twitched nervously, looking around with pricked ears. One last idea came to mind. He cupped his mouth and shouted out his own name, once in English and another time in Cheyenne.

Two braves appeared as if from a mist on a rise on the other side of the small valley.

Luke's heart jumped in his chest and his blood stirred.

The two stoically sat their horses, waiting for him to make a move. From this distance, being sure of anything was difficult, but Luke didn't think they had guns. Bows slung across their chests and quivers of arrows hanging from their saddles were visible. Not knowing exactly what to do, Luke held up a hand in greeting.

Several soundless moments ticked by before the larger of the two nudged his horse, and they began the descent to cross the ravine and come to his side.

Luke breathed deeply, excitement warring inside with his caution. These men might not have an inkling who he was or who he was looking for, and they just wanted to get closer to make killing a white man all the easier. He needed to stay on guard.

They reined up twenty feet away.

Being on the ground, Luke was at a disadvantage. Now he could see the larger of the two had lost his left eye. A long scar ran from the top of his forehead, across his empty eye socket, down his cheek, and ended just below his lower lip. The injury made him look fierce, as did his other eye, which was narrowed into a slit of suspicion. But he was thin, and his tattered buckskin shirt appeared too bulky in his emaciated state. Three eagle feathers stuck up over the crown of his head.

The other Cheyenne was much younger, maybe thirteen or fourteen years old, and might even have been the warrior's adolescent son. Over his bare chest hung a vest made from porcupine quills. A beaded arm band hugged his sinewy bicep. Two long braids, on either side of his head, reached all the way to his navel. They both sat their horses proudly, as if they didn't have a care in the world.

Luke had a care. He didn't want to get killed before finding help for Brandon. Charity needed him, too, and, of course, his own family. If these two were hostile, he wouldn't go down without a fight. "*Haaahe*," Luke said slowly. The word of friendly greeting was taught to him by Fox Dancing and Painted Bear Stone.

They just stared.

"Fox Dancing," he said in Cheyenne.

They looked at each other and then back at him.

Pointing to himself, he said as calmly as he could, "Luke McCutcheon." Nerves battled inside. He needed to try a sentence, but felt he'd butcher the words. There was nothing else to do. "*Netchiwaan*," he said slowly. "*Nee hosy.*"

The younger one's face brightened. "*Ného'éehe*?" he repeated, making Luke's butchered pronunciation sound the way Fox Dancing had said the words.

Excited they were making progress, Luke nodded. "Yes! *Ného'éehe*," he barked loudly, encouraged. "My father. *Netchiwaan*." He made the motion of his fingers walking. "Take me to him."

The older man grunted and stared.

The younger one rode two steps closer before

being halted by a growl from the other. Instead, the younger man put out a hand to the one-eyed Cheyenne warrior. "*Netchiwaan he'neho.*"

Luke heard what he thought was the word for brother, because it was what Fox Dancing had called him. Was the young warrior trying to say this fierce, one-eyed man was brother to his father? If that were true, then he was looking at his uncle. A bolt of hot fire flashed through Luke. He shook his head, amazed. Wonders never ceased.

When the older brave frowned at Luke's head shake, Luke quickly smiled. He wished he'd paid better attention when Fox Dancing had tried to teach him her language. Truthfully, he'd never thought he'd ever have to use it. "Fox Dancing," he said several times in Cheyenne. Unable to remember the word for sister, he just thumped his chest over his heart.

The older warrior, his uncle, if Luke was correct, rattled off a fast sentence to the younger man. Dialogue went back and forth contentiously. Darned if Luke didn't wish for Fox Dancing now. At least, then they'd be able to communicate a little better. Finally, they quieted.

"You stay," the younger brave said, pointing at the ground. "We go."

"But you're coming back?" Luke asked quickly, making a move to gather his reins. If he lost them now, maybe he'd never find them again.

"Wait," the young one replied. "Wait."

What else could he do? Luke just hoped they'd return quickly. Brandon's life depended on it.

He prayed this effort would not be for naught. He'd wait and try to relax as they went for either his father or Fox Dancing. The cogs in the system had begun to turn.

Chapter Thirty-Nine

Madison sat on a bench outside Lichtenstein's Provisions with her notebook and pencil on her lap, pretending to write, but she was much too excited to do anything except daydream about what the day might bring. She'd found a sunny spot close to the door, and with the help of Morgan Standford, who'd crossed from the boardinghouse to buy a can of turpentine before going to his shop just two doors down, moved the bench for her into the desired location. Madison planned to spend the day here, watching people come and go. Each time a person exited, she peeked inside to see if the letter remained in the upper-right mail slot.

As soon as the store had opened, she'd taken a few minutes at the notions shelf, picking out a few buttons so she could make sure the letter was still there. If Mr. Simpson hadn't been watching her like a hawk, she'd have found something to stand on and quickly taken a peek. But he'd raised a brow the moment she walked through the door, probably still annoyed she'd asked him to tell her who the letter was addressed to, and rewarded her by staying at the counter, even when a man asked for help finding something. He'd mumbled a reply and said he'd look a little later when he had time.

Her nerves were strung tight. Ethel had agreed to cover her shift at the Biscuit Barrel. She'd awakened at four o'clock this morning, feeling the joy and anticipation of Christmas. Nothing was more important than today.

"Madison?"

Turning, she found Heather Klinkner contemplating her with a tented brow. Two other young women stood at her side, smiling curiously.

"What're you doing?" A cloth-covered basket hung on Heather's arm. "Writing out here?"

Madison hated to be dishonest, but she didn't see any way around it. "Just jotting down some ideas as I watch how the people of Y Knot go about their day." A wagon rolled past with two dogs trotting at the wheel. "Like that." She pointed. "Until I came west, I had no idea how large some of the wagons were. I'm used to the smaller buggies and cabs I've seen around Frankfort and Lexington. Sometimes even a gig." The buckboard rattled down the street and halted in front of the bank. "Two horses are needed for such a large conveyance." She smiled and made a note on her pad. "It's the little things I'm looking to write about."

Heather nodded and gestured to the two at her side. "These are my friends, Kathryn Preece, another mail-order bride we spoke of the other day, and Poppy Ford, her sister. Poppy is engaged to Shad Petty, who works at the Heart of the Mountains Ranch. They're getting married soon."

Poppy smiled and lifted one shoulder as Heather circled her waist with an arm.

"Congratulations, Miss Ford. You must be excited. I can't imagine." And she really couldn't. A flutter of happiness inside made her think of Justin.

"Thank you." Poppy's face took on a rosy hue. "The days are flying by in the blink of an eye. I just wish Shad wasn't gone." She glanced at Heather and Kathryn. "These two are keeping me occupied so I can't fret too much."

They all laughed, all the while Madison stayed tense and alert at the mercantile door. "Kathryn, did Heather mention I'd like to interview the mail-order brides, if possible?"

Kathryn perked up. "She did. And we're all in agreement, even Evie Holcomb. Doing so might be helpful for other young women deciding if they want to entrust their futures to men they've only met through letters. Our three accounts have turned out well, better than any of us dreamed." She smiled warmly at Heather. "We're available almost anytime you are. We can meet at my house."

Heather leaned in and said in a stage whisper, "Kathryn has a beautiful parlor, something Evie and I both lack." She winked at Kathryn. "But she shares the room generously. Anytime you're ready. Now, don't let us interrupt your work any more than we already have." She glanced at the mercantile door. "I'm just stopping into Lichtenstein's to drop off eggs for Ina. And Poppy is checking to see if the wedding gift she ordered for Shad has arrived."

"How exciting!" Madison nodded and watched as her new friends disappeared inside.

A wagon came down the road from the other direction. Madison recognized Lynette and Saralee Hicks, the two women married to the loggers who supplied the Klinkner lumber mill.

A few feet away, Lynette pulled back on the long, leather lines. When the wagon rocked to a halt, she stomped her booted foot on the brake with the confidence of any man.

Three children she remembered, as well, from the Biscuit Barrel, all piled out the back and ran into the store in a clamor of laughter.

The women nodded their hellos as they passed and disappeared inside.

Either woman was the right age to be her mother. Had one gotten in trouble before they'd married, and now had other children? Anything was possible. As Madison was trying to decide if she should go back inside where she could keep a closer watch, she heard Berta May call out to her.

"Nice to see you, Miss Plumb. Getting some writing done?"

Feeling a pinch of worry, Madison nodded and stood. "I sure am."

"Good for you. Can't wait to read whatever it is you're writin'." Berta May pulled open the mercantile door to a jingle of bells and voiced a loud hello to the others inside.

When it rains, it pours! So many women inside the usually quiet store. What's my best course of action? Madison cupped her eyes and discreetly pressed her face to the window. The letter was still there.

Moody Lenore Saffelberg slipped by behind her with barely a word, followed closely by Lou, owner of the boardinghouse.

With her face on the glass, she hadn't seen them coming, but they'd certainly seen her peeking in. Feeling tense, Madison set her pad and pencil on the bench. She must get inside where she could monitor the situation more carefully. Once the letter was safely tucked away, all would be lost.

Trying not to attract Mr. Simpson's attention, she slowly opened the door. Even before the bells stopped sounding, she quickly slipped sideways, turned back to the window, and edged to the wall and a shelf of canned goods, attempting to be invisible. Gradually turning her head, she watched the happenings.

The cramped area was filled with chatting women. Heather's basket of eggs sat on the counter. At the side table, Heather and Kathryn showed Poppy some fabric, exclaiming over the rich softness. Lou conversed with Saralee Hicks smack in the middle of the entry. Lenore appeared from the narrow middle passageway with a small bucket. Laughter from the children reverberated from somewhere in the back of the store. With her arms filled with several items, Berta May looked over Poppy's shoulder and jumped in on the girls' conversation, saying she had a similar fabric at her store and to come and see it before Poppy made any decisions. Hers cost half the price.

Mr. Simpson, listening from behind the counter, plopped his hands on his bony hips and scowled. "Berta May! What've we said about you comin' in here and stealing our customers away? Ain't neighborly a'tall." He shook his head.

Berta May just laughed and waved him off.

The bells above the door sounded again. This time, Jack Jones, and the newcomer, Cole Mercer, came in one after the other. They both pulled up for a moment, and Jack gave a wide smile. He glanced at Mr. Simpson. "Don't mind us." He strode toward the rear of the store. "Just showing my friend, Cole, here somethin'. Carry on."

A woman Madison had never seen before opened the door, stopped to briefly glance around, and then stepped inside. She was nicely dressed and appeared to be in her late thirties or early forties. She was tall, regal, and her eyes seemed to smile on their own. Her light brown hair was fashioned in an elegant French twist. *A perfect candidate! Will she walk right up to the counter and ask Mr. Grumpy Simpson for her mail in the upper-right box?* Madison held her breath.

"Why, good morning, Mrs. Payne," Berta May said with her wide smile.

"Good morning, Berta May. What's all this happening in the store? I hadn't heard. Are you having a drawing of some sort, Mr. Simpson?"

"Certainly not," he grumbled back. "Can't get a lick of work done, either."

"It's serendipity," Kathryn said with a soft laugh, glancing around. "I think it's fun."

Jack and his friend reappeared, gave a quick wave to Mr. Simpson, then strode out.

Eavesdropping, all the while watching the letter, Madison learned the unknown, refined woman was the wife of the new banker. The couple had moved to town in the past three months. Her name was Bethanne, and his Daniel. Madison had met him the day she'd gone to the bank and placed the money she'd brought from Kentucky into an account for safe keeping.

A loud crash resounded from the back of the store.

Silence descended. All heads swiveled.

"Riley," Lynette hollered, still holding a lamp

chimney in her hands. She'd appeared from the farther shelves in the back of the store a moment ago and came to stand by her sister-in-law. "What's goin' on? You break somethin'?"

"Weren't me, Mama, but Dodger," came Riley's slow reply. "He dropped it on purpose."

"Dodger! Nancy!" Saralee screeched. "You know better."

"Just a little glass dish doohickey. T'wern't worth much, a'tall," one of the boys yelled back.

Saralee's face flashed apple red. "Get your rear end up here and bring the pieces so Mr. Simpson can put it on our account. Didn't I tell you not to touch? Your pa's gonna be mighty angry—"

"I know, I know," came the insolent reply. "I'll get a lickin' to save my life. *Big deal* . . ."

Madison sucked in a breath and looked down, embarrassed for all concerned. The boy had a brazen mouth, if she'd ever heard one. Disobedient and rude. Her parents, God rest their souls, would never have stood for such behavior.

Mr. Simpson grumbled loudly. His bushy white brows dropped stormily over his eyes as he searched around for the Hicks children. "Where are they?" he barked. "You gotta pay for broken items, Saralee. Tell your young'uns ta wait outside iffin they can't keep their hands in their pockets like I requested. This place is too dang crowded."

Riley came forward, hands stuffed in his

pockets and his shameful gaze riveted to the floor.

Madison remembered Lynette's son was the boy who had been kicked in the head when he was four years old and hadn't been the same since. Sadness welled, for he was good-looking in his own right, and she wondered about his future.

Lynette put a hand on his shoulder. "You wait in the wagon, son. I'll be out in a moment."

Mr. Simpson arched an angry eyebrow Madison's way as Lenore Saffelberg, who'd been as quiet as a mouse through the exchange, Mrs. Payne, and Saralee Hicks all crowded forward to the counter.

Lou also suddenly seemed in a hurry to get out of the store and edged in with the others.

Berta May turned. Her ample form bumped Madison, causing her to tilt dangerously to the left.

She almost fell into a three-foot-tall stack of canned prunes. Mr. Simpson wouldn't be pleased if she added to the confusion.

Heather, Kathryn, and Poppy stood wide-eyed as Dodger and his sister marched outside without looking at anyone or saying a word.

Madison noticed Dodger's hands were not where Mr. Simpson had requested they be. And he hadn't gathered the broken glass, as his mother asked.

Mr. Simpson wiped his forehead with his handkerchief. "Mighty hot in here. Anyone not intendin' to purchase something this moment, please wait outside, iffin ya don't mind. I can't hardly think straight."

He means me. The clerk had spotted her a few moments ago, watching the hubbub. Madison turned to go, but before she did, she glanced up to check the box one last time.

The letter was gone!

Feeling sick, she swiftly assessed the group, searching hands, baskets, and reticules, hoping to see the white corner of the envelope somewhere, either sticking out of a pocket or held in a hand. The person must have asked for it when the Hicks children broke the glass dish in the back of the store. Everyone had been distracted, including her.

This might be my only chance! What should I do? I could ask the women straight out, but they'd think I was crazy. And then, too, the whole town would know, and perhaps it would embarrass my mother and ruin her life. This is a private affair.

Had someone asked for the letter during the disturbance? Or perhaps slipped behind the counter and taken the envelope herself? Her heart raced, and she felt a sheen of moisture break out on her forehead.

As the women paid, or Mr. Simpson added to their accounts, they began to leave.

She needed to get outside. And do what? She didn't know. Maybe if someone left empty-handed, the mail was the only reason they came. Opening the door, she slipped out, feeling sick to her stomach. Bumping into Pauline Backus, she almost let out a groan.

Carlie was at her side.

Pauline pulled back. "Miss Plumb, are you feeling all right? Your face is rather blanched."

"Hi, Madison," Carlie cried, her excitement impossible to miss.

Madison looked down into Carlie's eager face and then at Lenore's retreating back. Lenore was too young to be her mother, Hildy having told her the waitress was around twenty-six or twenty-seven, but not Mrs. Payne, who gave her a brief smile and hurried on her way. Of all people to run into now, talkative Pauline Backus was the worst.

Chapter Forty

Fancy never went to the mercantile during the day, if possible, or any of the other businesses in Y Knot, so as not to scandalize the townswomen and embarrass the men. Oh, the men liked her well enough when they were in the saloon drinking, but that changed in a heartbeat when they encountered her on the street, especially if their wife or daughter was at their side. To avoid any unpleasantness, she usually came around the back of the mercantile after the store had closed and tapped on the door. Old Mr. Simpson, or the proprietor, Mr. Lichtenstein, allowed her inside with a smile on their face. To them, money was money, no matter where it came from.

But today was different. Abe was ill. She needed quinine powder or laudanum to help him rest. He refused to send for the doctor, because if men thought he had some infectious ailment, they'd stop coming in. A situation he couldn't afford. So, what else could she do, except look after him herself?

She stepped lively, still rattled from the events of the night before. Encountering Cole Mercer, face to face, had shocked her speechless. *I haven't thought of him in years.* When she'd first spotted him in the Hitching Post, she'd experienced a funny feeling inside at seeing his face, but she'd just chalked the sentiments up to her profession. She'd worked many places in her life. After a good number of years, towns, and saloons, one handsome face after the other began to look like all the rest.

She slowed her pace and glanced up at the sky, remembering. She'd been thirteen, and in town with her family. She was enjoying the sunshine at the riverside, collecting flowers and shiny, colored rocks to take home to her mother. She recalled the day clearly, because that was when her mother was still alive. Yes, work on the farm was exhausting, but her mother, who was raised with gentility in the South, attended to her two daughters with softness. Reading to them every night. Training them in the kitchen, as she passed along old family recipes. Fancy had adored those times concocting dishes more than anything else. Her mother had praised her and planted the seed that if she kept practicing, someday she might even have her own little bakery or restaurant.

Fancy's heart swelled, and she blinked at the heat behind her eyes.

This is why I never allow myself to look back. Life had been so good, and I didn't even know it.

At the river's edge, she'd accidentally slipped on a moss-covered rock and fell into the current. She struggled to stay at the surface, fighting against the long fabric of her best Sunday dress.

Going under once, she let out a piercing scream when she resurfaced.

Cole and his company of Union soldiers were stationed nearby. Hearing her cry, Cole came to her rescue, swimming out into the waterway without a thought for his own safety and dragging her out as if she were a wet puppy. On the riverbank's grass, he laid her on her side and pounded her back until she coughed up enough water to fill a bucket. Gasping for breath, and clutching his soggy shoulders, she gazed into his dripping wet face, wondering if an angel from heaven came down and had plucked her from a watery death.

He had. And his name was Cole Mercer. And I lost my heart and soul.

Until the day Cole's company pulled out, she'd found an excuse to go back into town to search him out. At the memories, a smile crept onto Fancy's lips. Being a full-grown man at twenty, he patiently endured her innocent attention, much to the amusement of his fellow soldiers. The night before he'd gone, she found him and had professed her love.

I love you, Cole. Please, don't forget me. I want to be your wife.

But years passed, and she grew older. Her memories of him dimmed as other young men, ones not so gallant, had noticed her. Her parents died, leaving her and her younger sister under the thumb of her older brother, Craig.

And now, here he was again, and all the old feelings rushed back the moment they stood face to face.

Chastising herself for allowing memories, she took a breath and continued. She needed to complete this errand, as uncomfortable as doing so was, then return to the secluded walls of the Hitching Post. Abe needed her.

Almost to Lou and Drit's Boardinghouse, where she'd cross the road to the mercantile, Fancy pulled up. Justin Wesley's judgmental and disapproving aunt stood on the boardwalk in front of the store, speaking with the newcomer, Madison Plumb, the young woman the deputy had taken a shine to. Fancy had never met Miss Backus in person, but she did have ears. Plenty of talk circulated in the saloon to get a good impression of what she was like. Fancy pitied Judge Wesley and his young daughter, as well as Justin, having to put up with her every day. The woman had a sharp tongue and wasn't afraid to use it. The last thing Fancy needed today was a public dressing down by the holier-than-thou Miss Pauline Backus, busybody in chief.

Should she retreat and come back in an hour? Fancy glanced around. The coast was still clear. The hour was early, and few were out and about. If Evie Holcomb was here, she'd take Fancy's arm and escort her inside, daring anyone to speak up against her. She wasn't Fancy's only friend, either.

Just as she'd decided to duck into the doorway of the dark bathhouse and wait for the woman to leave, Drit, proprietor of the boardinghouse, appeared before she had a chance and came striding down the steppingstones toward her. She cringed.

"Hello, Fancy. I don't usually see you out on the street." His voice was not overly loud but would easily carry across the road. "Getting some sunshine and air? I don't blame you. That saloon can be mighty pungent, at best." He grinned and looked around as if he thought his statement was humorous. "I almost didn't recognize you in a bonnet." He came close, smiling into her face, and whispered, "I guess some people just stand out, no matter what they wear."

Hell's bells! He doesn't have the common sense of a flea! Why not use a bullhorn?

Pauline Backus jerked upright, and she glanced across the street at Fancy and Drit.

Miss Plumb pulled up, too, and searched to see what the woman was glaring at.

Fancy prepared for the outcry. In moments, they'd scurry away as if she carried a plague that could ruin them for life.

"Excuse me, Miss Backus, but I *really* need to concentrate on my school paper," Madison said, panicked inside. She glanced at her tablet, thankful she'd had the foresight to quickly jot down a few paragraphs before leaving the hotel. "If I don't complete this thought, I'll lose it." Madison hated to be disrespectful or rude, especially to someone who had welcomed her so warmly, and was also Justin's aunt, but she couldn't help it.

My most important task is to find my mother. Nothing will stand in my way.

Pauline's brows crashed down for a moment as she seemed to digest Madison's surprising words, but then understanding eased across her face. "Of course, dear. You get back to your work, and we can—"

Both women looked over at the activity on the other side of the street.

"F-Fancy?" Miss Backus sputtered. "Y Knot's soiled dove? What on earth . . ."

Madison realized the woman speaking with the boardinghouse owner was the one Hildy had told her about. She'd weathered out the huge snowstorm with Hildy and the other townsfolk, trapped for days inside the hotel. In the evenings, when the hotel was slow, Hildy was a great source of information, not for spiteful gossip, but filling in Madison on the town and the recent happenings. She'd said, although Miss Aubrey rarely came out of the saloon during the day, when she did, Hildy found she liked the fallen woman. Miss Aubrey had been polite and helpful during the snowstorm. Madison had decided before today that speaking with her would be interesting. The woman's life story would be fascinating material, if she'd agree to talk. It appeared her conversation with Drit had ended, and she intended to cross to the mercantile. This was a golden opportunity for Madison to line up a date, since she could hardly go knocking on the door of the saloon.

Miss Aubrey was halfway across the road now.

Pauline sucked in a loud breath. "Madison," she said sternly, grasping Madison's arm with one hand and Carlie's hand with her other. "Come along with us." She began tugging Madison toward the hotel and sheriff's office.

Madison pulled away and stood her ground. Not only did she not want to miss speaking with Miss Aubrey, but she was not leaving the front door of the mercantile! Period. Pauline Backus's unwanted attention was getting out of control. Madison lifted her chin and squared her shoulders.

Pauline glared. "I really *must* insist."

Madison, forgetting herself, emulated the way her girlfriend at school dealt with her temper when she was at her limit and stomped her right foot. "I'm not leaving, Miss Backus," she said more softly. "You go on, and we'll talk later."

Fancy passed them by without a smile or nod and was reaching for the doorknob.

"Wait, Miss Aubrey," Madison cried. "May I please have a word?"

Fancy turned as Pauline backed away, slowly shaking her head.

"Did you want to speak with me?"

At Pauline's gaped mouth, Madison's heart sank.

The woman turned, stormed away, dragging Carlie with her.

She and Miss Aubrey were alone, and maybe no one would come out of the store just yet. "Yes, I did. My name is Madison Plumb, and I'd like to interview you for a term paper I'm writing for college. About life in the West." Heat prickled her face under Fancy Aubrey's gaze. "Might we talk sometime?"

Fancy smiled and let the door close softly. "Sorry to disappoint you, Miss Plumb, but I'm not interested in sharing the facts of my life with curious busybodies." She held out a hand, bouncing it softly, as if she were soothing a frightened puppy. "Not you, mind you, I think your heart is in the right place, but the good citizens of Y Knot and beyond. Our Deputy Wesley has told me about you and why you're here with pen and paper. I hope you understand. It's nothing personal." With a polite nod, she opened the door and was gone.

Stung, Madison could only stare. She hadn't contemplated what the saloon girl sharing her history might mean to her. Madison had been caught up in writing a paper to impress Professor Galbraith. She hadn't considered the ramifications for Miss Aubrey. Feeling contrite, Madison took a step back and watched the door, sure many of the women inside would rush out in one big surge now that Fancy Aubrey had entered. The thought made Madison sad. She'd liked Miss Aubrey's voice. And even the understanding in her eyes as she'd kindly dressed Madison down. Promising herself she'd do better in the future, she calmly waited for the flurry of activity about to explode.

Chapter Forty-One

Minutes later, Madison slowly made her way toward the sheriff's office. The exit of women hadn't provided any new answers. She counted the cracks between the boards at her feet, thoroughly discouraged. She'd started the day with such high hopes. Whoever retrieved the letter simply walked away, unidentified. Not only that, but she'd alienated herself, she was sure, from Pauline Backus. The look of disgust on Justin's aunt's face when Madison refused to leave because Fancy Aubrey was coming their way was etched in Madison's head. And poor little Carlie didn't know what to do as her aunt marched her toward Justin's office. Were they still there? Was Justin there? She wholeheartedly hoped he was. She needed someone to talk to, and he was the only one who knew her secret. Passing the hotel, she looked in to see Lenore at the counter, speaking with Hildy.

Almost to the sheriff's office, Madison heard Pauline's angry voice reverberating painfully out to her ears. Unable to discern the words, Madison pulled up just in time as Pauline barged out, Carlie still in tow.

Coming face to face, the woman visibly bristled and then passed by without another word.

Heaving a sigh, Madison wondered if she

should even go inside. Quietly stepping up to the open door, she glanced in to see Justin at his desk, head cradled in his hands. She was just about to move on when he straightened.

"I think I conjured you out of my thoughts," he said, low. "Come in, please."

Madison lifted a shoulder. "You sure I should? I know your aunt just gave you an earful about me. Maybe I'll go back to my room and begin my day over. I seem to have messed this one up beyond repair."

Smiling, he came to the door and ushered her inside. "Things aren't *that* bad. Tell me what happened."

"No? I heard your aunt's angry voice, and I know what she was talking about. I'm sorry, Justin. She's never going to forgive me for defying her."

"Somebody needed to." He chuckled. "Don't worry about her. I don't. I learned years ago to not take her too seriously. Now . . ." He pulled the side chair close and gestured for her to sit. After she did, he took his seat behind the desk. "What happened with the letter? The moment I saw you outside the mercantile, I knew what you were up to. Did you find out anything important?"

She shook her head, defeat filling her lungs. "The letter's gone."

His face brightened. "Well, that's good, isn't it? I looked in the window this morning, first thing, and the letter was still there. You've been stationed in front of the mercantile since the store opened. Who went inside?"

Madison ticked off her fingers, naming each woman. "Nine."

"Nine!"

"I know. The place was crowded. Mr. Simpson was none too pleased when one of the Hicks children broke something. But, getting back to my story, four of the ladies, Heather, Kathryn, Poppy, and Lenore are all too young to be considered."

"Lenore, too young?"

"Hildy told me she was around twenty-six or twenty-seven." Madison gave a tentative smile. "I just can't make such a stretch."

Justin sat forward and watched her, elbows on the top of his desk and his chin resting on his tented fingers.

Madison admitted to herself, she enjoyed his attention enormously.

"Who were the others?" he asked. "Don't keep me in suspense."

"Lynette and Saralee Hicks. Lou from the boardinghouse. Berta May. And Bethanne Payne, wife of the banker."

He sat for a long time without saying a word. "You realize you're not one-hundred percent positive the letter came from your father's attorney at all. Correct?"

"I do." She blinked, recognizing just how much she'd pinned her hopes on discovering something today. Going back to work at the Biscuit Barrel and her old routine would be difficult.

"Stop it," he said softly. "I can see you're discouraged. You've only just begun." He reached forward and brushed several wisps of hair out of her face.

The touch was intimate. She didn't know how she should respond. Her intention in coming to Y Knot hadn't been to fall in love. He was her friend. Her confidant. She looked down, still feeling his touch although he'd drawn back his hand. "I know. But it's difficult not to."

In a flurry of heavy breathing, a red-faced Mr. Lichtenstein barreled through the door.

Both Justin and Madison shot to their feet.

"The perpetrator has hit *my* store, Deputy," the German bellowed, anger making his accent all the more evident. "And not a small item this time. Have you made *any* progress in finding who is plaguing our small community?"

Madison took a step back, feeling out of place.

"When?" Justin inquired. "And what?"

"This morning. Mr. Simpson said the store was crowded, and with all the talking and commotion, and with his fuzzy memory, he can't remember exactly who was there. This pilferage must stop! Y Knot has turned lawless. We need . . ."

Madison closed her eyes and prayed the

proprietor didn't say what she thought was coming next.

"... Sheriff Crawford."

Justin straightened, the infinitesimal squaring of his shoulders apparent. He looked as if he was slowly counting to five.

"Deputy? The two small timepieces were worth at least twenty dollars! That's not a handful of change or a rack of ribs. *Something* must be done."

"I'm sorry, Mr. Lichtenstein, but Brandon won't be back anytime soon, as much as we'd *all* like him to be." His voice was stern. "I'm patrolling later and longer. I've spoken with the victims and collected any evidence, not that there's been much of anything. I'm doing all I can. But, just so you know, because of Miss Plumb, I know everyone who has been in your store all day, up until about ten minutes ago. I'll follow up immediately. When was the last time you saw the timepieces? Where were they kept?"

Mr. Lichtenstein's face relaxed, and he took a deep breath. "They were in the back storeroom with the other new merchandise I intended to put out today," he said in a much calmer voice. "I remember seeing the box and even looking inside. Whatever happened, did so this morning."

"Was the storeroom locked?"

Mr. Lichtenstein's face reddened again. "I believe it was, but there have been occasions in the past when Mr. Simpson goes in to retrieve something and forgets to relock it."

Madison softly cleared her throat. "Excuse me."

They both looked at her.

"I was in the store this morning. Heather Klinkner said one of their reasons for going in today was to check to see if the wedding gift Miss Ford ordered for her husband-to-be had arrived." She lifted a shoulder, not wanting to say what her statement meant about the case. Mr. Simpson had, indeed, gone into the storeroom to check and must have left the door unlocked.

"Justin?" a male voice called from outside.

A moment later, Francis stuck his head inside the open office door. Seeing her and a red-faced Lichtenstein he straightened and stopped.

Justin opened his desk drawer and took out a folded telegram. "The latest," he said, holding the message out. "Everything remains the same. You pickin' up supplies?"

Francis's unkempt appearance surprised Madison. Light brown whiskers covered his jawline, his shirt was smudged, and the dark circles under his eyes made him look fatigued. She'd yet to meet Brandon Crawford, but if Francis's condition meant anything, the sheriff was greatly loved, and anyone who knew him well was suffering with worry.

"Not in for supplies today," Francis replied, still standing in the doorway. "Mrs. McCutcheon couldn't sit still a day longer. She and Faith came into town to send their own telegrams. The other two women remained home with the young'uns. They've all been living at the main house with Claire the last few days, trying to keep calm." He stepped in farther, removed his hat, and ran a hand through his shaggy hair. "It's been tough, staying behind, and that's no lie. I'll be more than happy when Flood and the others get back. Waiting around is hard on the soul."

Justin brought him the telegram.

Mr. Lichtenstein just listened with a grave face.

The theft didn't seem quite so important, at the moment.

"Flood been told about Brandon yet?" Justin asked.

"No way to know. Claire had us send word to the stockyard office in Miles City to let Flood know as soon as he arrived and to send word back when he was on his way home. She also arranged for a man from the stockyard to ride out and look for the herd. That's big country out there. The drive isn't due in for a couple of days. And then they have the ride back." Francis shook his head and just stared at the floor.

A middle-aged gentleman with a noticeable limp came into the already crowded office. He wore a battered old cowboy hat, and his shirt tails were hanging out. He looked grizzled and grumpy.

Madison thought he must have something to do with the ranch she'd been hearing so much about. A young boy, with long hair that reminded Madison of Samson from her early Bible studies, followed in his wake.

"News?" the older man asked.

Francis held up the telegram. "The same, Lucky. Brandon's still lingering after the surgery." He took a deep swallow. "The women ready to head back to the ranch?"

The boy straightened and shook his head. "Nope. Went into the mercantile to pick up a few things. Looking for some doodads for the tykes—cheer 'em up. They all miss their pas."

Madison hid her smile. His adult statement sounded silly, coming from someone who'd been a tyke not long ago.

The older man named Lucky cleared his throat, now respectfully holding his hat to his chest. "Miss?"

"I'm sorry," Justin said. "Lucky, Hickory, this is Madison Plumb. She's new to Y Knot. Madison, this fine gentleman is Lucky Langer, cook at the bunkhouse up at the Heart of the Mountains Ranch. And this is Hickory." He lifted a brow and smiled. "Ranch hand."

Everyone nodded and mumbled. She could tell they weren't feeling their best. "It's my pleasure to meet you both."

"We'll be goin'." Francis placed his hat on and

turned for the door. “Justin, send word out to the ranch if you hear anything new.”

“You know I will. And the same goes for you. Let us know if you need anything. Or there’s something we can do to help.” He glanced at her and then Mr. Lichtenstein. “We’re all ready to assist in any way we can. All you have to do is say the word. Nothing is more important than Brandon making a full recovery and coming home.”

“Amen,” Lucky croaked, his eyes swimming in tears. “Amen to that.”

Chapter Forty-Two

The sun was just setting when Luke heard the approach of horses. He'd staked out his own mount so the gelding could graze, then he'd hunkered down under the shade of a mighty oak, unable to do anything else except wait—and think. Thoughts of Brandon plagued him. Of Charity, too. If the outcome of his actions—riding all this way and then waiting all day—turned out to be for naught, he'd never forgive himself. Hunger gnawed at his belly, but now, seeing the several riders, his hunger pains fell away, replaced with excitement and caution.

As the group came closer, Luke recognized the older, scar-faced warrior. Three other young to middle-aged warriors, fit and adorned in their leather and feathers, sat tall on their horses. They didn't look as underfed as the first two had, and he wondered if they went to the reservation more often than not. A handful of others rode in their wake. Was this a welcoming party they'd sent out to greet him? Or something else?

Surprised to see a woman among the approaching group, Luke wished for the hundredth time he'd paid more attention when Fox Dancing had tried to teach him the language. At the time, she'd chastised him for his indifference, but in a loving way. Discovering he'd had another sister other than Charity had been such a surprise and welcome gift. And now he might even have an uncle and nephew. What other surprises might he learn today? Dare he hope his father might be among this party?

Luke had been wrong, thinking he'd speak with the Indians where he was, somehow get his meaning across, and then head back to Helena. No, this had been a search party of sorts, to see if bringing him to the hidden village would be safe. Maybe they had to get somebody's approval. They'd stood around, making hand gestures and voicing the few Cheyenne words he knew, including those of his father and sister, as well as his new brother-in-law, Painted Bear Stone. Reading their reactions had been difficult, but all at once, something must have happened, and they'd mounted up and gestured for him to do the same. Since then, they'd ridden for almost an hour, going through narrow canyons, dense vegetation, and then, coming out into the open, they'd crossed a shallow creek. Within moments of that, they topped a rise and were now looking down on a medium-sized Cheyenne village. At least thirty tepees dotted the area, some with smoke rising from the smoke holes. Off to the west was a modest herd of horses, maybe twenty head strong.

Everyone reined up, and Luke followed suit. The same burning need to get back to the hospital smoldered inside him. Brandon and Charity were never far from his mind. This journey had already stretched on much longer than he'd anticipated.

A middle-aged man, one who'd arrived with the newcomers, rode up to Luke's side. His deeply lined face looked like leather. He waved his hand to the sight before them. "Village," he said in an accented voice.

Surprised, Luke gaped. "You understand?" Why hadn't they brought the old warrior out sooner, instead of waiting until they made the long ride to the village? He'd already talked his throat hoarse trying to say he needed the help of their medicine man and quickly.

The fellow pointed to the village again and nodded. The others were already riding down the hill toward the tepees. "*Netchiwaan*."

Shocked again, Luke blinked. Was he saying his father was down there? He, himself, pointed. "*Netchiwaan here?*"

The man nodded and nudged his horse forward.

The village was alive with movement once he and the fellow arrived a few minutes after the others. A warm wind held scents of leather baking in the sun, curing hides, and something rancid, as well as smells of wood smoke and tantalizing meat cooking. The men crowded around him, some bumping or shoving. The women stood back, their eyes narrowed. Three mangy, thin dogs followed his heels, probably looking for a scrap of something to eat. The overall appearance of the camp was hunger. Without the freedoms they had years ago, feeding a number of people would be difficult. From what he'd heard from Fox Dancing and Painted Bear Stone, they needed to be cautious, mostly staying out of sight and out of mind.

"Luke McCutcheon."

Turning, Luke found a woman. He couldn't gauge her age, but her skin was lined, and she had some wrinkles around her eyes and mouth. Her waist-length black hair was braided in one thick plait down her back, falling past her waist.

"My name . . . Biting Horse," she said haltingly.

Fox Dancing had told him she had two mothers, Biting Horse and Crow Foot Woman. He didn't know which one had brought Fox Dancing into the world. He also knew, when his own mother had been taken captive and given to *Netchiwaan* as a wife, until Claire had proven herself, his father's two wives had treated her cruelly, pulling her hair, slapping, and pinching her. Luke dipped his head respectfully. "Mother to Fox Dancing," he said slowly. "She told me about you and her village. Is Fox Dancing here?"

She shook her head. "Reservation."

Luke wondered if she'd moved there permanently. "Can I see my father, *Netchiwaan*?"

As if the decision had already been made, Biting Horse inclined her head and motioned for him to follow.

He was sure this was not the same camp where his mother had lived because she'd told him of the sweeping beauty of the land. The many trees and hundreds of tepees.

A handful of young braves followed as they meandered through the village, where others, the older men and women, hung back as if Luke's oddity had already begun to wear off and they were now uninterested. With the sun on his shoulders, he still led his horse, until they were almost to the middle of the tepees. At the tallest, decorated with painted horses and moons, Biting Horse held out a hand, motioning for him to stay, and ducked inside. He heard indistinguishable voices, one the deep resonance of a male and the other a female. *Crow Foot Woman?*

Finally, the flap lifted, and another woman stepped out, this one young and slender, her face oval where Biting Horse's was round.

"Crow Foot Woman?" he asked, somewhat thrown off. He hadn't thought his father's other wife would be so young.

With a laugh and dancing, dark eyes, she shook her head. She didn't try to speak but motioned for him to enter.

The darkness was heavily scented with wood

smoke. Tiny dust motes danced weightlessly on a beam of light that streamed in from the smoke hole. As Luke's eyes adjusted, he saw a man reclined on a stained and tattered old buffalo robe. A porcupine quill vest and several strands of beads covered his bare chest. Eagle feathers hung in his hair. His leather leggings appeared worn and dirty.

My father!

Luke fought the urge to go to him and gather him in an embrace.

Seeing *Netchiwaan* struggle to stand, Luke took a step forward to assist but was met with a loud negative sound.

Finally upright, his father proudly lifted his chin. "My great, white son!"

Luke nodded. He searched for a resemblance to himself but was unable to see any. "Father," he said, hoping *Netchiwaan* would understand more than a little English. He had so much to ask. To say.

"He understands and speaks some English. Your mother taught," Biting Horse said choppily from behind him.

Luke had forgotten the woman was still there. He didn't turn but kept his gaze on his father. He heard the others leaving.

"I have seen Luke McCutcheon. Three times. I go to ranch. Hide away until I see the seed of my loins."

Fox Dancing had told him this fact, which he'd found difficult to believe.

"When you three, then thirteen, and last, you young, strong man. Tall. Proud."

The words were as hard as flint but laced with pride. His gaze took in every inch of Luke, making Luke regret he hadn't learned more Cheyenne from his sister so he'd know better now how he should respond. "You should have presented yourself," Luke said. He stood stiffly, wishing they could sit together around the small fire. Get to know each other.

Netchiwaan's brow furrowed as if he hadn't caught everything Luke had just said.

Luke patted his chest with an open palm and then held it out in offering. "I'm pleased to finally meet you. The man who gave me life. My heart is full." His father must have understood because he smiled—and his face changed, softened. He nodded a few times, and Luke thought he saw his lips twist, as if he was holding back emotion.

Netchiwaan put out a hand and gestured to the small fire ringed with rocks. "I smoke with my son." He looked around for his pipe. "We talk."

The burning need to get back to Brandon was never far from Luke's mind. He must ask about their medicine man, then return quickly to Helena and St. John's Hospital. As soon as he and his father had a few moments of words, Luke would make him understand why, at this time, he couldn't stay longer.

Sitting cross-legged across from each other, *Netchiwaan* lit his pipe with the glowing end of a straw from the edge of the fire. The scarred tube was about two feet long, and each end was darkened from years of smoke. A decorative ring of green with diamond shapes circled close to the mouthpiece. Three feathers hung from the middle. *Netchiwaan* took several more puffs, causing the porcupine quills on his chest to rise and fall. Smoke flowed from his mouth into his eyes, enveloping his face. He puffed heartily again, as if enjoying the action, and then, with a nod, reached across the fire to hand the pipe to Luke.

Luke tried to figure his age, but he couldn't. He thought him younger than Flood and closer to his mother's age. He wondered why his father was in the tepee and seemed incapacitated in some way. Luke took the pipe and inhaled into his lungs, fighting against the urge to cough. His eyes watered as he willed himself to smile. He'd smoked from a pipe before with his friend Eagle Gray, but the smoke had not seemed so intense. "Good," he choked out, the smoke rushing from his mouth to flow, stinging, up his nose. He blinked away the moisture from his eyes.

Netchiwaan grinned, as if knowing the pain his son was hiding. "Good," he echoed. "Your mother, Yellow Hair Woman."

It was said as a statement, but Luke understood he was asking about her. "My mother is well. She had two more children after me. She was kind to Fox Dancing when my sister came. She surprised us with the Cheyenne words she knew but kept hidden all these years. She remembers her time in your village."

Netchiwaan's grin widened.

Luke thought he saw a little of himself in the delighted expression.

"She *good* woman. Didn't want to let her go. For safety of the village, had to be done."

Luke inclined his head and handed the pipe back, making the decision, then and there, he'd not tell anyone he'd met his father. Flood had already been through too much. This was a secret he'd keep forever. "Thank you for that. My *other* father, Flood McCutcheon, treats me like a true son. Never made me feel different when I was a boy or now that I'm grown. I respect and love him."

Netchiwaan puffed vigorously on the pipe. Smoke swirled upward to the top of the tepee and out into the sunshine.

"I have an uncle I met coming here," Luke said, when *Netchiwaan* didn't reply. Luke accepted the pipe when it was offered. "He is your brother? The one with the scar on his face." Luke drew on the pipe. This time, the smoke didn't burn as deeply.

"*Héehe'e*."

Luke recognized the word for yes.

"You have many relations here. The young woman who brought you in is daughter of uncle." He thought for a moment, as if searching for the correct translation. "Little Singing Deer."

More relatives? Why hadn't Fox Dancing mentioned that fact during her visit? Did she fear his curiosity would put him in danger by seeking them out? He should have been working to help his people. As soon as he was home, and Brandon was recovering, as well, he'd fix his oversight.

"Father, I have a request. My brother, Brandon Crawford, is ailing in the hospital in Helena. He's had surgery but does not grow stronger. We fear he might die. I'd like help from your medicine man."

Netchiwaan's face grew grave. "We all die, Luke McCutcheon," he said, a hint of anger in his tone. "Some sooner than we should."

Would his father be no help? Unwavering, Luke tried again. "Brandon is married to my little 'white' sister. I told her I'd do all I could to help her husband recover. She's expecting their first child."

"Like your mother was expecting *my child* when she was taken from me?" His father's face was suddenly unreadable. He straightened and laid the pipe to the side. "My brother, my people's medicine man, was killed by the whites on the reservation. Said he stole a calf, but they lied. They always lie. Their forked tongues eat the truth."

Frustrated, Luke knew his father had good reason to think such things. The way the Indians had been treated since they'd been rounded up and put on reservations was disgraceful. Uncountable thousands had perished from starvation, white man's illnesses, and murder. The flinty hardness of *Netchiwaan*'s eyes made Luke wary of pushing his request. Still, he had no other option. "I'm deeply sorry." And he was. "Is there another medicine man close? I don't want to return without obtaining what I came for."

The anger eased off *Netchiwaan*'s face, replaced with something else.

Compassion? Love?

"Even my son knows not the suffering of our warriors. Can't hunt. Watch family die. Our women beg at the reservation for food and then sneak back here, frightened of discovery and being beaten. I do not blame you, my son. The evil could not be stopped. The roaring tide overcame my people. *Your* people, too."

They stared at each other.

Netchiwaan broke the silence. "We have no more medicine men anywhere. Biting Horse's elder brother was healer before murdered. She knows many of his cures. She will tell you what you need."

Would that be enough? Luke didn't know. He'd like nothing more than to remain in the village a few days and get to know his father better. And his other relatives. Who knew? By the time he got home and sent a small herd of beef, they could all be dead. The thought was terrifying.

He inclined his head. "Thank you. It's been my honor meeting you. Something I've wanted for many years. My mother told me about you. Your kindness. Her days in captivity weren't all bad. She kept those words in her heart until the right time to share with me."

Netchiwaan's eyes widened. He hadn't expected to hear such news about his lost wife.

"Now, I feel a great need to hurry back to Helena. When I return to my home, I intend to supply your village with beef. To help you pass the coming winter in comfort."

"We will greatly appreciate your charity, something I would never have said twenty years ago."

They both stood.

"You will return?" *Netchiwaan* asked.

"I give you my word." Luke stepped around the fire when his father did, and they embraced.

Chapter Forty-Three

In the soft, pillowy bed, Charity turned to her side, enjoying the feel of the smooth pillowcase next to her cheek. She drifted in and out of consciousness, not thinking of anything. Y Knot was exceptionally quiet this morning. Reaching out, she found the other side of the bed empty and cold, which was not unusual. Brandon typically awakened at four thirty, lit the stove to warm the house, and was drinking his first cup of coffee by a quarter to five. With her eyes closed, she took a deep whiff, detecting no aroma. Strange. Had he gone over to the office without a cup at home first? She generally followed him over an hour later with a plateful of bacon and eggs.

The sound of the door creaking softly brought Charity fully awake. Expecting Brandon, the shock of seeing her brother, Matthew, threw her off. A split second later, she remembered. Brandon! Across the street, fighting for his life, and she was confined to her bed in order to protect the tiny life growing inside her.

"Good morning, Charity. You awake?" Matthew said, low. "It's still early. Six o'clock, Saturday morning. Mark's over with Brandon, and there's been no change overnight."

She was thankful he'd said the time and date.

Days ago, she'd stopped caring and had no idea of the passage of time. Would she ever hear her love had awakened and was asking for her?

"My intention was to poke in my head to see if you were awake, not wake you up. Then again, I thought you might be hungry. You didn't eat but what a bird would last night, and with the baby . . ."

She smiled and sat up, pulling up the dusty rose counterpane, then positioned a pillow behind her back.

He'd stepped inside and softly closed the door. He was dressed in one of the three shirts he'd brought along from home, his denims, and his boots. Dark whiskers covered his square jaw, and his hair and clothes were rumpled. Dark circles had formed under his eyes, and the whites were bloodshot.

He looked almost shy to approach the bed. "I was just coming out of a dream," she responded. "I was waking up in Y Knot, and Brandon had had his coffee and was already waiting for me at the sheriff's office to bring over his breakfast." She couldn't stop her eyes from filling, but she'd not cry. She'd already caused her brothers, who were trying to care for Brandon, more undue stress on top of the tragedy at hand. "He usually eats bacon and eggs."

Matthew crossed the room in three long strides. When he sat on the side of the bed, it squeaked loudly. He stroked the side of her hair. "Things'll take a turn for the better soon, Charity, I promise. You're going to be fine, and so is Brandon."

She rolled her lips painfully against her teeth to steady her voice. "I just wish I could be with him," she pushed out through her tight throat. Matthew was such a good big brother. Always knew exactly what to say. "And hold his hand. I think he's aware when I'm there and when I'm not. He must wonder. . . ." Her voice broke, and she couldn't go on.

"Shhh. Hold tight to your faith. I believe you're right about him knowin'. I told him last night where you were and why. He wasn't awake, but I slowly spelled out what had happened about you and the baby. Why you weren't there and about the doctor putting you on bedrest. I can't be sure, but I think he squeezed my hand."

She glanced up into Matthew's face and sat a little straighter. "He did?"

Matt nodded.

"You were holding his hand?"

He nodded again. "You bet. The human touch is powerful. I was sending him my energy, and . . ."

That was all he got out before Charity sat forward and threw her arms around him. "Thank you," she whispered earnestly through her strangled throat. "Thank you for loving Brandon as much as I do. And thank you for telling him where I was." Strong, warm hands went slowly up and down her back. He held her close, and she imagined she could feel the thumping of his heart.

"How're *you* feeling this mornin'?" he said against her head. "Any more pains? Or . . . anything else?"

She shook her head and got a hold of her tears. Sitting back against her pillow, she reached for her hanky on the bedside table and blotted each eye. "Nothing else." Not quite the truth. She'd carefully gotten out of bed around midnight to use the chamber pot. She wouldn't have lit the candle, except she'd had a small cramp and was frightened. Three tiny spots of blood were present, but no more. Nothing like the day before. "I just pray what the doctors said is true and the last episode didn't harm the baby." She took a deep breath and willed away her tears. Since she couldn't be with Brandon, her two brothers had an important job, and she'd not distract them with tears. "Any word from Luke? Or home?"

Matt nodded. "Mother continues to send telegrams every day to inquire, but we didn't say anything about you." His brow furrowed. "Are you sure you don't want her here with you, Char? She's going to be duly upset—and with every right—when she learns the truth."

"Me in this bed is just a passing hurdle." She gestured to her room. "I don't want to frighten her to death. I'll be fine in a few days, then the doctor will allow me to resume my spot at Brandon's side. Besides, it's a long journey. By the time she arrived, we might already be on our way home. This can't go on much longer." Blinking, she glanced at the window, realizing the enormity of what she'd just said. Brandon dying. She cleared her throat. "And Luke? You never said."

"He's out in open land and can't communicate." Matt smiled lovingly and picked up her hand. "I'm sure he'll be back later today or early tomorrow. He said, one way or another, he wasn't staying away long. You're not to worry."

The backs of Charity's eyes stung, but she swallowed down her fear. "Of course. I bet you're ready for a few hours' sleep in your bed. Is there anything . . ."

A soft knock sounded on the door.

Matthew stood and crossed the room.

Opening the door, Mrs. Hardie stepped inside. She held a tray filled with breakfast. "I hope you don't mind, but I heard some stirring up here and thought Charity might be hungry."

Charity forced a smile. Mrs. Hardie had been amazingly kind from the moment she and her brothers arrived. The thought of any kind of food soured her stomach, even though she'd long passed her morning sickness. If she took even a tiny bite, she'd choke, but she'd not hurt the woman's feelings. "It smells delicious, Mrs. Hardie," she fibbed. "Thank you so much. I'm famished."

Matt gazed at her with a tilted brow.

Her brothers knew her so well, she had no chance to get away with anything.

Smiling, Mrs. Hardie came forward and set the tray on the bedside table where Charity's hanky had been moments before. "That's wonderful to hear," she said softly.

The tray held a cup of coffee generously laced with cream, a plate of scrambled eggs, two flapjacks, butter and syrup, and a thin slice of ham. Everything *did* look delicious. "You've outdone yourself," Charity said, looking at all the fare. "I'm sorry you had to carry the heavy tray up three flights of stairs. I'm sure, by the time you reach the top, your arms are aching."

"I'm happy to do it," she replied. "And used to it. The exercise keeps me young. I should be thanking you." She shook out a burgundy napkin and laid it over the counterpane on Charity's lap, moving the tray there, as well. She glanced at Matt. "Your breakfast is ready, too, Mr. McCutcheon. Another guest checked in last night, so he's at the table, eating now. As soon as you go down, I'll pull yours out of the warmer."

"Thank you. I think I'll keep Charity company while she eats." He gave her another knowing look.

"That's perfectly fine. It'll stay hot until you're ready." She smoothed her white, Swiss dot apron. "You let me know if Charity needs anything else."

"I'm fine," Charity replied. She already felt stronger with a good night's sleep under her belt. "I can't thank you enough for all you've done."

Already at the door, Mrs. Hardie waved dismissively. "Oh, poo. I'm happy to help. I don't want to hear another word about it." She smiled and glanced at a cross on the wall. "Give over your worries, and all will be fine."

Charity wished she could believe her words. Was Mrs. Hardie right? So much was at stake.

Chapter Forty-Four

Feeling the wear and tear of doing both her and Abe's job, Fancy swung the saloon doors wide open and tied them back to allow fresh air to clear out the lingering scents of stale smoke, horse manure, and sweat. *The Hitching Post never opened this late on a Saturday morning.* Now and again on a Sunday, maybe, but she was surprised some of the locals weren't already at the door, angrily waiting for their beer and whiskey.

A ripple of anticipation ran through her. *Cole Mercer! Imagine that.* Would he come in again today?

That man made her feel young. His memory represented a magical time in her life—the cusp of her girlhood and falling into the valley of young womanhood. Discoveries and awareness of her body—*and heart.* Like a butterfly, she'd been shedding her childhood cocoon and blooming into a different creature. After meeting him, longings and dreams had kept her awake well past midnight. The world had been her oyster, ripe for the plucking—and could have played out so differently.

Her father, a private man, had never been much for showing affection to his two daughters. Her older brother had a hard shell he rarely came out of unless to criticize his sisters, or perhaps to show them the back of his hand. The truth of the matter was, she'd feared Craig. He was eight years her senior, with eyes she couldn't read. She sometimes wondered if he was fathered by someone else and was planted in their family to make life difficult—like the long-tailed cuckoo bird. That horrible parasite laid its eggs in the nest of other species. After hatching, the cuckoo grew quickly and soon overshadowed the other baby birds. The adults were worn ragged, trying to keep the monster bird fed. In the end, its sheer volume pushed the rightful chicks to their deaths.

Just like Craig did to me . . .

As she hurried to the storeroom for several bottles of whiskey to restock the backbar, she glanced up to the second story. Everything was still quiet. She'd served Abe some tea and toast for breakfast and given him a dose of quinine powder in a large glass of water. As soon as someone arrived who she could leave in charge, she'd check on him.

Taking the iron key from her pocket, she unlocked the door to the storeroom. The horrified expressions of the women in the mercantile yesterday floated before her face. The second she'd stepped into Lichtenstein's, all talking hushed, and a thick silence descended. Some of the ladies tolerated her whenever they met up. But yesterday, to save face with the other women present, decorum said they must keep a respectable distance. Etiquette insisted decent women must look down their noses on women like Fancy, or their own reputations would be called into question. She didn't mind. She was used to it.

Berta May, her secret friend, had given a clandestine wink before exiting with her purchases. On occasion, they met in Berta May's upstairs living quarters for tea and cake—her signal was a white handkerchief fluttering outside the fabric shop's window. When present, she was to slip over when the bar wasn't busy. The middle-aged seamstress with the big heart usually made a delicious walnut raisin crumb cake topped with sweet cream or an apple tart with an impossibly thin, flaky crust. They'd eat and giggle and talk about recipes.

Lou, too, was Fancy's trusted ally. The owner of the boardinghouse had taken Fancy under her wing like a mother hen two years ago. If Fancy was under the weather, Drit alerted Lou, and she'd cook up a pot of chicken soup with lots of vegetables and noodles. She marched uncaring of other's opinion of her through the saloon doors and took the stairs as if she owned the place. She always remembered Fancy's birthday with a small gift and note. Throughout the weeks, she'd waved through the batwing doors whenever she passed by, calling out a hello. Lou was a woman with a backbone as strong as her heart.

A warm feeling swirled around inside, and Fancy recognized the emotion as love. A few other women would give a hidden wink or a wave. She wasn't thinking of her male friends. She had *lots* of those. Starting with Brandon Crawford and all the McCutcheons, as well as more than a handful of shop owners and the deputy. They treated her respectfully and even asked her opinion. A soiled dove couldn't ask for more than that. Realizing she couldn't complain about much at all, Fancy smiled. But then, others like Pauline Backus . . .

Fancy's smile grew as she set the heavy whiskey bottles, clinking in her arms and full to their cork stoppers, onto the shelf, remembering her proclamation as she'd stepped through the mercantile door. "Excuse me, ladies, but Abe's under the weather," she'd said, holding out a short list of items. "Please permit me to gather a few things he needs. I'll be as quick as I can." She'd glanced at Mr. Simpson and gave him her most brilliant smile. "And even *quicker* if you help me, Mr. Simpson. You're so knowledgeable about medicinals and such." The cute old clerk had stammered a few times as his large ears turned as pink as a peach. He was probably remembering her last visit a week ago, when he'd talked her head off and they'd shared a cup of tea after closing time. He'd said she reminded him of his sister, back when the two were young sprouts growing up on a farm in Nebraska. Today, he'd remained silent as he'd clomped his way around the counter, preceding her to each item on her list, shelved in alphabetical order. She'd taken each article and gathered them into her arms.

Young Mrs. Klinkner and her friends, Mrs. Preece and Miss Ford, were just finishing at the register. They'd smiled weakly and then quietly went out the door. Fancy liked their husbands. Hayden, Tobit, and, of course, Shad, Miss Ford's intended. Fancy would like to get to know their wives, as well—on a woman-to-woman basis. *In another life,* Fancy chastised herself.

Hayden was so funny, he often had her laughing at the smallest comment. His quick wit was impossible to match. And the attractive farmer, Tobit, took himself much too seriously at times. She liked to tease him and get his goat—and joke about his *real* goat, Buddy, and how Tobit had to fight the scraggly billy off in a field of giant sunflowers—protecting his young mail-order bride. Fancy giggled, imagining the scene in her head. And then there was Shad Petty, oh my. He was much too handsome for his own good. And he possessed *such* a golden heart. One that prompted him, a cowhand, to raise his own brothers when his grandparents passed on. When he reminisced about his grandma Girdy, Fancy found holding back tears near impossible.

His words were so tender, touching. The women of this town just might have their eyes opened if they knew what *really* went on here behind the batwing doors. She hoped they took the time to listen to their husbands. Try to understand them. She'd never forget how Shad, concerned for her safety during the blizzard last year, came and fetched her to the hotel where others were safely waiting out the storm. He'd made a trip to the saloon through the biting whiteout and insisted she pack a bag and come to the hotel where there was food and warmth. *He even stood up to that Boston city buffoon when he demanded Shad show me the door.* Good men like Shadrack Petty were damned hard to find. She hoped those three young women knew just how fortunate they were to have such fine men in their lives.

Finished setting up, she glanced around, amazed Jack Jones wasn't here, as she'd been open a full eight minutes. The room was actually appealing, when empty of drinkers. Sometimes, in the early morning hours, after Abe had kicked out the last few drunks, Fancy came down in her nightgown and robe to sit by the potbelly stove and warm her hands and feet. She'd imagine herself in a sturdy little cabin on the top of some deserted hill. Once her imagination got going, she could think up one hundred different happy situations about how her life could have gone.

Male laughter sounded outside, and Fancy

knew her respite was over. Sam Green and Dennis Oats stepped inside, went directly to the bar, and claimed a stool.

"How's Abe?" Sam asked, glancing up to the second floor. "Feeling better yet, or has he died?"

She shook her head. *Not the men I want to leave the kitty alone with.* "Still in bed. I think he's pretty run-down. I hope Dr. Handerhoosen returns today. I'd feel better if someone who knew something about doctoring took a look at him. I can only do so much." Without waiting for them to order their usual beer, she went to the stack of newly polished mugs and drew them two. "Here you are, fellas, for having to wait."

Dennis's eyes went wide. "Thank you, Fancy. How'd you know we came by a while ago, but the place was locked up tight?" He slurped down half the mug, leaving a yellow foam mustache above his upper lip. "That's mighty kind of you."

"Because you come by every morning at nine—just like clockwork. Why would today be any different?"

"Good point," Dennis replied.

"She can afford to be generous with Abe's money," Sam Green said. "But you have my thanks, too, Fancy. Mighty classy of you." He raised his mug in salute.

The fool.

With the doors open, other men began to filter in, some taking tables and dealing out cards and others waiting at the bar for service. With the coffeepot empty and the trash bin full and needing to be dumped, she had a lot to do. Moving up and down the bar, she tried to minimize her steps as she accomplished her deeds, all the while worrying about Abe.

Shaking her thoughts because she couldn't shake her head, she turned, a small smile playing on her lips and thinking about how shocked Sam Green, the skunk, would be if he could see inside her head.

"Why the smile?"

Cole! The deep voice couldn't belong to anyone else. She stopped and took a breath. She cut her gaze to Sam and Dennis. "Just thinking."

Cole smiled. "I can imagine." He chuckled. "You have a lot to do. How can I help?"

She'd trust Cole with her life. "Really?"

"I wouldn't have offered if I didn't intend to follow through." He stood, came to the end of the bar, and tied on Abe's dirty apron.

"I need to check on Abe. Can you watch the bar while I do? I'll fill the coffeepot before I go and get those fellers at the two tables their drinks first, though."

"You go on. I can easily handle everything."

Looking back at her were the same green eyes as the day she'd almost drowned in the river. A shiver slipped up her back. How long since she'd felt like this? Why was he here? Was their meeting by chance? So many things she didn't know, but she did know she was happy to see him—and could use the help.

"Go on," he prompted, looking up and down the bar. "I'm itching to get busy, and I can't as long as I have you to look at."

She flushed warm. Cole Mercer, here in Y Knot. Trouble was just begging to happen.

Chapter Forty-Five

The warm evening air curled about Justin as he slowly made his way down the boardwalk. All the stores were closed, except the Hitching Post. He'd checked in the saloon a few minutes before and learned Abe was still bedbound, but the new man, Cole Mercer, was busy helping Fancy run the place. Justin was glad for it. Mercer was a large man. An army man. Nobody in their right mind would mess with Fancy with him watching over the saloon—and her. They'd had a good crowd tonight, but the place had thinned out by ten. She'd said they'd be closing soon.

Justin stopped and quietly tried the doorknob of the leather shop, not wanting to upset old Mr. Herrick by waking him with a rattling door—or getting shot in the process. The man was still angry about losing two new bridles, as well as the money. Justin was irritated, too. Solving this mystery was paramount for him *and* before his father returned. As much as Justin didn't like to think it, the shadow of his father's large reputation was hard to fill. As was Brandon's. Determined to stay up all night if he had to, he walked on, trying the door of Lichtenstein's and then Doc Handerhoosen. The doctor was still over in Pine Grove.

Madison had told him about Jack Jones coming into the mercantile with Cole Mercer at the time Mr. Lichtenstein said he'd been robbed. They'd said a brief hello to the women and then disappeared into the back of the store. They weren't there long before exiting the store again. Justin had followed up on the lead directly, exasperating Jack with questions.

The former deputy didn't like being under suspicion—since he considered himself a model citizen. He claimed to be showing Mercer some tools.

As crazy as that sounded, Justin had gone to the hotel and found Cole in the dining room, who corroborated Jack's story and then clammed up. Why tools?

That left the Hicks children, and Justin's assumption was Dodger Hicks could be responsible.

They'd been in the store at the right time, unsupervised in the back, where the theft had happened. Ever since Justin's arrival in Y Knot, he'd been rubbed the wrong way by Dodger Hicks. The insolent kid always had a smart remark at the ready, but never within hearing distance of his father, Jed. The boy was large and strong from moving logs with his father and uncle. Riley Hicks, a year younger than his cousin, was amiable and did his best to please. At fifteen, he was large and strong, as well. Was there any possibility Nancy Hicks was involved? She was only ten, and as quiet as a mouse, or acted so whenever Justin was around.

Unsure of anything, Justin lifted his shoulders, working out the strain. The thought of Brandon and what he was going through was never far from his mind. He'd never dreamed the sheriff would be so close to death's door. They'd all just believed he'd busted his leg. The thought of anything other than him recovering was unthinkable. Y Knot without Brandon Crawford wasn't an option he liked.

Stepping off the boardwalk with the intention to cross the alley to Standford's Fittings, Justin caught a scuffling sound and looked up just in time to see some sort of movement in the back of the mercantile. Was the perpetrator trying to hit Lichtenstein's again? Crouching, he skimmed along the brick wall and then held up before rounding the back. All was quiet. He waited for his heart to slow down. Continuing around the building, he slowly made his way back the way he'd just come on the boardwalk, passing the rear door of the leather shop with the newly replaced lock.

Approaching the back of Cattlemen's Hotel, he pulled up, sure now he'd seen a flash of white in the moonlight. Several small cottages took up the lot behind the hotel. One was occupied by Lenore Saffelberg, and another was rented by Harold, the young man who made his living by mopping the floor of any business willing to pay him. He also worked some nights at the Biscuit Barrel.

Justin had seen Lenore working in the hotel earlier tonight. Had she gone home yet? He didn't want her place to be broken into while she was there. Or Harold's, either. In the midst of a struggle, someone might be killed. These break-ins had been innocent enough up until now, except for Liechtenstein's. Seemed they were escalating, and the thief was growing bolder.

Carefully placing his feet, he slowly crept forward, his anticipation growing with each step. In a preemptive move, he unbuckled the leather holding his bullwhip gathered on his hip. Still attached but now unbuckled, his long leather friend would be ready, if needed.

Halting under a nearby tree, he studied the area. Still all quiet. Seeing light from Lenore's window, he decided she must be at work. She usually left a lamp burning inside on a small table and extinguished it when she went to bed. Moving closer, he carefully tried her doorknob, finding the apparatus locked. Walking around the structure, he stopped at the window. The lantern, on the small table by the window, gave a good amount of illumination. Justin took a quick look around the room to be sure no one had gotten inside.

As he turned to leave, an envelope under the

lamp caught his eye. Large and white. His heart thwacked against his ribs.

What are the chances? Many articles of mail arrive in Y Knot weekly. That can't be the envelope Madison is searching for. Can it?

He tipped his head, trying to see in the murky light. What was the name of her father's attorney? She'd mentioned it one time, but he hadn't committed the name to memory.

Turner, Scheller, and Robles, Attorneys at Law. And from *Kentucky!*

He straightened and looked off into the darkness, rubbing a hand over his face. This didn't make any sense. Hildy had told Madison Lenore Saffelberg was twenty-six years old. She would have been *six* when Madison was born. That tender age wasn't possible, any way you looked at it. Justin took a step away from the house, not wanting anyone to exit the back of the hotel and catch him lurking around Lenore's window, especially not her. Even though he was the deputy and was working, being here didn't feel right.

Should he mention this to Madison? He wanted to help her, not make matters worse. No, he'd wait. Give the situation a few days to shed new light. But he wouldn't keep the discovery from her for too long. Just enough time to figure out why a twenty-six-year-old spinster had a letter from Madison's father's attorney's office. But then, maybe this was some incredible coincidence. Did Lenore have any legal issues she might be consulting the firm for?

Major, Cole Mercer's dog, trotted up and stopped a few feet away.

Justin had seen the dog in the saloon, sleeping on a blanket in the corner.

The dog let out a loud bark.

"*Shh,* Major. Hush." Justin put out a hand and walked forward, unafraid. The animal knew him. He'd not bite.

The dog stepped forward and sniffed his hand.

Just then, Lenore came out of the back door of the hotel and stopped when she saw someone standing near her place.

"It's just me, Lenore," Justin called, feeling guilty as hell after snooping in her window. He'd had the right reason, but since seeing the envelope, another can of worms was open.

"Oh, Justin! You gave me a fright." She came closer. "And now I see you have Major with you, too." Her voice softened. "He's a good boy."

She still wore her white apron, which had a few blue splotches and another stain in brown looking like gravy. She'd been kind to him from the day he'd been hired. For the first few months, she'd stop in and say hello or tell him about something special, like Wednesdays at the Biscuit Barrel or the Twilight Singers performing the last Tuesday of each month in the gazebo. She made him feel welcome, although a bit apprehensive for all the attention she was showering. For a while, he had suspicions she'd set her cap for him, but when he hadn't responded duly, she kept their association one of friendship, never trying for anything more. Tonight, after her long shift in the restaurant, she looked tired. Two or three strands of her brown hair hung around her face, and her shoulders slumped. But she wore a smile for him.

Brushing her hair away, she looked around. "Is he out here causing mischief? Where's his owner?"

"The Hitching Post." Justin reached down and petted the dog. "I was in the saloon earlier, and Major was there, sleeping in the corner. I suppose he caught some scent and ran in pursuit. The batwing doors make keeping him inside difficult."

"Saloon?"

He nodded. "Cole Mercer's helping Fancy Aubrey run the place. Seems they're old friends. Abe's been sick and staying in bed." He pulled up when he realized he'd spoken so freely about Fancy. Usually, women didn't want to hear about a soiled dove.

She'd sharply looked away to stare at the moon.

He put out a hand in supplication. "I'm sorry, Lenore. I shouldn't have mentioned—er, her, you know, about the—"

"My sensibilities aren't so fragile I'll wilt at the mention of Miss Aubrey." She smiled at Major, who wagged his tail as the dog listened to the conversation.

The derisive tone in her voice made him wonder if he had, indeed, offended her—but then Lenore, being Lenore, didn't need a reason to sound offended, he guessed. "Anyway, I'll take the dog back to the saloon so he doesn't get into anyone's trash. I was out here looking around. Trying to catch the thief we have. I thought I saw something come this way, but I might have been mistaken. Just be alert. I'll be around most of the night."

"Bent on catching him?" Her tone had lost the hardness he'd first detected.

"You bet. Townsfolk don't feel safe with a robber amongst them."

She took a step to go around him, her signal indicating the conversation was over. "Good luck then, Deputy. You be careful, as well."

He dipped his chin and watched her fish her key out of her little brown bag. He'd lost his chance to tell her he'd looked inside. And what difference would the confession make, besides assuaging his guilt-ridden conscience?

She went inside and closed the door.

What must life be like, living in the tiny abode behind the establishment where you worked? The same four walls, day in and day out. He couldn't fathom. That was one aspect he liked about being deputy. Every day was different. And he was free to ride out to the Heart of the Mountains with a telegram or check on the lumber mill on Spring Street. Then he went home to his family, where Carlie was always excited to meet him with open arms and a big kiss. Life was sweet. He wondered what Lenore's connection was to the letter. He stood there a good three minutes, just thinking. When he saw Lenore's light wink out, he realized she might wonder why he hadn't gone.

"Come on, Major," he said and started off. "Let's get you back to the saloon so I can keep at my task. Our crook won't walk up and turn himself in." With one final look at Lenore's house, the two went down the alley and turned the corner.

Chapter Forty-Six

Feeling the worse for wear, Luke ran up the steps and under the portico gracing the front of St. John's Hospital. The three-story building loomed before him, the stones slick in the early morning mist. The turrets on each end of the red-brick structure were pointed, and a cross graced the top of each. Another cross capped the middle of the building where an open area allowed patients and visitors to go out and catch a breath of fresh air. Bells from the Catholic church a street over rang out for Sunday service as worshipers gathered for Mass.

Luke had ridden, hell-bent, through the night, praying every step of the way that Brandon had regained his strength, and what Luke had gone in search of—and was now tucked away in his satchel—wouldn't be needed. In his mind, Luke imagined walking into Brandon's room, seeing the bed gone, and the nurse telling him Brandon had made a miraculous recovery and was over at Mrs. Hardie's inn with the rest of his family, recuperating, as well as waiting for him to return before their long trip home.

Home.

Yes, Luke would be happy to get back home with his loved ones where they were safe and healthy and all this pain and worry was behind them.

Grasping the handle, Luke pulled open one of the double doors and removed his hat. Knowing the hospital layout well after their extended stay, he made a direct right and proceeded down the narrow hallway, dipping his chin at a surprised nurse as she approached. He still wore the fringed leather he'd purchased and hadn't shaved since he'd left. Windblown and unbathed, he must look a sight and was surprised the poor nun didn't turn and flee in the opposite direction. "Morning," he gritted out as they passed.

The hospital felt abandoned. No doctors. No brothers. Charity. Where was everyone? Almost to Brandon's room, he made a right and pulled up in front of the open door. Brandon *wasn't* there. Just like his vision, the room was quiet as a tomb. Shocked for a moment, he didn't know what to think. *Had* Brandon made a miraculous recovery? Had Luke's thoughts come true, or had he picked up on what was happening at the hospital while he'd been away?

Might something else have happened? his mind whispered. No, he wouldn't even think it.

Turning, he stared at the picture on the wall, having already seen the image many times before as he'd gone in and out of Brandon's room. The six Sisters of Charity from Leavenworth, Kansas, who'd come to Helena in 1869 to educate the youth, nurse the sick, and care for orphans. They'd been the inspiration and strength behind the hospital.

Feeling propelled by an invisible hand, he decided to cross the street to the Victorian but pulled up after hearing the well-known *tap-tap-tap* of a nun's hard-soled bootheels on the worn wooden flooring.

She came into sight.

"Excuse me, Sister," he called.

She'd reached a convergence of hallways and already turned in another direction. She appeared back around the corner.

When she saw him, her hand went to her throat.

"It's me, Luke McCutcheon." A bad feeling still rumbled in his gut. The stillness of the large building wasn't helping his concerns.

The fright on her face softened after hearing his name, and she swiftly approached.

Her usual smile was nowhere to be seen. He realized he'd spoken with her several times before as she'd tended to Brandon. In her hand was a stethoscope.

"I'm glad you've arrived back, Mr. McCutcheon," she said, her tone serious. "They're all on the second floor."

He didn't want to ask. "Second floor?"

"I'm sorry," she said, her tone now softened. "But your brother-in-law took a turn for the worse and is back in surgery. The doctors will tell you more."

"Why?" he asked forcefully. "Can't you say?"

Her eyes filled with compassion. "Doing so is against the rules. I've already said too much. I might give you incorrect information by mistake. Follow this hallway. The stairs at the end will take you to the second-floor surgery. You've been there before." She dipped her chin as she looked up at him. "I've been saying a rosary for Mr. Crawford. *And* your sister."

Charity! What does she mean? Has something more happened?

As he opened his mouth to ask, he felt her nudge his arm.

"You don't want to dawdle. Every moment is critical. God bless you and your family."

Feeling as if he'd just been punched in the gut, Luke sprinted down the hallway, not caring how much noise he made. The long-handled leather pouch Biting Horse had given him was slung over his chest and one shoulder and bounced against his side as he ran. At the commotion, another nun appeared in an open door and watched his approach, her face disapproving at all the noise he was creating.

Rounding the corner, he bounded up the steep stairs, his mind flashing in different directions. Was this really happening? Or was this a nightmare he'd wake up to praise God he'd imagined the whole thing? At the top, he glanced both ways.

Midway down the hallway, Matthew and Mark both bolted to their feet at his noisy arrival.

Breathing hard, he strode their way. “What’s going on?” His gaze went to the door of the surgery. A sign said Quiet in bold, black lettering. “Brandon’s in surgery?” He dropped his volume to a whisper. “Why?”

“It’s not good.” Mark shook his head. “He kept growing weaker. The doctors weren’t sure why.”

Both his brothers appeared worn out and defeated. He’d never seen them look so beaten. A McCutcheon always came out victorious. This wasn’t right. He glanced at Matt. “Tell me more. Where’s Charity? There’s no way she wouldn’t be here, unless something has happened.”

Matt nodded and put out his hand to the chairs lined against the wall. “Sit down, Luke. We have time to talk. We’ve been here for an hour already, and Brandon won’t be out for some time. The doctors suspect they might have missed something or didn’t remove all the infected area. Those are the only reasons they know of why he hasn’t improved. We’re not doctors to dispute them. We must trust what they say.”

Luke took a deep intake of air, tossed his Stetson onto one of the empty chairs, and collapsed down.

His brothers followed suit.

That *was* true. They couldn't second-guess the experts. Why come all this way and not do what they suggested? "All right. Where's Charity?"

"In bed at the Victorian. Sometime Friday morning, she experienced some pain and began to bleed." Matt's face was gray as death. "A good amount. Thankfully, she was in the hospital when it happened and was quickly seen by a doctor. She didn't lose the baby, but the doctor put her on complete bed rest. He thinks sitting with Brandon day in and day out was too much for her, in her condition. Mrs. Hardie is looking after her so we both can be here. Until this morning, and Brandon's second surgery, we've been staying with her. She's trying to be brave, but . . ."

Luke dropped his head into his hands, digging his fingers into his scalp. Fear streaked through him. What *else* could happen? Losing the baby, with Brandon on death's door, would crush her. She might ride and ranch like a man, but she was still his little sister, and her heart would be destroyed. He didn't like to think it. "How's she now? And does she know about Brandon?"

"She knows," Mark said. "Being Brandon's wife, she had to give permission for them to go ahead. And she insisted she wanted us over here with him. She's trying to keep a stiff upper lip, for the baby's sake, but we both feel"—Mark glanced at Matt—"she's ready to fall apart. We've never seen her so fragile."

Luke nodded. Of course, she was fragile. Who wouldn't be? He felt pretty fragile, himself.

"She's asked about you every time one of us goes to see her," Matthew said. "She's worried you won't return. Maybe you better take a few minutes and reassure her you're back and haven't been killed."

"Killed?" he barked quietly. "Surely, she doesn't think that."

They both nodded. "Surely, she does," Matt responded. "Go see her, Luke. Brandon won't be out for a long time."

What did you say to your little sister in the event her beloved husband might not live through his second surgery and she's fighting to keep her baby? As much as he wanted to see her, hold her in his arms, and quiet all her fears, he was skittish like a two-year-old feeling the saddle on his back for the first time. This was uncharted territory. He wished like hell Faith were here to tell him what to do, what to say.

"Go on, quit stalling." Mark handed him his hat. "Once you see her face, you'll find the right words. We've all been in your boots."

Chapter Forty-Seven

When the kettle sang out, Claire hurried from the front window toward the kitchen. She didn't want the sound to wake all her grandbabies, who were sound asleep upstairs. Faith, Rachel, and Amy, all worried about Brandon, had moved into the big house so they could console each other and help keep their minds from sinking into a pit of despair, as Amy had so rightly expressed. Each wife had taken their husband's old room and shared the bed with their younger children. The older children, Billy, Adam, Colton—and Dawn—after her persuasive speech on why she was old enough to sleep with her older cousins, even if they were all boys—were all crowded together into John's room. That child would grow up to be a lawyer, if not a ranch hand, which she proudly proclaimed every chance she got.

Claire smiled and shook her head, thinking about the spirited five-year-old. With each passing year, she saw more and more of Faith in Dawn's smile and eyes. In her determination, too. Luke would have his hands full when she hit her teens. Just like Charity. Claire was glad. Her antics would keep Luke on his toes. A man needed something of a challenge as he settled into his role of father and provider—so as not to get bored with his life.

Luke. Claire tried to tamp down her anxiety when she thought of her third son. As she poured hot water into her teacup, her hand jerked, and she spilled the scalding water onto the counter and splashed the floor. She jumped back and looked at the mess with dismay.

Harold had brought a telegram last evening, and because of it, she hadn't slept a wink. Now, up at four, Claire realized today would feel even more exhausting than the rest. The news stated Luke had ridden out by himself in search of a Cheyenne tribe he'd heard about camping somewhere around Helena. He hoped to find a medicine man who would return with him to the hospital. The telegram hadn't said how grave Brandon's condition must be, but the fact Luke felt compelled to try such an impossible deed said what the words did not. At the time the telegram had arrived, all her daughters-in-law had been upstairs, busy tucking the children into bed. Harold had come in and out in less than a minute, and Claire hadn't passed on the information, not even to Faith. She didn't see how adding another layer of worry was a benefit to anyone.

With a dishtowel, she cleaned up the spilled water and finished making her tea. The house was dark and quiet. Esperanza wouldn't be here until seven, because of all the children sleeping above. Let them rest.

Claire took a deep breath. Who would Luke

find? Fox Dancing? Possibly *Netchiwaan*? He'd been alive when Fox Dancing had shown up at Luke's barn party in June of '86. Then again, a year later, to help Luke escape from the burning jail cell. Claire's insides trembled. So many variables existed. Would the tribe, if Luke was successful in finding them, hurt him? Torture him? Maybe not knowing who he was? Or would he meet *Netchiwaan*? Luke must wish for that. She knew he loved Flood as his father, and no man, whoever he was, would ever take Flood's place in Luke's heart, but a chance to meet the man who'd sired him would be all-encompassing.

The memories came so fast, the forgotten teacup rattled in her hand. She made her way through the dark room to the large chair—Flood's chair—sitting closest to the cold hearth. The lamp they always left burning on the fireplace mantel gave the room a golden glow. Taking the thick, woolen throw folded across the back, she cuddled the warmth in her lap, wanting to thaw her chilled insides. Blowing on the hot tea, she took a tiny sip. A moment later, she closed her eyes and began to remember . . .

The first few moments of her abduction flashed through her mind. She'd been hanging out the wash on the line when the warriors rode into the yard. They must have known Flood was with the cattle, because they seemed unworried about their surroundings. Stifling a gasp, she bolted to the flowerbed where Matt and Mark, both just toddlers, sat in the dirt, playing with a spoon and some blocks. They didn't yet see the marauders and protested loudly when she yanked them up by their arms and half ran, half stumbled for the homestead door. She knew the gruesome stories of how warriors bashed the heads of white children on the rocks. Her legs felt weighted, as if sacks of sand were tied to each calf. Just as she pushed her boys inside, slammed the door, and was hefting down the bar, she saw a man reach through the small opening and grasp a handful of her hair. When he yanked, her head painfully struck the doorjamb. Stars danced before her eyes. She fell to the ground as he pulled her through. A second later, as he kicked her side, she heard the blessed thwack of the door bar landing into place. At least, the heathens wouldn't get her children. The frightening war cries had sliced through her mind, as real as when they'd happened.

Claire opened her eyes, her breathing labored. She blinked several times, trying to forget.

Beyond the window, the yard was still dark. Sunday morning had yet to arrive. Her heart thumped painfully against her breastbone. Looking down, she'd spilled more of the tea onto her lap robe. Carefully, she moved the cup with shaky hands to the small table beside the chair.

They'd ridden for hours that fateful night. Her

bound hands gripped the mane of the black-and-white horse, trying to keep balance, for she'd never before ridden bareback. The warrior who'd captured her had ripped her bodice and chemise when she wouldn't get up off the ground, knowing that as soon as she did, they might steal her away—and she'd never see Flood or her sons again. The torn garments gave the savages partial view of her bosom. Once the braves got her to her feet, she'd put up a fight, clawing and kicking. But then one punched her in the face, almost knocking her out. After that, she'd quieted and stopped struggling. She didn't want to be killed in the yard for Flood to find or for the boys to see from inside the homestead. A tinny slickness filled her mouth, and her side burned where he'd kicked her. She hadn't shared any of this with Flood or Luke. She'd take her secret to the grave. Along with the baby she'd only had suspicions about but lost three days later.

Where was Luke? Was he in trouble or worse? Over the year of her captivity, she had seen *Netchiwaan*'s brother, the medicine man, skillfully heal many people using nothing but herbs and other various plants. She'd seen well-being return with her own eyes. Could something so simple save Brandon? Or were everyone's lives planned out before their birth? Sometimes, the way her life had played out, she thought that might be so. If she'd not been abducted when she was young, she wouldn't have Luke, and the thought of life without Luke was something she didn't like to contemplate.

"Claire?"

Claire was jerked out of her thoughts.

Faith stood on the last step of the stairway, her long nightdress brushing the tops of her bare feet and a small blanket wrapped around her shoulders. "I hope I didn't startle you," she said in a hushed voice. "The pitcher in my room was almost dry, so I came for a glass of water. I couldn't sleep, anyway. Luke's been on my mind, as well as Brandon and Charity." She stepped forward. "But I didn't expect to find you up this early." She glanced around. "What time is it?"

"Must be quarter past four," Claire replied, thankful for a respite from her memories. Had her recollections and fear awakened Faith? Oh, how she loved this woman, as much as a true daughter.

"My goodness," she said, taking the chair on the other side of the hearth. "It's chilly in here. Should I build a fire? Might chase away some of our gloom."

The word fire recalled Claire's first night with the Cheyenne warriors. Nine of them had been present. The man who held the lead to her horse was the one who'd wrenched her from her life, the fiercest of the warriors, with narrowed eyes and several missing teeth. Scars covered his body, as if, at one time, he'd been mauled by a bear. Large sections of his scalp were gone, and she'd learned months later, after she'd been given to *Netchiwaan*, the renegade had indeed been attacked by a grizzly. The small band moved quickly, probably fearful Flood and a posse were tracking them. The higher they ascended in the mountain passes, the more quickly the temperature dropped. Nightfall had fallen before they made camp. How she'd survived, she didn't know. All she had for cover was her ripped dress. They'd taken her shoes, probably to keep her from trying to escape. The men lay close to a small-flame campfire, but she was left several feet away on the cold, hard ground, her wrists, and now her ankles, bound together. All she could think about were Flood and her boys. What would happen? Would she ever see them again? Freezing pains tormented her feet and hands while she cried inwardly. Numbness crippled her, especially her heart. Had Flood returned to the ranch to find the boys crying in the house? Were Matthew and Mark okay? Had they somehow been hurt in the attack or hurt themselves alone in the cabin? Would they remember this horrible day as the last time they'd seen their mother? The painful thoughts were too much. She'd allowed herself silent tears as she gazed at the stars above. The same wondrous sky she and Flood had studied with such love and admiration only the night before.

"Claire?"

Faith had risen and was touching her arm.

"I'm sorry," she said. "I've a lot on my mind. Did you say something, dear?"

"I asked if I should build a fire. But now I'm going to, after feeling your freezing skin. You're chilled to the bone."

Claire went to rise.

But Faith gently held her to her seat. "You've worn yourself out caring for all of us, women and grandchildren, alike. We don't want *you* to get sick. You stay put, and I can easily light this fire. Luke makes sure I can take care of myself, as well as the children, in case anything were ever to happen to him." Faith blinked and looked away.

Claire knew she was thinking how fast everything had changed for Brandon and Charity. What would Charity do if she became a young widow and had to raise their child alone? She'd never be the same. The thought was too heartbreaking to consider.

Chapter Forty-Eight

With the arrival of Sunday morning, and Abe still weak as a newly hatched chick, Fancy nailed up a notice on the front doors of the saloon. Closed. It was the first time the saloon had been closed on what Abe classified as a workday. The saloon stayed open seven days a week. Perhaps that's why Abe was so sick. His body needed a little time off. With the hammer still in her hand, she glanced up and down the quiet street.

Y Knot had been her home for the past two years. The town was much like others where she'd lived, in size and makeup, but she had found a measure of happiness in the walls of the Hitching Post—as much happiness a woman of her profession could, anyway. She had nothing to complain about. Abe was a good boss, and he pretty much left her to her own, pertaining to work. Looking at the sign, she felt a pinch of guilt, but not enough to make her change her mind. What Abe didn't know wouldn't hurt him. She'd take the day and give the place a good cleaning. When she'd been doing both her and Abe's job, she'd had to let things go.

Lenore came out of the hotel across the street and, stepping quickly, left the boardwalk to cut the deserted road diagonally, heading for the butcher shop. The restaurant must have run out of bacon or other meat. As if Lenore felt Fancy's gaze, she turned her head, and their eyes met. Lenore gave a small smile and raised her hand in greeting. Then she turned back and hurried on her way.

A moment later, Cole stepped out of the hotel doors, as well. Immediately looking Fancy's direction, he grinned. Crossing the road, he headed toward her, his stride eating up the distance between them.

She held her breath, wondering what he wanted on this early Sunday morning. He'd stayed until closing last night and then helped her clean up. They'd kept the conversation light, only speaking about the bar or Abe and what needed to be done. But every time she'd looked at him, she couldn't but help remember him all those years ago.

"Good morning, Fancy." Cole touched the brim of his tan hat. He glanced at the Closed sign on the door and raised his eyebrows. "What's this? Is Abe feeling worse?"

She shook her head. The longer she stayed out on the boardwalk, the more attention she'd attract. She'd meant to come out, tack up the sign, and disappear back inside. "We're staying closed for the whole day," she said, a bit defensively. She dared not look him directly in the eye, for all the feelings doing so created. She needed to keep a level head. "With Abe down, I need some time to give the place a good clean, restock bottles, and wash the place up properly. Each day, I get a little more behind."

He chuckled. "I can't imagine any drunk minding a sticky tabletop or smudged glass. And especially not if they must wait a whole day to get a snoot full."

She put one hand on her hip. "They might not, but I do. I can't abide this place when it goes to the dogs."

His eyes brightened. "Then, in that case, I'm glad I came over this morning. Let me help. I've nothing better to do. And when we're finished, which will be a lot quicker than if you worked alone, I'll take you on a buggy ride. How long since you got out?"

At the sight of two riders coming up the street, she turned and stepped inside.

He followed close.

She quickly shut the door. "I'm not taking a buggy ride with you, Cole Mercer. I don't do *those* kinds of things. And I'm not accepting any more help from you in the saloon, either."

His gaze slowly went from her lips up to her eyes and lingered. "You won't run me off, Fancy," he said softly, a look of determination on his face. "I've been hunting for you since I left the army. Your pledge of love stayed with me my whole life. Got me through those twenty lonely years. Thank you."

His smile pulled up a little higher on one side, and she was tempted to glance away. He always was the most handsome man she'd ever seen. He'd aged, but the lines on his forehead and around his eyes added to his attractiveness. She wondered how he'd gotten the scar on the corner of his bottom lip. His crowfeet deepened as she studied his face.

"What do you want to do first?" he asked. "Where's the mop bucket?"

Knocking came on the door behind them.

"Fancy? You in there?"

Glad for the reprieve from his earnest eyes and smile, Fancy turned to the door. "Jack?"

"Why'd you close the Hitching Post? It's Sunday, and I'm thirsty."

"Sorry, but you won't drink here today. I have chores to do, and I made the decision to stay closed. Don't badger me, Jack. My mind's made up."

"I saw Mercer go in there."

"Mind your own business," she responded. "Go to church. Maybe it'll do you some good."

All the while she was speaking through the door, Cole stood there watching, a humorous tilt to his brow.

"Fine," Jack said stiffly and then chuckled. "But you don't have to be mean." A moment later, his footsteps on the wooden boardwalk could be heard walking away.

Reaching for the door, Fancy fully intended to kick Cole out, as well. She had a surplus of hard work to get done and didn't need any distractions. If she fiddle-faddled her time away, why close at all? Who knew how long Abe would be sick.

Cole gently caught her wrist. "Don't," he said. "Allow someone in your life, Fancy. Let that someone be me."

Losing my heart to Cole will be disastrous. He'll get bored one day and disappear. He'll be on to a new life, but I'll never be the same. My life is good as is. Each day begins and ends the same. I like the monotony. That way, I never have any surprises to work around.

She shook her head. "Nothin' doing, Cole Mercer. I'm a mature woman, not the starry-eyed girl when we first met. I'm smarter. Tougher. The last thing I need in my life is a man. I'm good on my own and aim to stay that way." She gave a small smile. "Sorry to disappoint you, sugar."

Cole arched a crooked eyebrow. "As beautiful as you are, Fancy, you're cantankerous, too. Have you always been like that? I only knew you as a girl."

"Cantankerous?" She gazed at his hand, still holding her wrist. The sight made her insides quivery. "Is that what I am?"

"That, and a few things more."

"That girl you're enamored with is long gone—and she's not coming back." Fancy allowed her gaze to wander the room, saying the things she didn't want to spell out. He was a man and knew the score.

"None of this makes a whit of difference to me."

Cole let his hand fall away and came a step closer, close enough she could see the flecks of gold in his green eyes, even in the shadowy barroom. He might be older, but he was just as handsome as she remembered. She recognized that *something* she'd seen inside him all those years ago, something way down deep. Fear and excitement sliced through her veins. Worried he'd see just how much his closeness affected her, she took a tiny step back.

Boots clomped up to the door outside and stopped. The door handle rattled violently and then a few choice curse words filled the air. "What the hell's this about?" Sam Green hollered through the barrier and rattled the door again. "Closed! The Hitching Post is *never* closed. On Sunday—or whenever."

Cole put a finger to his lips.

He'd gussied up and looked nice. Up close like this, she detected a hint of spiced cologne, as well as the aroma of the coffee and syrup he must have had for breakfast. A moment of longing stirred. Having Sunday breakfast in the hotel, in the midst of a crowd of people talking . . .

"Fancy," Sam shouted. "Open up!"

The humor in Cole's eyes dissolved. He gently

set her behind him, and before she realized what he was about, he wrenched open the door, grasping a surprised Sam Green by his shirt front and yanking him close. They were nose to nose.

"Can't you read?"

"Yes."

"The sign says closed. So, hit the road."

Sam glared back, not moving an inch.

"I don't like you," Cole growled. "I don't appreciate the way you talk to Fancy. And I *don't* like the way you think you own this place. The Hitching Post is *closed!* Period. Now, if you want a beatdown on a Sunday morning, just open your mouth. If not, take your stinking hide out of my sight."

Fancy had to bite the inside of her cheek to keep from laughing. She'd never seen Sam at a loss for words.

Cole shoved Sam Green away.

On his propelled movement backward, he caught his heel on the boardwalk and fell on his butt.

Fancy was shocked when he didn't cuss or challenge Cole.

The man climbed to his feet, dusted himself off, and took himself back down the street as if nothing untoward had happened.

"You shouldn't have, Cole. You've made an enemy," she said, proud as all-get-out when he came in and closed the door.

He dramatically dusted his hands as if he'd just

taken out the trash. "No?" He smiled into her eyes. "He's had that coming for days. Actually, it felt good." He glanced around and began rolling up his sleeves. "Where do we start?"

She eyed him for all of five seconds and then smiled. "First thing is me checking on Abe and getting him fed, then I'm starting down here. I intend to give the saloon a good scrubbing from top to bottom."

"And then?"

She stifled her smile. Why was he persisting? She thought she might know but didn't like second-guessing herself. Her life was set. No changing could happen now. "Cole, I don't want to lead you on. Nothing can come of you helping me or sweet talking me. Or you spending your days in here, keeping me company."

He'd been looking out the window after something outside had made a noise. At her pronouncement, he turned back to her, slowly taking in her face as his gaze traveled from her lips up to her eyes. His crooked smile reappeared. "You might think that, Fancy. But I aim to change your mind. I'm not getting any younger myself. I'm not the green colt who you mesmerized all those years ago by proclaiming your never-dying love. I long for a helpmate at my side. I've decided you're her."

A feeling like warm honey spread through her being. "I won't give you a family."

He chuckled. “You’re not past that—even if you like to think it.”

“No child wants a barmaid for a mother, Cole. And especially not an *old* barmaid. That would be shameful.”

His gaze softened. “I never said anything about children. I said a wife.”

A hard knot of emotion stopped her response as she gazed into his eyes. There’d be no controlling Cole Mercer, she realized, so why even try?

Chapter Forty-Nine

Madison sat at the window of her hotel room, sulking. The slow progress of the Sunday morning townsfolk on the boardwalk kept her mind from spinning off into a thousand different directions. She'd been to church and now just wanted to be alone. She was no closer to finding her mother than when she'd left Kentucky.

Berta May had been at the church service this morning, as well as Lou and Bethanne Payne. She hadn't seen Lynette or Saralee Hicks or their children. Of all her possibilities, she realized she hoped her mother was Bethanne. Why was that? She knew Mrs. Payne the least out of everyone.

I adore Berta May; she's been kind and helpful since I've arrived. And I like Lou, too. As painful as the thought is to admit, I don't think I want my mother to turn out to be Lynette or Saralee Hicks. I'm a terrible person! I'm judging people on how they look and what they have. I don't mean to. Do I prefer Bethanne because she's tall and stately? Because she's the wife of a banker and makes a good appearance—and for what she's not?

Madison stood and paced across the room.

Do I think so highly of myself? I sound like Pauline and the dreadful way she treated Fancy Aubrey on Friday outside the mercantile. She practically ran from the saloon woman's presence. My mother could be any one of these women or even someone else. Justin said I might be wrong about the letter. I should remind myself, my mother hasn't invited me back into her life. Who am I to judge? Shame on me, shame on me . . . Who would want a horrible daughter like me?

Turning, she fell backward onto her bed and stared up at the ceiling. The gnawing girlhood uncertainties rushed back with force, gripping her chest. Her heartbeat raced painfully, causing her to gasp for breath. The ugly monster had first emerged after she'd learned she was adopted. No wonder her mother had given her away. She wasn't worthy of anyone's love.

Tears leaked from Madison's eyes, wetting the quilt as she gripped the fabric beneath her. She needed air. She needed to breathe. Why now? She hadn't had an episode in several years. She'd thought she was past the pain.

Forcing herself to calm, she sucked air in through her nose and held her breath, slowly counting to thirty. She thought of Justin and the way his smile made her feel. Closing her eyes, she gradually let the air slip away. She felt better, lying quietly for several minutes.

She needed to pull herself together. The only one she could talk to, who could help her make any sense out of her life, was Justin. He hadn't been at church. Had he stayed away on purpose, not wanting to see her? Had his aunt swayed him?

Thinking of him and her at the picnic last Sunday was the only way she could settle her racing heart. She had to fight against her self-incrimination. She must, or she'd never get anywhere.

A soft knock came on her door.

Madison swallowed down her grief and wiped her eyes. "Yes?"

"It's me, Hildy. I'm sorry to disturb you, but Justin is downstairs and wondered if you'd mind coming down? If you're tired, and would rather not, he said he'd see you another time."

Justin.

Pulling herself together, she stood. Should she open the door? Surely, her eyes were red, and Hildy would wonder why she was sad.

"Madison?"

"Yes, I'm here. I'm just resting." She needed to open the door. Besides Justin, Hildy was her closest friend. Madison could hear the worry in her voice. "One moment, please." Madison wiped her eyes again, softly blew her nose, and walked to the door.

Hildy's eyes went wide. "Is everything all right?" she asked tentatively.

Madison nodded. She hated to tell falsities anymore, but she had no other option. "I'm just feeling a little homesick. I've been here almost two weeks and haven't had a letter from home or my girlfriends from college. I'm sure something will arrive tomorrow."

Hildy's expression warmed. "I understand completely. No need to feel embarrassed." She reached out and rubbed Madison's arm. "How about I tell Justin you'll be down in a few minutes? He looks spruced up, and I believe he arrived in a buggy. I'm talking over myself, because I'm not sure of anything, but I think he wants to take you on a Sunday drive."

Hildy was so dear. For her, Madison was able to manage a smile. In doing so, the old, black feeling inside began to shrink until the dusky mist finally disappeared. "Yes, thank you. That's perfect." She ran her hand down the front of her Sunday dress. "I'm still dressed from church, and I'll just touch up my hair."

The quiet hush of two people whispering in the hallway made Hildy look over her shoulder. She was such a pretty girl. Madison wondered about her and her background.

Hildy turned back. "Arrived a few minutes ago," she murmured with a conspiratorial smile. "Newlyweds. I don't believe they're from around here."

See? A big world is out there, and Madison best remember that when she started to feel down. Would the end of the world crash around her ears if she never found her mother? Her heart tried to say yes, but she inwardly gave herself a scolding.

No, it won't. Life waits for no one. A saying her adoptive mother loved. *Make the most out of every day—and smile in the process*.

Yes, Mother, she thought and put on a smile. She'd been given a beautiful adoptive mother. One she'd never forget. One who had nurtured her love and creativity for the first seven years of her life. She'd been blessed.

And now, Justin was waiting for her downstairs. A girl couldn't get luckier than that.

Justin paced the lobby of Cattlemen's, feeling strung as tight as a guitar. He'd debated with himself for fifteen minutes whether he should seek out Madison before he knew more about Lenore and the letter. He didn't want to give her false hope. Lenore was too young to be Madison's mother. Something strange was going on in Y Knot, and he aimed to find out what. Until then, he hadn't been able to stay away. He'd missed church service, but Aunt Pauline told him, only after he'd asked, that Madison attended and sat with Berta May. He hadn't seen Madison since Friday, when she'd come into his office after her upsetting confrontation with his aunt and the fact she hadn't been able to see who'd taken the letter.

I know who took it, but I can't say.

Frustrated, Justin glanced around the quiet

room. The large potbelly stove all the lodgers warmed by during the hellacious blizzard last winter now sat cold and empty. Sounds of people eating drifted in from the dining room. He yanked down the ends of his suitcoat, feeling conspicuous, then ran his finger around his collar, made snug by a narrow black tie. Today was Sunday, after all. And he was calling on a beautiful young woman.

Trent Herrick came through the doors and pulled up, his crooked smile inching up his face.

Justin gave him a look of warning.

"I didn't say a thing," Trent said as he glanced around. "Is Hildy here?"

Wonderful. Now Justin would have to say she'd gone to fetch Madison, and everyone would know his business. At least, he'd worn his Colt but left his bullwhip at home. Didn't quite feel right for courting. "She is. She's gone upstairs for a moment."

"Oh?"

"To give Madison a message for me."

Trent hooked a thumb over his shoulder, his eyes widening. "That buggy out there yours?"

The sound of speculation in Trent's tone brought heat to Justin's face. "It is. What of it?"

"Stop being so touchy. Nothin' wrong with going for a buggy ride on Sunday. I think it's commendable."

Justin shifted his weight. "You do, do you?"

Trent nodded.

At the sound of footsteps descending the stairs, they both looked up.

When Hildy saw Trent, she blushed and blinked several times. She turned to Justin. "She'll be right down."

"Thank you," Justin mumbled, feeling stupid without his hat, his whip, and wearing these fancy duds. Maybe this wasn't such a good idea. When he'd told her he was going out, he'd received one of Aunt Pauline's censuring stares. She hadn't asked with whom, because why would she? Justin hadn't been interested in anyone except Madison since coming to Y Knot. He'd be sorely pressed if she got discouraged and returned to Kentucky. Last night, he'd tossed and turned, trying to figure out how he felt. But that was ridiculous. He knew. His heart knew. She'd come to town, and he'd fallen. That was it. If she didn't find her mother and returned to Kentucky, she'd take his heart, as well.

He turned to the window, not wanting to intrude on Trent and Hildy, who were speaking quietly at the end of the counter. She gave a soft laugh.

Then Trent chuckled.

A sound on the stairs made him turn.

Madison approached, looking rested. She was dressed in a pretty blue dress he'd not seen before, and his heart gave a little leap. "Madison," he said, in a sound of awe. "Thanks for coming down. I hope I didn't disturb your Sunday." He felt her smile all the way down to his boots.

"Not at all. I'm happy you came by. I was a little lonely in my room." She glanced around.

The silence became awkward. "I rented a buggy from June, and if you'd like, I thought we could take a ride. Or, if you haven't eaten, we can get a bite either here or at the Biscuit Barrel." This felt different than their prior friendship. He didn't want to spoil what they already shared.

"A buggy ride sounds lovely. I've not been since arriving. Thank you." She glanced out the window and smiled.

But he got the impression she was sad. "In that case, your carriage awaits." He gestured toward the door. "Thanks again, Hildy," he called. "Trent." Outside, and with her hand in his, Justin assisted Madison into the buggy, feeling excited, and yet thoughtful, too. What would her reaction be if she knew he was keeping some information from her? Would she understand? She looked beautiful and rested, but he noticed a kind of melancholy sense about her. And, if he wasn't mistaken, her eyes were somewhat red. Had she been crying?

Both now settled, he lifted the lines and clucked to the mare. Passing the jail, he made a right-hand turn onto Half Hitch Street, passed the butcher shop, and approached the schoolhouse. Other than the supper at his house, and then the picnic, they'd never really made plans to be together. She was being especially quiet, confirming her gloomy mood. The buggy caught a rock and violently rattled as he searched for something to say.

"Oh!" she gasped, a small smile appearing. "This can be bumpy."

Justin slapped the lines once, and the horse extended her trot, making the ribbons in Madison's hair sail freely out behind her. "Going left," he said as they veered onto the road taking them to the fossil field a quarter mile away. If they continued, the road eventually led to the Heart of the Mountains Ranch. Now out of town, he asked for more speed and clucked several times.

Madison laughed and gripped the side of the conveyance with one hand and the front bar with her other, her face alight with excitement. "Where on earth are you taking me, Justin?" she said loudly, to be heard over the horse's trotting hooves and the spinning wheels. "I can't imagine."

"Have you heard Y Knot has some fossils close by? Thought you'd like to take a look."

"Yes, I have. How exciting. I've been meaning to ask you about them. Hildy told me, and Ethel, too, at the Biscuit Barrel."

"Good. I thought some fresh air out of doors

would be nice. I wasn't sure if you'd be working today—but I thought I'd ask."

She looked at the horse, the buggy, and then him, amusement in her eyes and her lips softly smiling. "That was a lot of trouble, if I had been working." She let go and touched his arm. "Thank you."

He felt like a rat for not telling her right away about the letter. He returned her mischievous look, hoping she felt the same warm stirrings inside, sitting so close and having a private conversation. "We'll be there soon. Don't worry."

"I'm not worried at all. I'm enjoying the ride immensely. I can see why Ashley said she liked driving the buggy on the day of the picnic." She lifted a brow. "Do you think I might drive on the way back to town?"

Was the thought of driving the buggy making her so animated? He'd hoped his closeness was the reason. At least, she didn't look sad anymore. "Of course, you can."

The road swerved like a snake, so Justin asked for a little more speed, making Madison sway to his side. She connected with his shoulder. Shamelessly, he passed the right line to his left hand and steadied her with an arm across her back. She laughed and looked at him, seeming not to notice at all. Farther on, the road curved the other way, and he had to relinquish her to take the lines and direct the horse. Beyond, they climbed a small rise and then slowed under the shade of a line of trees. “Whoa,” he called, taking back on the lines.

The mare slowed, came down to a jog, and then a walk. They halted under the cottonwood.

Madison grinned from ear to ear.

Stroking his chin, he regarded her carefully, lifting one brow. “I’m happy to see your smile has returned. I don’t like to see you sad. You had me worried.”

Neither of them made a move to get out.

“Do you want to tell me about it? What has you so down?”

She glanced into his face. “I’m amazed you could tell.”

With a finger under her chin, he tipped up her face so he could see into her eyes. “I’m not amazed. I haven’t known you long, Madison, but I feel like I know you well. The fact you’ve shared so much makes me feel close. I hope you don’t mind.”

She shook her head. “I was a little homesick earlier today.”

He gazed at her, waiting, sure there was more to it. She just wasn’t ready to say. After a moment, and her not volunteering anything more, he set the brake and wrapped the lines around the bar on the dash. He climbed out, circled around, and helped her down.

The two of them walked out into the field to

the sound of birds and the soft sigh of the wind in the treetops. The way the sun played in her hair reminded Justin of something, and the delighted sparkle in her blue eyes and the dainty slope of her nose brought *someone* to mind. Who? He couldn't figure it out. Surprised he'd never noticed before, he wondered if it was her mother. Lenore Saffelberg's brown hair, the color always reminding Justin of a mushroom cap, didn't match Madison's in the least, nor did her features. Maybe he'd been going about this all wrong. Maybe Madison's mother was right under their noses.

Chapter Fifty

From the large goose down bed, Charity gazed out her bedroom window, her mind and heart across the street with Brandon. Surgery on a Sunday? Was Brandon strong enough to go through another procedure and live? He'd already lost so much weight. How she wished she could erase that fateful day. She wanted her old life back, when all she had to do was take care of her handsome husband and plan for the arrival of their child. Her eyes prickled. Why couldn't she have gone to the hospital, just for a few hours? She'd feel much better being close to him.

Mrs. Hardie sat by the bedside, her knitting needles going *clickity-clack.*

Surely, the woman had better things to do today instead of keeping Charity company—and from falling apart. Matt and Mark had left two hours ago after Matt had returned with news. Brandon needed a second operation. The physicians required her permission before they would proceed.

The door creaked, and she glanced over. Recognizing Luke as he peeked in, she smiled, her heart leaping with joy at his return.

When he saw she was awake, he opened the door farther and stepped inside.

Mrs. Hardie folded her work and stood.

Everyone seemed afraid to ask.

"Charity." Luke set his hat onto a chair as he crossed the room. He was at her side in seconds.

Mrs. Hardie waited, her hands clasped together in front of her skirt.

"I don't have any new news," he said. "I returned to the hospital, and Matt and Mark filled me in on what's been happening since I left. Brandon is still in surgery."

Luke's much-beloved tone felt like a warm, comforting breeze drifting over her.

He carefully sat on the side of her bed.

"I'll be going now, Charity," Mrs. Hardie said. "If you need anything, please don't hesitate to send your brother. And, Mr. McCutcheon, if you want to go back over to the hospital at any time, just let me know. I'm happy to stay with Charity. She's a good patient."

Luke smiled and arched one eyebrow. "Are we talking about the same woman?" he asked in all seriousness. "Charity's been a handful since she was five years old." He sent her a teasing smile. "I can't see why she'd amend her ways now."

Mrs. Hardie laughed and waved away his comment. At the door, she turned back. "When did you last eat?"

Luke didn't instantly answer.

"I thought as much. I'll have a tray for you in minutes. You must be famished." Before anyone could say different, she was out the door, pulling it closed.

Now alone, and with Luke back safe and alive, Charity couldn't stop her eyes from filling. Frustration burned through her. She'd thought all her tears were gone—but lately, crying was all she seemed to do. She must face reality. Tears wouldn't change anything. Still, when Luke turned back her way, she sat forward and into the arms he offered. Just like when she was a little girl, all her fears and insecurities were chased away. "I was frightened your leaving meant Brandon would die," she said softly against his neck. "I know that's illogical, but I was."

"I'm sorry he went back into surgery. But he's strong. He'll pull through."

Had her brothers told him about the baby, and what had almost happened? "Did they mention—"

He stroked her hair. "They did. But now you're fine, and nothing more is going to happen. Kick all those fearful thoughts out of your head. You'll be up in a day or two."

"Did you speak with a doctor?"

Luke sat back and looked into her face. "Well, no. I just know. You're a McCutcheon first and a Crawford second. That says it all."

Her gaze dropped to a small buckskin bag Luke carried, the long strap looped across his chest. "You must have found the Cheyenne."

He nodded. “I did. But they no longer have a medicine man. Biting Horse, a knowledgeable woman who has been doctoring, gave me some herbs we can make into a fortifying tea. She insists the concoction will help and absolutely won’t hurt—”

Charity reached out. “May I see?”

With a worn-out smile, he lifted the long strap over his head.

His face was rugged from hours in the elements. A light beard covered his jaw. Lines fanned out from the corners of his eyes, and the occasional grooves on his forehead were becoming permanent. Luke, to her astonishment, was aging. Maturing into someone else, who was as dearly loved as her dashing, half-Cheyenne hero. Oh, how she loved her brother, and thanked God he’d returned to them alive.

“Be careful, they’re all mixed. We’re to steep a spoonful for at least fifteen to twenty minutes. Feed him as much as he’ll take.” He gave her an amused smile. “The Cheyenne don’t measure much or are too concerned about timing. The tea will reduce his fever and help him grow stronger as it fights the infection.”

“Do you know what herbs and such?” She couldn’t keep the suspicion out of her tone. She didn’t want to insult Luke, but *everything* made her wary, even the medical procedures across the road.

"Her English wasn't perfect, but I caught some of it. Red clover for inflammation, buck brush, also known as hummingbird blossom, again for inflammation. Saw palmetto to promote Brandon's appetite in his recovery. Willow bark and meadowsweet to reduce fever. A little devil's claw for his digestive tract."

Charity sucked in a breath. "I'm impressed."

"So was I. Time will be the judge. Almost forgot cattail, too. Supposed to fortify and aid his recovery."

She reached up and, for a moment, laid a hand on his stubbled, windblown cheek. "Thank you, Luke. I'm touched you went to all this trouble for Brandon. He'll be so appreciative, as well, when he finds out." She swallowed, hoping she'd get to be the one to tell him. "I'm so grateful you returned safely."

"I'd do *anything* for Brandon and you, too, Charity."

She nodded. "Did you see Fox Dancing? Or Painted Bear Stone?"

Luke shook his head. "They were away."

"Were you able to communicate?"

"To a degree. I'll have to thank Fox Dancing when I see her for the few words she taught me. They came in handy." He gave a pointed stare. "You need to rest. Try to sleep."

"I'm relieved you're back, Luke. Go down and eat. Mrs. Hardie has made you something satisfying. Then, take a few hours yourself and sleep. If I know you, you haven't slept since you left."

He stood. "I don't need sleep, but food's a different matter. I'm sure you've heard my stomach grumbling about being empty."

She nodded and laughed softly. "A time or two." With her brother back, she'd indulge herself and even try to sleep. Put out of her mind wondering when news about Brandon would arrive.

Chapter Fifty-One

With a great sense of accomplishment, Flood hollered and hawed at the livestock as they rammed and knocked into each other, scrambling to fit through the gate and into the stockyard corral. When one pen filled, they moved to the next. Dust swirled in the air, and the sun beat down on their heads. The bawling steers made hearing yourself think near to impossible. This was the last of them, and Flood couldn't be more anxious to get off his horse and clean up. As much as he'd enjoyed every day of this cattle drive, and the comradery of the men, he was bone-weary and ached from head to toe. He looked forward to sleeping in his own bed, next to Claire—but to do that, he'd have to get through these final days first. A night next to Claire was still a good week or more off.

Smokey and Roady were on the other side of the gate, making sure the cattle kept filling the corral.

He and Shad worked this side, keeping the moving stream of livestock scrambling forward.

The other men were doing the same in other locations.

Flood slapped a fly from his sweaty neck and grinned at Shad, who'd just spurred his horse forward when a bald-faced two-year-old with a bent ear had tried to break out of the line and make a run for it.

They'd reached the outskirts of Miles City about two hours earlier but had taken their time not to rush the cattle at the end of their journey. They'd moved them nice and slow around civilization. Nothing worse than to get them this far with no mishaps, and then have a calamity where some unknown, unsuspecting person was injured or killed.

The men were looking forward to their time off in Miles City. He was anticipating a long, hot bath, a two-inch-thick steak in the best restaurant in town, as well as a whiskey, and then a soft bed. He'd earned it. His *old bones* had earned it. No wonder his boys liked to hit the trail so much. The hard work made the rest and relaxation feel so good. Even with all the aches and pains, he'd loved every moment of the drive.

Pedro rode up from behind and, in the confusion, bumped Ace, Flood's gelding, with his own horse.

Flood looked around.

"*Patron*," Pedro called loudly.

"What is it, Pedro?"

Ace, doing his job, jumped forward when another steer tried to break free, and successfully cut him back into line. The unexpected jolt almost unseated Flood. A pain flashed up his backbone, and he let out a grunt. This was why he didn't allow distractions around the cattle. They were unpredictable. He reined around for a second to be able to hear.

"Sorry, *Patron*," Pedro yelled. "You have a message waiting. *Important* message." He shrugged and frowned. "In the stockyard office." Pedro's gaze followed the bovine as the animals rammed and lumbered ahead, loudly bawling with each step they took.

Important message? Fear streaked through Flood. Claire usually waited for him to send a telegram home stating everyone arrived safe and sound, and then she'd reply. This was something else entirely. Had something dire happened? A thousand and one frightening possibilities sped through his mind. His children and grandchildren. All his daughters-in-law and Brandon. Claire, too! His ranch hands. *Hickory!* Every single person in his life was irreplaceable. Precious. A rare and cherished individual. With a constricted heart filled with fear, all he could do now was pray. "Thanks, Pedro. If you'll take my place, I'll go see what this is all about."

Twenty minutes after Flood had ridden off, leaving Pedro to work with him, Shad stepped off his horse and ran his bandanna over his sweaty face. Grub and a bath were going to feel so good. Saddle weary, he led his horse toward the outbuildings where the rest of the Heart of the Mountains ranch hands were waiting for Flood to return. Word had spread. They'd have a meeting as soon as they were all together.

"What do you think?" Jonathan Burg asked, a hand-rolled cigarette dangling from his lips. The smoke hung in a cloud around his head on this windless day.

Roady and Chance, both husbands and fathers, had taken off to find Flood as soon as they'd heard their boss had received an urgent message.

The rest of the men just waited, wondering what was afoot, hoping for the best.

Shad lifted a shoulder. "I'm sure we'll find out soon enough." He looked at Tanner, who was slumped against a fence post. At his age, nothing much rattled him.

The shrill ring of the chuck wagon triangle clanged through the air.

"That must be Ike, with coffee." Shad glanced around and then over the stock pens. "Where's he parked? Anyone know?"

"Back the way we come," Smokey answered. "Maybe an eighth of a mile. Saw him pull over as I drove in the last of the steers. You goin' for coffee?"

"Naw," Shad replied. "I'm waiting. Flood should be back anytime." He flexed his tight shoulders, hoping all was well in Y Knot and the ranch.

"Here he comes," Pedro called.

Chance and Roady followed alongside.

The men gathered up.

Shad watched as Tanner stood and ambled over, his face ruddy from sun and work. His brother had grown up two-fold since hiring on at the Heart of the Mountains.

Flood's face was grave as he strode toward them, his gaze on the ground in front of his boots. His clothes were covered in a sheen of fine dust, and he had a smudge on one of his sweat-stained cheeks. His old chaps he loved so much flapped around his legs. Where he'd been filled with energy before, talking about the cattle drive and enjoying the campsite talk, even on the last day, now he just looked old and tired.

Chance and Roady stood, one on each side.

"Men," Flood began, his stance wide with authority. "I've received word from Y Knot. There's bad news about Brandon. He's taken a turn for the worse. Doc said he twisted something inside when he fell. Surgery is required, lest he die. This message is quite a few days old."

If not for the lowing of the cattle, Shad would have heard the descent of silence. Instead, he read the fear on all the men's faces. None of them had ever had an operation. Setting of bones, yes, as well as bullets dug out, extractions of slivers, bandaging of puncture wounds, lancing of boils, curing a colicky stomach, and pulling of teeth.

But Shad couldn't remember anyone having an operation.

"Did Handerhoosen do the procedure?" Jon asked, his hands clenched at his sides.

Flood shook his head. His chest heaved out as he took in a deep breath. "No. Said he couldn't. Sent him to Helena, where there's said to be a good hospital with excellent surgeons."

Downhearted murmurings went around the group. Every face looked as grave as death itself. Shad couldn't imagine Brandon being incapacitated. Seeing him in a cast was strange enough. The day Shad had gone into the ranch house to pay his respects, just seeing him lying in bed with his leg propped up on pillows, dark circles under his eyes on a pale face, and a whisker-covered jaw, had been a shock. Last year, Brandon had requested Shad stay at Cattlemen's Hotel when the blizzard hit and watch over everyone. The responsibility the sheriff had trusted him with had won Shad's loyalty and admiration. Sheriff Brandon Crawford was a man to be reckoned with, not one to die in the prime of his life.

"How'd he get to Helena with his broken leg and insides twisted?" Smokey asked, giving a long, low whistle. "That's a long trip. Last I saw him, he was in bed upstairs at the big house. Didn't look as if he could move an inch." He shook his head. "Poor Brandon."

"All my boys went. Matt, Mark, and Luke. Charity went, too. Francis rode along as far as Waterloo to help carry Brandon onto the train and then to bring back the wag—" Flood's voice broke, and he cut his gaze away. He struggled for a few moments, grappling with his emotions. "Wagon," he finally finished. "They built a platform, so Brandon could recline on the train."

For the first time since Shad had met him, Flood McCutcheon looked beaten.

"He's in a lot of pain," Flood went on. "And his chances aren't good. I'd be grateful," he said in a hoarse whisper, "if you'd keep him in your prayers. Charity, too. I'm sure she's suffering. Can't be easy, with her in a delicate way."

Shad didn't know where to look. "Will do, Boss," he said. "What's *our* orders? How can we help? With all them gone, the ranch is pretty shorthanded. Not many to hold down the fort, so to speak."

"That's what I'm getting to. I've checked the train schedule, and I'm heading to Helena in about an hour. I know I promised all you men a few days off, and I feel mighty bad about going back on my word, but I'd feel better if you'd head straight home. Well, after your horses rest a few hours, and you get a good steak meal. I don't like Claire and the women, and all my grandbabies, at the ranch with three men and a boy. I know they're not alone . . ."

"No need for more words," Pedro said. "We all feel the same."

Flood nodded. "Good. I believed you would. Chance and Roady will stay back and finish up at the stock office and collect payment on the cattle, then set off. That'll take a day or two more." He nodded at both men. "They're anxious to get back, as well." He looked around the group. "Jonathan, you travel back with Ike and the chuck wagon. That'll take the longest."

All the fellas nodded. Everyone considered Brandon's life more important than a few days hanging around Miles City. But what about Shad's intention of seeing a doctor? Someone with a good medical degree. Once Shad had decided, the second opinion was all he'd been able to think about in his bedroll. He owed Poppy at least that. Maybe give her good news about his condition. His heart sank. This was her life he was contemplating.

"That's about it, men," Flood said. "You're a good lot. The Heart of the Mountains is lucky to have you. And on your return trip, don't push your horses too hard. It's been a long sixteen days. Don't tarry, but don't run 'em into the ground."

Roady clamped a supportive hand on Flood's shoulder.

What should Shad do? Maybe a doctor could see him tomorrow, or the next day, and then he could set off with Chance and Roady. Maybe even sooner. But possibly the appointment would take days, or even a week, to get. He had no idea about these things. He looked up, trying to make a decision. He'd been digging in the dust with the toe of his boot, weighing his options. None of them good. Most the men were headed away, going for their mounts. Shad called out to Flood as the older man turned to go. "Can I have a word?"

Flood nodded.

Shad looked around and then moved closer to the corral fence to be sure they'd have privacy.

Flood followed.

Unsure where to begin, he just looked at Flood.

"Go on, Shad. What is it?"

"I'd planned to see a doctor here in Miles City."

Flood's brow creased. "A doctor? Why?" He looked him up and down. "Are you sick?"

"No, not sick. It's of a personal nature, with my approaching wedding." Finding the right words was difficult. He hardly understood the inner workings of his manhood himself.

Flood shifted his weight.

Shad couldn't blame him for wanting to move. He had a train to catch. "You remember when I first hired on at the Heart of the Mountains? Same day when one of your breeding bulls got kicked in the testicles."

Flood nodded. "I remember. A darned shame and waste."

"Breeding season was in full swing," Shad went on quickly, not wanting to drag this out any longer than necessary. "As hard as he tried, he didn't get any of the heifers bred. Because of it, he went to the stockyards."

Flood's face softened. "A bull's got to perform. What're you trying to tell me, Shad? Don't be shy."

For Poppy. He had to say everything for Poppy. "Years ago, I suffered the same fate. Well, at least, the first part. A fractious old bull head-butted me in the groin. When I could manage it, I went to a doctor. After an examination, he determined my siring offspring days might be over before they even got started."

Flood wiped a hand over his mouth and stubbly chin. "Does Poppy know?"

Shad nodded. "She says the doctor, *the ol' sawbones,* she calls him, is wrong. Or, if he's not wrong, she'll be happy with just me. But you know as well as I do the stock women put in babies. Especially their *own* babies! Anyway, while we're here in Miles City, I had hoped to get a second opinion. Maybe see a doctor who has a certificate from a medical school. An expert who might put my heart at ease. That's what I was planning to do with my days off. Would you mind if I stayed back? I wouldn't ask if Poppy's happiness wasn't at stake."

Several moments passed as Flood stared at him.

He'd like to know what his boss was thinking.

"I have a better idea, Shad," Flood finally said. Now he was the one to clamp a hand on Shad's shoulder. "Come with me to Helena. Claire's telegram said the hospital had the finest doctors. You can see one of them."

Shad stared as he let Flood's proposition sink in. "Helena? You sure?"

"More than sure. I should have thought of bringing a man along in the first place. I'll appreciate the company on the train ride. And my sons will be grateful for the help you can give them at the hospital. Claire's telegrams mentioned the boys don't say as much, but they must be worn to the wick. Sound good? You willing to go?"

Unexpected jubilation crashed through Shad. "Yes, sir. Thank you!"

Flood hitched his head. "Then get moving. Grab your saddlebags, take your horse to Tanner, and then get some grub. I'll meet you at the train office just as soon as you can be there. Don't be late."

Shad turned, snatched his reins from the fence post, and jogged away, not having to be told twice. He would get an answer for Poppy. He just prayed the outcome wouldn't break both their hearts.

Chapter Fifty-Two

Sweeping the dust from one of the back cells of the jailhouse, Justin told himself he shouldn't feel real rushed in notifying Madison about the letter he saw on Lenore's window side table. The correspondence wouldn't up and disappear. This was only Tuesday. He could wait a few more days and hope for more information to present itself. Being the deputy sheriff with Brandon away was giving Justin a small dose of the heartfelt decisions his father must have gone through in his years as circuit judge. As well as the more serious criminal cases. Much needed to be considered—especially in situations where a hanging resulted at the end. Justin not only desired to help Madison, but his obligation was to also honor the privacy of Lenore. And what was *that* about, anyway? Could Lenore actually be Madison's mother? A birth when Lenore was quite young wasn't totally impossible—but close.

He shook his head and reached under the cot with the broom. Next, he set the stool upside down on the blankets in his effort to clean every inch, ridding the place of dirt and dust. Brandon liked to keep the jail as neat as possible—something Jack could never accomplish. With a heavy heart, Justin contemplated Brandon. The sheriff had taken a chance on Justin a year ago. He'd become a close friend, as well as his boss. Justin had received word Brandon required a second surgery. Doctors were now watching his recovery closely. That was a telegram he'd hated to deliver.

From outside the jail's barred window, Justin heard a female voice call a greeting to someone. The tone brought to mind Madison, and the buggy ride they'd taken two days prior. Madison had been introspective and more than homesick, like she'd claimed. She'd done her best to hide her sad mood from him but failed miserably. The fossil field, as much as the scientific discovery had delighted her, had not softened the defeat of losing the trail of the letter. He'd taken more than a few walks down the alley between the hotel and sheriff's office, just thinking about Lenore's cottage in hopes of spotting something new. But nothing.

And what about Dodger Hicks? Justin was almost certain the troublemaker was the culprit bothering the town, but unless he caught the scoundrel red-handed, the boy would deny any wrongdoing. And Dodger was sure to have all the evidence well hidden. Justin didn't want to accuse Dodger and then, if he couldn't back up his claim, rescind the charge. Sloppy work wouldn't do.

Still, he needed to keep an open mind. As much as Dodger fit the bill, last night on his rounds Justin had run into Harold, just past midnight. The young man was behind the Biscuit Barrel in the dark. He claimed he'd lost his watch the day before and was searching the places he'd previously been. But at night? That story was fishy. Being a mop boy, he did empty lots of buckets of water out in different locations. That thought hurt. Justin had a great respect for Harold and his excellent work ethic. Discovering he was responsible would be a shock.

And then there was still Jack Jones. Twice now, Justin had bumped into him after one in the morning strolling down the boardwalk as if he didn't have a care in the world. Alleged he had trouble sleeping and the night air helped.

Whoever the culprit was, he seemed to have a dark sense of humor. One of the two new bridles stolen from Trent Herrick appeared like magic, hanging in this jail cell this morning. Justin went directly to the leather shop and knocked until Trent opened the door, since they hadn't opened yet. The bridle was his, all right. The offender was taunting him. Thought he was untouchable. Well, Justin would just see about that.

Justin stopped and leaned on the broom handle, thinking. He needed to be outside at all times. Four days had passed since the theft at Lichtenstein's. Dodger might be feeling bold, since his luck was holding out. Maybe he'd try in the light of day. Justin had inquired with Dodger's mother, Saralee Hicks, how often her son came into town. Instantly suspicious, she'd become indignant. Said the high and mighty always blamed the less fortunate. Justin didn't understand. The Hickses made a good living in Y Knot.

Justin rubbed his chin. *Perhaps the lady doth protest a bit too much.* The line from Hamlet made him smile and renewed his resolve to catch the thief.

With invigorated purpose, Justin swept several dust balls into the dustpan, heading next for the back door. Now he'd make another sweep of the town, so to speak. Still early, people were just unlocking their doors. He'd visit the alleys and side streets. Watch the back lots. Dodger was large for his age, and perhaps, with the constant heavy hand of his father, might think he had something to prove. Justin intended to be there to interrupt his plans.

Twenty minutes later, as he rounded the corner behind Standford's Fittings, a flash of blue caught his eye.

Four buildings down, Fancy appeared in the open doorway of the Hitching Post Saloon. Taking off at a nice clip, she walked the alley, keeping her focus on the ground in front of her.

Curious now, he watched as she slowed her pace behind the hotel but, instead of going to the back door of Cattlemen's, like he'd expected, she turned and headed for the small cabins.

A moment later, she stopped in front of Lenore's cottage and knocked. When the door opened, she stepped inside, and the door closed.

The area was once again quiet.

Funny, in this whole year he'd lived in Y Knot, he'd never witnessed Fancy visiting Lenore. He *did* recall Abe telling Sam Green Tuesday mornings were Fancy's time off. The drunkard hadn't been happy when she wasn't there to sing and give him luck in his poker game. Who was minding the Hitching Post? As of last night, Abe was still bedbound. Justin hadn't seen the fellow, but that's what Fancy and Cole had told him when he'd stopped in late. Maybe he was recovered enough to give Fancy her time off. She'd been working long hours and duties since he'd taken to his bed.

Justin rubbed the back of his neck. What was bothering him? Fancy must have friends around. What was so special about her visiting Lenore? There wasn't anything unusual. The two, both being somewhat loners, had become friends. End of story.

But was it? He stared at the house for a moment longer, remembering when he'd looked in the window. He wouldn't go there again. He still felt guilty for not telling Lenore about the first time. But he could check in at the saloon, he decided, and headed that way, instead.

Leaning over the batwing doors, Justin glanced around. Same crowd. Sam Green, Dennis Oats, and Chet Fender played cards at a table in the middle of the room. Where did they get the money, when none of them held down a steady job? Emerging from the back room, Cole Mercer carried several bottles to restock the whiskey shelf. He wore a white apron around his waist and a towel was slung over one shoulder.

His dog slept on his blanket. Sensing him, Major looked up and thumped his tail in greeting.

Taking that as an invitation, Justin stepped inside to the musty smell of cigar smoke.

"Deputy," Cole said in acknowledgment. "How's your mornin'?"

Justin leaned on the bar and smiled. "Just checking in on Abe." He looked up at the quiet rooms at the top of the staircase. "It's going on five days. Will Abe make a recovery? I'm gettin' worried."

"The doctor's back in town and checked on him last night. Says he's more run-down and tired than anything else. Abe'll be on his feet in a day or two."

Who was Cole Mercer, really? Seemed he and Fancy had a past they weren't sharing.

Justin wondered if Abe was aware the fella was now minding the store. Justin liked Cole, but something about the situation felt odd. "So, you working for Abe now?" Justin asked under his breath, for Cole's ears only.

Cole glanced up from pulling the plug on the rinse water. The sink made sucking noises as the water drained. His brows drew together. "Just helping out Fancy so she can have some time off."

His tone was guarded. What did he have to hide? "You never said why you came to Y Knot, but your friendship with Fancy tells me you knew her before your arrival."

Cole smiled, but the gesture didn't reach his eyes. He straightened.

Justin was reminded the newcomer was larger than most. "Am I right?" Justin persisted.

"Fancy is pretty tight-lipped about her past," he said, studying Justin's face. He lifted a shoulder. "If you want to know, why don't you ask her?" He took up wiping the bar. "You want something to drink? A cup of coffee?"

Justin chuckled and shook his head. "No, thanks. I didn't mean to pry. I just saw Fancy visiting Lenore and wondered who was watching the saloon."

"Then you know about Lenore?"

Shocked at the question, Justin kept his gaze on the window, trying to hide his surprise. *Then you know about Lenore?* How far could he push Cole Mercer? "About Lenore? What's to know?"

"Ask Fancy that, too."

CHAPTER FIFTY-THREE

"More tea?" Lenore asked as she set her cup into her saucer. She lived for these days. Lenore told herself each month she'd escape to a larger town where, perhaps, she'd have a better chance at finding a husband. Here in Y Knot, everyone knew her as the town spinster. She'd been branded—story closed. If she wanted a different life, she was responsible. But the months and years rolled on, and she stayed put in this little cottage behind the hotel.

"No, thank you." Fancy stretched her legs out before her on the stool. A plate of oatmeal cookies sat on a small table nearby. "I've had three cups already. It's delicious, Lenore. You always amaze me with your concoctions. What kind of tea is it? I can taste the cinnamon. What else is mixed in?" She held up her cup and smiled. "It's really good."

"A sprinkle of lavender and a pinch of ginger. It's one of my favorites."

Fancy took another sip. "You have such a knack. Seriously. Do you think you could wrap me up a little to take back to the saloon? I'm happy to pay you."

Lenore's face warmed. Fancy always lavished her with praise about everything. In all honesty, the admiration felt wonderful. That's why she never canceled their Tuesday morning dates. Fancy had come to town two years ago, and at that point, Lenore's life had become bearable.

Fancy turned in her chair. "And I adore your new curtains," she said, gazing at the window. "The design is clever. The bows are perfect. I love the way they puddle on the floor. I know I told you the same last week, Lenore, but seeing them a second time, I just have to applaud you again. You're very clever. And the green brocade brings out the green in your eyes." She tipped her head in thought. "Do you have any dresses this shade? I don't recall."

Poor Fancy shouldn't try so hard. Just being in the same room together was enough for Lenore. "I have one, but I need to restitch the hem where it's come loose." She took a sip from her cup.

"You should think about rectifying that," Fancy said. "I've been meaning to ask. If I supply the fabric and paid you, can you make a simple curtain for Abe's window? He has a blanket and nail. The sight troubles my heart, even if it's in a saloon."

"Of course. And if you try to pay me, I'll be offended."

"I'll compensate you. That's the only way. You'd have to work on your time off."

Lenore gave a quiet laugh and then shook her head. Once she set her mind, Fancy got her way, and especially about money. She was strange that way. She acted as if she owed something to Lenore, but she didn't. She'd do anything for Fancy. "Since I won't win this argument, I'll give in right now. Yes, I'd love to. Would he like something short or all the way to the floor, like these?"

"Short and basic. I'll purchase a thick fabric to keep the light out. Maybe corduroy. What do you think?"

Lenore nodded.

"He's much better," Fancy went on. "And might even be up and about right now. He said he was going to, and I think he's ready. His color is back, and he looks much stronger. He scared me for a while, refusing to eat and getting so tiny I almost lost him in the sheets."

Lenore smiled. She loved to listen to Fancy go on and on about simple things. She didn't get much of a chance to just chat in the saloon. "Getting the fabric is easier for me to do, Fancy," Lenore offered. "I'm going to Berta May's later today. I'll go 'round back of the saloon and eyeball his window for size. Doesn't have to be exact."

With her hand clasped in Fancy's, Lenore felt a rush of love.

"Thank you. What would I do without you?" Fancy whispered. "You're an angel without wings. You keep me sane."

"You'd probably move on and find a larger, nicer place to live, that's what. You don't fool me. By the way, what's this about you and the new man in town? Is something brewing?" If it were, she'd be hurt if Fancy hadn't said anything to her first.

Fancy's cheeks bloomed pink.

"So, there *is* something?"

Fancy shook her head. "No, you're wrong. He's been lending a hand while Abe was out. If not, I wouldn't have been able to visit today. He's handy around the saloon. The regulars give him respect they don't give me. Have you met him?"

Anxiety gripped Lenore like a fist around her throat. Fancy was tight-lipped about her work and about men. She never shared anything of those matters with Lenore. "Not really. I've served him a time or two in the hotel. Seems like a nice fellow." Dread sprang to life at the light shining in Fancy's eyes. Had she fallen in love? She remembered Justin's comment about them being old friends. If that were true, wouldn't Fancy tell her? "And he's handsome, too," Lenore heard herself saying. "Even the scar on his lip seems to enhance his looks." Why was she going on so? She didn't want to share Fancy with anyone. "What do you think? About his looks, I mean?"

"I'm sure he's turned many heads. Doesn't change my mind about my life and where it's going, or not going, though." The smile that appeared on her face at the mention of Cole Mercer widened. "He has a nice dog. I've always been partial to black with white markings."

Lenore wished to change the troubling line of conversation. She stood and went into her bedroom, returning with the letter she'd picked up four days prior. She held it out to Fancy.

CHAPTER FIFTY-FOUR

Charity heard the muffled sound of someone climbing the staircase. Standing in front of her mirror as she buttoned her dress, she looked to the door. A quick knock sounded, and then her father appeared. With his sweat-stained bandanna still knotted around his neck and soiled shirt, he evidently hadn't bathed since stepping off his horse. His Stetson dangled loosely in his fingers. His shaggy hair appeared windblown, and he needed a shave. Still, he'd never looked so beloved and inviting to Charity in her life.

Twenty minutes prior, the doctor had examined her and given her permission to get out of bed and pay a brief visit to Brandon across the street. Luke was coming to fetch her back after she'd had some time to clean up and get dressed. That's who she'd been expecting now, and the sight of her father's treasured face brought a new round of tears to her eyes, but she didn't allow them to fall.

"Charity," he said in a gravelly voice and rushed forward, wrapping her in his arms. "Thank God nothing more has happened. I was shocked to hear about you. You should have sent for your mother directly!"

His arms felt so good. When she was in them,

nothing bad could ever happen to her. All her life, he'd been protecting her and watching over her. Her eyes stung at the thought. And yet, he hadn't been able to protect her from this. "I know, but I didn't want her to worry," she choked out. "The ranch was already so shorthanded." Her mother would be upset with her, and rightly so. But, at the time, her decision had felt right. "I thought we'd be on our way home in just a few days." What a dream that had been. "I'm sorry."

"Shh, shh, I wasn't scolding you. I understand your feelings, and I would have done the same. I'm just concerned about all you've been through. I thank God your brothers were all here to help and support you both."

"So am I, Pa, so am I." She buried her face in his chest, loving the scent of horse and sweat. "Brandon's getting stronger," she eked out between the hurt jamming her throat. They rocked back and forth, strong arms around her, her father's cheek pressed firmly to the top of her head. She heard his sniffles and knew he was crying, too. "He's going to live."

"I know, darlin'," he said in a thick, hoarse voice. "We went straight to the hospital from the train station, thinking you and your brothers would be there. That's when I learned about what happened to you." He pulled back and looked down into her face. "And the scare with the baby."

She nodded, blinking back tears. "I get to see Brandon today," she whispered, as if she said the statement too loud, the doctor would return and tell her to get back into bed. "The first time in three days. It's been horrible. But he's hung on. Survived the second surgery and is now actually able to rest. *And* he's coming around, something he didn't really do before. I can't wait to see him, Pa. I love him so much. I feel like my heart will explode when I think about seeing him. I'm ashamed to say, many times these last three days, I lost hope. My faith wasn't strong enough. I believed Brandon would die, and he'd never see our baby."

"Shhh," he crooned softly. "Remember, my daughter, faith and courage go hand in hand. Courage is nothing but fortitude, and that's a *virtue,* not something you can dredge up on your own. You must pray, and God will provide. I can't tell you how many times in my life my courage withered up like a sun-scorched vine. Searching for your mother after she'd been abducted by the Cheyenne was one of those occasions. Month after month passed with no results. I prayed for strength and courage to lift my foot. Walk the next step. Another time was in the early years on the ranch. We had a hellish drought. Cattle were dying. After all the years of toil building the stock, the possibility of losing everything felt devastating. But God brought us through. Then again, one time when I was traveling with Joe Brunn, a blizzard surprised us. I can still feel the tips of my toes and fingers burning like fire. That night, curled up to the trunk of a large bull pine, I said my prayers, thinking they'd be my last." He chuckled dryly. "Not everything goes the way we'd like it to, but God never gives you more than you can handle."

She enjoyed listening to his deep, calm voice. His arms tightened.

"Your grandpa, Augustus McCutcheon, used to tell me to grow my fortitude each morning before heading out to do my chores. He meant it, too. He was a tough man. Strong in his faith." Flood took a breath and said in a deep imitation, "Don't forget your prayers, Jefferson—he liked to use my given name—because without 'em, at the first sign of trouble, your fortitude will vanish like mist on a pond. Take heed to grow it every day of your life." Flood gave her an extra squeeze. "I wish you could have met him, Charity. He'd have recognized your strength and grit and been proud."

Her father's face glowed from the memories. "You don't speak of your father often, Pa. Why not? What was he like?"

Flood rubbed his whiskered chin, still just as strong and square as his sons'. "He was tall and strong of arm. His hair was the same color as Matt's and Mark's. He was serious and could sometimes have a temper, but he also had a funny bone. Didn't mind playing a joke on us boys, now and then. He respected your grandmother, Sarah, with staunch faithfulness and demanded the same from his sons. Those two were a team and loved each other fiercely. I guess I don't say much about those days because doing so makes me feel bad. When I left home, my pa didn't want me to go. Neither did my ma. My younger brother, Gideon, had just run off without a word, and they were still mourning that surprise. I guess I added to their hurt." Flood took a deep breath. "But I do feel I was *supposed* to end up here in Montana. I can't imagine raising my family anywhere else. And, too, I think my leaving gave Winston room to grow as large a ranch as he wanted without us stepping on each other's toes. We both could." He nodded, his eyes still filled with his recollections.

He chucked her under her chin like he used to do when she was just a little girl.

"I'll talk more about him now. After the reunion a month ago, I feel resigned. What I did back then was good for all concerned. I want *you* and *all* my grandbabies to know their roots. Where they come from and what kind of stock runs in their blood. That's mighty hard to do if I never speak about Augustus McCutcheon and Sarah Fitzpatrick, now, isn't it?"

Feeling so much better, Charity gave him a bear hug.

He chuckled. "What's that for?"

"Because I love you so much!"

"I'm glad to hear that, daughter. Now"—a half smile pulled his lips—"no more talk of Brandon dyin'. Your husband opened his eyes and smiled when he heard my voice. The measures he'll go to for a little attention are beyond me."

She gasped and pulled back. Seeing her father's cherished smile brought a glimmer of sunshine to her heart. She smiled, too, and wiped away her unshed tears with shaky fingers.

"I always said he was hardheaded," Flood went on, encouraged by her smile. "Maybe allowing the two of you to marry was a mistake." He lifted a sardonic eyebrow. "As if I had any say at all in the matter."

She stepped back farther and searched her father's face. "He smiled at you?"

Flood nodded.

"I can't *wait* to see him." She quickly took up where she'd left off on her bodice buttons over her chemise. Being shy in front of her father was the least of her worries.

"Yes, ma'am. And everyone noticed, cheering him on." Flood shook his head. "I don't think I've ever seen your brothers so concerned about anything. You and Brandon *both* have them walking on eggshells."

Finished with her dress, she tied the sash around her expanding waist, creating a nice bow.

"Who came with you? You said *we* when you first came in the room. Roady? Smokey?"

He glanced over, tilting his head to one side. "Shad Petty."

"Shad?"

"Just thought another man might be helpful. The train trip took almost twenty-four hours." He looked down at his clothes. "Sorry about my attire. We came straight from the stockyards, only having time to grab something to eat before the last train left for Helena." He scratched his whisker-covered jaw. "I hope I didn't scare you."

She actually felt a tiny bubble of laughter. "You'd never scare me." She rubbed a hand over her stomach, thankful her brothers had filled him in so she didn't have to. Almost losing her baby had been a nightmare she didn't want to repeat.

His brow puckered. "You feeling all right?"

"Better than all right. You're here now, and I get to be with Brandon in a few minutes. I've been lying in this bed for much too long with nothing to do but worry."

"Well, you won't be staying there like you were before. The doctor said for a couple of hours and then you're to come back here, rest, and eat properly." He gave a tender gaze. "You need to take care of my little Charity in there." He looked at her tummy. "Nothing else will do. I can hardly wait to welcome her and hold her in my arms."

Charity went to the dressing table and began

brushing and plaiting her hair in an easy side braid. "How do you know I'm having a girl? Not even the doctors know."

He eased a shoulder against the tall post of the walnut bed as he watched her. "Because you look like your mother did before she had you. Just something different. I'd lay money on it."

Finished, she turned to him.

He put out his arm. Without another word, they exited the room and slowly took the stairs. At the bottom, they came upon Mrs. Hardie, a bag of groceries in her arms.

The innkeeper's eyes opened wide. "It's a blessing to see you up, dear."

"Thank you, Mrs. Hardie. I feel the same. This is my father. Pa, this is the wonderful woman who's been caring for us since we arrived."

"My wife and I are much obliged for all you've done, ma'am," Flood said. "Caring for our children when we couldn't."

Mrs. Hardie's face colored up. "Well, I don't know about all that, but meeting the McCutcheon family has been a delight and blessing. I ran into your brother, Mark, across the street when I was coming back from the mercantile. He alerted me your father, and another ranch hand, had arrived and would need rooms if I had them available, which I do. And also that the doctors think, if Mr. Crawford keeps growing stronger at the rate he's doing now, he'll be here soon, too, for recovery.

I'll prepare the larger room on this floor, so he won't have any stairs. You both can stay there."

Unable to stop herself, Charity stepped forward and gave Mrs. Hardie a hug, bag of foodstuffs and all. They both laughed.

The woman patted her back. "Now, you be off. I'm sure Mr. Crawford is anxious to see you after these days away." She blinked several times over watery eyes.

Charity could hardly wait to see for herself how Brandon had improved. Their time apart felt like years.

All the fellas surrounding Brandon's bed looked to the door, and Brandon thought Charity must be arriving. He was still weak, but at least his head wasn't filled with troubling thoughts about dying. Leaving her a widow. Never holding his child. He'd been surprised to hear Flood's voice earlier today, and even more to see Shad Petty had also made the trip to Helena. "Charity." His barely audible voice sounded strange even to *his* ears.

And then there she was, standing in the doorway.

A murmur went around the men. Matthew, Mark, Luke, and now Shad turned in unison and headed quietly for the door.

As soon as the others were out of the room,

Charity dropped Flood's arm and hurried to his side.

As she came forward, his whole being filled with light and anticipation. He couldn't speak from the raw emotion holding his tongue. At times, he'd thought he'd never see her again. And then, when Matthew had carefully, and painfully, told him of her condition, and why she'd been confined to her bed, he thought he'd die from grief. So much had transpired since he'd broken his leg all those days ago. Never again would he take even one second of his life for granted.

She placed her warm palm against his cheek as she searched his face. "My love," she finally whispered. "You have given us all a scare."

"I'm sorry." He couldn't stop tears from spilling from his eyes and running down onto his pillow. "I'm so sorry."

She carefully kissed his lips, lingering for many seconds as he breathed in her scent. Laying her cheek against his, she couldn't seem to get close enough. "Are you in pain?" she asked softly.

"Only from missing you. And from the knowledge of how you were suffering. You must have been terrified, Charity. I'm sorry about that, too."

"Stop. Nothing was your fault. The important thing now is you. Growing stronger. Gaining back the weight you've lost. Going home, where we can welcome this baby into our lives."

He closed his eyes as she carefully wrapped

him in her arms. Would he fully recover? Could he be the man she, and their child, needed him to be? Or was that all just wishful thinking?

Shad stood quietly outside of Brandon's room, listening to the others. Flood had pulled Brandon's door closed, to give them privacy. They were both still covered with grime and dust, and he felt like he smelled like a cattle yard. The brothers had been surprised to see him, but when they were over their shock, they thanked him for coming with their father. The men were circled up, and Shad could see relief in Luke's and his brothers' eyes at the arrival of their father. If he was in their shoes, he guessed he'd feel the same.

"He's not completely out of the woods yet," Matthew said in low tones. "But since the second surgery, the doctors are finally speaking optimistically, which is a great relief to us all. Until today, we"—he looked at Luke and then Mark—"had begun to think they didn't know much of anything."

Luke shifted his weight from one foot to the other. "His recovery here will be longer than we expected. Maybe even a month. Someone'll need to stay with them."

"That someone will be me," Flood responded. "Your wives and families need you back at the ranch. And Shad has a wedding to attend to.

Claire will join me as soon as I send a telegram. Francis can travel with her."

The group nodded.

"Not sure if you've heard," Mark went on, keeping his voice lowered. "Luke struck out on his own, found a tribe of Cheyenne, and retrieved some herbal plants known to fortify an ailing body. Brandon's first dose was early this morning, when he woke up."

If Shad wasn't wrong, Luke looked a mite uncomfortable.

Flood caught Luke's eye and lifted his chin. "That so?"

"We didn't have any better ideas," Mark added.

"Guess we'll never know what to credit Brandon's reversal to," Matthew said. "The second surgery or the brew of magical medicine Luke supplied. At the smell, I was worried." He smiled at Luke. "I'm just kiddin' ya, little brother, don't take offense. I don't think any of us care the *why,* we just thank God Brandon's finally coming around. You're a brave man to take on such a challenge. I might kid around, but I couldn't be prouder if I tried." He glanced at the closed door, and then they all moved to the side of the narrow hallway to allow a nun to swish by. "And then we had the scare with Charity." Matt rubbed a hand over his face. "Her losing her baby, on top of everything else, would have been devastating if the worst came to pass. I don't like to think it."

Flood shook his head and stared at the floor. "I never dreamed something of this magnitude would happen when we were away." He looked at Shad. "We were moanin' and groanin' over the campfire, homesick and wondering about the great time everyone was having back in Y Knot. That'll teach us not to speculate."

"And the cattle drive?" Luke asked. "How'd it go?"

"Fine," Flood said. "Couldn't have been better. We had no mishaps and got a good price per head. Roady and Chance are bringing back the banknotes. The rest of the men headed back to the Heart of the Mountains about the same time we boarded the train, giving up their free days in Miles City in concern for the others at the ranch. They have a few days' ride ahead of 'em, but the going is much faster without the herd."

Mark chuckled as he nodded. "No explanation needed, Pa. We've all pushed a herd to Miles City more times than we can remember. Congratulations."

A grin split Flood's face. "I tend to forget you're all grown men." He glanced around at each of them and even gave Shad his warm regard. "Does a man good to see the next generation step up and take charge. Especially when you're all such fine examples."

Chapter Fifty-Five

Fancy glanced at the letter in Lenore's hand and then up into her eyes. "What's this?"

Lenore shrugged. "I'm not sure. Arrived on Friday."

Fancy hesitated.

"Go on, it's from Kentucky."

Fancy didn't want to take it. She felt something was unmistakably wrong. Her heart ratcheted up, and her mouth went dry. "But we've already received a letter this year. In January."

"Don't be frightened," Lenore said in her soothing tone, her eyes softening. She set the letter on the table by the plate of cookies and went to the kitchen, returning a moment later. "I just need a splash of hot water to warm my tea. Are you sure you wouldn't like a little, too? The water is heating."

Fancy knew this Lenore extremely well. Sweet. Caring. Her nurturing way always knew just what to say and do to make things right. In truth, she was a worrywart, and held agonizing issues inside for much too long. No one ever got to see this side of Lenore, except herself. She kept others at bay. Fancy glanced at the letter again. Why was it so frightening? Quickly picking up her cup and saucer, she held them out to Lenore, not even trying to hide when it rattled dangerously in her hand. "I would, thank you."

Lenore took both cups and headed for the tiny kitchen.

Fancy had no other option. Lifting the correspondence, she slowly, carefully, slipped her finger under the sealed edge, taking care, as she always did, not to rip the envelope.

> Dearest Ma'am. It is with great sadness that I inform you the adoptive father of your daughter has passed away. This occurred in February. The kind gentleman went peacefully in his sleep. His death was not too much of a shock, since his health had been in decline for some time. As you must realize, because both her parents were only children, themselves, this leaves your daughter alone in the world—except for me, her faithful nanny and housekeeper, although I'm now retired, and the friends she's made here in Frankfort and in college. She is a wonderful young woman, as I've written to you in the past, and has taken her new life circumstance in stride, although she misses her father greatly, as we all do.
>
> Rest assured, you would be extremely proud of your daughter if you knew her. She's beautiful and bright, as I've

expressed often. She's determined and principled and has a high moral code. Her father, until his death, hoped for a young man he worked with, encouraging a relationship between them. I'm sure his desire was to get her settled before he'd been called home. But she was not interested in marrying, just yet. She has other aspirations on her mind.

Since we never receive a reply to our correspondence, we are unaware if these letters ever really reach you. I hope they do. I have something important to request. I think of my sweet girl as my granddaughter, not a charge. I only want her happiness. Since the day twelve years ago when she learned she was adopted, she's longed to find her mother. Not to create a problem. Or ask about the circumstances for her being given up at birth, but because she longs to meet you and to know you. She wants nothing more. She understands you might have married and have a family. She begrudges you nothing.

Unable to stop the tremor in her hands, Fancy set the letter aside because she couldn't read the words jumping around on the page. She took a deep breath.

Lenore returned with the cups and set them both on the table. "Would you like me to read it aloud?" she asked softly.

Fancy shook her head. She almost knew intuitively what Mrs. Goodheart was about to say.

> I understand what I'm about to tell you is against all the rules. If Mr. Turner knew what I was about, he'd not send this letter. I'm lucky he's a busy man and has long since stopped reviewing the letters I provide. He believes I'm only writing to inform you of her father's passing and that no more correspondence will be forthcoming.

With a shaky hand, Fancy slipped the first sheet behind the second. Doing so, she looked up and caught Lenore's gaze. Feeling an urgency within, she continued.

> Almost a month ago, your daughter, with my blessing and encouragement, set out to find you. All she knows is your most current address for these yearly correspondences is Y Knot, Montana Territory. The attorney addresses them, so we don't know your name. If she has not found you yet, I pray with all my heart, if

and when she does, you welcome her with open arms. She could be a good friend, if not a daughter. Please, ma'am. Please don't reject her when you meet.

You must wonder why I've written to you without her knowledge. Like I said before, I love her like a granddaughter. I long for her happiness. I hope, by meeting you, she can stop the constant ache in her heart and concentrate on her own life, her future, find a loving man and start a family all her own. I don't believe that will happen until . . .

Feeling numb all over, Fancy went to the third page.

. . . she knows her past and comes to terms with it. Only you can help her accomplish that. I wish I could, but it's proven impossible. I've accepted long ago nothing can take the place of a mother's love. Because of how wonderful she is, I know you must be an extraordinary woman, as well.

Wishing you peace and an abundance of God's grace.

In your service,
Mrs. Goodheart

Chapter Fifty-Six

The midmorning sun beat down on Justin's head, making him feel like a slice of bacon on a hot skillet. Perspiration made his shirt cling, causing the clothing to catch and rub as he flicked back his whip and took several deep breaths.

Earlier today, he'd moved the old bench behind the jail out into the alleyway between the modest home where Brandon and Charity lived and a towering old pine. He'd found ten pine cones and, after balancing them upright on the bench seat, he'd been going after it for the last fifteen minutes. He needed practice to keep his razor-sharp edge. Besides, he found deep thinking easy when snapping his bullwhip back and forth. Many of his problems were solved during his intense concentration.

A burning ache deep in his bicep felt good. His back muscles twinged and strained. If he'd been alone, he'd have stripped off his shirt and let the sun bake out his disturbing thoughts, but he didn't want to scandalize any of the women of Y Knot who might unexpectedly come upon him.

He hadn't seen Madison since Sunday, when they'd taken a buggy ride. He supposed she'd worked on Monday, as she usually did, but he'd kept his distance. And he'd actually searched the street from the window before exiting the sheriff's office to see if the coast was clear. *What a coward!* Guilt over not sharing about Lenore's letter was eating him alive. Nothing about this quandary made any sense at all. Having just replaced a second batch of targets, he coiled his whip and let it fly.

Crack! The first pine cone on the long bench flew into the air.

Wiping his forearm across his sweaty brow, he slowly recoiled his whip. Another irritation, while setting up this practice spot, he'd discovered a small pile of rib bones by the backdoor of the jail. The odds of the bones appearing by chance were none. Another taunt by Dodger.

Crack! The second cone flew off to the right. It hit the trunk of the bull pine in a burst of dust, fell to the ground, and rolled to a stop.

The fact Major hadn't found the bones before Justin did was astonishing. Or, maybe, Dodger was around, watching him. Could be the scoundrel had just put them out. Justin wouldn't put anything past the Hicks boy. At least, Justin felt he could be certain the perpetrator lived in Y Knot. What did the law do with lawbreaking boys?

Hearing footsteps, Justin turned to find Jack Jones coming his way. The former deputy looked at the lineup of pine cones and then back at Justin. "Practicing?"

"No, I'm baking a cake." He really shouldn't poke the bear whenever he had the chance. Doing so wasn't nice. "Sorry, Jones. I haven't seen you around much. Thought you might've moved on."

"Only in your dreams, Deputy."

Justin chuckled as he slowly coiled his whip. "Maybe so. Maybe so." He straightened and readied himself, wanting to get back to practice. He liked to get in and get out before he drew too many spectators who eventually appeared to see what the unusual sound was and who was making it. "You need something?"

"What's the latest on Brandon? Have you heard?"

"I have. And good news, to boot. I've permission to pass on that Brandon had a second surgery. Since then, he's gaining strength. Flood went to Helena and Claire's going up there, as well. Seems Brandon's recovery won't be short. But the telegram assured he would get better if nothing else unseen or unexpected happened."

Relief slid across Jack's face. "That's darned good to hear. Thanks for letting me know."

Jack was being awfully nice. Agreeable. And had been mostly the same since returning to town. Was he planning something, or had he actually changed? "So, Jack, you ever going to tell me what you're doing in that broken-down shack next to Standford's Fittings? The suspense is killing me. I see you in there from time to time, poking around, but then the place never seems to change. I haven't really even seen you in the saloon?" He lifted a curious brow. "What's your game?"

A smug smile appeared on Jack's lips. "Just have to wait and see, Deputy. You'll find out when everyone else does."

Justin lifted his arm and let his whip fly.

Crack! The third pine cone, which was quite rotted, burst to pieces. Snapping again in quick succession, cones four, five, and six leaped into the air.

Crack!

Crack!

Crack!

"That's somethin'!" Jack thumbed back his hat to widened eyes. "I've been wonderin' if you could use that whip of yours or if it was just for show. Now I know."

The praise felt good, even coming from Jack. The sound of a door opening drew Justin's attention to the cabins not far away.

Fancy stepped out. Without a backward glance, she started out at a good clip, headed for the alley, but when she saw him and Jack, she pulled up. Her wide, startled eyes were red as if she'd been crying. And her mouth was a hard, straight line. Not only that, but she also clutched a large, white envelope in her fist.

His gut twisted. The letter?

Without a word, Fancy spun on her heel, reversing course to take a different path to the saloon.

Justin watched her go. His time had just run out.

Abe came slowly down the stairs, a tight grip on the handrail.

Cole noticed him right away. The room was busier than it had been in all the days Cole had been in town. Several tables were filled with card players, and five men sat at the bar. He found he enjoyed working the saloon. The mindless job was better than his days in the army. He'd had some good times when he was young, but more often, he was on a patrol looking for someone or something with a group of his comrades riding in line. He didn't like shooting at people—white, black, or red. He was tired of watching men die. He'd rather watch them drink. Other times, before he'd earned a higher rank of captain, he'd worked in the mess tent more times than he liked to remember. Or was put on watch, where he'd stand guard through long nights in freezing temperatures. No, sir. He enjoyed working at Fancy's side. The job was like being retired. Easy work during his twilight years. He'd earned it.

"Abe, I see you made it down." He grinned at the short, slim man. Abe must have lost a considerable amount of weight, because his red suspenders gaped at his shoulders. His scant, fuzzy hair was wet from combing. "How you feel, ol' timer?"

The saloon owner gave Cole a sideways glance. "I'm not much older than you, *ol' timer*."

Cole chuckled. "Fair enough. I'll tell Fancy your humor has returned."

The man struggled to take a seat on a bar stool. Once settled, he leaned his elbows on the countertop and sighed. "Thought I just might up and die in my bed, alone and sore from all the lumps." He glanced around. "Busy in here. This suits me better."

"You ever think about retiring, Abe? You have family around the area? Or do you plan to stick around till you die?"

"Pour me a whiskey," he answered.

Cole ignored his request and instead poured him a water, while admiring the squeaky-clean glass he'd just washed. The Hitching Post looked much better since Fancy—and he—had taken charge.

Abe narrowed his eyes, looking at his drink. "What's this?"

"Fancy would be mighty displeased if I undid all her nursing. When she gets back and says you can imbibe, I'll pour you a drink then. But not before."

Loud laughter sounded from a table at the back of the room. The fellas must be almost ready for another bottle. He was getting to know the drunks and their habits. If they wanted to get dog-faced inebriated, who was he to tell them no? As long as they had the money to pay, he'd keep pouring.

"But I own this place . . ."

Cole glanced around, admiring the tall, walnut backbar and mirror. The piano in the corner. The tables and chairs. Now clean, the establishment didn't look half-bad.

"Cat got your tongue?" Abe asked. "You interested in buying? Is that why you're prying into my business?"

Cole had disappeared into deep thought and glanced up at Abe's question. "I hadn't considered it before—but that's not a half-bad idea." That way, he could be around Fancy and convince her to marry him. The task wouldn't be easy, or fast, but he had all the time in the world. He gave Abe his most engaging smile. "If you're selling, that is. Wouldn't want to twist your arm."

Abe harrumphed.

Fancy came through the back door in a terrible rush.

Before Cole had a chance to say hello, he watched her turn at the stairway and proceed up. He felt a little hurt. As much as she tried not to lead him on—those were her words—she still had a way of making him feel special. More special than he had a right to feel. She was kind and thoughtful. He could see her yearning for him behind her eyes. Hiding that was impossible.

Why this reaction now? She'd been looking forward to seeing Lenore. Had something happened? Did they have words? All he knew was, Fancy was hurting. He aimed to find out why and make it better.

Chapter Fifty-Seven

At the sound of the approaching stagecoach, Justin coiled his whip and hooked it back onto his gun belt. He went to the water pump behind the jail and worked the handle until a strong flow of cold water splashed out into a bucket on the ground. In cupped hands, and being careful not to drench himself, he slapped some water onto his face and scrubbed, and then used his shirttail to dry. He needed to look presentable for any newcomer who might be arriving today. Aware Jack Jones was still present, watching, Justin pondered why the man was being so friendly.

From the street, Justin recognized June Pittman's voice, the owner of the livery, as she arrived to water the stock. He gave Jack a nod and then strode out to the road.

"Justin." A deep voice boomed.

Justin cut his gaze to the back of the coach. "Pa. You're back early." He hurried to his father's side.

The driver and shotgun messenger fumbled around on top of the conveyance with luggage and a trunk.

Embracing, Justin thumped his father's back a couple times and then stepped away, giving them both room to talk. "Why'd you cut your plans short? I didn't expect you home for another week." They almost stood eye to eye. Years ago, Justin lamented whether or not he'd ever be as tall as Harrison Wesley. At six foot two, Justin fell only two inches short of reaching his goal. "You've barely been gone a week and a half. That's a long way to travel to just . . ." Justin left his sentence unfinished, seeing the contentment on his father's face.

Harrison lifted a shoulder.

His father looked rested, a healthy glow emanated from his eyes, and he appeared incredibly happy. A set of new, stylish clothes looked good on him. Something had transpired during his father's time in Denver, something substantial, or his name wasn't Justin Wesley.

"The wedding I went to officiate took place the day after I arrived. Then I saw the people I wanted to see. Visited a few sights." He grinned again. "I missed everyone here." He took a deep breath and glanced around, smiling and nodding. "How's Carlie? She faring all right under Pauline's critical eye?"

Something felt off. His father never avoided Justin's gaze. That could be a problem, sometimes. "She's fine. Pauline's fine. Y Knot's fine. I hope you didn't hurry back because you were worried about things here. And me being on my own in the sheriff's office."

He slung an arm over Justin's shoulders.

"My son is *so* suspicious. You'd think he was a lawman or something." Harrison chuckled and then shifted his attention to the men as they brought down his travel bag and an additional trunk.

Justin gestured to the crate his father must have bought in Denver, because he didn't leave with one. "What's this?"

"Couldn't go to Denver and not bring some surprises home to everyone." He gave a wide smile and winked. "Carlie *and* Pauline would never forgive me."

Okay, Justin was sure. He'd get to the bottom of things.

"First off, what about Brandon? How is he? I've been praying for that young man the whole time I've been gone. Has he returned to Y Knot? Although, if he has, his recovery would be exceptionally fast."

Justin filled his father in on the latest updates about Brandon.

Harrison listened, rubbing his chin all the while.

"That's all just transpired within the last two days. Luke and his brothers are keeping us all well informed."

"And you? How did everything go in town? Any troubles?"

The shotgun messenger set Harrison's things on the boardwalk and bid him "Good day."

"Thank you, young man," Harrison responded. "I've enjoyed speaking with you."

Justin waited until he had his father's full attention. He was thankful to have him back, even after all his assertions about handling Y Knot on his own. "We have some issues."

His father nodded. "Go on."

Harold came out of the hotel. "Judge Wesley! Welcome home."

"Thanks, Harold. Mighty glad to be here."

Harold pointed toward the trunk and other smaller luggage. "Want me to fetch your items home for you? I've just been at the livery, and the buckboard is still hitched up."

"That would be helpful, Harold." He slipped a half dollar from his pocket and handed the tip to the young man. "Thank you."

"My pleasure."

"Come on, Justin," Harrison said. "You can tell me everything as we walk to the house."

After weighing all the important issues about Madison and her mother, Justin felt happy to stroll along. No doubt, the short distance would take twice as long for all the welcoming home his father would receive. They could barely move ten feet before someone new saw him and came to say hello. Justin had a new respect for all the difficult decisions his father had made during his lifetime as a judge and lawman. Nothing was ever simple when the good of others was involved.

They passed the hotel and approached Lichtenstein's Provisions. "And how is Miss Madison Plumb? Still in town, writing up a storm about the American West?"

Justin's face heated, and he was thankful his father was so intent on looking around that he wouldn't notice. "She is. And doing well."

"She still working at the Biscuit Barrel? I'm a bit hungry."

"She is. But I'm not sure if she's working today."

His father glanced over.

Justin knew that look. His father was weighing every clue, trying to figure out if Justin was still sweet on her. Or, if maybe the two had cooled on each other. He wished he knew.

Across the street, Lou stood over Drit as he worked on the gate to their short picket fence. When she looked up and saw them, she waved. "Why, Judge, you're back. We missed your smiling face, sir!"

"And I missed yours, as well," he called over. "I'll be in soon for one of your fine, home-cooked meals, Lou. Just thinking about your lamb stew, oat bread with the crunchy crust, and your molasses cake makes my stomach rumble."

A red-faced Drit climbed to his feet and was now smiling, as well.

"We're always ready for you," Lou went on.

"Lamb stew's planned for tonight, and meatloaf tomorrow."

The judge chuckled and glanced at Justin. "Y Knot's a grand town, son. Denver can't hold a candle. No sir, indeed."

Those words were a relief. Perhaps, once his father returned to the city they'd lived in for years, he'd regret his move to such a small town. Hearing him say different was good. So then, what was this strange feeling Justin still had about him?

Harrison pulled up in front of Standford's Fittings. "Let me poke my head in and say hello to Morgan. I'll let him know he can count on me tomorrow and the rest of the week."

"You go on," Justin replied. "I'll wait here. Take all the time you'd like."

Standing out front, he had a nice view of the Biscuit Barrel across the road. Several horses were tied on the side hitching post and two buggies parked on the other side. He longed to go inside to see if Madison was there. Sunday felt like a lifetime ago, and he missed her. He wondered how she felt. Had she gotten any word from home? From the woman, *Mrs. Goodheart,* she'd spoken about several times? Madison seemed quite fond of her. Or her classmates and Professor Galbraith? Every time he heard, or thought that name, he wondered about his age and their relationship. Justin was constantly fearful she'd give up her search. With no reason to stay in town, she'd go back to Kentucky. What would he do then? What would he *really* do? He knew he loved her. Felt more for her than he'd ever had for a woman. Would he follow her and give up his life here in Y Knot? Give up his family? His friends?

Shocked at his inner turmoil, Justin glanced into the sky. The sun tracked west, soon to give them a respite from the heat.

I wouldn't want to leave everyone, but I would, for Madison. Still, he had no idea how she genuinely felt about him. He was her confidant because she had no one else to entrust. No one else to help her. Maybe he was still just a friend and always would be. Turning when his father appeared in the doorway, he pushed away his agitated thoughts.

Morgan Standford appeared behind his father and waved to Justin. He approached alongside, his noticeable limp making his gait uneven. "You see what Jack Jones is up to over there?" Morgan hitched his head, covered with thick, black hair, to the shack standing five feet to the west of his shop. The place was quiet, at the moment.

Harrison straightened. "Jack Jones! What's this about that scoundrel? I'd think he'd not have the nerve to show his face again around here."

Morgan and Justin exchanged a look. "I'll tell you all about that, too," Justin said. He glanced back at Morgan. “Not a clue, but he’s up to something. Was baiting me earlier today.”

They walked on and crossed the road.

Madison stepped out of the Biscuit Barrel, her apron draped over her arm. When she spotted them, she pulled up, and a troubled expression filled her eyes.

His father nudged him with his elbow. “Miss Plumb, how nice to see you.”

She smiled and came closer.

Justin took in her face, so dear, and noted her eyes weren’t quite so red today. She gave him a quick smile, but nothing like he was used to. He’d been giving her mixed signals, and she felt hurt, he could tell. Adding to her pain was the last thing he wanted to do. Suddenly, in the way she tipped her head as she looked up at his father, he knew exactly who Madison reminded him of. Fancy! The truth was right before his eyes all this time. And Fancy had the letter in her hand when leaving Lenore’s house moments ago. Why the letter was addressed to Lenore instead of Fancy was still a puzzle. Still, he held little doubt the woman Madison was looking for was Fancy Aubrey. Soiled dove of Y Knot!

“Justin?”

Justin cut his gaze to his father, who stared at him.

“Where are you, son? Miss Plumb just asked how you are. You have cotton in your ears?”

Justin shook his head and looked at Madison. Anyone who didn't see the resemblance was blind. Fancy Aubrey was a beautiful woman—and so was Madison. But how would the proper young lady take the news? Would she rather not know? "I'm sorry," he finally said. "I'm fine. Just been a bit busy, trying to catch the town thief in action. I'm sorry I haven't looked in on you, Madison."

Harrison took a step back. "Town thief?"

"Something else I'll fill you in on later, Pa." Justin wished they were alone, so he could take Madison's hand and tell her how much he'd missed her, even after only a couple of days without seeing her. He was having a difficult time dragging his gaze away. Same nose, same eyes, same beautiful, wheat-colored hair. By gosh, she was almost a spitting image.

"I best be going. Today, I'm on a split shift and must be back at four o'clock." She looked off down the street, as if eager to be away. "Time waits for no one."

Justin needed to talk with her, but what would he dare say? Her situation was critical. He wished he knew how she'd take the news. Leave town instantly? Anything was possible. "Can I stop by a little later?" he heard himself saying. When had he made that decision? He thought he knew about Fancy but wasn't absolutely sure. Calling this too soon was a gamble for everyone.

A small, cautious light came back into her eyes. “That would be fine, Justin,” she said. “I’ll be at the hotel.”

His father had fastened his attention on a strip of horizon showing over the treetops, as if he’d never before seen the view.

Justin touched his hat brim and bade her good-bye, all the while silently praying he’d find the right words when the time came. Revealing Fancy as her mother could go either way.

Chapter Fifty-Eight

Seated at their kitchen table, Harrison studied his son closely as Justin filled him in on all the events transpiring in Y Knot since he'd been gone. The house was blessedly quiet, since Pauline had taken Carlie to visit one of her new friends from Sunday school. The child, roughly Carlie's age, was the niece of the new banker's wife and, being an orphan, lived with the couple.

Justin shared about Jack Jones's return to Y Knot and also about the burglaries occurring around town. Justin was probably correct about the culprit being the Hicks boy. That wouldn't surprise Harrison in the least. Especially with the juvenile way he was taunting Justin with the return of the new bridle and the rib bones he'd lifted from the butcher shop. But something more seemed to be bothering his son. Something he wasn't saying. They'd just finished roast beef leftovers from the previous night's supper, and Harrison felt sated. Pushing back his chair, he took a deep breath.

He wasn't saying everything, either. How he'd met a female friend from his youth at the wedding, and sparks had ignited. So much so, he'd been spooked. He wasn't interested in another wife, just yet—or, at least, so he kept telling himself. His life had just calmed down with this move to Y Knot. Confronted with strong feelings, he'd run like a scared rabbit back to Montana. And this was where he intended to stay.

"Pa?"

"Sorry, I guess I'm a bit tired from the long ride, and now the big meal. I wouldn't worry too much about Jack. Once the McCutcheons return, he might change his tune about staying in town. From what you've said, he seems to be walking a straight line. He's harmless, unless he locks you up in a burning cell." They exchanged a knowing look. "And I have every faith you'll catch the scoundrel with sticky fingers. You can't do any more than you've already done with one man short. Just stay alert, as you've been doing. You've got a good head on your shoulders. I'm extremely proud of you, son, even if I don't say it often."

"Thanks."

That was all? Now Harrison was sure something was bothering Justin. He was staring into his coffee cup with the concentration of a fox watching a mole hole and hadn't even looked up at the praise. "Justin? More on your mind?"

Justin sighed deeply and sat back in his chair. "I'm just struggling with a situation. Involves two people. One or the other might be in for a big hurt, and I'm not quite sure how I should proceed." He gazed at his father, this time not as a son, but as an equal.

"Go on."

Justin rubbed a hand over his mouth. "This dilemma has brought greater appreciation for all the decisions, many life-and-death, you've had to make over the years. It's tough. I'm not sure I'm able. There's a lot at stake."

"Yes, you can. I have every confidence in whichever outcome you decide. It will be thought out and measured. Two sides always exist for every situation, which means someone will be pleased and someone won't. Can't be helped. Or, you might be surprised when both parties feel your decision is the right one—*or* the wrong one. I assume this decision is something you haven't shared with me?"

Justin nodded.

"Does the outcome involve you in any way?"

Justin sat for a long time without answering. And then he nodded. "Indirectly, but I won't let that alter my reasoning."

"I see." *Something involving Miss Plumb.*

Justin shook his head, as if he'd just read Harrison's thoughts. "You probably think you know, but trust me, you don't. This is big, life-changing. Getting this right is imperative."

Intriguing. When had his little boy turned into such a man? Maybe it was the trip he'd just taken, and before that, he'd been seeing Justin as he'd been five years ago. This large fella across the table was strong of arm and wide of shoulder.

He'd matured into a fine mixture of himself and Justin's mother. Theresa would be so proud of him. Justin had inherited Theresa's lighter hair and blue eyes. And he often saw her in his smile. Harrison's heart warmed. They'd married when they were both only eighteen, with stars in their eyes and a love so big it reached to the moon. "When I was on the bench, I never allowed fear to hinder my judgments in any way. Fear can harness your intellect. Don't let that happen. You might find this surprising, but I never shied away from consulting God, as well. He's always there to listen."

Justin just stared.

"If the situation calls for action, don't hesitate. Indecisiveness only makes matters worse. God gave you a brain. *And* a heart. The law gives you authority. Being a lawman isn't an easy job, but someone has to do it. Brandon Crawford would echo what I've just told you. As a matter of fact, I think I remember a conversation like this one over a game of checkers a handful of years ago." He smiled into his son's troubled eyes, believing every word he'd just said.

Chapter Fifty-Nine

Fancy steeled herself to the relentless knocking as the sound reverberated around her small room. She wasn't ready to face Cole. What could she say? The words in Mrs. Goodheart's letter kept rolling around in her head, mixing her feelings with her intentions, her memories, her longings, and tossing them into a jumble. She needed to get out of Y Knot before the truth came out for everyone to talk about and sneer at. Or, more importantly, ruin her daughter's good reputation and social standing.

Her daughter was here! Or soon would be. The unbelievable thought made her shiver. Mrs. Goodheart hadn't revealed her name. Was that intentional? Could Miss Madison Plumb be her daughter? She looked to be the right age and resembled Fancy, with her cookie-dough-colored hair and vivid blue eyes. Their brilliant hue had struck her the day they'd come face to face, and Fancy had thought what a fortunate young woman she was. She could attract any young man she wanted.

As greatly as her heart yearned to take time and get to know her daughter—*maybe Madison Plumb*—she just couldn't. Madison had no idea about Fancy. She might want to find her mother *now,* but she'd be sorry after the fact. Then the damage would be done. Her status would be ruined. Marred from a mother who had led a fast life and whose shady past was never far away. Fancy had given her sweet baby girl up for adoption to assure she'd have a good life and respectability, with a mother and father to love her. Dress her in nice clothes. Nourish her with healthy and abundant food. Give her a good education, so she wouldn't be at the whim of anyone. Back then, Fancy didn't have two nickels to rub together. She'd never married. And then the life she took up would brand her daughter forever. She just couldn't do it. Her eyes welled and finally spilled over.

"Fancy! What's wrong? Please open the door."

She placed her hand on the shabby wooden divider, knowing she couldn't put off Cole for long. "Please, Cole, give me a moment to collect myself, and then I'll let you in. Can you do that?" She looked at her bed, thinking about her traveling case stored beneath.

"Open the door, Fancy," he said sternly. "Did something happen to upset you? Is Lenore all right? Did someone stop you in the alley and try something?"

Oh, how she wished this issue was as straightforward as some simpleton trying to paw and fondle her. Men's advances didn't bother her much. She'd learned early how to take care of herself with perfected, scathing lines and escape tactics. She'd had lots of practice.

Taking a calming breath, she steadied her voice. "No, no, nothing like that, Cole, I promise. Give me five minutes and I'll tell you everything." Would she? Today's stage had already come and gone. She'd heard the rattle as clear as day after she crossed the street and headed for the saloon's back door. How could she get out of town? Time was of the essence.

"Fine. You have five minutes to do what you need to do, but I'm standing right here with my shoulder against the post."

She heard the click of Cole's pocket watch lid flip open as he checked the time.

He snapped it closed.

One thing about Cole, he was punctual. With single-minded resolve, she pulled her valise from under the bed, laid it on her quilt, and threw open the lid. Going to her highboy, she opened the bottom drawer, grasped an armful of clothes, and began stuffing them in one by one.

She stopped. Looked at the almost-full container and then back at the highboy. Cramming them in would never work. Taking out the garments, she examined each and then carefully folded the items she couldn't live without, strategically trying to make them fit. She'd collected a few extra clothes since coming to Y Knot, but she wouldn't miss them once she was gone. The important thing was to get away before Madison learned the truth and tracked her down.

Cole tapped on the door. "Time's up, Fancy. You promised to open up. I'm holding you to your word."

Cole, oh, Cole. Just like she'd feared. Her life had changed when he'd shown up. Became light and breezy. She'd told her heart to stay away, but it hadn't listened.

"Fancy?"

He wouldn't be put off again. She wiped the silent tears and went to the door. With a shaky hand, she unlocked the latch and pulled it open.

He stepped into the room. A few seconds passed as he looked at the open valise on the bed and then back into her face. "Goin' somewhere?" he asked calmly.

Her lips wobbled. "I am."

"Why?"

The way his gaze searched her eyes, she knew *he knew* the gravity of the situation. His playful half smile was nowhere to be seen. "For reasons I'd rather not say."

"Sorry, Fancy, you'll need to do better. I think you owe me that small courtesy. I've told you how I feel about you. *And* I'm concerned." He touched her cheek where her tears left a damp trail. "I won't let you leave without an explanation. A *good* explanation."

The panicky feeling was back, raking her heart

with sharp fingernails. Slicing her insides to tiny pieces. "Marry me, Cole. You asked me before. Well, I'm saying yes now. I'm sick of Y Knot. I've stayed too long and feel the urge to move on."

He just stared.

"As long as you take me away immediately. Once I've made up my mind, I can't abide waiting. Today's the day."

"Today!" he blurted.

Voices from downstairs carried up the staircase, and she looked at the door.

"Just the fellas gettin' drunk."

"You're up here in my room! What will they think?"

"Do you care?"

She did now. *Especially* now. She'd never brought anyone into her room. Not even Abe. The women of Y Knot might think otherwise, but they were wrong. She nodded. "I *do* care. I might be a saloon girl, but I'm not a soiled dove." Her voice dropped to a whisper. "At least, not anymore . . ."

His face softened. "Still the little girl I saved from drowning. Even if you were, it wouldn't matter a lick to me." He took her hand and led her to the bed. He gestured for her to sit and did the same beside her. "I'm not marrying you to help you run away from some problem rattling your mind. Tell me what it is, and I'll help you figure it out."

Fancy had no other option. Her past was here in town. If she wanted to save her daughter from ruining her life, she needed to act fast. "It's not a *problem,* Cole, it's a person." Her breath came out on a shudder. "When I was sixteen, I gave birth to a little girl. A perfect, beautiful angel. *My daughter.* Her adoptive parents have now passed on, so she's taken it into her head to find her real mother. She's coming to town to look for me. Or, maybe, she's already here."

As he studied her face his expression relaxed. "How do you know?"

"A letter from the woman who's been her nanny since she was small. Mrs. Goodheart—ignorant of the truth about me—sent me a letter in supplication. Imploring me to accept her. Befriend her. I believe Miss Madison Plumb might be my daughter." Her voice broke. Unable to go on, she dropped her gaze to their clasped hands as she wrangled her emotions. At his silence, Fancy looked up. "Can you imagine, Cole? That beautiful young woman?"

Cole was smiling. Gazing at the ceiling with a look of wonder. "A daughter?" he said, his tone full of reverence. "Fancy, that's remarkable. Yes, Miss Plumb must be her. Thinking on it, she looks remarkably like you." He picked up her hand and kissed her fingers. "Yes, I believe it completely."

"She knows *nothing* about me, Cole. Doesn't

know I'm a—well, she doesn't know who or what I am. I aim to keep it that way, no matter what. She's educated and refined. If the truth comes out, everything will go up in smoke. She'll be ruined. I know how cruel people can be, even when they know nothing about you. If you won't marry me, I'll go away by myself. Start over in a different town and change my name." She lifted a shoulder. "The name Fancy Aubrey is made up, why not try a new one?" She dashed away a new round of tears on her face. "That's the only way I can protect her."

Cole stood and dragged her to her feet, wrapping her in his arms. "You're not leaving town, and I'm not marrying you. Not under those circumstances, at least. Not to help you run from your past. You're not thinking about this in the right way. You're fortunate this young woman has hunted you down. Her actions are the only way for you two to have found each other. Ponder that. You have a chance to be a real family. Maybe have some grandchildren someday. I wish I could say the same, Fancy. I truly do."

"But the people of Y Knot. What will they—"

"Who the hell cares! You've got to leave the decision up to Madison. She's the only one who matters, and I can tell you, she'll love you the instant you meet. You're a wonderful, caring woman."

His deep, warm gaze did funny things to her.

Magical things, as if he could make her life right. When she considered meeting Madison on these new terms, her insides froze up like a January blizzard. She couldn't do it. She had to think of her daughter. Somehow, she needed to make Cole understand and get him to promise to keep the secret until she could get out of town. She just had to.

CHAPTER SIXTY

Justin made the only decision that sat well with his conscience. *It's not enough to speak, but to speak true.* His favorite line from *A Midsummer Night's Dream*. He'd talk to Fancy first, and make sure his suspicions about her being Madison's mother were true, and then go to the hotel and speak with Madison. How the news would be received, he wasn't sure.

Justin liked and respected Fancy Aubrey as much as he did any of the women in Y Knot. She was one of the funniest, brightest women he knew. He never thought less of her because of her occupation, but Aunt Pauline did. Could his aunt change the way she thought of Madison, too? She'd been plenty angry with Madison for just speaking with Fancy outside the mercantile after Pauline had tried warning Madison away. Madison had no control over her maternity, but small-minded people wouldn't care. Frustrated with the situation, he shook his head.

As Justin strode down the boardwalk, he saw Mr. Tracy step out of the telegraph office. The short man waved a greeting, but Justin didn't have time to stop and talk. Important business needed addressing. Like his father had advised, he'd not put off the inevitable.

Stepping into the Hitching Post, he stopped to let his eyes adjust to the dim, smoky room.

Abe stood behind the bar, and Fancy was nowhere to be seen.

"Fancy here?" he asked, stepping up to the bar.

Abe's eyes narrowed.

"Something wrong?" Justin asked.

"Don't know. You tell me."

Not in the mood for games, Justin squelched a sharp retort. "What's that supposed to mean, Abe? All I did was ask a simple question."

Abe took his time drying the beer mug in his hands. Finished, he carefully placed it on the top of the pyramid of mugs stacked on the back of the bar. He turned and leaned with both hands on the counter. "She's in her room. Cole's up there with her. Heard some pounding on the door a while back and some words exchanged, then quiet. I haven't heard a peep since she let him in."

Justin looked up. He'd never seen a man—or *anyone,* for that matter—go in or come out of her room before. He shook his head and looked away. What she did wasn't his business. All he wanted was to speak with her so he could talk to Madison. "Do you know what the pounding on the door was about?" He doubted Abe would say any more, but he had to try. The time to address Madison was slipping away if he wanted to catch her before she went back to the Biscuit Barrel.

Abe's face softened. "I sure don't. But I don't

like to see Fancy cry. And she was when she snuck in the back door and tried to get to her room, sight unseen. Cole didn't like it, either. Seems he's taken quite a shine to my Fancy. And, unless I'm a blind bison, the feelings are returned. I'm plumb scared, thinkin' I might lose the best saloon gal I've ever had. Nobody sings like Fancy."

Abe didn't know the half of it. "Don't suppose I can go up and knock on her door?"

Abe bristled like a banty rooster guarding the henhouse.

Justin scuffed his boots. "Guess that was a dumb idea. I really need to speak with her. It's important." He glanced at the second floor, mulling over his options.

A door opened, and Cole stepped out. He descended the stairs, looking tired.

Did he know the truth of things? Would bringing him in on the situation be a violation to either woman's trust? Cole came toward them, a contemplative expression on his face. "Mercer." Justin felt Cole knew the situation. But would the man talk? He'd been protective over Fancy before. "You have a minute?"

Cole glanced at Abe, who lifted a shoulder.

Justin gestured toward a lone table in the corner by the front window where they could talk in private. They walked over and got comfortable. "I know about Fancy," he said low, under his breath. "I've been putting two and two together for a few days." He didn't want to be too specific, in case Cole really didn't know anything. Or in case Justin was wrong. "What's she planning to do?"

"And what do you think you know, Deputy?" Cole replied softly. "Just this morning, we had the same conversation, only *that* time your questions were about Lenore."

"Don't you mean Lenore, Fancy's *sister?*" Justin threw it out, guessing. No other reason made sense why Fancy would have a letter from Kentucky delivered to Lenore. The two women didn't have a strong resemblance, but a lot of siblings didn't.

Cole sat back. His eyes narrowed, and he crossed his arms over his chest.

From behind the bar, Abe watched their conversation, not even trying to cover his curiosity.

"All I want is five minutes," Justin said. "Can you go up and ask her?"

"I assume you have more information you're not sharing."

Justin nodded. "You'd be correct. Just like you're trying to protect Fancy, so am I. As well as somebody else. It's important. Life-changing. All I'm asking for is a handful of minutes."

"Nothin' doing, Deputy. I've just had a long discussion with Fancy. She's not bending. I think you and I see this thing the same way, but she doesn't."

"What's she planning?"

Cole just stared.

"She's leaving town," Justin guessed again. "Doing what she thinks is best. Running to protect the truth from coming out."

Still, the steely hard stare from Cole.

The man wasn't saying, but he wasn't denying anything, either. What now? Surely, Fancy would be on the stage tomorrow. If she changed her name and went to some big city, say San Francisco or New York, or a hundred other places, finding her would be impossible. She'd disappear, and Madison would never see her dream fulfilled. He rubbed a hand over his face. Did he dare tell Madison without solid proof?

A hoot went up from a table and the sound of chips being racked to the side. Someone was having a good day. The question was, would Justin end up a winner or loser when Madison learned the truth?

Chapter Sixty-One

Justin knocked on Madison's hotel room door, anxious to see her. He would have sent up Hildy, but the hotel clerk wasn't around. It was only one o'clock, so Madison still had a few hours before she needed to be back at the Biscuit Barrel. Silence filled the musty hallway. Was she napping? Nervously, he worried the rim of his hat dangling in his fingers.

The door opened, and Madison's eyes widened.

He smiled and forced a chuckle. "What? I said I'd try to come by. I guess you didn't believe me." She didn't come out or invite him in, which wouldn't have been proper, anyway. "Would you like to take a walk?" He looked past her into the room. A beam of sunshine entered her window and sliced the small space in two. "That is, if I'm not interrupting anything important."

She tipped her head, as if trying to decide.

"I hope you weren't sleeping."

"Oh, no. I was writing some questions for my interview with the mail-order brides. I need to concentrate on my *real* work occasionally. Seems life keeps getting in the way."

"So, does that mean you'd like to take a walk? Or go back to work? I'd never want to stand in the way of progress. You have a few hours before you must return to the restaurant. You could get a lot accomplished."

She set a hand on her hip. "Are you trying to talk me *out* of your invitation, Deputy?"

He cracked a smile. "Nothing could be further from the truth. I just don't want you to feel obliged. I thought I'd go over to the livery and look in on my mare, Scout. It's been a few days since I've taken her out. She enjoys a good brushing now and then."

Madison's eyes lit up.

He knew she liked horses. And the livery was close and usually quite private. He'd not want anyone to hear the information he intended to share.

"If you'll wait for me in the lobby, I'll be down just as soon as I change my dress."

No turning back now. Feeling a stone drop in his stomach, Justin smiled and dipped his chin. "Take all the time you need."

Excited for some time away from her troubles, Madison walked at Justin's side as they passed the sheriff's office and crossed Half Hitch Street and into the livery yard. Gravel crunched beneath the soles of her boots as the musty scent of horseflesh greeted her. As unladylike as the thought was, she loved the smell of horses, and all being around the animals entailed. She hid a half smile, remembering her girlfriends back in Kentucky pinching their noses at the sight of a fresh mound of horse manure.

She followed Justin into the quiet dimness of the large barn, hearing the *clang-clang-clang* of hammer on anvil and the occasional neigh of a horse. A few chickens scratching around in the dirt scurried away when they walked in. A bright-colored rooster in the rafters crowed their arrival. She flinched at the sudden sound and then laughed.

"June must be shoeing a horse," Justin said over his shoulder as he looked around. "I'll just let her know we're here." He disappeared through a wide door that must lead to the forge.

Madison let out a deep, relaxing breath. She'd met June Pittman several times before. Once at the fabric shop, once in passing on the boardwalk, and another time in the mercantile, when Madison had gone in to check her mail. The straightforward young woman worked and acted like a man. She wore dungarees, cowboy boots, and scraped her long, brunette hair back in a ponytail. For all that Mrs. Goodheart had preached to Madison about manners and being a lady to catch a young man's eye, acting like the stronger sex hadn't stopped Morgan Standford from falling for the lady blacksmith. Their story was poignant.

Over a cup of hot cocoa at the restaurant, Hildy

told Madison the two were in love, and June was ready to marry, but Morgan couldn't—or, at least, felt that way. His family, back in Saint Louis, was large. Ten children in all, counting his sisters, Heather Standford Klinkner, one of Y Knot's mail-order brides, and Sally Standford Guthrie, who came to Y Knot, as well, and married one of the ranch hands at the Heart of the Mountains. Morgan, second to the eldest, had followed Sally and found he liked Y Knot enough to stay and set up his furniture shop. The issue was, Morgan's father was dead, and Morgan took it upon himself to send most of his earnings home to help support his mother and siblings. If Morgan and June wed, the next natural step, children, would soon follow. Then his earnings would be needed here to support his wife and family. Hildy said the situation was frustrating for them both.

Enjoying the solitude of the large barn, Madison went to a stall door and looked in on one of the horses. It had its muzzle deep in a mound of greenish-brown hay and looked to be enjoying the treat immensely.

The animal raised its head but didn't come over to say hello.

"What's he saying?" Justin asked, a playfulness in his tone as he approached.

She turned and smiled. "Don't disturb me when I'm eating." She was relieved to see his dancing eyes. He'd been so serious of late. And she hadn't seen much of him. She'd grown used to their many meetings around town, when he came into work for a quick cup of coffee and a slice of pie, or inside the quiet sheriff's office. His face was what she looked for the minute she stepped out of the hotel. She'd feared her newness had worn off and he'd moved on. Or maybe he was tired of her hopes and need to find her mother. For all she knew, that letter was nothing. A million envelopes could look the same. She was probably driving Justin mad with all her talk and solicitations for help.

"I can understand," he replied. "I don't like if Aunt Pauline wants a recounting when I'm trying to enjoy a meal." He took her elbow and turned her to the barn aisle. "Come on. I'll catch Scout and bring her inside so we can clean her up. Caring for a horse can be calming."

She tipped her head. What an odd thing to say, although it did sound exactly like what she wanted to do today. Stop the crazy thoughts running through her head. The bliss of repetition and calm. She glanced around. "Where is she?"

"Out behind the barn, in the sunshine." Justin went to the wall pegs and gathered a halter and lead rope. They walked in companionable silence until they emerged into the sunlight, where several small paddocks were filled with horses and a few mules.

"There she is." Justin pointed to a group of five

animals in the left enclosure. "Can you pick her out?"

She'd run into Justin on his horse a couple of times when she'd been on her way to the restaurant or coming back after her shift. The horse was tall, and she'd had to crane her neck to look up into Justin's face. She glanced between the animals.

He smiled at her now.

"Well," she said, thinking how much they all looked alike. She realized, when she'd encountered him astride, she'd noticed more about the attractive man than she had about the horse. "She's not the mule," she said on a giggle.

"Very good—although sometimes she's as stubborn as one."

"And she's not the black. I remember . . ." She went closer to the fence, where she'd have a better view. "Hmmm . . . yes, she has a white marking on her forehead between her eyes."

He nodded. "Again, right. That's called a star, or a blaze, if it's long. But I see the three remaining have the same."

She glanced up into his face, already knowing he was teasing her. "I'm narrowing down my options."

"This might help—she's the only mare out there. The others are geldings. Do you know how to tell the difference?"

Heat surged to her face. She dared not look at

the area Justin had alluded to. She'd guess and hope for the best. "She's on the far right of the bunch."

"Congratulations! You did it." He gave a whistle.

Scout, already looking their way, slung her head to the side and trotted over.

Justin opened the gate and stepped inside. He slipped the halter over her head and led her out, closing the gate behind him. As they walked toward the barn, he held out the lead rope to Madison. "Would you like to lead her?"

Excitement zipped inside Madison, mixing with a little fear. The sound of the *clop-clop-clop* on the hard, beaten earth was wonderful. She'd always liked horses, and now was her chance. "All right," she said, taking the lead rope as he scooted to the outside, placing her between him and the large animal. She glanced down, watching the hooves as they came forward, plunked down, and then moved back as the opposite leg came forward. She looked up at Justin. "She's nice."

Justin nodded. "She's gentle. Carlie rides her here in the back paddock. You can, too, if you'd like. She doesn't get enough exercise these days."

Madison just smiled. She wasn't sure if she was ready for that, but offering was generous.

At the back door of the barn, Major, Cole Mercer's dog, rested in the sunshine, chewing vigorously on something.

"What's he have?" Madison asked. "It doesn't look like a bone."

"A clipping he must have pilfered from the horse June is shoeing. Dogs love 'em."

Not understanding, her eyebrows shot up.

"The clipped-off toenail."

At the disgusting thought, she clamped a hand over her mouth. All the places the hoof had stepped flashed through her mind. Since the dog didn't seem inclined to move, they walked around him and went down the aisle toward the front of the barn.

Once there, Justin took the lead rope and tied it to a metal ring attached to the wall.

Feeling a sense of accomplishment, she patted Scout on the neck, still warm from the sunshine.

From a bucket of grooming tools, Justin handed her a brush and showed her how to slip her hand underneath the leather handle. "Don't be frightened. Like I said, she likes to be groomed. By the way, you never told me how you picked Scout out of the group."

She liked Justin's warm gaze and attention. She knew he was tall, but she'd never really stood so close or realized just how tall he was. She felt tiny between him and Scout. Wanting to change the direction of her thoughts, she turned and swished the brush along Scout's back. "I just thought she was the prettiest. Since you said the rest were boys, I figured . . ."

Justin barked out a laugh.

She stopped brushing and stared.

"I agree with you. She has a nice, refined head, and good conformation," he added quickly. "But your reasoning for her appeal tickles me."

She raised a brow in mock protest.

"Although it shouldn't, I guess." His attractive half grin appeared, and he looked apologetic. "Makes total sense."

She smiled at his flirtations. She was flirting with him, as well, something which was becoming too difficult to deny. He stood at her side, and she focused on his hand holding the grooming tool as it moved along the horse's back. Large and strong, she'd noticed his hands many times before. In the Biscuit Barrel, eating a slice of pie. Or when she'd visited him in the sheriff's office, and he was writing something in the daily log. And again, on their Sunday picnic after church. His long, tapered fingers made tingles tumble around in her tummy. "I've never seen you snap your whip, Justin. Can I watch sometime?"

"Of course. The next time I practice, I'll let you know."

She smiled and ducked her head back to the job before her.

Major trotted up, his prize still clenched in his jaws. He sat a few feet away and wagged his tail.

Madison stopped brushing and glanced at him.

"He's a good boy, most of the time," she said, holding back a laugh.

"Only most of the time?"

She nodded. "He comes to the Biscuit Barrel with Mr. Mercer and waits outside and gazes in the window with the saddest expression. Sometimes, he sneaks in when someone opens the door too wide. He quickly looks for crumbs until Mrs. Larson notices and gives him a tongue-lashing, escorting him out the door."

Justin laughed and circled around Scout's hindquarters and gazed at Madison over the horse's back. "Then I guess you don't have to sweep."

"That's not the way it works." She glanced at the dog. "I certainly don't mind his visits, but he gets scolded so often, I don't know how he remains so cheerful." She smiled at Major. "Mr. Mercer gets a tongue-lashing, too, although a nicer, calmer one. Mrs. Larson would never run him off completely. He's too good a customer."

Justin stopped brushing.

His peculiar expression was one she'd never seen.

"Cole Mercer's a quiet fellow," Justin said. "What do you think of him?"

What a strange question. "He's quiet, all right, and extremely polite—and patient. I wish I could say the same of everyone who comes in to eat." She cocked her head. "Why do you ask?"

The way Justin quickly went back to work made her suspicious.

"Just wondered what you thought. He's new to town and holes up in the saloon most days."

"As do a lot of men, I've come to learn since I've arrived in Y Knot," she quickly replied. "Something I'll add to my term paper. I don't hold that against him—or anyone else, unless they're drunk and bothering people."

He dropped an arm over Scout's neck. "Anything else?"

"About Cole? No. Not really." Madison went to the bucket of grooming tools and exchanged her brush for a comb. Scout hadn't moved one hoof since her beautifying effort had begun. Madison combed a few tangles from the mare's medium-length, reddish-brown mane. "It's time for me to figure out my next move," she said softly. "I hadn't intended on staying at the expensive hotel this long, but I've grown to love my cozy little room and Hildy's friendship. Having the restaurant downstairs is handy, too." She glanced up at Justin over Scout's neck. That strange expression was back in his eyes. He was acting odd. Had he brought her out here for a reason other than spending time with her?

CHAPTER SIXTY-TWO

Justin had talked himself around in a circle, trying to conjure up his courage to tell Madison her mother worked in the Hitching Post, singing, serving whiskey, and entertaining men. *I like Fancy Aubrey. She's a good woman. A kind woman. Madison will love her once they get to know each other.*

The memory of Madison's arrival in Y Knot, and the moment she'd stepped from the stage and onto the dirt of Main Street, flashed in his mind. The sophisticated dress. The matching hat with net trim. Her delicate, white lace gloves. She'd been raised a lady.

I've made my decision to tell her, and I can't change my mind now. Fancy is leaving town. Would Madison ever forgive me for robbing her of the choice that is hers, alone, to make?

At his silence, Madison looked up at him with questions in her eyes. "Actually, Justin, I'm thinking about returning to Kentucky. Coming was a fool's errand. I never really had a chance of finding my mother. Communications move slowly. She could have died or moved away. And that letter could have come from anyone. I'm deluding myself."

Tossing the brush into the bucket made Major jump to his feet.

Justin circled back around his mare and took Madison into his arms. Relief and love flowed through his body so strongly, everything became clear. He just needed to walk softly. She hadn't pulled away. "Please don't go," he said against her ear, and then looked down into her expectant face. "Finding your mother isn't impossible. And if you must move from the hotel, inquire with Ina Klinkner. Their home has several empty bedrooms. She lets out a room to Ashley Adair, the schoolteacher. I don't want you to leave," he said, his voice husky. Should he say more, not knowing how she felt? She'd never expressed anything more than fondness for him, and now today, a little innocent flirting. Nothing he could say would convey the enormity of his feelings for her. Words would fall short. Perhaps he'd show her, instead. He leaned down and pressed his lips to hers.

The kiss was light and brief, but for him, packed a powerful wallop. He needed all his strength not to wrap her in his arms and kiss her properly, the way he'd been dreaming about for days. Her empty hand came up, and she gently placed it on his chest, as if not knowing what to do with her arms. He should tell her before they got any more involved. Their faces were still close as he gazed into her vivid blue eyes. Had he ever seen anything more beautiful? He took a halting step back. "Madison, there's something I need to tell you."

Wonderment from their kiss was still etched on her countenance. Her cheeks turned a dusky pink. "Yes?"

Taking the comb from her, he tossed the tool into the bucket and took hold of both her hands. "Do you mind sitting?" He gestured toward a small bench along the wall.

"Is something wrong?"

"Just give me a minute." To the clanking of June's hammer in the other room, he led her over to the seat. Perhaps he should have given this a little more thought. "I discovered something," he said, after they were settled facing each other, their knees touching on the small seat. Dust particles danced in a beam of sunshine only a few feet away. The chickens had gone away somewhere to roost and had stopped clucking. "Something about your mother."

Madison straightened, the glow on her face turning into excitement and wonder. "What?"

He rubbed his palms together, thinking. *How is the best way to say this?*

"Justin. Tell me!"

"The letter. I saw it. At Lenore's."

Confusion shone in her eyes and she looked away, but only for a moment. "Lenore's? How do you know it's the letter I'm looking for? And how did you find it?"

“When I was patrolling the town Saturday night, I thought I saw someone or something around the cabins behind the hotel. Investigating, I noticed the letter placed on her table under the light. The return address was from a law office in Kentucky.”

Her eyes went wide. “You saw all that? Looking in her window?”

It *did* sound terrible. “I knew she was at work, and I was making sure no one was inside,” he explained quickly. “I couldn’t help but see the letter. And knowing how important to you finding your mother is, I read the return address.”

Madison’s shoulders slumped. “Then the letter means nothing to me. Lenore is too young. She must have some other legal business that has nothing to do with me.” She huffed out a disappointed breath. “And you waited three days to tell me because you didn’t want to hurt me. You know the letter is my only lead.” She timidly laid her hand on his, which rested on his leg. “I understand, Justin. You don’t have to worry.” Her gaze moved over his face and wandered to his lips. “I could never be angry with you.”

Her soft touch stirred all kinds of feelings inside. He didn’t have much experience with women, since his growth spurt was so late in his teens, and then he didn’t have much confidence, but perhaps experience didn’t really matter when true love was concerned. He held her gaze. “There’s more.”

A small smile appeared. “My, you’ve been busy.”

“That’s why I haven’t directly sought you out for a few days. I wanted to be sure of my findings before I said anything.”

Her brow crinkled, and she nibbled her bottom lip.

Her hand still rested on his, so he rolled his over and took both of hers into his own. So small and warm. He wanted so much to make her his own.

“Please don’t drag this out. I’m not a child. Whatever you have to say can’t be as bad as you’re making it seem. Trust me.”

“Lenore is your mother’s younger sister. So, in actuality, she’s your aunt.”

A thousand expressions crossed Madison’s face as she tried to put the pieces of the puzzle together, but that wasn’t possible without his help.

At that moment, Drit marched into the barn, making Major jump again to his feet and Scout look around. The boardinghouse owner’s gaze found them together on the bench. One of the man’s overall straps wasn’t buckled and hung down over his belly, as if he’d dressed quickly.

“The thief has struck *again!* This time, the boardinghouse. Berta May said she saw you coming in here a little while ago. You need to come right now, Deputy. Lou’s spittin’ mad.

Whoever's accountable stole her favorite cookie jar passed down from her ma!"

Justin wasn't going anywhere now. He'd not leave Madison hanging. "I'll come, Drit, but not right this second."

Drit glared at Madison's hands in his own. "Courtin's more important?" he grouched and shook his head.

"We're not courting." *Yet.* "We're discussing an important matter." He gave her a sideways glance. "I'll be down to investigate as soon as I'm finished here." Beside him, he felt Madison getting ready to bolt, and he slightly tightened his grip. Who knew what was going through her mind?

Grumbling loudly, Drit turned and stomped out the way he'd come.

The clanging of metal on metal stopped. Silence engulfed them.

"Who is my mother?" she whispered.

"I'm not absolutely sure, but I believe—"

"Justin!"

"Fancy Aubrey." He held his breath.

She blinked. Her hands trembled, but she didn't pull away. "Fancy," she repeated softly. "Fancy Aubrey is my mother."

Such wonder was in her tone, he didn't know what to think. Did she believe he'd made the whole thing up?

"And you know this how?"

She sure wasn't giving out any clues to how

she felt about the revelation. As he watched her stare at their clasped hands, he gently cleared his throat. "After I saw the letter Saturday night, I began watching Lenore's house." He lifted a shoulder, still feeling like a Peeping Tom. "Not looking inside, just observing to see if I could learn anything more. This morning, Fancy went to Lenore's. With Abe still feeling under the weather, I decided to go to the Hitching Post to see if he was up and feeling better, but instead, I found Cole Mercer behind the bar. He and Fancy seem well acquainted for him being so new to town, so I asked him a few questions. He wasn't pleased. When I mentioned Fancy visiting Lenore, he asked then if I *knew* about Lenore. As if whatever he was alluding to was a secret." Madison seemed to be holding her breath. He hoped she didn't swoon.

"And?"

"I thought that a peculiar thing to say. So I asked again, and he clammed up and told me, if I wanted to know anything about Fancy, I'd have to ask her and not him."

"Is Cole my father?"

Her face had gone white, and she gripped his hands like a lifeline. With trying to figure out who Madison's mother was, the possibility of Cole being her father hadn't dawned on him. But the prospect was real. "I don't know. I guess anything's possible."

She let go of his hands, stood, and walked back to the stall she'd been looking in when they'd first arrived and gazed at the horse inside.

Justin followed her over and stood behind, waiting for her to say something. Did she want to hear his opinion? She wasn't asking, but he'd give it, anyway. "Madison, I like Fancy Aubrey a lot," he said softly. "She's always been kind to me and has, on occasion, given me good advice. In my estimation, she's a fine woman."

Madison turned to face him, tears shimmering in her eyes. "I believe you. I've only spoken with her once, but recalling that moment now, I remember thinking that I'd like to get to know her. She was interesting and straightforward." A large tear slid down her cheek, and she quickly wiped it away. "And she's extremely pretty."

Madison was only inches away. He thought about pulling her back into his arms. "*Beautiful,* you mean! And the two of you look just alike."

Her face pinked.

"I'm shocked I didn't see the resemblance sooner."

She glanced down for a moment and then back up into his face. "I want to go to her and meet her." She swallowed nervously. "Should I just go to the saloon and knock on the doors?"

CHAPTER SIXTY-THREE

Why was Justin taking so long to answer? Only moments ago, she'd been thinking about his strong arms, and now this revelation about her mother had her lightheaded and dizzy. "Justin? That's where she lives, isn't it? Or, at least, I've always assumed saloon girls resided in a saloon. Is there somewhere else?"

"Yes, she lives at the Hitching Post, but, ah . . ."

When she stepped back to study his reaction, she felt the stall door. "You told me your suspicions so I could meet her." Warmth infused her cheeks and tears swam in her eyes, making him look blurry. Why was he being so mysterious? "Justin, you're scaring me."

"I'm just not sure you should go to the saloon. Women don't usually go inside. And maybe Fancy should have a little warning, so she can get her thoughts together, as well."

"She can come to my room. We'll have plenty of privacy there. You tell her."

He shook his head. "I don't think she'll agree."

Uncertainty of the situation swirled within. Was he trying to keep them apart? "I've dreamt of this day since I was eight years old, Justin. I don't want to wait a second longer than I must."

"I haven't heard it from her lips, Madison. Maybe I'm wrong."

"I'll admit, I was a bit shocked, but I'm fine now and filled with excitement. All I want to do now is speak with her and make sure it's true before I let all my feelings run wild. I've found my mother!" She breathed out. "No, *you* found my mother! I'll be grateful to you for the rest of my life."

He rested his hands on her shoulders, as if to keep her feet on the ground.

She felt as if she might float away with happiness.

"Let me go talk to her and set up a meeting at Lenore's place. You'll have privacy there to work this out. No one will be the wiser."

He smiled, but the gesture didn't reach his eyes. Was there more he wasn't saying? "What's to work out?"

He swallowed and glanced away from her gaze.

I'm not imagining things. There is *more.*

The ten-foot-tall barn door between the livery and the forge opened. June led a gray horse through and approached, her face sweaty from all the strenuous work. A bandanna held her hair away from her face. Sweat stains marred her shirt at the neckline, and she wore short, leather leg coverings, flapping each time she took a step. She looked between them briefly but didn't say a word. Going to an empty stall, she led the horse in and reemerged a moment later with the halter in hand. Closing the door, she smiled as she passed them and was gone.

"Please, Justin, be honest with me. Don't try to protect me."

He let go a deep sigh. "You're right. You've come this far. When I went to the saloon, Abe told me Fancy went to her room and hadn't come out. She seemed upset. Maybe even was crying."

"And she had the letter?"

"That's what I saw. *A* letter, anyway. I assumed it was the one from Kentucky."

What Justin said was prudent. Madison shouldn't just barge in on Fancy without some advance knowledge. Justin's theory said she'd read a letter, and whatever was inside had upset her. A thought Madison hadn't considered before hit her. Perhaps the letter was what they thought it was, and Fancy didn't want to have anything to do with her long-lost daughter. She'd given her up at birth, and that was that. Fear, larger and deeper than anything she'd ever felt before, gripped her insides with the strength of a bear. "She doesn't want me—*again*."

"Don't jump to conclusions. You've had years to consider a reconciliation, but Fancy hasn't. Let me speak with her to set up a meeting. You seeking her out in the saloon, and causing an unneeded stir, isn't prudent for either of you. Go to work, and try to forget about anything other than serving open-faced beef sandwiches covered in gooey gravy and slices of pie," he said with a slight chuckle. "I'll let you know as soon as I have more information. You've waited this long, a few more hours, or maybe even a day or two, won't make a difference."

She didn't resist when he pulled her back into his arms. He was warm and safe, and she liked the way he smelled. The shadowy barn was quiet and felt like a sanctuary. He held her close and rubbed her back. Was Justin right? Would Fancy welcome a meeting, once she knew her daughter had searched her out, unbeknownst to her? Or would she be upset her life had been disrupted? Madison had heard once some women have no motherly instincts. Fancy Aubrey might be one. She'd gone into an occupation most women wouldn't choose, hadn't she? She hadn't married later and had other children. All the signs pointed to the fact she was a loner and most likely wanted to stay that way. And Lenore? What about her?

"And I think it'd be best if you didn't go searching out Lenore just yet, either," Justin said, as if reading her thoughts. "Our first and only move will be *me* speaking with Miss Aubrey." He leaned away and smiled down into her face. "Now, on to other matters. Thank you for the kiss, Miss Plumb," he said playfully. "I hope you liked kissing me as much as I liked kissing you."

He was changing the subject. Their first kiss

on this monumental day! He'd known then about Fancy. Was more going on than he was letting her know? "I did," she replied, warming at the memory. "Very much."

A small smile played around his lips. "I'm glad. Promise me one thing."

She gazed at him. "What?"

"Whatever happens in the next few days, promise me you won't run off to Kentucky. Let me help you work this out." He gently brushed back several strands of hair dangling in her face. "What seems enormous now can change quickly. What my earlier kiss said is that you mean a lot to me, Madison. It's true, You're special. I feel it in here." He tapped his chest. "I want to get to know you better and court you, if you'll have me. Help you find another place to live and see you settled in whatever you want to do. But I'm not sure your aim was ever to stay in Y Knot forever after finding your mother. You have college and your last year coming up. I hope, if my assumptions are right, they've now changed—and you feel the same about me as I do about you."

The feel of his fingers touching her temple was sweet. So much was happening. And so fast. Justin was waiting for an answer, and she didn't know exactly what to say. When she took too long to reply his smile faded. "I promise I won't leave town without telling you first," she murmured, knowing her words weren't the ones he hoped to hear. As much as she hated to hurt him, she didn't have a reply. Everything and more were jumbled inside her. Years of longing, thinking. She took a tiny step back.

His arms fell away.

His dear face was stoic.

"That's all right," he said softly. "You've had a shock. I understand."

But did he? Did he, really? In the midst of the chickens and horses, she nodded. Her life had taken a huge turn in some direction, she just didn't know which one.

Chapter Sixty-Four

Justin strode into the Hitching Post, ready to climb the stairs even if Abe tried to throw him out. Too much time had passed. He'd told Madison on Tuesday afternoon about Fancy, imploring her to give him ample time to set up a meeting between the two. Today was Thursday morning—and he'd yet to track down Fancy. He had no option now but to seek Madison out later today and give her an update. If he didn't, she'd take matters into her own hands. He was surprised she'd endured this long. Fancy needed to face facts. Madison wouldn't be put off much longer. They'd have a face to face, whether Fancy wanted it or not.

Inside, neither Cole Mercer nor Fancy was anywhere to be seen. "Abe, where's Fancy?" he barked, glancing to the upstairs balcony and then around the quiet saloon a second time.

Abe scowled and clonked the bottle down onto the bar top none-too-gently. "I *told* you yesterday, whatever's going on with her is none of my business *or* yours. I ain't seen her since Tuesday, when she ran upstairs crying—same as you. Ain't heard her in her room, either. Could be, she snuck out in the middle of the night." He gave a low whistle. "Sure am gonna miss my gal."

Frustration ripped through him. Fancy hadn't left town on the stage. Justin had watched closely. No one had gotten on or off today except a bag of mail and supplies for the mercantile. "And Mercer?"

"Same goes for him. Ain't seen hide nor hair—now I'm running this place alone." Abe's scowl faded, and he gave a deep, conceding sigh. "You got any new news on Brandon? How's the sheriff doin'? Sure never expected him to be gone so long."

Justin remembered the telegram in his pocket. He'd deliver it out to the Heart of the Mountains as soon as he'd spoken with Madison and hopefully found Fancy and talked some sense into her. Madison would be on her morning shift at the Biscuit Barrel, by now. "I do. He's doing well and should be able to be moved from the hospital across the road to the boardinghouse where the McCutcheons are staying anytime. His recovery is progressing since the second surgery."

Abe nodded along with his news. "That's darn good ta hear! He's much too young to die."

"And Flood's arrived in Helena from Miles City, and by now, I'm sure, Mrs. McCutcheon might be there, as well. It'll be a while before they're home in Y Knot—but, at least, Brandon is out of the woods." Justin was grateful. Not only his friend and upstanding citizen and sheriff of Y Knot would be fine and return, but when he did, Justin could go back to being the deputy and following orders until he was ready to become a sheriff himself. He missed those days. He'd followed up with Lou at the boardinghouse about the theft of her cookie jar. But he was back to square one with no real evidence. Dodger Hicks was responsible. Justin just needed to catch him in the act.

A sound behind Justin made him turn.

Cole Mercer stood in the doorway, one hand on each batwing door.

He looked as if he were about to turn and skirt away, sight unseen. "Mercer!" Justin called. "I want a word with you."

Cole stepped inside.

Justin tipped his head to the private corner by the window where they'd talked before. They ambled over but didn't sit down.

Abe shook his head and turned away.

"Where's Fancy?" Justin asked, keeping his voice low. "Abe says she's moved out. She needs to face the facts. She can't avoid what she thinks she can."

Cole fastened his narrowed gaze out the window, as if weighing his next words carefully. The muscle in his jaw tensed. "You can't make Fancy do something she's set against. And been set against her whole life," he said under his breath. "*Nothing* will change her mind. Believe me, I've tried and talked myself blue in the face."

"Dammit," Justin growled. "This decision isn't just up to her! A meeting between the two is inescapable."

Cole just gazed back.

Exasperated, Justin pulled off his hat and beat the Stetson against his leg. "If you're still in town, Fancy's still here, too. Where is she? I want to speak with her."

"Ease up," Cole said. "Just so you know, I agree with you. I think she's making a big mistake." They stood eye to eye. "I know you won't say who you're referring to, but we all know it's Madison Plumb. She looks just like Fancy and showed up in town at the right time. They have the same eyes, mouth, and hair." He glanced off for several long seconds. "I can't divulge where Fancy is because she made me swear, but I *can* tell you, she's meeting the stagecoach tomorrow after it passes through Y Knot and before it takes the south fork toward Pine Grove. At the stage station about an hour out of town. She intends to keep going and catch a train east. Has friends in New York she anticipates looking up."

Justin clenched his jaw against the frustration boiling inside. "And you're just going to let her go?"

"Hell no. I intend to marry Fancy and start over here in Y Knot, where she can remain close to Lenore, and hopefully her daughter, too."

This was a pickle. He couldn't just allow Fancy

to slip away before the two women had a chance to meet, but if he brought Madison out to the stage stop and Fancy rejected her there, Madison would never recover. Not a second time. And what would Madison think if she knew Fancy really *was* running away again, just like she'd said? For her daughter's own good, of course, but still. Fancy being young and afraid years ago was one thing, but having a second chance at a relationship and then throwing it away like day-old garbage was something else entirely. He might be forced to fudge the truth to make this work out for the best.

Chapter Sixty-Five

Shad Petty strode swiftly down the long, third-floor corridor at St. John's Hospital, his heart a beating snare drum. Rubbing his clammy palms against his thighs, he dreaded the conversation and examination to come.

A nurse headed his way.

He was as anxious as a five-year-old on his way to the doctor's office for his first shot. In reality, this examination would be far worse. In his disconcerted state, he'd wrongly gone to the third floor, looking for the doctor's office, only to be instructed by an orderly that Dr. Marlow's office was on the first floor. The slip of paper Flood had clandestinely handed him earlier this morning resembled chicken scratch. The writing, not Flood's, was next to impossible to decipher. The number one, after Dr. Marlow's scribbled name, had looked like the number seven. Now he'd have to hustle to arrive on time. "Sister," he said politely as they passed.

She smiled and nodded but gave no response, the *clip-clip-clip* of her shoes fading away as she continued past.

Taking the stairs two at a time, Shad descended the flights, glanced at the numbers and arrows on the passageway wall, and strode as quickly as he could without running and arrived at an office only three doors down from the room Brandon had occupied all the days he'd been a patient.

Filling his lungs, he grasped the knob and plunged inside, determined to get good news for Poppy. He'd sent a telegram as soon as he and Flood had arrived in Helena, explaining the change of plans and that he'd return home as quickly as possible. He hadn't mentioned *why* he'd gone with Flood but would explain everything when they were together. No secrets would come between them.

Inside, a young woman looked up at his abrupt appearance. She sat demurely at an oak desk kitty corner in the room closest to a closed interior door, a pen in her hand and papers in front of her. Three empty chairs sat along the wall. One dark eyebrow winged up. "You must be Mr. Petty, I assume?"

His throat went suddenly dry. "Yes, ma'am," he got out, his voice scratchy. "That's correct."

"Very good. The doctor will see you shortly. Please, take a seat and make yourself comfortable. Can I get you anything? A cup of water?"

He shook his head. A glass of any kind of liquid was the last thing needed now. He'd probably spill the whole thing down his shirt. His hands trembled like a bridegroom's since the moment he'd stepped into the room. "No, thank you, ma'am, I'm fine," he replied, gripping them together. He glanced to the chairs and took the one farthest from the young secretary. At least, that's what he assumed she was. She wasn't dressed like the other nurses, gliding down the hallways, taking temperatures, and bringing trays of food. She wore regular clothes and appeared prim and proper.

She smiled and then went back to whatever she was doing before he'd arrived.

Happiness or heartbreak teetered in the balance from today's outcome. He'd hardly slept a wink the last two nights, circling all the possibilities. Taking a deep breath, he willed himself to relax. He'd done this before. Being anxious was foolish. His everyday routine on the ranch was more dangerous than suffering an embarrassing examination by a stranger. If he wasn't getting married, he wouldn't be here at all. He'd accepted his fate years ago. A person couldn't direct destiny. The acknowledgment had taken some time, but as they say, what was done was done, and the past couldn't be changed. Now, he hoped that wasn't true. His ardent wish, after marrying Poppy, was to give her the child she wanted so much and rightly deserved. Even after all their talking, he wasn't sure he'd be able to go through with the wedding if children of their own weren't a possibility. He'd told her he would, but in his heart, he knew such a fate wouldn't be fair at all to her.

The interior door opened, and a man around thirty or forty stepped out. He handed the secretary a slip of paper.

She took it and scribbled something in a thick ledger. “Very good, Mr. Eberly. Have a nice day. We’ll see you next month.”

In anticipation of being called in, Shad’s heart began thumping again. Several moments passed and nothing happened.

The woman went back to work, shuffling envelopes, and then opened a drawer and took something out.

The door to the outer hallway opened.

The same nun he’d passed on the third floor stepped inside.

When she saw him, she pulled up in surprise, but only for an instant. She went to the desk, and the two women began a quiet discussion. The conversation continued softly, reminiscent of the quiet hum of a bee colony.

One woman said something, he couldn’t tell which because the nun had her back to him and blocked his view, and then the other giggled. He wrung his hands and tried to relax.

The nurse turned and went to the hallway door.

The young woman stood. “It won’t be much longer, Mr. Petty,” she said and smiled, after which she disappeared into the examination room.

This was it. The moment had arrived. Taking a deep breath, he closed his eyes.

Dear Lord, he began. *I don't have much to offer a woman like Poppy. Just my love and devotion. She'll be my first thought in the morning and my last before I fall asleep at night, after You, that is. But, Lord, she deserves children of her own. I've not asked for much over the years, just a job, and a roof over my head—oh, and jobs at the McCutcheon ranch for my two brothers. I've thanked you for that many times. But I'm asking for something now, Lord, for both Poppy and me. From my heart. Please, if it be your will, allow my seed free rein and the ability to reach her—"*

The inner door opened, and the young woman leaned into the room, one hand still grasping the doorknob. "Dr. Marlow will see you now."

With a shuddering breath, Shad stood and forced a smile. Whatever the outcome this morning, at least he'd know he'd tried everything. For Poppy. Always for Poppy.

Madison calmed her agitation and worked at the stubborn smudge of blueberry on the counter of the Biscuit Barrel café, applying more elbow grease. Several tables of customers dotted the dining room. She'd expected Justin yesterday, but to no avail. When would she get to speak with her mother?

The bell above the door sounded. Justin came through, his hat dangling from his fingers.

His handsome face made her cheeks warm as she remembered the kiss. Seeing him place his Stetson on the hat rack, she noticed his hair appeared damp. Had he washed up on her account? Excitement swirled inside. He must have news. She'd be meeting with Fancy today! Yesterday, as the hours crawled by with no word, she'd had to corral every ounce of willpower to trust his plan and not to go to the saloon unannounced. Or seek out Lenore.

She hurried to the end of the counter to the stool where he normally sat. "Justin," she said as nonchalantly as possible as he took his seat.

"Good day, Miss Plumb," he replied respectfully for others to hear, although his eyes danced with a secret.

Mrs. Larson sat at the other end of the counter, working on the schedule. She glanced up for a second, smiled at Justin, and then returned to her work.

"The coffee fresh?" Justin asked.

Hardly able to contain her excitement, Madison rushed for the coffeepot without even answering. Returning, she set a mug before him and poured to the brim.

He glanced at her boss and then asked, "How was business yesterday? Wednesdays are usually busy for the café."

Madison stifled a deep sigh. She didn't want small talk, only news of Fancy. "People bursting out the door. I was surprised you didn't come in for your usual slice of blueberry pie."

"Howdy, Deputy," Renee said and smiled at Justin as she came out of the kitchen with two plates in her hands and proceeded to a table by the door. "Missed you yesterday," she called over her shoulder.

Madison lifted a knowing eyebrow. Exasperated from the lack of privacy, she widened her eyes. "Do you have news?" she whispered.

He took a drink of his coffee and nodded. "A meeting is set up for tomorrow. Out of town."

Out of town? A pit dropped in Madison's stomach. Why couldn't they meet at Lenore's, if her mother was worried about being seen? Out of town sounded quite drastic.

"Do you work tomorrow?"

She cut a glance to Mrs. Larson, who didn't seem to be paying any attention. Madison shook her head. "Luckily, I don't," she replied under her breath.

"Good. Come by the sheriff's office around eleven in the morning. I'll have a buggy ready and waiting."

Something in Justin's tone made her wary. "So, you've spoken with her, and she's agreed to meet me? She knows I'm her daughter? In the livery, you just said you'd seen her crying while holding the letter we both believe was from my father's attorney."

He shifted uneasily on the stool.

"Order up, Madison," the cook called from the kitchen.

"Justin?" Something was wrong. Desperately wrong. She could feel it in every inch of her being. Hear it in what he wasn't saying.

"Madison?"

Mrs. Larson stern tone made Madison glance over.

"Did you hear Cook?"

She nodded. "Yes, ma'am." Twirling, she hurried off. A hundred bad feelings made her hands tremble. Thankfully, the order was only one plate filled with six-inch-wide flapjacks and topped with a mound of scrambled eggs. She smiled at Mrs. Larson as she breezed by, feeling anything but happy. She needed to speak with Justin in private.

Finished, she went to her other table and gathered up the three empty plates. Experienced now, she stacked two greasy plates up her left arm and held the other with an empty coffee cup balanced on top. "Will there be anything else?" she asked the man and two women.

"Nope," the man replied. "Just the check."

From the corner of her eye, she could see Renee speaking with Justin.

He said something.

Renee laughed.

The man cleared his throat. "The check?"

"Oh, I'm sorry. I'll have it right away." Carrying the dirty dishes and rattling cup and utensils, she crossed the café in quick strides, sounding like a peddler's wagon, uncannily aware of Mrs. Larson's watchful gaze. Her employer stood and followed her into the kitchen.

"Is something wrong?" Mrs. Larson asked, watching her unload the dishes at the sink. The steamy kitchen was hot from the cookstove. "You seemed distracted yesterday—having two different tables sending back food. You certainly seem anxious today. Is there a problem you'd like to share?"

Heavens, no! "I'm sorry, Mrs. Larson, I, er, am just trying to decide if—well . . ." *What can I possibly tell her?* "If my decision to come to Y Knot was completely thought out? And if I should stay living at the hotel. Just little issues, is all."

Mrs. Larson's eyes bulged. "If you decide to quit, I hope you'll give me ample notice to replace you. Yesterday's Wednesday was the best day in Biscuit Barrel history. Word has spread far and wide, and it's not just the McCutcheon ranch anymore who plan their week around dinner here. We couldn't have survived without you."

Madison nodded eagerly. "Oh, yes. Don't worry, I'll give you heaps of notice, but right now,

I need table three's check before the gentleman becomes angry and leaves without paying."

Mrs. Larson's face brightened. "That's good thinking. You're a good girl, and I appreciate you greatly. We'll worry over other matters later."

Madison breezed by Justin without a sideways glance. Something was amiss, and he was protecting her. The humming smile was a dead giveaway.

Chapter Sixty-Six

After the physical examination, Shad sat up and pulled the chilly sheet closer. The experience hadn't been as bad as he'd anticipated. A lot of probing and pressing, some on his belly, then lower. Staring at a small crack in the office ceiling, he'd thought of anything besides what the doctor was doing below. Spring roundup, the color of Poppy's sky-blue eyes, and once, when Tanner was only three, he'd snuck out of bed in the middle of the night and gone outside. Grandma Girdy was beside herself, hysterical, in tears until Tanner was found in a dirty barn stall, playing with a handful of chickens.

Dr. Marlow, a short, slim man, wearing a white coat over his brown slacks and street shoes, leaned back against a small counter that held several doctoring tools, folded his arms, and regarded him intently. His bespectacled countenance had an air of calm. From the start, he'd been kind and extremely professional. He'd listened carefully, taking notes as Shad went over what had transpired with the bull, giving him his reason for the doctor visit today, as well as the fact that he was set to be married in the near future.

"From what I can ascertain from my exam,

nothing seems to be amiss, Mr. Petty. I didn't even find any scar tissue. That said, that does not mean you are as you were before the accident with the bull."

Hope surged.

"Truthfully, I can't imagine how the doctor you saw in, ah . . ."

"Colorado," Shad filled in.

"Yes, well, how he could have known much of anything by the superficial examination you described, and then given the kind of diagnosis that he did. I can't do something like that with all the best equipment offered here at one of the most respected medical institutions in the country. That's not to say he was wrong, but he shouldn't have given you the prognosis so quickly—and without examining a specimen. You say you were in a lot of pain for an extended amount of time? That might only have been the result of extensive bruising, and perhaps not something being crushed irreparably."

Shad could hardly trust what he was hearing after all the years he'd believed he was sterile. "You think I'm okay then, Doctor? That I'll be able to give my future wife children of her own?"

Dr. Marlow's face softened. He removed his glasses, rubbed his eyes, and then positioned them back on his nose. "I can't say that quite yet."

Shad slumped. He had hoped for something a

little more solid. *You're a stud, Mr. Petty. I see no issues with you getting your beautiful wife with child every year.* He stifled a small smile that threatened to appear at his wayward thought.

"Only time will tell—as well as the results of the sample you'll give me."

Heat sprang to Shad's face.

"That's why we call this practicing medicine. We try, regroup, and try again. But, if issues *do* arise, and you have no success say, in six to twelve months, there are some options you can try. The medical industry has made giant strides in helping couples who experience infertility problems. Just four years ago, in Philadelphia, Dr. William Pancoast successfully completed the first recorded case of human artificial insemination that ended with a live birth, a concept that's been in the works since 1850. I, myself, have helped three women carry a healthy child to term." A bright smile broke out on his face.

"That's remarkable," Shad said. "But if my sperm is blocked, you can't get out any to inseminate with, right?" Shad's shyness had disappeared, and he now felt as if he were speaking about livestock on the ranch. Whenever a bull was rendered sterile, and stopped getting heifers in calf, he was no longer needed and soon ended up on the butcher's block.

"Very astute, Mr. Petty. You're asking about Azoospermia, where no sperm is present in the ejaculate due to a blockage. We're working on a procedure called surgical sperm extraction or testicular sperm aspiration, but we have not yet been successful. Retrieval of viable sperm remains at a low percentage rate—but progress is being made." He held up a hand. "I'm not saying this is *your* case. You can only know for sure by trial and time. If you fail, your wife can always be inseminated by a donor, and she'll have her baby, truly *her* baby."

Shad rubbed a hand over his face, suddenly feeling impossibly tired. A baby by another man? That might be their only option. Still, at least they *had* an option. He'd shelf his pride for Poppy. He'd do anything to assure her happiness.

"As a matter of fact, the first successful artificial insemination I spoke of was achieved with a donor, but Dr. Pancoast didn't volunteer that information until many years later. The problem was assumed, as in most cases, to lie with the wife. But, after an examination was done on her older husband, Dr. Pancoast found, because of the man's earlier case of gonorrhea, he had relatively no sustainable sperm to work with. Shrewdly, he told the man he only needed some medicine, and then he'd be able to impregnate his wife by artificial means. After the patient completed a round of treatment, Dr. Pancoast then chose his best-looking medical student and inseminated the woman using *his* sperm instead—and was successful."

Shad just stared. Living so many years under the cowboy code of honesty and morality, that sounded like a dirty trick.

"Don't look so defeated, Mr. Petty."

The doctor misread his expression.

He reached into the cabinet behind him and took out a small glass vial, handing the container to Shad. "I have a feeling you'll do just fine. When the four-legged devil knocked you into the fence, he didn't know the man he was dealing with. I might be speaking ahead of myself, but since I can't detect any scar tissue, and everything else seems fit as a fiddle, I believe we'll have good news." He gestured toward the vial. "I'll expect a card sometime next year, if not sooner, telling me your wife has delivered a gurgling baby boy or girl wearing cowboy boots and a Stetson." He laughed and then nodded to Shad's clothes. "You can get dressed as soon as you give me a sample to study. Just leave it there." He pointed to a small cabinet separate from the others. "I'll take a look directly, and you can stop back in a couple hours for the results." He scribbled something onto a small sheet of paper, handing it to Shad. "My secretary will handle everything else. Good day."

Shad sat for a few moments after the doctor closed the door, considering the new prognosis.

Rubbing a hand over his mouth, he suppressed the image of Poppy receiving the good news. “I’m gettin’ ahead of myself,” he mumbled. “Fate is a fickle friend, as Grandma Girdy used to say. I’m not out of the woods yet. No sir, not by a long shot.”

Chapter Sixty-Seven

Fancy paced the porch of the Wells Fargo station, waiting for the stagecoach to arrive. Fresh horses were already harnessed and ready to be switched out with the spent livestock.

Cole came from inside, his face set in stone. "You're makin' a mistake, Fancy. You have time to change your mind."

Her heart ached. Not only was she running out on her daughter—*again*—but she was also leaving town without speaking with Lenore. Her sister had been her confidant and ally for years. She'd never let Fancy just up and leave without a fight. And there was no time for a fight now. She had to get away while she could make a clean break.

"Everything I've done over the last twenty years will be for nothing. I don't mind giving up this"—she spread her arms wide—"if I know Madison will have a good life. If I stay, and everyone finds out who I really am—"

Sounds from the tree line where the road approached made Fancy snap her mouth closed. She stopped and looked around. Instead of the stage, a buggy driven by Justin appeared, the horse moving at a brisk trot. Madison sat at his side. A ray of sunshine, through the tall trees, illuminated the pretty fabric of her blue dress. The plume on her hat fluttered in the breeze. The first thought flashing through Fancy's mind was, *What a beauty. My girl. My daughter!*

Cole stepped to her side.

She glanced into his face to see he'd been aware of the plan.

"It had to be done, Fancy. There was no two ways about it."

The station offered nowhere to run. To hide. Taking a deep, cleansing breath, she watched the buggy approach, thinking how lovely Madison looked. The last time she'd seen her, she hadn't known the young woman asking her questions outside the mercantile was her daughter. But now she did, and a great, welling pride filled her chest. She was a stunning young lady, proper in every way.

"Whoa," Justin said as he drew the buggy to a halt a few feet away, leaving the spot empty where the stage would need to be. "Miss Aubrey," he said. "I have someone I want you to meet. This is Miss Madison Plumb. She believes she's your daughter and would like to speak with you. If you'd like to climb in, then I'll take the two of you a few minutes beyond, where there's a bench set on the edge of a meadow and out of view of the road. The stage was just pulling into town when we left and should be here shortly."

• • •

Madison swallowed down a lump of worry as the buggy pulled away, leaving her and Fancy at the secluded spot Justin had mentioned. She didn't dare look at her mother. Everything she'd rehearsed last night had flown out of her head the moment they'd pulled out of the trees and she'd seen Fancy Aubrey packed up and ready to flee. Ready to begin another life over again, somewhere without her. Was meeting her a big mistake? Maybe her mother disliked children. Madison couldn't believe that, but the hard set to Fancy's mouth had her insides trembling. Was she causing her mother undue and unasked-for pain and remorse? She'd made the choice years ago to give up Madison. Maybe Madison should have respected her decision and left matters alone. They moved like stick figures, stiff and slow, and sat on the small, rickety bench, appearing weathered by a hundred winters. "I wonder who built this seat?" Madison forced out to break the ice. Someone needed to, and Fancy didn't seem inclined.

Fancy ran a hand on the branchlike armrest but didn't look at her. "I wouldn't know."

Her voice was small and soft, making Madison's heart tremble. "I'm sorry to spring this on you," Madison said, feeling air once again filling her lungs. Her strength had returned. She'd be able to hold her emotions together and have a decent conversation. She'd had a brief dream last night about meeting Fancy. Her mother had taken her into her arms and told her how much she'd missed her. Loved her. Said giving her away all those years ago was a mistake. Madison glanced over, feeling nervous. "I only learned on the way out here you're planning to leave Y Knot. Justin worried, if he told me sooner, I'd take your actions to heart and return to Kentucky without meeting you." She softly cleared her throat. "No matter what, I couldn't do that."

"I see." Fancy looked at her for the first time. "I'm sorry if my plans hurt your feelings."

"I don't want anything from you, uh . . ." Madison stopped. She didn't know what to call her. Certainly not Mother.

"Please, call me Fancy. It'll make everything easier."

Madison nodded. "Yes, well, I don't want anything, Fancy. I just wanted to meet you and speak with you." Happiness brightened Madison's insides. Even with her mother's stiff posture, her voice was soft and calm, encouraging. The tightness around her mouth had disappeared. "I've dreamt of this since I was eight years old and learned I was adopted." She glanced around at the tall, silent trees, the only witnesses to their conversation. "And now I'm here." She couldn't stop herself and reached forward to briefly touch Fancy's hand, but Fancy didn't react. "Truthfully,

I can't believe I'm actually sitting here with you. I want to pinch myself to make sure this is not a dream, too." A bird in the nearby tree twittered softly, and a gentle breeze made the feather on Madison's hat flutter into her face.

"You're a beautiful young lady," Fancy finally said, not much more than a whisper. "I'm happy you persisted. Means you're determined. That's a good quality in a woman."

"Thank you." She wanted to refute Fancy's claim, but her adoptive mother had taught her contradicting a compliment from an elder was impolite. If Fancy knew how many times Madison had wanted to quit and go home, she'd change her mind. "I think *you're* incredibly beautiful, Fancy. It's difficult for me to look away. I've wanted to know you for so long. Would you mind terribly if I gave you a small hug?"

Several moments passed before Fancy shook her head. "Not at all."

Scooting forward, Madison gradually put her arms around Fancy, marveling at how small she felt. Her shoulders were slightly built but sturdy. Madison couldn't stop herself and pulled Fancy closer, tighter, and buried her face into her mother's neck, feeling three years old again. Fancy smelled wonderful. Not of strong perfume, but clean and fresh, with a slight scent of summer daisies. Without warning, a strangling sound escaped Madison's throat, followed by a gasp.

She clutched Fancy to her with every ounce of strength. The spring of moistness stinging her eyes turned into a waterfall of tears.

"Shhh, hush now," Fancy whispered as she held Madison. "You're not a little eight-year-old now, Miss Plumb. You're a sophisticated, full-grown woman." Fancy tried to sit back.

But Madison wouldn't let her. She needed to feel Fancy's arms and hear her voice. Without warning, her tears came harder.

"Aww, sweetheart," Fancy whispered. "You're here now, and I'm so happy to meet you and hold you. To be honest, I've dreamt of this day, as well."

Madison took a wobbly breath and sat back to study Fancy's face. She looked sincere. Was she telling the truth or just trying to make her stop crying? Madison gathered her emotions and dried her face with the hanky she drew from her sleeve. "Is Cole Mercer my father?"

A ghost of a smile fluttered across Fancy's face. "I wish he were, sugar. Cole's a good man. At least, then, you'd have his wide shoulders to lean on. But no, he's not. I met him three years before I met your daddy, the latter a smooth-talking salesman who came by our farm once a month." She patted Madison's knee. "Few men are as honest as Cole Mercer."

"Oh."

"I'll have no lies between us. Your daddy was

too handsome for his own good. He'd come by, hawking his cookware and giving me the eye behind my brother's back. By then, Mama and Daddy had died and my brother, Craig, who was eight years older, standing six foot three, was head of the household. I was fifteen, and Lenore was only five. Your daddy professed his love and begged me to marry him. Said I was the most beautiful girl in the world, and he couldn't live without me." She gave a rueful smile. "He promised I could bring Lenore, as well, since Craig was such a beast, always yelling and screaming about something. Anyway, the month after your daddy declared his love for me and promised me the moon, he came by right on schedule—but this time, he waited until Craig had left the house for the fields before knocking on our door. Lenore was gone, having walked the short quarter mile into town for a small sack of flour, since all hell broke loose because there was no bread for his breakfast. Craig gave me a shiner for my stupidity of letting the flour run out and told me I wasn't to go to town with Lenore as punishment. Town was our only reprieve."

Madison's heart hammered at the thought of such treatment.

"Being alone in the house, you can imagine what happened. Your daddy claimed I didn't love him enough because I wanted to wait until after the wedding. He held the prize away unless I gave in. Determined to get Lenore and me away from the farm, I did. You see, if I might be so blunt, for the few months prior, Craig had begun visiting my bedroom after dark, watching me sleep. I was scared. One night, he came in and sat on the edge of my bed, whispering soft words. Lenore woke in the loft with a bad dream, scaring him off. I saw your daddy as salvation, a way out." Fancy took a deep, fortifying breath.

Madison's stomach felt queasy at the revelations, but she forced herself not to look away.

"The next month was the first in a year the peddler wagon didn't pull into our yard. I made every excuse in my head why: he was sick, or busy, or his wagon had broken an axle and he'd be along shortly." She shook her head and frowned. "But another month passed, and then another. Soon, my pregnancy was too difficult to hide. I was five months along when Craig beat the truth out of me. He called me trash and threw me out of the house. Said I was never to step foot on the farm again. He locked Lenore in the root cellar so I couldn't take her along."

"How horrible! Did you go find him then?" Madison asked. "My father?"

"Asking around town was difficult, because hiding that I was in the family way was impossible. Everyone knew I was unmarried. The wife of the postmaster had always been kind to Lenore and me. She inquired around and learned your daddy had already said his 'I dos' at the end of a shotgun in Louisville. He'd impregnated another young girl and wasn't coming back again. I was on my own."

Madison couldn't hold in her remorse. "I'm so sorry. What a terrible thing to do to you."

Fancy nodded. "That's true. There's a special place in Hell for men like him. And men will take advantage, if you let them. But I'm to blame, as well. I have no allusions. I could have said no."

But then I wouldn't be here.

"Your face gives you away," Fancy said with a trembling smile. "And I've thought the same thing often. Life is strange. There's good and bad in everything. You can't pick and choose one or the other but must take what comes."

Madison nodded. Her mother was a wise woman, indeed. "How, then, did Lenore receive the yearly letters from my adoptive father's attorney? I don't understand."

"That kind lady, Mrs. Petunia Hanson, the wife of the postmaster, took pity on me. She gave me her address and said I could send mail to Lenore through her, and Craig would never find out. Lenore went into town, and Mrs. Hanson invited her in for cookies and milk and any correspondence I might have sent. When I had given birth, made my decision, and contacted the attorney the midwife had given me as a man who arranged adoptions, I lied and said I was Lenore and gave him Mrs. Hanson's address. I thought doing so was a way to protect you from learning my identity and, in so doing, safeguarding your reputation." She wiped tears from her cheeks.

"I'm sorry," Madison whispered. "I didn't mean to cause you pain." She reached out and took Fancy's hand into her own. The appendage was small and cold. What a life Fancy had led. One heartache after another. "You don't have to tell me any more."

"I want to. This is the first time I've told anyone everything. I've carried the truth around so long in my heart, sharing is a relief."

"Good, then, because I'd like to know it all."

"When Lenore was older and wanted a life of her own, she contacted the attorney and gave her new address where she'd settled and found a job."

Should she dare asked the question? The horrible possibility was frightening. "Fancy, what about Craig and Lenore alone on the farm?"

A dark shadow crossed Fancy's face. She raised a shoulder. "I don't know. She's never said. I had warned Mrs. Hanson, who'd promised to watch as much as she could. Other than that, I believe it was my older status that attracted my brother. He never seemed to notice Lenore, and when he did, he treated her more as a daughter. I can only pray . . ."

"How did she end up in Y Knot?"

"She'd read about a job in a hotel in Waterloo, Montana Territory, working as office help. She's extremely well read and good with numbers. She applied for the position by mail and was assured she had the job, but she learned on arrival the position had been filled. They suggested she try in Y Knot. The town had a fine hotel and restaurant. She's worked at Cattlemen's ever since. Getting older, I finally decided I needed some family and moved to Y Knot, myself, about two years ago—never in my life thinking you'd track her down and find me."

"Do you mind terribly?" Madison held her breath, frightened what her mother's response might be.

CHAPTER SIXTY-EIGHT

Fancy leaned forward and ran her hand down the side of Madison's hair, marveling at the softness. "Mind terribly? How could I? Do I want to turn you over my knee? Never. After living with Craig, I'll never strike another human being, except to protect the ones I love." Looking into the face of her lovely daughter, Fancy couldn't stop her smile. A real smile she felt all the way into her heart. Madison Plumb, *her daughter,* and real lady, sat before her, looking like a princess.

"And what has happened since you've left Kentucky?"

Fancy's heart swelled at the look of love in Madison's eyes and the worried tilt to her brows. "Nothing I feel compelled to share with you. You're not to blame for any of this. You're innocent. And you're not to blame for your father's sins, either. You have his vivid blue eyes and corn silk hair, but that's where the resemblance ends. I can tell you don't have a devious bone in your body."

"Will you still leave Y Knot?"

Madison looked to be holding her breath. How could Fancy leave now? The sight of her daughter sitting before her was like a man dying of thirst and looking at a clear mountain stream. She wanted to gather her up and never let her go.

She wanted to see her first thing in the morning and be the last person to kiss goodnight. She needed to know how she thought and what her hopes and dreams were. So much needed to be learned and so little time. If they were both living in Y Knot, surely, someone would discover the truth. Five people already knew: Justin Wesley, Cole Mercer, Lenore, Madison, and herself. And Mrs. Goodheart, who had written the letter. That temptation was all too risky. Truth would get out, and then Madison's reputation would be ripped to shreds.

"Mother?"

Fancy tipped her brow. "I *insist* you call me Fancy. Not because I don't like the sound of Mother, but because saying the word aloud is playing with fire. We mustn't conduct ourselves with such reckless abandon." Her lips pulled up, and she winked. "We're cleverer than that."

The sounds of the stage arriving filtered through the trees and over the small meadow where they were carefully hidden away. Shouted curse words mingled with the neigh of a horse. A few minutes later, the rumble of wheels on the hard ground were heard on the other side of the thicket. The stagecoach passed and rolled out of earshot.

"You never answered my question, Fancy." Madison clenched her bottom lip between her teeth. "Are you still planning to leave Y Knot? I don't want you to. Since I've found you, I want to know everything. Please, don't go."

"You don't know what you're asking. Now you think it's a grand idea, but the ramifications are just too dangerous. If anyone found out I am your—"

"I don't care who knows. It's up to me, isn't it? If I'm the one to supposedly be hurt, then I should be the one to make the decision. Don't you think? Nothing is more important to me than you."

"If you won't consider for yourself, and all your adoptive parents have done for you, consider for your children. You'll have a few one day, you know. What we do now will affect them, as well. That's why Lenore and I have been so careful about our relationship. For *her* sake. She still has dreams of marrying someday and having children. Not everyone in town is open-minded like you, Miss Plumb."

"Madison."

"Oh, no, it's Miss Plumb to me. Today and always. For propriety's sake."

Madison stomped a foot. "And not everyone in town is as close-minded as you might think. I can list a handful of women I can't believe would change if they discovered our relationship to each other."

Seemed Madison was hardheaded like herself. "I've lived with discrimination and intolerance;

you're only hearing about it for the first time in your life. Being shunned is more hurtful than you can imagine. You won't change my mind. You might have delayed my going for a day or two, but not much more."

Madison's eyes welled again with tears.

"That is, unless you agree to my stipulations." Fancy couldn't stop herself and pulled Madison back into her arms. "Now that you've found me, my love, I can't give you up. But I will, unless you agree to keep our relationship secret. We can meet from time to time at Lenore's." Still in an embrace, a smile crept onto Fancy's lips as she gazed up into the treetops, thinking how good Madison felt in her arms. "For now, you and I will do as Lenore and I have done for two years." She pulled back to study her daughter's face. Could she trust Madison to keep the bargain? If she didn't, her daughter's life would be ruined. "Madison? Will you promise me and stick to your word, no matter what? You might hear things about me. Suddenly taking my side would seem suspicious. You must remain indifferent."

Madison's forehead wrinkled and she frowned. "Yes, I'll agree. I'll keep our secret. But, just so you know, I've already taken your side before I knew anything."

Fancy's smile widened as her chest filled with love and pride. "That's my girl. Now, here is what we'll do . . ."

Chapter Sixty-Nine

The smooth feel of the buggy lines grounded Justin in the moment on the return trip to Y Knot. None would be the wiser a critical meeting had transpired. He felt pleased he'd been able to make it happen. He cut a quick look at Madison on the other side of the narrow seat. She seemed fine, happy since he'd helped her into the buggy, and they'd started off. Now, slightly turned, she gazed off into the treetops. He was trying to be patient, waiting for her to open up and tell him about the meeting. Was it really any of his business?

Yes. She's the girl I intend to marry. Everything about her is my business. Maybe it's time to let her know.

"Madison?"

She looked over. Her eyes widened. "I'm sorry. I'm being mean."

He lifted a shoulder and smiled. "We're already three quarters of the way back."

"It's not that I don't intend to tell you, it's just I'm so amazed at everything that's happened since coming to Y Knot." She smiled. "Thank you, Justin. If not for you, Fancy would be on the stage and, most likely, I'd never be able to find her again. How can I ever repay you for fixing my life before everything was ruined?" The feather on Madison's hat bobbed with each stride the horse took.

That was a good start. "I didn't do much," he said, relieved she'd started talking. "But you must know I'd do *anything* to make you happy. I knew speaking with your mother would." They were on the edge of town and would soon be coming up on the shack Jack Jones was fixing up on the left and the Biscuit Barrel on the opposite side of the road. He slowed the horse to a walk, wanting to put off their arrival at the hotel for a little longer.

"Will you stay in Y Knot now?" he asked slowly. "To be close to her?" Madison had college and friends back in Kentucky. *And* Mr. Galbraith. Both she and Fancy had been born there. When he held up his crossed fingers, Madison's smile reappeared.

"In a fashion."

What did *that* mean? His heart dropped into his boots as the buggy rattled along.

"My moth—*Fancy,*" she corrected quickly, "insists I call her Fancy and, if the occasion arises, she will refer to me as Miss Plumb. She also insists we keep our relationship a sworn secret. Like she and Lenore, *my aunt*—and that's the last time I can say that, as well—have done. She gave me up so I could have a better life, with two parents and a home. And to protect me—that has not changed, she says. I'd tell the whole world, if she'd let me, and everyone else could bite a lemon if they didn't like it."

Justin couldn't stop a chuckle. "You mean Aunt Pauline? I'd like to see that." She looked enchanting as she described the encounter, and he longed to pull her into his arms.

She covered her mouth. "Please, I didn't mean her specifically. But if I don't agree to Fancy's terms, she'll be forced to leave town. Meaning she'd lose her sister, who she's just recently been reunited with. I could never be so cruel."

A deep despair filled her eyes at her last statement. Fancy must have shared a lot.

"I just can't do that to her, Justin," she reiterated. "I hope you understand."

A death knell.

"But you should have seen her," Madison went on quickly. "She's so sweet and kind. Everything she did was for my welfare. And in the beginning, before me, she was looking out for Lenore. I *must* do as she requests. There's no alternative."

Here again, Justin's uneasiness gave way. "What does 'in a fashion' mean, Madison? And 'I hope you understand'? Let's start with the first . . ."

"It means I'll remain in Y Knot to finish out my summer break, which ends in early September, and then return to Mary Sharp College. Not to graduate would be unkind to my adoptive parents. They were well off, but not rich. My mother and father spoke often of a higher education for me. And I'll always be grateful they went to the hardships and expense. And, Fancy thinks a college education is a wonderful achievement, too. She says she's incredibly proud. The small trust my father and mother set up for me won't be available until I'm twenty-two. But the other inheritance will afford me this option."

He'd been watching the road but now turned to look at her, and their gazes locked.

She blinked and glanced ahead. "Fancy insists staying any longer in Y Knot would tempt fate. She believes Lenore will gladly take me in while I'm here." Madison's smile returned. "So, I'll be able to get to know Lenore well and learn about our family. My grandparents and their farm. Fancy says Lenore's bedroom is large enough to easily fit another small bed. And, if the coast is clear, once a week, Fancy will visit."

"September?" He needed everything spelled out for him three times. Right now, his brain felt like a pot of mush.

"Yes."

She said the word so willingly, as if leaving Y Knot, *and him,* suited her just fine. With the way he felt for her, he could hardly believe his ears. They hadn't known each other long, but sometimes months and years weren't needed to feel sure about something. "Just like that?"

She nodded and tried to smile, but her eyes

betrayed her. She couldn't hold his gaze, and her lips trembled.

With his heart beating wildly, he eased back on the lines and guided the buggy to a halt under the shade of a tall alder tree.

"Why are we stopping?"

"I wanted a little more time to talk before we reach the hotel. I've been doing a lot of thinking these last few days, and, well . . ." He took her hands into his, causing her eyes to go wide. "Actually, *Miss* Plumb," he said slowly, trying to achieve a light, teasing tone, incredibly difficult under the dire circumstances. "I didn't really need to do much thinking at all. I've known for some time how I feel about you. I don't want to lose you. Now or ever. I'd hoped you felt the same."

She sucked in a breath, and briefly, the sadness left her eyes.

Several seconds skipped by. "Don't say anything now," he said, low and quick. She was too fresh off her conversation with her mother. Nothing he said now would change her intentions. But he could try to show her how he felt. Fancy might be her mother, but *he* wanted to be her husband. And he'd known her longer. He was sure he'd seen love in her eyes. Her face always glowed at the first sight of him. Didn't that mean anything?

Madison should have some say as to what would make her happiest. Justin was of the same mind she was about the situation in Y Knot. People couldn't control their parents' past. They shouldn't be blamed for their actions. After a few days or weeks, nobody would remember a thing. Life would go on. He thought of Aunt Pauline. Well, *some* of them would. The others could just bite into a lemon, as Madison had so sweetly said. Or move. He wouldn't care. He had about a month and a half to woo her and win her heart.

Seeing Madison ready to respond, he released one of her hands and gently placed his finger on her lips. "Ah, ah, ah," he whispered, smiling into her eyes. "No reply from you, remember?" Gently tugging her closer, he wrapped her in his arms and found her lips. She complied. Melded to him. They remained together for several long seconds, the warm air, her soft breathing, and the buzz of insects creating a moment he'd never forget.

The horse fidgeted, and the buggy rocked.

As much as he hated to, Justin pulled away, hoping to see happiness in her eyes. The same love he was feeling—and it *was* there for a brief second but was quickly replaced with the *I can't love you* look. The reality of what Fancy was insisting on. He'd felt Madison's willingness moments before. She'd enjoyed the kiss, even pulling him closer. No matter what she said, he knew she *did* care, even if she didn't want to admit the scary fact to herself.

Chapter Seventy

Five days had passed since Brandon's second surgery. He'd gained strength and color, and his humor was returning, as well.

"Be careful, be careful," Charity repeated over and over, holding Brandon's warm hand as she walked at the side of the cot carried by her brothers and father. Each man had a death hold on their corner pole as they left St. John's Hospital and crossed the rutted road toward the tall, three-story Victorian house where Mrs. Hardie held the door, ready and waiting.

Claire walked alongside Brandon's casted leg, protecting the limb from any accidental bumps.

Shad Petty was gone, having taken the five a.m. train.

"Everything's ready," the proprietress called, her voice laced with the excitement everyone was feeling. "As you know, we're keeping him on this level, so you don't have to attempt the long, winding climb to the third floor."

Although Charity heard Brandon's assurances he was fine and all his pain was gone, she wasn't quite sure she believed him. If the men jostled him the smallest amount, then his mouth pinched tight. He was on the mend, but weeks would pass, and maybe even longer, before he was back to his normal self. Now inside the inn,

Charity and her mother preceded the procession into Brandon's room where a beautiful, blue canopy covered a four-poster bed. He'd remain here for at least three to four weeks before the doctors would release him from their care to go home. The large window on the street side of the room was already open, allowing in fresh, clean air. Being out of the hospital was a joy. Charity took in her three brothers, wishing John was there with them. Nothing brought family closer together than heartbreak.

At the side of the bed, Mark and Matthew took two handles each, allowing Flood and Luke to transfer Brandon into the turned-down covers.

"I feel like a crippled calf," Brandon complained, as her father and brother carefully situated him and his casted leg. "I don't like all this smothering—and worried expressions. I keep telling everyone not to make such a fuss."

Charity gazed down at him, so thankful he was alive. "No complaints from you, my love. Each day is a gift, and I'll not allow you to think otherwise." With the men finished, she plumped his pillow.

Mrs. Hardie waited at the door. "I have a pot roast with all the fixin's ready to be eaten. You've all been through enough worry for ten years. Charity, I'll bring you and Brandon a tray, and the rest of you can now relax in the dining room. I won't take no for an answer."

Smiles blossomed around the room.

"That sounds lovely," Claire responded. "We can never thank you enough for your kindness. You've gone far above and beyond the call of Christian duty."

"Nonsense, nonsense," the woman replied. "I've enjoyed having you all here." She smiled and then hurried out the door.

A lull wafted around the room. They'd all been going full tilt for so long, finally having Brandon here, and in recovery, felt strange. Charity needed to say something fast, before her emotions got the best of her—*again*. She'd been a weepy mess for the last week. "We'll miss you, boys," she said to Matthew, Mark, and Luke, snagging each of their gazes for a brief moment. "Brandon and I will never be able to thank you enough for everything."

Brandon reached out and took Charity's hand.

The gesture made the lump in her throat expand exponentially. "These sixteen days have meant everything," she went on. "Life and death."

Luke's gaze momentarily dropped to her middle.

She knew what he was thinking. Not only for Brandon, but for the baby, too. "So much has happened, I've forgotten what home is like." Her gaze shifted to her mother and father. "And I'm so happy you're both staying on. In the morning, when the others pull out, I won't feel so alone."

"Be sure Luke takes the medicine tea he's been

forcing down my throat back to Y Knot when he goes," Brandon said and made a show of very carefully rubbing his belly. "I can't stomach another drop."

Charity was thankful for the mischievous glint in her handsome husband's eyes. He knew she was close to tears again and was lifting the mood.

"And deprive you, brother?" Luke quipped. "I wouldn't do such a thing. What do you think is behind your swift turnaround?" He glanced at Matt and Mark. "My brothers may gainsay and believe the second surgery is responsible, but I know different." He fingered the small rawhide bag, the long strap draped across his chest, and lifted the pouch over his head. "You're in charge of this from now on," he said, handing it to his mother. "Make sure he consumes a large mug twice a day."

Everyone chuckled.

Matt grasped Luke by the shoulder and gave a good shake. "I guess we'll never really know the truth, now, will we? All that matters is Brandon will be back in Y Knot in time for the Fall Festival to dance a jig with our sister."

Those words were music to Charity's ears. *Home*. It couldn't come soon enough to suit her.

Luke sat by the parlor fireplace, staring into the glowing embers. The inn was quiet. A lamp by the door provided soft light. Everyone had turned in an hour ago, and he'd been sitting here ever since. The satisfying meal Mrs. Hardie had served them had been a celebration of sorts. Brandon would recover. Charity hadn't had any more issues with the baby since she'd come off of bedrest. And he'd met his Cheyenne father. *That* had been a revelation—and something he hadn't anticipated when he'd set out to find the Indian village. He'd dreamed of *Netchiwaan* for years, and yet, had he ever really believed a meeting might happen? He was anxious to get home to Faith. How he missed her, their talks, their home, and their children.

Stretching out, he crossed his ankles. He really should get to bed. They'd be up early to catch the five a.m. train south, but something inside wouldn't allow him to relax. If he tried to sleep now, he'd end up being serenaded by his brothers sawing logs.

From somewhere, a door creaked open, and then footsteps padded.

"Luke?" Charity came forward, a teacup and saucer in her hand. She stopped by his side. Her hair was down, and she wore her robe over her nightgown. "You're still up? Can't you sleep?"

He stood and stretched. "Sure can't, little sis. I guess I'm excited to get home."

"You miss Faith."

He nodded. "Guilty as charged. And the little ones, too."

When she glanced around, as if intending to join him, Luke fetched another chair close to his so they could talk without disturbing anyone. "How's Brandon?" he asked after getting comfortable. "Still resting easy?"

She nodded. "He is. No fever. I finally feel like we'll return to Y Knot together. I haven't allowed myself to believe until now."

"Charity, you should have told me. We could have tried to soften your fears—although I've been feeling much the same." She looked all of thirteen in the soft light of the lantern. He should have been more attentive. "I'm sorry."

She glanced up into his eyes. "Don't be sorry. You and the others have done everything humanly possible. I couldn't have done any of this without you all." She took a deep breath.

"And you? The baby? Everything's good there?" Even in the wan light from the hearth, he saw a hint of a blush.

"I feel fine. But I'm being careful. Not overdoing, and putting my feet up now and then. If I was home, I'm sure I'd be doing more." She gave him a long look. "So, what were you thinking about when I disturbed you? You looked like a little boy lost."

He chuckled.

"Let me guess. The Cheyenne village?"

Luke nodded. "You know me pretty well. When I was locked up in Priest's Crossing, preparing to die, a Cheyenne death chant, one I didn't even know I knew, came out of me. It must have been somewhere deep inside—in my blood. The feel was soothing. This encounter was a lot like that."

"We've yet to really talk."

"The people were thin. Breaks my heart. There wasn't much time, but an old warrior and I smoked a pipe."

"Really?"

"His gaze was like a hawk's and didn't miss a thing." Luke reached up and fingered his face. "Had sharp cheekbones more obvious than mine. There was a hardness to him. And wisdom. Yet, he listened."

"Will you tell them these details? Mother and Father, I mean?"

Luke shook his head. "No. They don't need to know everything. I've wrestled with the choices. After the uneasiness Fox Dancing's arrival caused Ma and Pa, and even strained my relationship with Flood, doing so again would be unforgiveable. But I do intend to help the tribe. I'll give enough detail so Flood will understand why I'm compelled to." The concerned tilt to Charity's brow gave him pause. "Don't worry," he went on. "I can be discreet, when I want to be. Those two have already suffered a lifetime's worth over me. I don't intend to add more." He cut his gaze away to the hearth.

"Luke?"

"Growing up, I was different from my brothers, making me anxious and short-tempered. You're too young to remember much, but I was a hothead. Always pining for a fight. Looking for a small infraction to validate my feelings about my darker skin, almond-shaped eyes, and black hair. I didn't know who I was or where I'd come from. Getting older, of course, I knew then, and Ma and Pa were sure to shower me with love and understanding, but those things didn't solve all my difficulties. I'm sure my behavior got old. For Matt and Mark, too. John, being younger, was spared much of my temper."

"And then you met Faith, and she changed everything."

"True. She was my angel come down to earth."

But it wasn't all Faith's doing, but Ma's secret she finally shared on that dark night when I discovered Faith was lying about her past. Some things are too frightening to share, she'd said. Or sometimes, the time wasn't right. Be patient, be loving, be supportive. Love her for who she is now, and forget the rest. Then Mother had shared her secret story, in a soft, dreamy voice I'd never heard before. She hadn't suffered all badly when she was married to Netchiwaan *in the Cheyenne village. I wasn't the product of a rape, but something different . . . She said she couldn't tell such a thing to Flood, who had been crushed by her capture, and I understood. The secret that changed my life is* still *safe between us . . .*

"Dawn and Colton will never get to know their roots because their father is dead. Their uncle and grandfather, too. As they grow up, they'll have many questions, and they might be fearful to ask because they won't want to hurt my feelings, or Faith's. We'll need to watch closely. Be ready." He took a moment and cleared the emotion from his throat.

"You're such a good man, Luke," Charity whispered as she reached out and caressed his arm. "I'm honored to be your sister. Have I told you lately how much I love you?"

"You have, but you can tell me again. I never get tired of hearing those words from my little shadow."

She leaned forward and whispered them into his ear.

"Thank you. And I love you. I told the Cheyenne I'd be back. Bring some cattle to help stave off starvation. That's a promise I won't break. Time is running short."

She sat straighter. "I'll go with you."

"No, you won't. Your days of trailing after me are over. You're married, and soon you'll have a little Brandon or Charity to wrangle. But rest assured, you'll be with me in spirit, as you always are."

Chapter Seventy-One

At the sound of whooping and hollering, Justin stepped out of the jailhouse to survey the street. Just as he'd thought, several ranch hands from the Heart of the Mountains who'd been on the cattle drive reined up in front of the saloon and strode inside. Tanner, Smokey, and Pedro. Half a minute later, Nick and Francis galloped up behind to join them. Seemed the men had stopped in at the ranch and then came straight to the Hitching Post after checking in and getting the news. Greetings were shouted.

In the doorway, Smokey turned and waved him over.

The town felt alive again. At peace again.

"Must be the returning ranch hands from the Heart of the Mountains," a soft feminine voice said beside him.

He didn't need to turn to know who'd quietly appeared. "Mornin', Madison," he replied. Turning, he gave what he thought was his most charming smile. She looked beautiful, and his heart ached. He missed her terribly. The sun, playing in her golden hair, made his fingers itch to touch the spun glass. She appeared rested and happy. For the last three days, he'd purposely stayed away. Given her miles of space to contemplate what he'd said and remember their kiss. He'd also stayed away from the Biscuit Barrel, although he surreptitiously watched her walk down the street on her way to work. Before he'd dropped her at the hotel the morning after his profession of feelings and kiss, he'd offered to help her move her things to Lenore's house when she was ready. But she'd declined. During the exchange, they'd been shy and awkward. She'd said she had little to move, and Harold could easily take her one trunk over, but only after Lenore had given her permission.

"Good morning, Deputy," she replied, coming alongside him. "I didn't see you in church this morning."

Her unasked question hung in the air. At least, she'd noticed his comings and goings. "Actually, I'd planned to go and was dressed for the part, but Shad Petty arrived back in town and stopped in the office. He'd taken the train from Helena and then rented a mount in Waterloo. He's on top of the world. Seems the dark cloud that's been hanging over his head for a while has been lifted. I've never seen him so happy."

She pursed her lips. "He *is* getting married, you know."

"Yes, of course. But the exuberance seemed like more. Like he'd found an enormous pot of gold at the end of a rainbow. His thoughts switched back and forth faster than a brood of hens competing for a handful of scratch. He wore me out with his pacing and planning. Wanted to know if the gazebo would be available next weekend if he and Poppy moved up their wedding date. That's where they're planning the reception. I said the gazebo is mostly always available, and they could certainly have the site, if they wanted."

Madison laughed and pulled back. "I wonder if Poppy knows?"

"I think she must by now or will soon. He said he was headed to the Heart of the Mountains for a bath, shave, and clean clothes before proceeding to the Preece farm. I was wondering if you'd like to go to the wedding with me. He extended an invitation for whenever the wedding takes place—next Sunday or in a couple of weeks."

Her face brightened, and the smile she'd been wearing since she'd arrived got larger. "Did I tell you, the three mail-order brides sat down with me yesterday and I finally got my interview? Of course, I didn't. I haven't seen you."

Justin scuffed his boot on the boardwalk to hide his smile. "Yeah, I've been busy. Trying to catch the thief. At least, he's been quiet of late. No new break-ins."

Her gaze momentarily searched his face. "I went to the Preece farm, and Poppy was there, too. She invited me to the wedding, as well."

He dipped his chin in response. "There you go. You're making friends all over the place."

He noticed her eyes stray across the street and a couple buildings down to the saloon and wondered what she was thinking. Had she seen Fancy or spoken with Cole Mercer since their talk? She looked adorable as she attempted a businesslike demeanor. "How did the interview go?" he asked. "And how did you get out to the farm? It's too far to walk comfortably."

"Very well, indeed. They shared firsthand information, which will make for fascinating reading. I can't wait to get started. And to answer your question . . ."

"The first or the last?"

She arched a censuring brow. "The last. The getting there. Heather and Hayden Klinkner were so kind as to pick me up in the surrey. I've never been in one before. On the way, we stopped and collected Evie Holcomb, too. Her little boy, Garth, is adorable. And I loved seeing the Holcomb ranch and all the cattle, the chicken coop—and the massive stove Evie learned to cook on." Madison laughed, and her smile pushed up into her eyes. "She has several funny stories about her first attempts. I guess her husband will be home soon, too, if the cowhands are returning." She gasped and briefly touched his arm. "And the dog, Dexter. The day before, he'd chased a skunk and was sprayed. I've never smelled anything so horrible!"

Justin chuckled, a little sad he'd missed her

experiencing all these firsts. *First ride in a surrey, first visit to the Holcombs and Preeces, first tangy stench of skunk.*

"Ah, Dexter's favorite pastime. Can't seem to stay away. Sounds like you had a real nice time. I'm glad." He was, but he would have liked to have been the one to drive her out. That was all right. Patience was a virtue. He had formulated his plan and had to play a little hard to get. "What are some of the things you'll include in your paper, about the mail-order brides, I mean?"

"Let's see." She tapped her finger on her lips. "Well, that Evie has kept up her cooking lessons with Ina Klinkner. In fact, Mrs. Klinkner's one student has expanded into a class. Heather assists, since she already is incredibly talented in the kitchen, having had to help at home with all her brothers and sisters. But Kathryn, who was raised with servants all her life, had practically no experience when she married, so she attends. As well as Hildy from the hotel and Ashley Adair, Francis's intended. They claim it's incredibly fun, and at the end of each month, they have a get-together, and each brings a dish they've learned."

Justin was sure to appear intent on Madison's words, when really, he was counting the little freckles dotting the bridge of her nose. Had they been there when she'd first arrived? "That's interesting. Your hand must be tired from writing all your notes. I wonder, do you enjoy cooking, Miss Plumb?"

Her lips tipped up at his playful tone.

"A class with all those young women mixing this and that, blending and boiling. Sounds inviting?"

"Maybe you should join?" she parried with ease. "I'm sure Ina would have you."

He barked a laugh. Her quick wit was something he loved. Rubbing his chin, he said, "I'm sure she would, but Aunt Pauline might get jealous. I wouldn't want to hurt her feelings. If not, I'd definitely inquire." He folded his arms over his chest, enjoying the conversation. "Any other gems of information you'd like to share?"

Madison nodded. "Kathryn, who is an accomplished pianist, gives lessons twice a week, and her client list is growing. She even has two adults. She's also taken to making floral arrangements with the sunflowers her husband raises. Some fresh and some dried. She commandeered a corner in their massive old barn to work and sell her wares. She calls her rustic shop *Kathryn's Corner*. When ranchers come to the farm to purchase and pick up hay, their wives ride along and do a little shopping."

"That's amazing."

"It *is* amazing, when you think of her pampered upbringing. She's adapted to farm life surprisingly well."

He shrugged. "A good man will do that."

Her eyes twinkled as a dark stain inched up her neck and into her face. "And the sheriff? Brandon Crawford?" Madison inquired, businesslike. "How is he? What did Mr. Petty say?"

"It was good to finally get firsthand information about Brandon, instead of all these telegrams. Brandon will be fine. He's being moved across the street to the inn where all the McCutcheons have been staying." He arched his brow. "He'll remain there about a month as he gets back his strength. That way, the doctors can keep an eye on him."

"Sounds perfect," she replied. "I'm sure you'll be glad when he returns."

"Indeed. I hope that's before you leave. I'd like the two of you to meet."

Silence descended around them. Her brows pinched together and she glanced about, as if she'd run out of things to say and was contemplating leaving.

"Are you dodging my question, Miss Plumb?" he teased before she could get away. "I invited you to go to the wedding with me, and you have successfully avoided answering. Maybe you'd rather go alone? Catch the eye of all the newly returned cowboys?"

Her face flashed scarlet. He hadn't known a blush could happen so fast. He'd just add a little fuel to the fire. "You *are* the new girl in town.

And they've not had a chance to even see you yet. I'm sure Nick Petty chortled the news the minute the ranch hands stepped through the bunkhouse door." He held her gaze, smiling. "You still have time for a summer romance. Might be fun. I'd understand if you'd rather go stag. I can surely visit with you there . . ."

She placed a hand on the bodice of her pretty blue dress. "I'm sorry, Deputy. I thought I already responded. I'd be honored to go with you. You've been my friend since the day I arrived. I remember the moment, the beautiful clouds, Main Street, with its hustle and bustle, as clearly as if it were yesterday."

"Pretty much was."

She laughed. Seemed she liked the safe banter. No talk of love and forever. But she'd have to do some thinking herself. Time was of the essence. September would be here in the blink of an eye. The intense feeling inside him blossomed and grew. Staying away for three days had been agony. He'd caught himself several times mindlessly walking to the Biscuit Barrel, whistling a happy tune, and had to turn around. Madison Plumb was the sunshine in his day and his star-filled sky at night. She was his everything. He couldn't live without her.

Chapter Seventy-Two

Madison stood at the small sink in Lenore's tiny cottage, washing the bowl she'd just used for an early dinner. She and Lenore had made a stew together yesterday, laughing and talking. At first, her aunt had been bowled over at Madison's claims, but then her face had glowed with happiness, truly changing her countenance from one of night into day. They'd hugged for a good five minutes. No time was wasted procuring a small bed from Lichtenstein's and, with Harold's help, moving the furniture and Madison's things from the hotel.

Lenore had spent two days, in between their shifts, filling Madison in on the family history, her uncle, Craig, and lots of endearing—*and heartbreaking*—details. In turn, Madison had shared about her early life with her adoptive parents, as well as her experiences at Mary Sharp College. Lenore had been enthralled.

Finished washing the bowl, Madison dried her hands, and then the dishware, and placed it back in the cupboard. She felt a little lonely. Her mother was off-limits, and Lenore, dressed in her uniform and white, starched apron, had headed over to the hotel an hour ago to set up for the dinner shift at Cattlemen's.

Again, Justin had stayed away.

She understood his actions. And she didn't blame him. Their attraction could not be disputed. Since the day in the buggy, she'd thought of little else. But searching him out would be wrong, knowing their relationship couldn't go anywhere. They were already more than friends. She shouldn't have accepted his invitation to the wedding, but he'd taken her by surprise, and she'd been weak. Declining now would be downright mean.

Ambling from the kitchen to the window in the front of the house, the one with Lenore's pretty new curtains, she glanced at the sheriff's office. Was Justin there now? Writing in the town log, buttoning up things for the day? Often, as she walked to work, she'd see him on the opposite side of the road, chatting with someone. Mr. Tracy, the telegraph operator, or Drit, on the boardinghouse porch, even Berta May. He was undoubtedly a handsome man, a commanding presence wherever he went.

As the gloaming settled around the trees and buildings, she sighed. Madison's loneliness swelled like a waterlogged sponge. Seeing nothing of interest, she turned her attention the other direction, to the back of Herrick's leather shop, Lichtenstein's, and farther, all the way down behind Standford's Fittings.

Major wasn't even out nosing around the trash barrels behind the businesses.

Maybe she should walk over to the hotel and see if Hildy was free for a cup of tea. During her stay, the two had partaken nearly every night. She shrugged and shook her head. She couldn't go back so soon after moving out. She'd feel silly.

What could she do? Most certainly, what she *should* do was begin writing her term paper. The project wouldn't write itself, and the days before she headed back to Kentucky were melting away like new snow on a sunny day. The thought brought another pang of melancholy. She mustn't dawdle too long. One thing she wasn't was a procrastinator. Her parents had made sure of that, devising a reward system when she was just a little girl.

She smiled, remembering. Fancy had done a wonderful thing, giving her to a stable home. And because of it, she'd had an incredible life, filled with attention and love. Fancy hadn't recounted the years between giving her up and then landing in Y Knot. How difficult had survival been for her? Their two lives couldn't be more different.

Blinking, she caught movement of some kind in the area behind Standford's Fittings. She narrowed her eyes and tried to see in the dusky light. Someone was down there. Could be Mr. Standford doing something, or even Jack Jones, since now he owned the building next door. At this distance, she couldn't make out who was there, but she did notice the dark clothing.

Suddenly, the person crouched low behind a tree, as if someone was close by and they didn't want to be seen.

Was the thief at work again? Justin mentioned whoever was responsible hadn't done anything for a while. Trying again now, when most people were home having some supper, would make sense.

She cut her gaze back to the jail. She needed to tell Justin. He'd seemed disappointed he had yet to catch the offender. Taking a moment to see if she could still spot the shadowy person, she narrowed her eyes again. Yes. Still there, but prowling closer behind the mercantile now, moving slowly. Stopping and starting.

She had no time to lose. Gathering her shawl, she snatched the house key on the second shelf of the cupboard and went out. She took time to lock the door and all but ran over to the back of the sheriff's office and down the alley, because she knew the back door was usually locked. Grasping the doorknob, she threw open the door and rushed inside.

"Madison!" Justin bolted to his feet, a mug of coffee in his hands. With a rueful grimace, he glanced down at the splotches of coffee splattering the papers laid out on his desk.

Breathing hard, she held up both hands. "I'm sorry to frighten you. But there's someone dressed in dark clothing down the way, behind the mercantile. I've been watching him. He looks suspicious. Could be the thief!"

He pulled out his handkerchief and began blotting at the puddles marring his work, his rueful grimace turning into a comely smile. "You don't need a reason to come visit, Madison," he said softly. "How are you? Been another couple of days since we've seen each other. You must have picked up on my thoughts, because I was just thinking about you, as well. About your term paper. Have you started writing yet?"

Panting, she ran up to his side. "What's wrong with you? I'm not making this up. If you don't get out there this moment, you'll lose your chance to solve this crime spree. And Mr. Lichtenstein may lose more merchandise."

He stood there, taking her measure.

"I thought you wanted to catch the thief?"

"You're not teasing? I thought, perhaps, you missed me just a little and were in need of one of our lengthy conversations. I wouldn't hold your actions against you, if you did. I miss them, too." He searched her eyes. "And you, too, of course."

Reaching up, she took hold of his shoulders and gave him a good shake. "Justin! Snap out of it. I'm not teasing or making this up! There's a person about to break into the mercantile!" She momentarily cut her gaze away in exasperation, and then drilled him with a stare. "He's probably inside by now."

Justin's forehead puckered. "You're *not* joking."

She shook her head.

Justin's eyes lit keenly, as if she'd just struck a match. His hand slid down, checked his revolver, then his whip, unsnapping the keep. "You stay here. I don't want to worry about you. *Promise* me."

She nodded.

"Thank you."

Before she knew what he was about, she felt him place a quick kiss on her forehead and was out the door.

Several seconds ticked by as she stood in the now-silent office, wringing her hands. A thousand possibilities flashed through her mind. What if Justin needed help? Maybe he'd been wrong about Dodger Hicks. Maybe the perpetrator was a cold-hearted murderer. Justin could be killed! She glanced at the door and then the desk, thinking until her decision was made.

Gathering the dangling ends of her black shawl, she tied them firmly together around her shoulders so the garment wouldn't fall, picked up the iron poker Justin used to stir the coals whenever he wanted to revive the stove, and stepped outside.

Chapter Seventy-Three

On the boardwalk, Justin took a quick assessment of the town. Piano music floated across the road from the Hitching Post, and Fancy was singing. The bank was dark, and so was the downstairs floor of Berta May's. He started to walk, sweeping his gaze back and forth across the street, looking for a figure clad in black skulking around. He planned to continue down the street, pass by Lichtenstein's as if he were just on his regular rounds, and then skirt between Morgan's furniture store and the shack belonging to Jones. He'd have a good view of the back alley from there. Cursing himself for not taking what Madison said to heart sooner, he slowed by Morgan's, turned on his heel, flattened his back to the building, and inched along. Pausing, he listened. A scraping sound caught his ear. And then a low curse.

Must be having some difficulty. That buys me some time . . .

At the edge of the building, Justin carefully peered around, searching first the immediate area, and then the back of Lichtenstein's one building over. Darkness had overtaken the shadows only minutes before. In a crouched position, he took three large strides and slipped around the trunk of an old oak large enough to give him cover. He'd been correct.

The Hicks boy grumbled something as he looked around and then went back to the padlock protecting the mercantile.

Justin stepped out. "Give up, Dodger! You've been caught. You won't be harassing the town any longer."

The boy spun around.

Just enough light shone from the moon to display the angry slant to his mouth. Seemed this was more than a prank to him.

"You ain't got me yet, Deputy," he hissed.

"Just settle down," Justin said, slowly approaching. "You don't want any more trouble than you already have."

Faking left, Dodger bolted right.

Not willing to draw his gun on the youth, Justin cursed under his breath and gave chase. He didn't relish the thought of fighting him, either. When he was close enough, he launched himself and landed on Dodger's back, taking him down. They hit with a thud, which slammed Justin's elbow painfully into the ground. They rolled, with Dodger kicking and scratching. Dodger was strong! Even stronger than Justin had anticipated, knowing he was the son of a logger and often had to help like a man. With a bark of surprise, he realized Dodger had bitten him in the neck. His own fury now unleashed, Justin brought a strong uppercut with his right between their bodies, striking Dodger on the chin, cracking his teeth together and knocking back his head with a loud snap.

A sharp intake of breath from a grouping of trees made Justin think Madison had not kept her promise to stay put but was somewhere close, watching. She better not try to intervene.

Still being held in his hold, Dodger bucked violently, knocking Justin to the side. Before Dodger could scramble to his feet, Justin butted the side of the boy's head with the top of his own, wrapped an arm around his throat, and then ground his face into the dirt. They both scuffled with their feet, trying to gain purchase.

"Give up!" Justin gritted through his pain. He felt warm blood creeping down his neck. His knuckles were skinned, and the fingers on his left hand were still numb from his elbow striking the ground. Flexing his arm, he applied more pressure to Dodger's windpipe. "You going peacefully?" He waited as Dodger continued to struggle. Pulling his arm tighter into Dodger's neck, he gritted out, "Answer me, before I lose the last shred of my patience. Give up!"

Unable to reply because of the arm on his windpipe, Dodger inclined his face into the dirt several times.

Justin remained ready as he lessened his hold. He'd felt the fury contained inside and was relieved this wrestling match was just about over. Still, he didn't put anything past Dodger Hicks.

Grasping Dodger's arm, he hauled him to his feet.

In an unprecedented move, Dodger twisted and did a back roll, pouncing up onto his feet and kneeing Justin in the belly.

Gasping and stumbling back, Justin saw the glimmer of a ten-inch blade clutched in the scoundrel's hand.

"I'm not going with the likes of you, you skunk." Dodger's voice seethed and oozed hatred. "You're just like my *father!* All knowing! Ready to strike as soon as say hello. I'm gonna cut you good."

Justin crouched, arms bent, ready for anything. "I'm taking you in, boy, one way or the other."

"Don't try it. I was born with this knife. I can trim your eyelashes and not touch your face." He sneered. "And you won't shoot, anyway. I'm only a boy. What would the townsfolk think?"

Deep laughter from the street spooked Dodger.

He turned and bolted straight for the trees where Justin now saw Madison, raising the poker from the sheriff's office in defense. He couldn't allow Dodger to reach her. Flipping out his bullwhip, he gave one swift crack and dropped the boy, the supple leather wound tight around his ankles.

Dodger went down like a mighty oak, himself, ten feet in front of Madison.

She screeched and backed away.

Running forward, Justin kicked the knife out of reach and then whipped out his handcuffs, securing Dodger's arms behind his back. His eye was cut, and blood trickled from his nose.

He didn't resist.

With the threat gone, and Dodger unable to move, Justin hurried to Madison, who quivered uncontrollably.

He wrapped her in his arms, holding her head to his chest. He'd never felt such panic as when he'd watched this delinquent run directly for her, his ugly weapon clutched in his hand. "What were you thinking, Madison, following me out here? Didn't you promise you'd stay in my office? I distinctly remember you nodding."

"I couldn't let you face him alone. I was the one who saw him first. Told you about him. If something horrible happened to you, I'd *never* forgive myself."

She was still trembling, and he was loath to let her go. Still, he leaned back to see her. "You wouldn't?"

Her gaze searched his face adoringly, and then her eyes went wide. "Oh, your poor, handsome face, Justin. Must be very painful." She slowly reached up and touched the side of his temple. "And your neck! It's horrible."

He'd never seen her eyes so huge. Embarrassed, he fished in his pocket for his handkerchief.

"No, I wouldn't ever forgive myself," she whispered, finally answering his question. "You mean a lot to me, Justin. I wanted to tell you in the buggy, when you told me, but I couldn't."

Her gaze shifted over his shoulder, as if she were looking past the mercantile, across the street, and to the Hitching Post. He understood what she was alluding to. "You never mind about that," he whispered low, so Dodger couldn't hear. "We have lots of time to work this out. Don't you have another year at school?"

She nodded.

"Just think how many letters you can send to Lenore and whoever else might like to hear from you. A lot can change. Also, I was thinking, perhaps my father could step in for me at Christmas time, be deputy for Brandon, so I can make a trip to Kentucky. I'd like to see Mary Sharp College and meet your friends, as well as Mrs. Goodheart. December wouldn't be long to wait after your departure in September. Just three months. That is, if you want me to."

"Oh, Justin . . ."

Her tone held all the reverence in the world. He felt her shiver, and this time, he knew the response wasn't from fear, but excitement. And maybe even something else, too.

Chapter Seventy-Four

Sunday arrived with all the fanfare of a delayed wedding now moved forward. In the days prior, Madison had watched much of the preparations at the gazebo from the large window of the Biscuit Barrel, since the grounds were right next door. First, two days earlier, a group of men, she believed were from the McCutcheon ranch where Shad Petty worked, arrived to clean up the place, give the structure a fresh coat of white paint, and deadhead the rockroses climbing the five sturdy posts of the gazebo and covering the entire lattice top.

They worked happily, with big smiles and laughter.

She recognized Nick and Francis, but the others were strangers.

In the middle of the day, they came in for a hearty meal and teased Renee and Ethel until their faces were as red as Renee's hair. But when addressing Madison, they were all shy and polite, barely saying more than "Yes, ma'am" and "Thank you, miss."

Then, yesterday, Poppy and the mail-order brides had stopped out to inspect everything.

Today, Justin escorted her on his arm into the small blue church on the hill behind Standford's

Fittings. Butterflies fluttered in her tummy. Justin had met her ten minutes earlier at Lenore's, looking incredibly handsome in trousers of fine material, a coat to match, and a cream bandanna instead of a tie, to cover the teeth marks left behind by horrible Dodger Hicks. The injury was healing, but not fast enough to suit Justin. At least, a scar wouldn't form.

She glanced around the already-packed church. Every pew was crowded full to overflowing.

"Uh oh," Justin leaned in close and whispered in her ear. "Where did all these people come from? Out of the woodwork?"

"My, my," was her soft reply. "Do you see Poppy and Kathryn's parents? Would you know what they look like?"

He shook his head. "They couldn't get to Y Knot on the short notice, but Shad said Poppy wasn't bothered and agreed with moving up the wedding. Her parents have promised a huge reception with all the pomp and circumstance in Boston, just as soon as the fall roundup work is done on the ranch." Justin chuckled. "Shad is actually looking forward to it."

Her lips rounded as she glanced at him. "Shouldn't he be?"

"Of course. Just, cowboys are usually a bit uneasy around pageantry of the upper crust." Justin tipped a knowing eyebrow. "He said he'd give them something to remember, as well. And wants to see the ocean. He was talking pretty big last night. I'd like to be a fly on the wall, to tell you the truth."

She gazed at him in amazement. "He said all that?"

"His bachelor party was last night in the saloon. He was talkative after a couple whiskeys." Justin gave a slight shake of the head. "He didn't get drunk, though."

"Aww, now I understand." Before she could ask him where they were going to find a seat, a new group of four came in behind them. When she looked around, she saw there were more than thirty people on the way in, as well.

"Excuse me," Reverend Crittlestick said from the front of the church. "It seems our bride and groom have overestimated the seating of my humble church. I've spoken with them, and they've decided to move the ceremony out to the gazebo. So, if you'll just take the short walk down the hill, we'll get started soon. Since you'll all be standing, I promise to keep my sermon to a minimum."

The assembly chuckled.

"There you go," Justin said with a smile.

Gathering the skirt of her fanciest dress with one hand, she held his arm with her other. Once they were outside, she kept her gaze on the path, watching for uneven places. She didn't want to fall and make a fool of herself. Her good slippers were thin, at most, and she could feel every pebble.

She'd yet to wear this dress, finding the garment too dressy for everyday Y Knot.

Mrs. Goodheart said the soft blue fabric made her skin look velvety and brought out her eyes. And the drop waist was complimentary. She hoped that was true. Personally, she loved the delicate white lace adorning the modestly scooped neckline. Since Tuesday night, all she could think about was Justin, what he'd said in not-so-many words, about changing Fancy's mind, and him visiting her at Christmas time. If he did come to Kentucky, all her girlfriends would be starry-eyed.

"Almost there," he said. "I can hear the horde behind us."

Judge Harrison came alongside and gave them a smile. Pauline and Carlie were walking a few feet behind with Bethanne Payne and her niece.

"Miss Plumb, you look exceptionally beautiful today," Harrison said. "I hope my son realizes just how lucky he is."

Her cheeks flashed hot as Justin squeezed his arm, pressing her hand to his side.

"You better believe I know, Pa." Justin took another look at her and gave a long whistle. "I practically passed out when I got my first glimpse. Miss Madison Plumb is an original."

Harrison laughed. “Well said, son. Now, how’s your prisoner? Has he stopped his grumbling?”

Justin shrugged. “Sometimes. I believe locking him up until Brandon was back in Y Knot was prudent.” He leaned toward his father and lowered his voice. “What he revealed about his pa’s temper and heavy hand, I thought it best to keep the two apart until his father had a chance to cool down.”

“You returned all the stolen items?”

Justin nodded. “Every one, except the rib bones.” He laughed. “Keeping Dodger locked up gives me some time to try to help him, too. He reads well enough, so I lent him my copy of Samuel Smiles’s *Self-Help* Grandpa gave me years ago. You remember the book?”

Harrison nodded. “Indeed, I do.”

Justin flashed a grin and leaned toward Madison. “Contains helpful tips that’ll benefit the boy, if he’ll only take them to heart. Inspirational stories, too, how hard work can raise him through the ranks. The deal is, for every hour he reads, I’ll take off an hour of jail time. Even though he hasn’t said so, I think he’s enjoying it.”

Harrison leaned over and winked at Madison. “My boy gets his smarts from his father.”

Enchanted, Madison took the opportunity to pull Justin’s elbow a little closer. He never ceased to amaze her. And his father was wonderful, too. Justin looked at her with a puckered brow and silly grin, as if he had no idea what she was thinking.

"And the knife?" Harrison asked.

"Locked up until Brandon returns."

At Justin's side, she walked by the Biscuit Barrel.

Cole Mercer stood on the porch, watching the parade of townsfolk.

Major, sitting by his side, gave a bark of greeting.

The dog wandered into the sheriff's office often and visited her at Lenore's, as well. When she caught Cole's eye, her heart gave a soft twitter, wishing so much she was free to visit Fancy any time she wanted. *How is she? Is she thinking of me?* The day on the hidden meadow bench twelve days prior felt like an eternity. Madison missed her. Fancy hadn't come over to Lenore's yet, but Madison was hopeful she'd come by this week on Tuesday, her regular visiting day for Lenore—and only two days from now.

Cole smiled and then touched the brim of his hat.

She didn't miss the way he noticed her holding Justin's arm, his countenance a lost, faraway emotion.

Not ten minutes after the considerable crowd had settled around the gazebo, but still leaving a wide, meandering path running from the Biscuit

Barrel to the structure for the wedding party to walk, the fiddle player of the Twilight Singers group began a soft, westernized rendition of "Jesu, Joy of Man's Desiring."

Recognizing the melody immediately, Justin cast a look at Madison.

She smiled. "Bach. One of my favorites."

He struggled to get words past the emotional lump the music brought to his throat, as well as the love he felt. If he was right, he saw the same shining in Madison's eyes. "Mine, too."

First, a gaggle of four young girls appeared, wearing matching pink-and-white dresses. Their faces beamed as they dropped rose petals from small wicker baskets they carried.

"That's Dawn, Cinder, Beth, and Holly," Justin whispered, making a curl of golden hair by her ear stir as his breath touched her face. "All the female children from the Heart of the Mountains. But you must know them already from the Biscuit Barrel Wednesday nights." He discreetly pointed to the edge of the gazebo. "There're all the mothers, encouraging them on."

"They're adorable. Faith made the flower girls' dresses."

"Shad and Poppy have postponed at least twice before. Everything was ready for the earlier dates. Came in pretty handy." He glanced at Shad, standing beside the gazebo with his two brothers and Tobit Preece, his soon to be brother-in-law, watching with smiles as the giggling girls took their time being sure the path was generously coated with fragrant petals.

Hickory stood with the men, as well.

Madison glanced at Justin and tapped his arm. "Hickory?"

"Heard tell, he's standing in for Luke. For reasons I don't know, Luke turned around and went right back up to Helena after he'd checked on his family and made sure they were fine. It's nothing about Brandon. Something else. Hickory was supposed to be the ring bearer, a duty he wasn't happy about, believing he was much too old. Being a groomsman is more to his liking." He chuckled. "He's lived in the bunkhouse for a while now with Shad and the others. He's like a little brother."

Hildy Hallsey came down the path next. She was followed by Evie and then a pregnant Heather. They carefully went up the steps and onto the stage. Kathryn came next.

Finally, Poppy appeared. She had the arm of Tobit's grandpappy, standing in for her own father. Her eyes were fixed on Shad's face, her radiance breathtaking.

At the steps of the gazebo, Reverend Crittlestick asked, "Who gives this woman to be wed to this man?"

"I do, Reverend," Isaiah Preece chortled. "As her *honorary* grandpappy. It's fittin', cause I gived her sister away, as well." His lips wobbled when he glanced at a pregnant Kathryn and then over at his grandson, Tobit. Swiping his eyes, he leaned in and kissed Poppy on the cheek.

From there, Poppy took Shad's arm, and they proceeded up the steps to the center of the stage where someone had set up a small, cloth-covered altar where a three-foot cross stood in the middle.

All settled, the reverend cleared his throat, calling for silence.

The giggling flower girl cousins wiggled onto their knees at the edge of the stage, trying to keep their excitement contained.

"Ladies and gentlemen, we're gathered here today in the sight of God," he began, lifting his arm toward the cross and then up to the magnificent sky filled with puffy clouds, "to witness the happy, *long-awaited* marriage of these two fine people."

A soft twitter went through the townsfolk.

"You might wonder why matrimony in the sight of God is important, so I shall enlighten you. First, the effect of the sacrament blesses their union. Second, it gives them the grace to put up with each other if a difference of opinion might arise. And lastly, it enables them to raise their children righteously, with a love of God. I believe Shad and Poppy already understand why patience and kindness are important, as they've had a few setbacks. They know about love enduring, for the same reason. I'll just remind them, from chapter ten of Mark, verses six through nine, and I quote, 'from the beginning of creation, God made them male and female. For this reason, a man shall leave his father and mother and be joined to his wife, and the two shall become one flesh. They are no longer two, but one flesh. Therefore, what God has joined together, no human being must separate.' "

Glancing at Hickory, Reverend Crittlestick held out his hand.

The boy promptly handed over the ring.

After a brief blessing, he gave the band of gold to Shad, who placed it on Poppy's finger.

Turning to face each other, they joined hands.

Reverend Crittlestick looked at Poppy first. "Do you, Poppy Alexandria Ford, take this man, Shadrack Bartholomew Petty, to be your lawfully wedded husband from this day forward, to have and to hold, in sickness and in health, in good times and in bad, to love and to cherish, and never to forsake, as long you both shall live?"

Poppy, already standing straight, gazed into Shad's eyes.

No one could doubt her feelings.

"I do," she said clearly, and then smiled, making her dimple appear.

The minister looked at Shad. "Do you, Shadrack Bartholomew Petty, take Poppy Alexandria Ford, to be your lawfully wedded wife, from this day forward, to have and to hold, in sickness and in health, in good times and in bad, to love and to cherish, and never to forsake, as long as you both shall live?"

Shad, his eyes swimming with emotion, nodded. "I do. And, Poppy, I promise to do everything in my power to make you happy. And give you every desire of your heart. I love you, darlin', so much so, I think my chest just might burst."

At his unscripted vow of love, Poppy sucked in a breath and melted into his arms.

Justin felt Madison shiver at his side. The ceremony hadn't taken more than fifteen minutes, but it was one he'd remember.

"Hold on, hold on," Reverend Crittlestick murmured. "I've yet to pronounce you husband and wife."

The couple pulled apart, their gazes locked on each other's.

"By the power vested in me by Montana Territory, I now pronounce you husband and wife. You may kiss the bride."

CHAPTER SEVENTY-FIVE

Cole stepped inside the Hitching Post to see Fancy meandering through the poker tables, singing "My Old Kentucky Home." Her voice, melancholy, was the first tell. The saloon was busy for a Sunday, and Abe moved up and down the bar, pouring whiskey, a smile on his face. Fancy didn't look so happy. Why would she be? Practically everyone in town was at the wedding, including her newly found daughter, and she was stuck here, inside these four walls. When their eyes met, she gave him a poor imitation of a smile.

He hitched his head, watching her come his way. "How ya doin'?" he asked quietly.

She shook her head and looked away. A large tear escaped her eye and slowly inched down her cheek.

"Hey, what's this?"

"Nothing."

"Come on, Fancy, spit it out." He took her elbow and brought her close to the wall, where they could have some privacy. "I recognize that look in your eyes." She gazed at him with slumped shoulders and quivering lips, as if everything she'd ever loved had been lost. "Can we go upstairs for a minute, so we can talk?"

Her countenance changed, and she shook her head. "That would give the wrong impression."

"The storeroom, then? I want to know what has you so sad." *As if I don't know.*

Without answering, she turned.

He followed her across the room. No one noticed when they slipped into the small room under the staircase. He heard the scratch of a match and waited as she lit the lamp.

Turning, she faced him in the musty, confined space.

He was thankful the gilded light allowed him to read her eyes.

"Why didn't I keep her, Cole?" she whispered, her words barely audible. "Why didn't I, at least, *try?* Years of regrets have my heart in a firm grip. I feel like I can't breathe. Especially now, after meeting her, and seeing what a brave, beautiful, and clever young woman she is. I should have kept her. Raised her. Had all those years together. I wasted my life! *Our* life! And now there's no changing it."

"Fancy," he crooned softly, cuddling her to his chest. He hated to see her so fraught with regret. "Don't do this to yourself. Every living person has mountains of things in their past they'd like to do over. Misgivings. Guilt. It's human nature. You can't help it. Thinking back and wanting to change the past will kill you. I know. I've done my share."

Leaning back, she dashed away her tears. "You?"

"Of course, me. You were just thirteen when I pulled you, in your bedraggled state, from the river. You were young, but not that young. Those days were the sweetest of my life. Why didn't I write? Come back to you? You'd proclaimed your love. Said you wanted to be my wife. That beautiful young woman could have been ours, made from our love. And, too, then I wouldn't have spent years in the army, conducting raids and operations where killing was involved. I weathered twenty years doing things I despised. And all the while, I pined for you. It was stupid. *I* was stupid. I threw away the best thing in my life. I wish I could go back and do everything over." He ran a hand along her soft hair. "But I can't. And I don't want to allow my regret to spoil what I've found now."

Her tears had stopped, and she listened intently. Still in his arms, she took a deep, steadying breath. "When Madison leaves in September, my heart will break for good." Her eyes filled again with the devastation her daughter's leaving would produce. "I'm thankful to have met her, but now I'm going to miss her *so* much, aware how the piece of my heart, lost to me twenty years ago, looks, smiles, and loves."

"I know you will. We all will."

She began to tremble. "Still, I should have tried

harder, looked for another way, gone to . . ."

"Hush. You did the right thing. The *only* thing, if you wanted her to be safe. You being a beautiful, young, *unmarried* woman with a baby would have attracted all the wrong kind of men. Your life would have been pure hell. What if, during your struggle to survive, Madison had been hurt, molested, or even killed? What if you couldn't get enough food, and she starved? Most certainly, she wouldn't have had such a fine upbringing and college education. God made sure she went to the right couple. They loved her greatly. And now she's found you. That's a true blessing. You should be thanking God, not looking back."

She just stared, her expressive eyes large as she took in every word.

"But, if my suspicions are correct," he went on, "you're not going to be able to hold back fate. Madison might leave in September to finish her schooling, but I believe she'll be back. There's more than you who's drawing her to Y Knot. That young deputy you like so well has eyes for her, and if I'm right, the feelings are mutual. You better prepare yourself and start planning. You have about a year to get your ducks in a row. I'll be by your side every step of the way." He leaned in and gave her a quick kiss on the lips, which she didn't rebuke. "Fate always has the last say, Miss Fancy Aubrey," he whispered close to her lips. "You, my dear, might be a grandmother before you turn forty."

Her eyebrows shot up. "Are you saying I might be in-laws with Pauline Backus?"

He gave a deep chuckle. "I wouldn't bet against it."

Chapter Seventy-Six

The evening was winding down, and Madison couldn't remember when she'd enjoyed a night more. Shad and Poppy made a beautiful couple. They'd danced the night away, looking like royalty. Even though Madison had yet to meet all the ranch hands, she'd gotten a chance to get to see their personalities from all the antics at the wedding reception. They were a handsome lot and funny, too. The party had been wonderful.

"Come on." Justin appeared at Madison's side, where she stood by the cake table and the remains of the cake. "Shad and Poppy are getting ready to leave. I didn't think you'd want to miss out." He placed a fistful of rice in her hand. "A present from Kathryn. The buggy will be pulling by any minute."

Madison learned the wedding couple were spending their first night in the bridal suite at Cattlemen's Hotel, and then taking the stage to Waterloo, where they'd catch a train to Bozeman to spend a week. She felt a delicious flicker of warmth curl in her belly. *What would being alone with Justin be like? Just the two of us? Day and night?*

Justin edged into the line of spectators waiting to toss rice beside Morgan Standford and June Pittman.

Madison smiled at June, having gotten to know her a little better tonight.

"They should be right along," June said, glancing up and down the line of people.

Madison nodded. "Yes. Can't wait. Tonight's been a fun evening." June looked so pretty in a blue dress, displaying her feminine figure much better than the men's denims she usually wore. Madison hadn't recognized her at first glance when the livery owner had addressed her earlier in the evening.

June inched closer. "Did you hear Morgan and I are making a trip to St. Louis in early October? One of his younger brothers is getting married and his mother really wants him to come—and me, as well. Heather will be too pregnant for the trip, and traveling would be difficult for Sally with Gillian. Plus, Roady will have the fall work at the ranch, him being foreman and all." Her eyes twinkled with excitement.

Madison remembered what Hildy had told her about why the two hadn't married up to this point. Perhaps, with the siblings growing older and getting married, those circumstances might soon change. "That's wonderful, June. I've been to St. Louis before. You'll love the city. There's so much to see." *And I hope it brings you closer to your heart's desire.* "Who will watch the livery when you're away?"

"Harold. He's a good young man to have

around town. I think he works harder than all of us combined." Her face brightened. "Found his watch the other day in a stall. He was glad to get it back." She shrugged. "If there's any shoeing work needed doing while we're gone," she said, going back to the topic at hand, "Smokey, out at the Heart of the Mountains, has done his fair share of blacksmithing. For anything bigger, they'll just have to go into Pine Grove or wait for our return." She leaned closer. "I'm not going to allow myself to worry about it." She threaded her arm through Morgan's. "And Harrison Wesley will mind Morgan's shop until we're back."

"Sounds like a perfectly well-thought-out plan."

"You're darn tooting. I wasn't going to allow anything to disrupt my chance of meeting his family. It's meant to be."

Madison wondered what June was referring to. The trip or her marrying Morgan.

At the sound of the jangling harness, everyone quieted. A moment later, the buggy approached, and showers of rice filled the air, first twenty feet away, and then around Madison when the buggy was right before her. She laughed and tossed up her handful, taking in a beaming bride and groom. Poppy was wrapped in one of Shad Petty's strong arms, smiling and waving the best she could. Then she turned, and they passionately kissed, almost making Madison glance away—*almost,* but not quite.

The cheers were deafening.

With a hearty whoop, Shad gave the lines he held in his other hand a hard flip, and they smacked across the horse's back. The conveyance jolted forward, amid the clatter of empty tin cans, old boots, spurs, and even some unmentionables, tied behind in long and short lengths of twine. Soon, the new Mr. and Mrs. Petty disappeared around the curve in the road, taking a bit of the party atmosphere with them.

Morgan and June said their goodbyes. Others were milling about, getting ready to depart.

Justin turned to Madison, his face still split with a wide grin. "Well, that was fun! I can't thank you enough for coming on my arm, Miss Plumb."

Whenever he wanted to tease her, he called her Miss Plumb. They'd danced closely tonight, whispering, laughing, and getting to know each other more fully. He'd even stolen two brief kisses, when they were alone in the shadows. She'd held his arm, and his hand, and his touch on her back as he escorted her to the dance floor brought waves of excitement each time they happened. No, they were anything but just friends, and her heart trembled at the thought of what that might mean. Looking up into his face now brought a rush of emotion and desire.

His smile faded, and his gaze dropped to her mouth. Leaning forward, his lips had just touched hers when she heard a woman call out.

Justin jerked away.

"Miss Plumb! Miss Plumb!" Belinda Bowie hurried their way. "I heard from Ina Klinkner you intend to return to Kentucky the second week in September. My plans are much the same. Who knows? Perhaps we'll be lucky enough to depart on the same stage. I so enjoyed our conversations."

Madison felt the tension in Justin's arm. Was she making the biggest mistake of her life? "That's correct, I am. But I'm not sure of the date just yet."

"Oh, we have plenty of time to make plans." Miss Bowie glanced between them, a knowing look in her eyes. "Now, I'll let you two young people be on your way. I just wanted to catch you, since I'm usually out at the mill. I've not had much of a chance to speak with you." She patted Madison's arm and was gone.

Justin glanced down at her, his expressive brows drawn together over his eyes. "She's right, Madison. It's still early August. You've plenty of time to plan." He ran his thumb across her hand. "Now, I better get you back to Lenore's house before she sends the law after me." His grin reappeared. "Wait, I *am* the law," he said with a chuckle. "Guess we can take our time, after all."

Silence fell around them as they made their way

to the buggy Justin had rented. He was so good at putting her at ease and hiding his real feelings. He was a good man, and she'd never find better. And she didn't want to.

Chapter Seventy-Seven

On her way to work, Madison studied the boardwalk, deep in thought. A month had passed since Poppy and Shad's wedding. The newlyweds had returned from Bozeman the week after, all smiles. The hay growing and selling business Shad was partners in with Tobit, his brother-in-law, was going exceptionally well since they were the only farmers in the area selling alfalfa and oat hay. Poppy had told her, she and Shad planned to build a small place on the farm soon, by a stream. "On acreage unsuitable for growing anything except herds of children," Shad had proclaimed proudly.

Madison felt a little down. Her departure was tomorrow. She'd asked for today off, but with the Wednesday night crowd expected tonight, Mrs. Larson had pleaded with her to work. The new girl, a daughter of a friend of Berta May's who'd come from Pine Grove, wasn't adapting well to waitressing. She'd already broken three plates and four cups. Madison didn't have the heart to refuse after Mrs. Larson, Renee, and Ethel had thrown her a nice going-away party.

The last four weeks had flown by in a breath. She could hardly believe it. Since Shad and Poppy's wedding, she and Justin had devoted all their free time to each other. She loved Frankfort well enough. She'd grown up there. But the people she loved were here in Y Knot. Not only that, but she'd grown fond of the smallness of the little cowboy town, knowing practically everyone she passed on the street. And the beautiful skies, with their billowy white clouds, or artfully painted sunsets, never failed to take her breath away. And much could be said for being able to reach anything you needed within a short walk.

I'm kidding myself. It's Justin! I love this town because of him. And Fancy and Lenore, too. How will I ever be able to leave?

Besides buggy rides, escorting her to church, and two additional suppers at his house, Justin had given her several riding lessons on Scout. Once, when she was ready, he'd taken a rental horse, and they'd gone on a long trail ride. First through town, where she'd smiled and waved at everyone she knew, and then continuing out toward the Heart of the Mountains Ranch, stopping in a secluded area where they'd enjoyed a small picnic, shared their love of literature, debated politics, and stole sweet kisses until they had to hurry back, not to be missed. The way they never ran out of things to discuss amazed her. When she heard him use the word onomatopoeia, she'd been astonished. She'd never knew the word existed before last year in her third-year literature class, when they'd been discussing poetry and the use of words that sound remarkably like their meaning.

Regrettably, she'd only seen her mother twice since their first meeting in the meadow because Fancy was terrified someone would notice her stepping into Lenore's home, where Madison was living. The fact no one had noticed before in the two years Fancy had been visiting Lenore, except for Justin, who'd been purposely watching, did no good to sway Fancy's resolve. She was holding to her resolution. In her mother's mind, Madison was to return and never come back, live a beautiful, well-respected life, and be happy. Since she'd agreed to Fancy's terms in the meadow, they stayed far away from the subject, sticking to safer ground and getting to know each other better.

Fancy filled Madison in on the portions of her life she was willing to share. Her mother enjoyed working with her hands, baking, and mixing creations in Lenore's tiny kitchen on her days off. On those days, she was truly at ease. Madison shared highlights of her upbringing, like tea parties with her mother before she died. And then, when she was older, the Kentucky Derby and a trip to Philadelphia for the World's Fair with her father. Last year, with her girlfriends from college and Professor Galbraith, the inauguration of Simon Bolivar Buckner, the thirtieth governor of Kentucky. When they were all laughed and cried out, they'd taken turns reading the twenty years' worth of letters, first written by her adoptive mother and then by Mrs. Goodheart, leaving them all teary-eyed with happiness.

During the telling of all her extravagant doings in Kentucky, Fancy's face had absolutely shone. Madison hated to let her down, but she'd already lived that other life and had experienced all the adventure she wanted to. She wanted to be here, in Y Knot. And if it was up to her, she'd tell the world her mother was Fancy Aubrey, singer, dancer, and entertainer. Those other things she'd had to do to survive, which Madison was still mostly ignorant of, were just a few measly side notes in the book of her mother's life. They were dust in the wind, as far as she was concerned. Madison didn't care one wit about them, except for how they'd affected Fancy and how she had suffered.

"Miss Plumb?"

Madison recognized the beloved voice calling. She was on the opposite side of the road than she usually walked. Justin had just stepped out of Lou and Drit's Boardinghouse and headed her way. He stopped beside her and briefly touched her hand, sending a jolt of warm awareness up her arm. He smiled, but his eyes looked bleak. Was he feeling as low as she was?

He affectionately looked her up and down.

"Thought that was you. You look beautiful. On your way to work?"

She nodded.

"Just as I thought. I planned this out perfectly."

She laughed, wishing she could turn back the hands of time one month. She'd grown used to their conversations and how his gaze made her feel. "You do seem to catch me each day. I had wanted this day off."

He stepped closer. "I've spoken with Mrs. Larson. As soon as the night slows down, which should be around eight, she's promised to let you off. I'll be there, and I'm taking you to Cattlemen's for your last night. Be sure not to eat before, because I have a special meal planned. I think you'll love it."

As I love you. She desperately wanted to say the words, but their future was so unknown. "That sounds wonderful, Justin. Thank you. I was hoping we'd have a little more time together." She looked up the street where a wagon appeared and turned onto Clove Hitch Street.

"Can I walk you the rest of the way? It's in my plan, you know."

"Of course. I was hoping you'd offer." They started off.

Justin briefly glanced back at the saloon. "Has Fancy said anything else, with the time running short?"

"No. She seems cold-stone-firm. I don't know

if your idea will work." She glanced at him and, unable to stop herself, she took his hand. "What if she never gives in? I promised her, Justin. Going back on my word would be a horrible thing to do—especially to my mother. I can't even contemplate a thing like that, but I don't want to lose you, either." *I love you. I love you so much it hurts.*

"You're not going to lose me. Granted, I'm a little amazed she hasn't cracked yet, but we have a whole year to work on her. And with all the letters you'll send her through Lenore, and my sharing about you, she'll relent. I'm sure of it."

The thumb he rubbed across the back of her hand was rough and warm, sending tingles up her arm.

"Look," Justin said. "Luke's back in town."

Justin and Madison were directly across from Standford's Fittings when Luke McCutcheon, surrounded by several ranch hands, rode slowly down the street. They pulled up in front of the building Jack Jones had been furiously working on the last few days.

At the same time, a large wagon filled to the brim with lumber approached from the other direction, driven by Cole Mercer. Major sat attentively at his side on the bench. Cole pulled up and pushed his hat back with his thumb, watching.

Jack stepped out the door with a post hefted

across his shoulder, his face sweaty and red.

"Well, I'll be," Luke said with a lazy grin. "I heard you were back, but I thought the men were pulling my leg. How you been, Jack?"

Jack heaved the post off his shoulder and, once one end was on the ground, he let the wood drop with a thump. "Been good, Luke. Good. Thanks for askin'. Glad to hear Brandon's doing better. Had us all scared. Saying our prayers. You headed to the Biscuit Barrel tonight?" he asked, a nervous, high-pitched quality to his tone.

Nick and Tanner, as well as Smokey, were giving Jack the evil eye. Tension crackled in the air. No one had forgotten how Jack had treated Luke in Priest's Crossing.

"Sure am."

"And the family?"

"Headed in, too, when supper rolls around." Luke palmed the saddle horn with both hands and gestured with his chin to the building behind Jack. "What do ya got goin' here?" he asked. "Been told you're keeping it secret."

Jack, the color of his face back to normal, lifted a shoulder. "It *was* going to be a barbershop, but I've recently changed my mind."

"Oh?"

"That's right. Took on some partners, so, with the extra funds, things expanded." He chuckled and pointed to the lumber in the wagon. "Or are just about to."

When he glanced at Cole, who patiently sat in the front of the buckboard, Madison sucked in a breath and squeezed Justin's hand. "What's this about?" she whispered.

"Don't know. It's news to me."

"And . . ." Luke prompted.

"We're building a restaurant," a feminine voice called out. Fancy stepped into the doorway. She wore men's work overalls, and her wheat-blond hair was pulled back in a messy ponytail. She didn't resemble her other self at all. For one fleeting moment, Fancy's and Madison's gazes touched.

Madison thought she saw a tiny smile.

"You have a problem with that, Luke McCutcheon?" Fancy placed her hands on her hips, no hint of fear in her voice.

"I sure don't, Fancy. I believe everyone is entitled to a second chance." He glanced at Jack with a half smile. "As long as he keeps to the straight and narrow."

"Does your generosity extend to saloon girls, as well?" Her chin was high, but a teasing smile played around her lips.

Madison couldn't have been prouder if she tried.

"You, Fancy? Why, you've never needed a second chance to try anything you wanted." He looked around at the fellows at his side.

They all nodded and shrugged.

"Everyone likes and respects you. We'll all be fortunate to have another eatery in town—and by the looks of the lumber, it's not going to be some small hole-in-the-wall."

"That's right," Smokey threw out, "especially when there're no tables to be had at the Biscuit Barrel on Wednesday nights. Might be nice to give 'em some competition."

"Happy to hear it." Cole set the brake and climbed down from the wagon seat. "Cole Mercer, partner number three," he said, sticking out his hand. "I've heard about Luke McCutcheon. Glad to finally meet you."

"Likewise," Luke said, grasping Cole's hand.

Jack came forward, but Fancy stayed in the protection of the doorway.

Madison felt she wasn't as sure of herself as she'd been acting. That was all right. Everyone had a year to get used to the changes.

"By the way," Jack said, stopping at Cole's side, "heard tell you and Smokey took a small herd of cattle when you returned to Helena." He scratched his chin for several long seconds. "That was a peculiar thing to do. Mind sharing why you'd go to such trouble?"

Luke smiled and shook his head. "I do, and that's the kind of thing that'll get you back in hot water, Jack. You best mind your own business."

Jack raised his hands, palms out. "Was just a simple question. Didn't mean to rile you."

"I'll *bet* you didn't," Luke gritted out in a steely tone.

"Come on, fellas," Smokey said. "We have business to attend to before pie tonight."

Madison gripped Justin's hand tighter as they watched the cowboys ride by. Luke, including the others, gave them a smile and respectful touch of the hat. *My mother, owning a restaurant! I can hardly believe my ears.* So much was changing so quickly. Her heart trembled with excitement. As Justin had said, time and prayers are a cure for anything. Would everything really work out?

Chapter Seventy-Eight

Earlier than needed, and with a heavy heart, Madison made her way to the sheriff's office. The stagecoach was scheduled to arrive in an hour, but she wanted to spend as much time with Justin as humanly possible. What she'd really like was to be alone with him. Have a heart to heart. With her departure looming, all her doubts and fears were gathering like a storm. Neither she nor Justin had ever said the words. She anticipated he would at dinner last night, but she'd been disappointed.

Instead, Lenore served them a wonderful meal with all the fixings.

Madison drank two glasses of champagne, making her laugh and giving her a fuzzy head. They whispered and held hands across the table. Truly, the night was magical.

Still.

Does it really matter? I know how I feel in my heart. I believe I know how he feels, as well.

Turning from the alley, she entered the sheriff's office and pulled up short. Justin was nowhere to be seen. Was he in the cell where Dodger Hicks was locked away? She didn't want to open the door leading to the cells to find out, so instead, she crossed the office to stand by the woodstove. Out of curiosity, she lifted the coffeepot to find it about half-full. He'd been here. A coffee mug sat on his desk. Something must have drawn him away. She wouldn't pout about it. After all, he was the acting sheriff and just doing his job.

In the cool silence, she spotted a book on his desk next to the mug. Curious again, she went over and picked it up. *Autobiography of Benjamin Franklin.* His bookmark was placed halfway through. She smiled. Justin never ceased to amaze her. She'd be sure to read a copy before her return, so they could discuss the contents at length. A telegram lay open-faced on the desk, as well. Before she realized what she was doing, she scanned the short communication.

SENDING MY THANKS ON A JOB WELL DONE STOP Y KNOT FAIRED WELL IN YOUR CAPABLE HANDS STOP I'M INDEBTED STOP FEELING MUCH BETTER STOP WILL BE HOME AS SOON AS I CAN STOP BRANDON

Again, she smiled. Justin had passed with flying colors. The arrival of a person made her spin away from her snooping. "Justin!"

He slowly came forward with narrowed eyes. When he reached her, he wrapped his arms around her waist and pulled her close, capturing her lips.

The kiss was long and heartfelt. Heat rushed

through every inch of her being. Tasting of coffee, and something else, he took her breath away. Eventually, they broke apart.

"I'm sorry I wasn't here to greet you, *my love,*" he said as he searched her gaze.

She felt her eyes go wide.

"What? Are you so surprised? You are my one and only love, you know." As if knowing he'd shocked her speechless, he hurried on, but he kept her in his strong embrace as he smiled mischievously. "I had an important errand. A visit to the stage office. Since there is absolutely no way I can escort you home, as I'd like to do, I've arranged for someone else to."

Her hands, resting on his tall shoulders, tightened. "Justin! No. I don't need anyone."

"I know you think that, but with the several train robberies of late, I'd just feel a little better."

What on earth? This is totally out of the blue.

"And I've been thinking about this for a long time."

Did he just read my mind?

He pointed to his bulletin board. "The wanted poster came in yesterday about the robberies."

"Please, Justin. I'll be embarrassed. I traveled here on my own, I can certainly make the return trip without going astray."

He went on as if she hadn't protested. "Who better, if not me, than my father? You'll have lots to talk about, with both your backgrounds. And you'll get to know him better." His eyebrows jumped up and down playfully. "For when you return."

She shivered as he leaned closer and rubbed his lips to hers, not quite a kiss, just enough to make her need for him expand exponentially. "Oh, Justin," she pushed out on a heavy breath.

"Oh, Justin, is right . . ." He silenced her objections with the promised kiss until they were both breathing heavily.

She tried to hide her quick breaths as she pulled away. "I'd rather he didn't."

"He's enthusiastic. And has promised to cover for me in December. And again in June, when you graduate, so I can attend that, as well. I'll be the proudest man there."

How could she deny him? His kisses were deadly. If sending his father meant so much to him, she'd gladly accept the company. Belinda Bowie, who, indeed, was traveling today, just might appreciate a big, strong gentleman along, as well.

"Justin?" she said again, loving the sound of his name on her lips. She so longed to hear the words and didn't want to say the endearments first, but she would, if she must. They were so close; he was just lowering his head to hers when someone in the doorway cleared their throat.

Madison pulled back, still in a fuzzy, longing haze.

Justin didn't let her go.

"I'm sorry to interrupt."

Lenore, looking sweet, was dressed for her shift at Cattlemen's in her long, black skirt and white, high-collar blouse. Her apple-red face appeared painful. The familial love Madison was growing used to feeling shivered in her heart.

When she took a tentative step in Madison's direction, Madison rushed her way, and they embraced.

"I just had to say goodbye one more time," Lenore whispered. "I'm so thankful you were brave enough to search us out, our dear Maddie. Our lives have changed for the better in such a huge way, I can hardly believe my good fortune. *Our* good fortune." Her gaze slid over to Justin and, if possible, the sentiment in her eyes deepened even more. "If I'm correct, each and every day will keep getting better and better from here on out."

When they parted, Justin put his arm possessively over Madison's shoulders. "Maddie, is it?" he asked with a smile. "Has a nice sound." He looked at Madison. "Are you holding out on me?"

"It's what my auntie started calling me." She covered her mouth and whispered, because she wasn't supposed to admit the relationship, "I like it."

He nodded. "So do I. Now, is your trunk packed

and ready for me to fetch it to the stage office? I'm not allowing Harold to do my task again."

Lenore winked and kissed Madison on the cheek. "Have a safe trip, and write to me every week. *We'll* be waiting." In an action unlike her, she rubbed Justin's arm. "And I don't mean *him*. I can imagine he'll get his own letters often enough." She reached into her pocket and drew out an envelope. "From you-know-who, to read when you're home."

Standing next to the Wells Fargo stagecoach, Madison worked to keep back her tears. Her trunk had been loaded to the top and her carpetbag placed inside. She didn't want Justin to remember her all teary eyed. Still, December was so far off. How would she get through her days without Justin there to talk to, laugh with, and kiss? Her heart trembled almost painfully. Was this what a broken heart felt like?

Lots of foot traffic was on the boardwalk today. Most people in town knew her by now, and that today was her day of departure. Some had come to say their goodbyes.

Belinda Bowie stood by the hotel window, chatting away with Ina Klinkner, both speaking at once.

Madison wondered if either woman heard a word of what the other was saying.

"Bless you, my dear Madison," Berta May

said. She'd just arrived in a flutter of skirts from across the street. From her watery eyes, she was holding back tears. "Have a safe trip home. Be sure to send a copy of your paper, when it's done. We'll all be interested in reading it."

"I will. And thank you for everything."

Berta May finally left.

Justin took Madison's hand and led her to the other side of the stage, in the street, where they'd have a modicum of privacy.

"All aboard the stage to Waterloo," Bradley Renfro, the shotgun messenger, shouted from the boardwalk, where they couldn't see him. "Get your goodbyes said and climb on up."

Alarm streaked through her. "Justin!" Her voice filled with panic. "I don't want to leave."

"No tears," he replied with a smile. "You have a year to fulfill at college. It's the right thing to do for your parents. And for *you*. And me. But don't you forget about Y Knot. Your mother is here, waiting. Your aunt, too." He squeezed her hands. "*Especially* me. I know you expect me to say, 'Parting is such sweet sorrow.' Yes, Shakespeare is correct, parting *is* such sweet sorrow, and I hate to let you go. But this particular quote paints more perfectly how my heart feels at this moment." He leaned back a little to study her face. " 'I love thee with a love that shall not die, till the sun grows cold and the stars grow old.' "

As she sighed, she felt his lips cover hers. The kiss lingered.

Moments later, he pulled back and whispered against her mouth, as if he were loath to let her go, "I love you, Maddie Plumb. And I'll have an important question to ask you at Christmas."

Surprised and excited, she pressed her lips back against his warm ones. Oh, how could she leave? "I love you, Justin. Y Knot was not only calling me here to find my mother, but to find *you,* as well. I love you so much. Please don't forget about *me*. I wish I knew some famous quote to recite."

He wrapped her in his arms, and they rocked back and forth in the warming sun, oblivious to whoever might be watching. "No love quotes needed for me to feel your love. You just remember us here in Montana, waiting for your return, and don't let Professor Galbraith turn your head."

She gasped and pulled back. "Professor Galbraith?"

"Don't look so shocked. You've spoken of him several times. What am I to think?"

She giggled, her sadness dispelling in a blink. "Mr. Galbraith is a lovable bear. *Everyone* loves him."

"Exactly what I mean. That's how they sneak up on you. Guard your heart, and I'll do the same with mine. December is just around the corner."

"Time's up, folks. Load up!"

Hand in hand, they circled around the back of the coach to the boardwalk. With one final kiss, Justin handed her up inside to the crowded coach and his father. Not only Miss Bowie and Harrison, but Aunt Pauline and little sister, too.

"Surpriiiise," Carlie cried loudly, the sound reverberating around the cramped interior.

Justin leaned in as Madison claimed her seat on the far side of the rear bench, closest to the saloon. Looking across the road, she saw Fancy standing out front of the Hitching Post, a pretty scarf subtly waving in her hand. Madison returned a discreet smile and patted her heart in full view of the window so Fancy could see.

"What's all this?" Justin asked.

"Harrison has already had one trip to Denver," Pauline said. "Carlie and I want to come along." She smiled at Madison. "To help see Miss Plumb home, and then to spend some time in Frankfort and Lexington." She patted Carlie's leg.

Justin's little sister squirmed with excitement.

His father gave Madison an apologetic smile. "Hope you don't mind."

"Of course not," she answered, taking Carlie's hand. "The more, the merrier."

The conveyance wiggled and jerked as the driver and shotgun messenger climbed aboard.

She caught Justin's gaze as he backed away and secured the door.

"You keep her safe, Pa," he called out in a strong voice. "I'll see you in December, Miss Plumb! Don't you forget."

Madison was filled with so much sentiment, all she could do was bite her bottom lip and nod, seeing his face through brimming tears. As they rolled off, and she couldn't see Justin anymore, she leaned out the window and blew a kiss in the direction of the saloon. She smiled as Fancy caught the kiss and held it to her cheek, where it remained until the stage turned onto the road to Waterloo and everyone she loved so dearly was out of sight.

Author's Note

When I began my journey writing *Montana Surprise*, I knew I wanted something a little different. I'd just finished *Montana Reunion*, a book that was chock-full of all the McCutcheons. Texas, Montana, Arizona, you name it! That's when Justin Wesley, deputy of Y Knot, popped into my head. He's a newer character, and up until now, the parts he's played have been minor. Son of our formidable judge, Harrison Wesley, he had large shoes to fill. And I have to say, I enjoyed making sure he's done just that. Paired with Miss Madison Plumb, another new character, but one with a shocking tie to one of our most beloved personalities, Fancy Aubrey. For me, Justin and Madison kept suspense, attraction, and heartbreak twirling from my fingertips. I have many secondary characters that I love as much as the main ones, and I couldn't help but continue to filter in their stories as well.

Researching St. John's Hospital in Helena and the six Sisters of Charity—who founded the institution in 1869—was of great interest to me. I can easily lose myself down a rabbit hole when I get hold of fascinating history. That, as well as the history of artificial insemination in humans, was a lot of fun. I'm always amazed at the little gems of antiquity floating out there that I would miss if not for the research I do for my writing. Funnily enough, my developmental editor had the same reaction Shad Petty did when Dr. Marlow retold how in 1884, Dr. William Pancoast accomplished the first successful recorded case of artificial insemination resulting in a live birth—clandestinely with the sperm that was not from the woman's husband—but the doctor's best-looking student! Shad's shocked inward response was much the same as my editor's note in the margin—which gave me a good laugh.

As promised, Belinda Bowie, loyal reader and winner from my December 2022 newsletter, became a character in *Montana Surprise*. A cousin of Ina Klinkner, she made two appearances in the story, arriving on the stage with Madison, and again towards the end of the book when she interrupts Justin and Madison's kiss at Shad and Poppy's wedding. (You know, every romance must include at least one interrupted kiss.) And was also mentioned by Madison to Heather Klinkner in the mercantile.

When I was creating the innkeeper who so carefully ministered to the McCutcheon brothers in Helena, as well as to a brokenhearted Charity, a certain someone came to mind. Mrs. Hardie is fashioned after my dear friend Michelle Hardie. (I'm hoping she likes the surprise.)

Acknowledgments

I didn't create this book alone. Heartfelt gratitude goes out to my editing team as well as my small group of pre-readers/beta readers, who are never too busy to read ahead of launch day! You're all the best and incredibly special. I can't imagine this process without each and every one of you. Your expertise and guidance keep me out of trouble, help me sleep at night, and make every step of the process enjoyable. Thank you from the bottom of my heart!

Gratitude to Paul Salvette at BB eBooks for the excellent formatting. Also Adam Fyffe, for his expertise in crafting a newsletter for me that shouts to everyone *Montana Surprise* is available!

Always thanks to my family! Michael, husband and first reader, for always being available to toss around ideas, search for the perfect word, keep me on track, and encourage me along the way. My sons, Matthew and Adam, for moral support, business advice, encouragement, graphic needs, and anything else a mother might need. My beautiful daughters-in-law, Rachel and Misti, who put a smile on my face and a song in my heart. And my darlings, my grandchildren, Evelyn and Hudson—you're both the apple of my eye. Then too, soon-to-be *new* baby girl (and apple of my eye)—we'll meet in a few short weeks. To say we're excited around here is an understatement.

Thanks to my supportive and amazing sisters, Sherry, Jenny, and Mary (and Shelly in Heaven), who are only a quick phone call or email away. I appreciate and love you all.

Ongoing appreciation and love to my readers, who saddle up for the ride every time a new book is available. Thank you! You make it possible for me to do what I love every single day. I truly treasure your love and support.

And, of course, profound gratitude to our awesome God, who has blessed me mightily in my faith, family, friends . . . and writing.

About the Author

USA Today bestselling author Caroline Fyffe has written twenty-six western historical novels to date. She was born in Waco, Texas, the first of many towns she would call home during her father's career with the US Air Force. A horse aficionado from an early age, she earned a Bachelor of Arts in communications from California State University-Chico before launching what would become a twenty-year career as an equine photographer. She began writing fiction to pass the down time during long days in the show arena, channeling her love of horses and the Old West into a series of Western historical novels. Her debut novel, *Where the Wind Blows*, won the Romance Writers of America's prestigious Golden Heart Award as well as the Wisconsin RWA's Write Touch Readers' Award. *Where the Wind Blows*, book one of her award-winning Prairie Hearts series, is also her first novel to be adapted into a feature film, now planned for release this fall. She and her husband reside in the Pacific Northwest and have two grown sons, two beautiful daughters-in-law, and three adorable grandchildren.

Want news on releases, giveaways, and bonus reads? Sign up for Caroline's newsletter at: www.carolinefyffe.com

See her Equine Photography:
www.carolinefyffe.com/equine-photography
LIKE her FaceBook Author Page:
Facebook.com/AuthorCarolineFyffe
Twitter: @carolinefyffe
Write to her at: caroline@carolinefyffe.com

Center Point Large Print
600 Brooks Road / PO Box 1
Thorndike, ME 04986-0001 USA

(207) 568-3717

US & Canada:
1 800 929-9108
www.centerpointlargeprint.com